A Highland Knight to Remember

Highland Dynasty Series—Book Three

by

Amy Jarecki

Rapture Books
Copyright © 2015, Amy Jarecki
Jarecki, Amy
A Highland Knight to Remember

ISBN: 978-1942442042
First Release: May, 2015

Book Cover Design by: Amy Jarecki
Edited by: Scott Mooreland

To Moriah.

Chapter One

The Scottish Highlands, Late Fifteenth Century

Gyllis Campbell forgot the pain in her backside when Dunstaffnage Castle came into view. It was all she could do not to dig in her heels, slap her riding crop against her mare's rump and overtake their dreary entourage. But Mother would surely admonish such a display of unladylike exuberance.

In the castle foreground, blue and white striped tents festooned with colorful flags flapped in the breeze. The sight made butterflies flit about her stomach. If only she could hop off her horse, she'd be able to walk faster than the guards leading them. Gyllis had been looking forward to the annual Highland fete for ages. At long last they'd arrived and the rain had stopped. It would be Beltane on the morrow—May Day. And it couldn't possibly rain on the opening day of the games.

Gyllis cast an excited grin toward her sister. "What is the first thing you plan to do?"

Helen licked her lips. "I can already smell the honeyed cryspes."

Food?

Though only a year younger, Helen could be incredibly dull. She even opted to wear a veil and cover her lovely honey-colored locks, though she was a maid and within her rights to flaunt her beautiful tresses. "Sounds delicious," Gyllis managed a disinterested reply. She set her sights on more interesting fare and scanned the scene for Highland warriors. *Where is he?*

"And you?" Helen asked.

"Hmm?" Gyllis focused on a gathering of well-armed knights ahead. *No handsome lad with a head of thick dark locks among them.* She could picture Sir Sean MacDougall in her mind's eye as if she'd seen him only yesterday. She adored everything about the knight including his long, athletic legs she'd admired many times when he sparred in the courtyard as one of her brother's Highland Enforcers. A potent and powerful man, Sir Sean's face was as equally rugged and handsome as his form. It had been six months since she'd last seen him before he left to patrol the borders. But forever burned into her memory was the way his azure eyes had stared at her from across the table during last year's Beltane festival. No man had ever gazed upon her with such fervent hunger. More so, his stare had awakened a longing deep within Gyllis's soul that would not be forgotten.

"What will be the first thing you'll do, silly?" Helen asked again.

Gyllis waggled her brows. "I want to watch the games."

"But they do not start until the morrow." Helen tsked her tongue. "Bless it, you are incorrigible." She leaned toward Gyllis. "I know what you're doing."

"So?" she snorted. "Eoin will be here, too."

Helen whipped her head around so fast, she nearly fell off her mount. "Wheesht. Ma will hear you."

Gyllis glanced over her shoulder at her mother and younger twin sisters. Bogle's bones, she and the lassies would all need to find husbands soon. She had long past attained the age of twenty. Many highborn lasses were wed by ten and six—the same age as Alice and Marion. Yet her brother, the all-powerful and domineering Lord of Glenorchy, frowned upon every available noble who passed through Kilchurn Castle's gates. Well, Gyllis had decided it was time to take matters into her own hands, lest she end up a spinster. If her brother deemed no one suitable to place a ring on her finger, she would follow her heart—a love interest she had harbored for years.

"Gyllis?" The commanding tone in Mother's voice made her sit straighter. "Have you seen Duncan?"

I'd prefer it if my overbearing brother remained on the borders. "Not as of yet."

"His missive said he would meet us at the gate."

Gyllis eyed the barbican and the long pathway leading to Dunstaffnage's immense grey stone walls. "Perhaps we shall see him when our entourage proceeds closer to the castle."

"Can we not stop and look at the wares first?" asked Alice, Gyllis's youngest sister—aside from Marion who was born moments later.

Mother cleared her throat. "No one will be doing any browsing at the fete until we are settled in our rooms."

Gyllis rolled her eyes to the sky. "The servants will see to that. We'll be in their way."

"Oh?" Mother said. "And how will you know where you'll be sleeping?"

Gyllis grinned at Helen. "You can tell us, Ma."

"Ungrateful children," Mother sighed. "It shan't take long. Together we will proceed to our rooms and I'll hear no further argument."

With a wink, Gyllis leaned toward her sister and whispered, "You'll have to wait a wee bit longer for those honeyed cryspes."

"And you must put off ogling Sir Sean."

Her heart fluttered at the mention of *his* name. She flicked her riding crop at Helen. "I'll wager you'll be dancing with Sir Eoin MacGregor this eve."

Helen grasped the crop and yanked it from Gyllis's hand. "You are shameless."

"And you are ungrateful." Gyllis snatched the whip back. "Remember, I am the one who intends to keep the Campbell sisters from spinsterhood."

***

Sean MacDougall left his horse with his squire and removed his helm. He inhaled a deep breath of Highland air. The sweet scent of home enlivened him. He'd been looking forward to the Beltane games as he did every year and now even more so.

After spending six months patrolling the borders with the Highland Enforcers, he needed clean air and good sport. He scrubbed his knuckles against his scalp and marched from the stables toward the smell of roasting meat.

"Where are you off to in such a hurry, nephew?"

Sean stopped on the path leading to the castle's main gate and turned. He'd recognize his uncle's timeworn scowl anywhere. "If it isn't the Lord of Lorn, himself." He held out his hand for a firm handshake. "I see you've outdone yourself this year. The collection of merchants is grander than ever before." Indeed, the tents sprawled across Dunstaffnage's foreground posed an impressive sight.

Lorn chuckled—though not a tall man, he had a deep voice. "We do bring in more tinkers every year." He rubbed the tips of his fingers together. "And with it comes more coin—as long as they can keep their thieving hands to themselves."

In the past six months, Sean had endured enough of backstabbers and thieves to last a lifetime. At times he'd reckoned fate must have doled him out a parcel of bad luck. But he aimed to rectify his lot starting now. "I wish you well controlling the roustabouts. I'm here for the games."

"I would assume no less." Lorn chuckled and squeezed his arm. "And I expect you to be victorious— I've wagered a nicely sum upon it."

Sean grinned. "I aim to give it my best."

"Good lad." Lorn smoothed his fingers down his grey, pointed beard. "I haven't seen the Laird of Dunollie as of late. Will he be dining at the high table with me this eve?"

"Unfortunately, Da needs rest. He was a wee bit fevered last eve, but I expect him to come round before the end of the games."

"Very well."

Above the crowd ahead, Duncan Campbell climbed the steps leading to Dunstaffnage's inner barbican. Sean waved and Duncan offered an exaggerated bow, his black hair dropping into his eyes. They'd been friends since the age of ten and four when Sean's father sent him to Kilchurn Castle to foster with the late Lord of Glenorchy, Duncan's da.

"Are you still riding with that Campbell blackguard?" Lorn asked.

Sean raised an eyebrow. "You surprise me, Uncle. Duncan is one of my closest allies."

"I'd watch my back with friends such as he."

"It would be in our best interest if we Highlanders could manage to end our feuds."

Lorn scrunched his nose as if he'd just tasted a bitter brew. "'Tis easy for you to say, but I must find some way of keeping Campbell fingers off my title when I'm laid to rest. To my chagrin, my sister off and married the Earl of

Argyll—if I pass without issue, the title will go to him, the bastard."

Sean regarded his uncle. Blood ran thick in the Highlands, but he cared not to taint it with hatred for friends. He thumped him on the shoulder. "You can always marry Dugald's mother and legitimize your son. That should solve all your woes."

"But marrying so far beneath my station would cause consternation at court," Lorn growled, drawing his thick brows together. "If only I had a legitimate heir like your father."

Sean headed off with a chuckle. "You must start on that, uncle—before you're too old to get a rise out of your cock."

Lorn fell in step beside him. "Insolent lad. You should talk—how old are you now? Nine and twenty?"

"Aye." Sean had never thought about aging, but the way Lorn said it, he already had one foot in the grave.

"You'd best be sowing your seed soon, else you'll find yourself in a similar predicament." Lorn jabbed his elbow into Sean's ribs. "There's no better time to find a ripe lassie than Beltane. You ken the legends."

"Ballocks to that." Sean slapped a dismissive hand through the air. "I'm off to fill my belly and enjoy the sweet Highland air. I've plenty of time to worry about marriage *after* the games."

Having had about all he could take of his uncle's babble, Sean raced ahead and followed Lord Duncan through the gatehouse. The inner courtyard was filled with nobles dressed in brightly colored blues, yellows, and more red velvet than he'd ever seen outside of court. A tall man, it wasn't difficult for Sean to push through the crowd, straight into the castle's tapestry-lined great hall. The smell of roasting meat and baking bread made his mouth water and his stomach growl.

From the high table, Duncan stood and beckoned him. "We're not too late for our nooning."

"Thank the good Lord for small mercies." Sean slid into the seat beside the baron. "And where is your wife?"

"Lady Meg opted to remain at Kilchurn with the bairns. The wee ones are still too young to travel."

Sean reached for a ewer and poured himself a tankard of ale. "And how are the twins?"

"Elizabeth has a healthy set of pipes for certain— though her brother Colin can hold his own."

"Was the birth worth returning from the borders early?"

Duncan bit off a chunk of bread and winked. "I'll say. Bloody miserable reiving thieves I can live without. A turn at home did me some good as well."

A servant placed a trencher of chicken on the table and Sean swiped a leg. "And Lady Meg, has she recovered from the birth?"

"Aye, she's as feisty as ever."

Sean laughed. He'd never forget the night they stole Duncan away from Edinburgh gaol. They were riding like hellfire when Sean realized someone had followed them. He'd set a trap and nearly killed Lady Meg before she uttered a word. If it weren't for her shrill scream, Sean probably would have run her through. He still shuddered at how close she'd come to meeting her end. *Feisty and fearless.*

High-pitched giggles across the hall pulled Sean from his thoughts. A lovely picture indeed. Gyllis Campbell and her sisters gaily flitted into the hall as if a ray of sunshine had brightened the entire room. Sean stopped mid-chew. It had been quite some time since he'd seen Gyllis. "God's teeth."

"What?" Duncan asked.

Sean swallowed as he wiped his mouth with the back of his hand. Tall with willowy limbs, Gyllis had always reminded Sean of a meadow nymph. Chestnut locks framed porcelain skin and her moss-green eyes encircled by rings of black could captivate any man. "Your sister grows more radiant every time I see her."

"Which one?"

Bloody hell, Duncan knew. Sean gripped his tankard and took a long pull on his ale. "I suppose Highland lassies are more appealing after a man's taken a turn in the Lowlands."

"Aye?" Duncan frowned. "Well, nothing's changed. Friends and sisters do not mix—*Lusty Laddie*, you've tainted my opinion by all the womanizing we did as lads. Bloody oath, you'll never put those lecherous hands on one of my sisters. You may be the best man I know with a sword." Duncan glanced at Sean's crotch. "And I'm referring to the one you carry on your hip. Pray you keep that in mind over the next few days."

True, Sean liked the ladies as much as the next man— mayhap better—and he'd earned the moniker Lusty Laddie, but it appeared Duncan had forgotten his own wayward womanizing. Those carefree days hadn't been all that long ago. Sean cleared his throat.

Gyllis caught Sean's eye and stopped mid-stride. She pursed her pouty lips as if gasping. Then she smiled and fluttered a wave. The corner of Sean's mouth turned up like a simpleton.

"MacDougall?" Duncan jabbed him with an elbow.

Sean glanced at his friend. "How do you recommend I react? Pretend your sister doesn't exist?"

"Aye, that's exactly what you should do."

"There's nothing wrong with a little healthy admiration. Besides, I'll be heading back to the borders in a fortnight, thanks to you." Sean bit down and tore a piece of meat from his chicken leg. "How have you fared finding a match for each of your *four* sisters?"

"Wheesht." Duncan eyed him. "That is none of your concern."

"Too right. And as I recall, *you* lifted lassies' skirts first and asked their names after." Sean picked up his tankard and guzzled it. Christ almighty, he didn't come to the games to flirt with some bonny lass deemed too good for him due to his friendship with her brother. Nay, it mattered not that he was to inherit the Chieftainship of Dunollie. Nothing Sean could say would make a difference to Duncan Campbell, the Lord of Glenorchy, unless he agreed that his sisters all marry above their stations.

He swallowed and glanced up. Then he nearly spewed his ale across the table. Bloody hell, Miss Gyllis stood opposite him, looking more radiant than she had at the far end of the hall.

"Good afternoon, Sir Sean," she said with a smile and a curtsey. "'Tis lovely to see you at the games again this year."

Must the temptress sound like a heavenly angel?

Sean's chair scraped the floor as he hastened to stand. Then the flimsy piece of furniture clattered to the floorboards. "Miss Gyllis, how delightful to see you." Bowing, he feigned his best attempt at nonchalance, ignoring the toppled chair behind.

The lassies around her giggled.

Sean bowed again. "Ah...All of you." He grinned at Gyllis like he was still wet behind the ears.

"Take a seat and eat or be gone the lot of you," Duncan said. "Pick up your chair MacDougall. Bless it, you act like you've never seen a lassie before."

"Pardon me, ladies." Sean hoped to God he hadn't turned red and stooped to right his seat. "It has been several months since I had the pleasure of such fair company." He raised an eyebrow at Duncan, the bastard. He might be a close friend, but he was a complete arse when it came to his sisters.

"We've already dined." Helen tugged Gyllis's arm. "Come. I'm dying to see all the wares on display."

"A moment." Gyllis smiled, looking sultrier than any young maid ought. "Will you be at the feast tonight, Sir Sean?"

"Aye."

She blessed him with a radiant smile. "Will you dance with me?"

"Gyllis." Duncan rapped the butt end of his eating knife on the table. "It is not your place to ask a knight to dance."

Sean would have liked to grasp her hand across the table, but the blasted board was too wide. He settled for a deep bow. "It would be my pleasure, Miss Gyllis."

"I shall see you this eve then." She dipped her head politely before being steered off the dais by her sisters.

Her tresses hung down her back in waves and swished across her shapely hips. Even with layers of skirts, her feminine form enticed. Sean rubbed his fingers together, imagining her hair to be finer than silk. No other lass in the hall came close to Gyllis Campbell's beauty. Unfortunate. If Sean had a mind to court anyone, it would be she. But the Lord of Glenorchy sitting beside him would ensure things never progressed that far.

Duncan pointed to the trencher. "Are you planning to eat that?"

"Huh?"

"The breast." Duncan reached across and snatched the last piece of chicken. "Are you entering all-around, or are you specializing this year?"

Sean's shoulder ticked up. "No use being here without going for a chance to win the purse."

"I thought as much."

"You as well?"

"Aye, as long as I'm here keeping an eye on your uncle for my uncle, I may as well enjoy myself."

Sean chuckled. "Lorn and Argyll—the age-old feud. By rights we should be fierce enemies."

"If it was up to our betters we would be." Duncan shoved the last bite of chicken into his mouth. "Thank God my father saw the benefit of uniting the clans. No one in Scotland can match the enforcers."

Sean held up his tankard. "And so may we continue to keep the peace."

Duncan raised his cup and tapped it to Sean's. "*Slàinte.*"

"*Slàinte.*"

Sean glanced toward the doors. Every muscle in his back clenched. That damned Alan MacCoul had Gyllis's hand clasped between his filthy mitts. Worse, she was smiling at him, giggling even. Her voice rang out above the hum of the crowd.

He grasped his chair's armrests, ready to spring, watching the bastard bend at the waist and plant a kiss on the back of her hand. Gyllis nodded politely, just as she had done to Sean a few moments ago.

Duncan sat forward. "What's that slithering snake doing?"

Sean shot him a sidewise glance. "Proving he's an unmitigated arse. Unfortunately, he's a member of my clan. I shall deal with his impertinence." Sean pushed back his chair, but by the time he strode to the dais stairs, Alan MacCoul had already shoved through the crowd as if he were planning to dine at the high table.

He traipsed directly to the base of the steps. "MacDougall, I thought I'd find you near the food."

"'Tis a common place to gather at the noon hour." Sean failed to understand why Alan had always been able to skate by with his impertinence. Even when they were lads Alan had been a bully—and older to boot. Sean would turn up with a black eye or worse, and the Chieftain of Dunollie would grab Sean's chin and pinch. Hard. "A little bullying will make you strong, son. Next time Alan challenges you, stand your ground—prove to me you're worthy to be chieftain."

Well, that had been close to impossible when they were lads, given three years difference in age. However, now that they were grown, it was another story. Sean stood a good hand taller than Alan, and fighting the weasel would provide no sport whatsoever.

Alan didn't try to mount the steps to the dais, but Sean could have sworn he caught a covetous glint in his eye.

The slithering snake smirked. "I'm surprised to see you here with news of your father's illness."

Sean knit his brows. He'd only had a fleeting moment with Da prior to departing for the games. He'd been home long enough to gather fresh clothing. Aside from a fever, Da had a cough, but dismissed it as a passing ailment. What more did Alan know? The bastard always had his nose in the family's affairs. Why, Sean wouldn't be surprised if he'd served his father with a tincture that had made him sick. "Da said he'd be along in a day or two." Sean shrugged. "But 'tis no concern of yours."

Alan's eyes grew dark.

Duncan moved in beside Sean. "State your business, MacCoul, then I suggest you head further down the hall and sit with your own kind."

The shorter, but stocky man sneered. "Just came up to tell Sir Sean I aim to win the tournament this year."

Duncan threw his head back with a deep, rumbling laugh.

But Sean clenched his fists. If the hall weren't full of women and children, he'd gladly challenge the errant scourge to a duel of swords. *Now isn't the time.* "Well then, it will be my privilege to hand you the purse should you be victorious." He'd meant it as a jibe and it sounded so.

"That would give me great satisfaction—though I believe I'd prefer the gift to come from the Lord of Lorn's hand. After all, he's an earl."

Duncan clapped Sean's shoulder. "Come. Lady Meg gave me a list of items to purchase at the fete. I could use a hand."

Alan blocked the stairs, the corner of his mouth turned up in a smirk. "Two knights heading out on a woman's errand?"

Sean clambered down and stood on the bottom step, towering over the cur. "A knight's code of chivalry is something *you* would know nothing about."

Duncan barreled down and pushed past Alan's shoulder. "Come MacDougall, we've no time to wag tongues with a sniveling whoreson."

Sean gave Alan one last glare—narrowed his eyes so he'd know this wasn't over. Perhaps it was a good thing he'd have the chance to beat Alan MacCoul in the games. He'd issue the smug toad some long-awaited humble pie.

Chapter Two

For the first evening feast of Beltane, Gyllis sat in the great hall with her sisters wearing a green damask kirtle and matching veil, held in place by a bronze circlet. All the lasses were dressed to astound—one thing Mother never failed to impress upon the Campbell sisters—*Clothes maketh the lady*. Gyllis did not admire fine gowns as much as Ma, but she couldn't discount the fact that a noblewoman's dress indeed was important to society.

Mother and Duncan had gained places at the high table with the Lord of Lorn at one end and the Earl of Argyll at the other. The two highest ranking men in the hall glared at each other like caged dogs and Gyllis was happy to be sitting away from the stuffy posturing and politicking upon the dais.

Alice pointed toward the door. "Alan MacCoul just arrived with an impressive retinue. Is he a knight?"

"He looks gallant like a knight," said Marion.

Gyllis tore off the butt end of bread and tossed it at the twins. "Sillies. Do you not know anything? He's a *bastard*." She cringed. Alan had stopped her earlier that day and had been a tad too familiar, grasping her hands and telling her how lovely she looked. She'd tried to be polite though there was something sinister in his stare.

Gyllis couldn't put her finger on it, but those lignite eyes made her uneasy.

Helen raised the ewer of watered wine. "Looking at his ceremonial armor, I'd say he's a wealthy bastard."

Alice craned her neck to better see him, making a blatant show of ogling. "Aye, he must have ample property."

"Good heavens, Alice, turn around. You're making a fool of yourself." Gyllis eyed her sister across the table. "You'd best set your sights a wee bit higher. Duncan would never approve of an untitled man." She leaned forward to whisper. "No one even knows who his father is."

Alice clapped a hand over her mouth. "That does sound like a scandalous story."

Marion giggled. "At least he's handsome if ill-bred."

A servant placed a trencher of roasted meat and stewed vegetables in front of Gyllis. "Thank heavens the food's here. Your minds have run amuck from hunger."

"Pardon me, is this seat taken?" The deep voice came from behind.

Gyllis cringed. Alan MacCoul had moved out of sight. *Please no.* She feigned an annoyed frown and turned. Her heart hammered in rapid succession. "Oh my." She smiled broadly and scooted aside on the bench, squeezing into Helen. "Of course, we would love to have you join us."

Sir Sean grinned. He could melt an entire slab of butter with his smile—straight, white teeth, bold jaw with a neat and closely cropped beard. His shoulder-length, dark brown hair and azure eyes made him look devilishly dangerous.

The bench was so crowded, his thigh and shoulder pressed against hers. In any other venue, such touching would be indecent, but Gyllis couldn't have moved if she'd wanted to. Her heart fluttered and she leaned into him a bit more.

"Sir Sean, Why are you not wearing your ceremonial armor?" Alice asked.

"Honestly?" Sean shot a puzzled look to Gyllis. "That sort of pomp is only reserved for weddings and court appearances. I'm far more comfortable wearing a plaid and doublet."

"Alan MacCoul has donned his ceremonial armor." Marion pointed. "Even the Lord of Lorn is sporting a silver breastplate."

Sir Sean's shoulder ticked up, but a tempest brewed behind his eyes. "Mayhap I incorrectly assumed this eve to be a more casual affair. I'm afraid my uncle makes Beltane a greater spectacle every year."

"The church is insisting we call it May Day." Gyllis lifted the trencher of meat and smoothed her shoulder against his as she offered it to him. "I think you are admirably dressed."

"My thanks." Sean selected a thick piece of roast lamb with his eating knife.

She replaced the tray. Helen nudged Gyllis with an elbow and she scooted flush against Sean's thigh. Though she wore layers of skirts, his leg felt hard as stone. *Goodness, with flesh as solid as his, he needs no armor.* She dared glance his way. "Apologies. The hall is awfully crowded."

Sean faced her and lowered his lids, fanned with long, dark lashes. Gyllis liked that he had to cast his gaze downward to meet hers. So often she was self-conscious about her height, but Sean MacDougall stood at least a head taller.

"Are you looking forward to Beltane?" he asked.

"Aye," she said. "The games will be great sport."

Helen leaned forward. "I hope the weather remains in our favor."

"Me as well." Sean held up his eating knife. "I prefer running on dry ground."

"I'm looking forward to the Maypole dances," Alice said.

Marion licked her lips. "And pigs on the spit—nothing better than pork roasted over an open fire."

"Mm, I can practically taste it now." Under the table, Sean's fingers brushed Gyllis's thigh. "And you? What are you looking forward to on the morrow?"

"Everything." She inhaled, her heart hammering like a snare drum. Sir Sean smelled of rosemary soap and spice. *How undeniably intoxicating.* Her eyelids fluttered while her head swooned. "Would you care to sit on our plaid...weather permitting of course?"

He reached for his tankard as if considering.

Gyllis could have kicked herself. *Oh heavens, I've been too forward. He most likely has other plans.* She flicked her hair with a toss of her head. "I'm certain Mother and Duncan will enjoy your company. After all, we haven't seen you at Kilchurn Castle in ages." *Now I've done it. Why can I not keep my mouth shut?*

Sean sipped then offered a nod. "I'm not positive Lord Duncan will approve, but I would be remiss if I did not accept your generous invitation."

"You will?" Beneath the table, Gyllis clasped her hands, trying to quell her excitement. "Very well, then. I shall ensure I bring along a plaid of ample size for us all to sit upon."

She hesitated for a moment, wondering what she should say next. Did Sean agree because they had been friends for such a long time? Nine years her senior, she'd known him nearly all her life, looked up to him when she was a wee lass, and as a teenager, admired him. They'd shared many a glance across Kilchurn's great hall, especially since she came into her majority. Gyllis had always interpreted meaning into those glances. However, Sean had never been more than courteous—though he was a good dance partner when he wasn't off on the king's business with Duncan. She stole a sidewise glance at him then quickly looked at her plate.

He's staring at me. Surely that must mean something.

The musicians moved into place on the balcony above—a fiddler, a drummer and a piper.

Alice clapped her hands. "It looks like his lordship has planned country dances for this eve."

Gyllis stole another look at Sean—he was still staring and now grinning at her. "Ah…It looks like a plaid and doublet were the perfect choice for this evening's dancing."

The fiddler started in on a reel and benches scraped across the floorboards. Sean stood and offered his hand. "I believe I owe you a dance, Miss Gyllis."

Her heart thrummed in tandem with the foot-stomping music. "You're ever so kind, sir knight."

"You must dance with us all, Sir Sean," Marion chimed.

Gyllis wanted to tell her sisters to go find their own dancing partners. But that wasn't the way of things at a Highland gathering. Everyone danced with everyone. At the moment, however, Gyllis rested her palm atop Sean's powerful hand. Though they were barely touching, gooseflesh rose across her skin. She prayed this would be a very long reel indeed.

***

Sean probably shouldn't have agreed to sit with Gyllis and her family at the morrow's Beltane feast, but her eyes had looked so hopeful, he couldn't say no. Since his father was ill, as future Chieftain of Dunollie, Sean should keep company with his clan. But he wouldn't worry about that now. He led the lovely lass to the dance floor, his thigh still tingling where it had been flush against hers. All he cared to do at the moment was watch her gracefully twirl in the crook of his arm.

In a fortnight he'd return to the borders, sleeping in stables with a mob of smelly warriors. He could allow himself a modicum of enjoyment over the next sennight, even if Duncan Campbell didn't exactly agree. Besides, the coming months would have no such pleasures. Sean was never one to buck a challenge, and he'd had been enamored with Gyllis since...since...honestly since she'd turned from a spoiled gap-toothed lass into a stunning woman.

"Have you had much opportunity to dance as of late?" Gyllis asked.

"None at all. I'm afraid all there was time for was riding, eating, sleeping and fighting the English." Sean's belly squeezed when she smiled, her dimples dipping into the high color of her cheeks.

"Oh my, that does sound tedious." She assumed her place in line, standing across from him. "Do you remember how Mother used to make you partner with us during our dancing lessons?"

"I shall never forget." At the time, he'd considered Gyllis an annoying child. He chuckled—he'd been sixteen and she seven. And as a young squire, Sean hated being forced to partner with the lasses. He had more important things to conquer during his fostering—like proving himself to the Lord of Glenorchy and earning his knighthood. As a matter of fact, he'd rarely had time to think of anything except enforcement work. But he did love it. Duncan called him a ghost because Sean's strengths lie in tracking and ambush.

The fiddler stamped his foot indicating the dance was to begin and Sean locked elbows with Gyllis. Her arms were long, yet lithe. *Willowy.*

She fluttered her lovely eyelashes at him. "I always thought you would rather be elsewhere than dancing with us."

Sean reached over and patted her hand. So small beneath his callused fingers, her skin was softer than silk. "Perhaps as children, but right now there is no place I'd rather be."

The dancers formed three large circles. Sean held Gyllis's hand while another woman danced in the center. He scarcely noticed the woman to his left. Gyllis's intoxicating scent of fresh cut flowers and honey captivated him. The bodice of her green gown was cinched taut around her waist. Creamy white breasts swelled above the neckline—not too small, and most certainly not too large. Her cleavage provided plenty to captivate his interest.

She glanced up at him and grinned. Afraid he'd been caught staring at her breasts, Sean snapped his gaze to her eyes. By God, they were the most tantalizing color of moss. He looked closer. He'd always thought she had black rims around her irises, but the more he studied them, the more he could swear the rings were navy blue. "Exquisite."

"Pardon?"

"Ah, your ey…."

Gyllis released his hand and skipped into the center of the circle. Sean studied the others with no clue as to where they were in the reel. Well, at least if Gyllis was in the ring, she'd spin with the man directly across then return to twirl with Sean. That was the good part of dancing—if he had a lapse of attention, he could usually pick the steps back up.

As he expected, Gyllis skipped toward him, her inordinately long chestnut tresses swishing behind her. He locked hands with her and spun. "Did I tell you how bonny you look this eve?"

She giggled and slid back into place. Irritated to turn away and join elbows with the woman behind, Sean continued with the reel. They wound their way around the circle until again he held Gyllis's hand in his. "You've become quite an accomplished dancer."

"Thank you." She blessed him with her dimples again. "I daresay you could use a lesson or two from me."

He chuckled. Someone had noticed his inattentiveness. "It would be my pleasure to take advantage of your offer someday soon."

Her mouth twisted. "But you must return to the borders."

"Aye, for a time." The music stopped. "But I shan't be away indefinitely."

"Miss Gyllis." Alan MacCoul stepped beside her. "Would you dance with me?"

Sean's gut churned. If only he could challenge the bastard on the spot. But a friendly gathering was no place to make a scene. His jaw twitched. *One dance.*

She cast Sean a questioning look. He tightened his grip on her hand and leaned to her ear. "Meet me in the courtyard after this tune."

Her gasp was barely audible, but she met his gaze with more than trust filling her eyes. The excitement written on her face made him yearn for more than a kiss, though that was all he could hope for.

Sean released his hold and bowed. "M'lady." Then he spun on his heel.

Why does that bastard plague me every time I turn around? And what the hell is he doing dressed like he's going to a king's coronation?

As he headed outside, he ground his fist into his palm. He had no business arranging a secret meeting with a woman, especially his best friend's sister. *It must have been her eyes that caused my lack in judgment. I shall keep the conversation light and see her back to the hall before anyone realizes Gyllis has slipped away.*

Chapter Three

Gyllis could hardly wait until the dance with Alan was over. She glanced at the great hall doors every time she had a clear view of them. Had Sean honestly whispered in her ear and asked to meet her in the courtyard? At long last her dreams were finally coming true.

Her palms perspired as she skipped along in a serpentine pattern, grasping the other dancers' hands. When she completed the circle and again clasped hands with Alan, she shuddered. With his black hair combed away from his face, he was handsome, but the way his dark eyes regarded her made Gyllis uneasy. She could never trust someone with such an intense stare. He seemed almost crazed, and starved. Alan couldn't possibly be hungry, they'd only just dined.

She spun outward. From the dais Duncan watched her, sitting on the edge of his chair as if he could spring across the hall any minute. Why her brother was so overwhelmingly protective was beyond her. *Heaven's stars, he's more watchful than a father.* She harrumphed. *At least they want their daughters to marry and make alliances with other clans.*

When the music ended, Gyllis's stomach swarmed with an attack of butterflies.

"Would you care for another dance?" Alan asked.

Her gaze darted to the doors. If she told him she planned to take a turn in the courtyard, he'd surely follow her. "Thank you, but I would be remiss if I didn't suggest you dance with one of my sisters."

He grasped her hand. His touch was rough like Sean's, but firmer and nowhere near as inviting. "But I'd prefer to dance with you."

Gyllis pulled her hand away and rubbed it. "Perhaps another time." She curtsied and made the pretense of moving toward the wall while watching Duncan out of the corner of her eye. Fortunately, he'd turned his attention to a conversation with the chieftain beside him. When certain Alan wasn't following her, she skirted toward the door. With one last glance over her shoulder to ensure no one was watching, she slipped outside.

She stood for a moment, blinking her eyes to help them adjust to the darkness.

A hand grasped her elbow. "Walk with me."

Her heart stuttered. "Sir Sean, you are full of surprises."

He slid his hand down her forearm and threaded his fingers through hers. "Apologies. I hope you do not think me untoward."

"Not at all. We've know each other since I can remember." She leaned a bit closer to him. "Duncan trusts you—I trust you."

"Aye? Mayhap too much." He looked at her, the whites of his eyes glowing in the moonlight. "I shouldn't have asked you to step out with me."

"But I wanted to."

He drew her hand over his heart. "I cannot chance sullying your reputation."

Of course Gyllis knew what he meant, though she still looked over both shoulders. "That is why I was careful to ensure no one was watching when I slipped out of the hall."

He led her into the shadows at the far side of the well then turned and faced her, clasping both her hands between his much larger palms. "When I said you look bonny this eve, I really wanted to say you are more radiant than any woman in the hall." His voice grew deeper, the rumble of it making gooseflesh run in tingling waves over her skin.

They were standing so close she could have sworn Sean could hear her heart pattering. She emitted a nervous laugh. "You exaggerate, but I thank you." Her insides were about to bubble out of control like a tankard too full of ale. "I cannot say how happy I am you were able to come to the games. I prayed you would be here."

"You did?" He sounded surprised. "I would have thought a lass with such a well-respected family would have far greater things on her mind than me."

"You are the heir to a chieftainship. I think that would qualify as a suitable subject to occupy any noble lassie's thoughts. Unless…"

"Unless?"

She had to ask. "Are you promised?"

A deep chuckle rumbled from his chest. "Nay. I've been too busy keeping peace in the name of King James to become mixed up in a betrothal."

"Oh." Her shoulders tensed. *What did he mean by mixed up?* She started to step away, but he tugged her closer. So near, his warm breath caressed her forehead.

"Forgive me," he purred. "I shouldn't have jested."

She bit her bottom lip. "I'm afraid I'm being overly serious. After all, we've been friends all our lives. Why should you not jest?"

He brushed an errant lock of hair under her circlet. "Gyllis?"

"Aye?"

"Have you ever been kissed?"

"I—" Before she could utter her next word, Sean's lips brushed hers in the most feathery kiss she'd ever imagined. Her head spun. With a sigh, she swooned into him. "I've nay been kissed like that before."

"That was no kiss." He wrapped his arms around her as if creating a protective barrier where nothing in the world could harm her. His face looked incredibly bold in the moon glow—desire filled his eyes, yet the dark shadow of his beard and long, wavy hair gave him a look of danger.

Hot blood thrummed beneath her skin as he studied her lips. His breath smelled of mint laced with a hint of aged whisky. Her tongue slipped out and wet her bottom lip.

Please, kiss me again.

With a tilt of his head, Sean plied her with his sultry mouth. Gyllis's knees wobbled, making her body crush into his hard chest. Her breasts molded into him, filling with desire. She closed her eyes and melted. If there was a heaven, she'd found it in his arms.

He spread his lips slightly and probed with his tongue. Gyllis's eyes flashed open and she tried to tug her head away, but Sean's hand slid up and cradled her crown. Relaxing, she parted her mouth. It felt too good not to play along. Then he stroked her tongue. Shivers coursed through her body.

This kissing is earth shattering.

Again closing her eyes, she followed Sean's lead while he swirled his tongue with hers, as if their mouths were dancing. Then he trailed feathery kisses along her neck.

"Now that was a kiss, lass." His deep voice rumbled with intoxicating resonance.

Floating. I must be floating. "I cannot tell you how long I've wanted you to do that."

"Aye? I reckon I've thought about it for quite some time myself."

"Honestly?" Gyllis still could not believe she stood there in Sean's arms. "Why did you wait so long?"

He chuckled. "Your brother isn't overly fond of the idea, considering he and I are both the king's enforcers."

"If it were up to my brother, I'd live in spinsterhood the rest of my days."

"I doubt that, but 'tis hard for him to see his younger sister in the arms of a man."

She skimmed her finger along his bearded chin. "Would you feel that way—if you had a sister, that is?"

"Aye, I suppose I would." His breath skimmed hot on her face as he drew nearer and kissed her cheek. "I cannot bear to think of another man kissing you."

She grew bold, rose on her toes and kissed his lips. "I like kissing you."

"Mm." Sean slid his fingers along her neck and splayed them through her tresses as his mouth again plied hers with the most rapturous kiss imaginable.

Swooning in his arms, Gyllis wanted this moment to last forever. If only she and Sean were completely alone and not at a fete with people mulling about, she'd keep her arms wrapped around him and kiss him until the sun came up.

"Unhand her, MacDougall," demanded a gruff voice. "Taking advantage of the Lord of Glenorchy's sister? I always kent you were a cur."

Sean tugged Gyllis behind him and faced Alan MacCoul. "You're prying where you have no business."

"Am I now?" Alan sauntered toward them. "You were holding the lady in your arms and I've heard not a word of your betrothal."

Gyllis started to step forward. "Mr. MacCoul—"

Sean stopped her advance with a straight arm, glaring at Alan. "Why are you always poking your nose in my affairs?" In an instant, Sean's voice had gone from soothing to a deadly growl.

Alan fingered his dirk, his eyes narrowing. "I've never been able to tolerate a spoilt chieftain's son."

His dirk hissed from its scabbard. In one motion Alan lunged.

Gyllis screamed.

Sean sprang to the side and grabbed Alan's arm, twisting him away from Gyllis. The dirk dropped. As she skittered against the wall, Sean flipped the blackguard onto his back. Before she could blink, the MacDougall warrior had him pinned to the ground with his fingers clamped around his neck. "Why my father tolerates your shite, I'll never know."

Alan choked and kicked his feet to no avail. "You-you've no clue who I am, do you?" he croaked.

"What are you talking about?" Sean leaned in. "I ought to—"

Duncan barreled into the courtyard, brandishing his enormous sword. "Gyllis! What are you doing out here?"

She clutched her fists under her chin and shot a panicked glance to Sean. "I...I...I..."

"Get your bonny arse inside and find your mother. Bless it, must I weld a ball and chain around your ankle?"

"But..." She scooted past Sean and Alan, her hands trembling. "He protected me."

Sean kept his eyes on Alan, but inclined his head toward her. "I shall see you anon, Miss Gyllis."

"Until the morrow, Sir Sean." She hastened to the door, but before entering, turned to watch.

Duncan pointed his sword at Alan's temple. "Be on your way MacCoul. This is a time of truce, no matter your quarrel with MacDougall. All can be settled with a bit of healthy competition."

Sean released his grasp and stood, palming a dagger. "I shall relish such an opportunity."

Alan scrambled to his feet, retrieved his dirk and shook it at them both. "This will *never* be over. I will imprison you in irons and laugh while your body rots in a dank and musty cave." The hatred in the man's voice was palpable.

Why on earth is he so bitter? Chewing her lip, Gyllis darted inside and skirted around the noisy hall before Duncan could chastise her yet again.

Clasping her hand taut to her chest, she raced toward Helen.

"Gyllis, Ma has had us searching all over for you. Where have you been?"

She grabbed Helen's hands and tugged her toward the stairwell. "Hurry. I'm bursting at the seams to tell you."

"What is it? You look like you could dance on the rafter beams."

Gyllis waggled her eyebrows. "I probably could if someone gave me a lift." She raced up the winding steps and into the tiny chamber where all four sisters were appointed to sleep. She closed the door and caught her breath. "You'll never believe it."

"What?"

"I know not what was more romantic," Gyllis bubbled. "The kiss or that he fought for my virtue."

"A kiss?"

Gyllis grasped Helen's hands and spun her in a circle. "Aye. At last Sir Sean kissed me."

Helen giggled. "Honestly? How scandalous—and here at Beltane with so many people about?"

Spinning off across the room, Gyllis hugged herself. "Aye." She stopped and swayed in place. "It was glorious, Helen. I felt like I was floating away on a wispy cloud."

Her sister drew her hand to her lips. "And you said he fought for your virtue?"

"After he kissed me, Alan MacCoul came out and drew his dirk—said all sorts of vile things."

"Oh no," Helen gasped with her eyes wide. "That dreadful man."

"Aye, but in the blink of an eye, Sean disarmed him and wrestled him to the ground. Why I've never seen a man move so fast."

"Did he hurt him?"

"I do not think so." Gyllis rolled her eyes. "Then Duncan came charging out of the hall like a mad hornet and sent Alan on his way." Her shoulders dropped. "And then he ordered me inside, the brute—spoilt all my fun."

Helen pulled her onto the pallet and sat facing her. "Goodness, it sounds as if you had enough excitement to last the duration of the games."

Emitting a long sigh, Gyllis grinned. "The best part?"

"Aye?"

"'Tis only the first day."

Chapter Four

The next morning, Sean found a place behind the stables to stretch his aching limbs. Though he was accustomed to sleeping on hard ground, the floorboards in the great hall provided no comfort. At a gathering like this, rank mattered not. A single man spread his plaid in any available space, unless he was an earl.

"There you are." Gyllis strode toward him, smiling like sunshine. She held out a white kerchief. "Will you take this for luck?"

He accepted the token and turned it over in his hands. Embroidered with bluebells, he couldn't help but hold it to his nose. *It smells like a mountain of heather.* "My thanks." He offered a sheepish smile. Duncan had given him a good earful last eve, and he'd been right. Sean never should have asked Gyllis to meet him in the courtyard—especially after dark, without an escort, and with so many clansmen about. Any number of people could have assumed the worst and tried to ruin her reputation. Bloody hell, Sean could have been forced to marry the lass on the spot.

"Is something wrong?" she asked.

He blinked, thinking for a moment that marrying her would have been rather fun. "Nay." *Blistering barnacles.*

Sean didn't have time for a wife even if he could convince Duncan he was worthy to marry his sister.

"Then why are you looking at me as if I've got the ague?" Gyllis was too perceptive. But that's another thing he liked about her. Not only beautiful, she was sharp as a hawk and quick with her tongue.

He resisted his urge to grasp her hand and pull her into his arms. Instead, he nervously wrapped her kerchief around his pointer finger. "I've a fair bit on my mind."

She looked at the cloth and then her gaze trailed sidewise. "Would you…um….prefer not to carry my kerchief?"

Damn his hesitation—he'd offended her. He took a step in and cupped her cheek. "I am honored to carry it."

She turned up her face and pursed her lips, eyelids fluttering closed.

Sean couldn't help but take note of all the people mulling about. *Bless it, I cannot kiss her here.* The resulting scandal would be unmitigated. It would ruin her for certain and send Duncan and the Campbells after him like a pack of wild dogs. Sean clasped her slender fingers and drew them to his lips, giving her a quick peck. Forget the heather. The scent of her skin smelled fresher than a pool of fragrant water lilies. He closed his eyes and inhaled again, until she slid her fingers from his grasp.

With a look of bewilderment she cradled her hand and stared at it, as if she were no longer willing to look at his face. "I'm told the piping and drumming competition will be during the feast this eve."

"Aye? That should liven things up."

"Gyllis." Helen came from around the stable's corner. "Mother is looking for you. We must take our places for the race."

She grinned at Sean—though her smile had a twist, as he might have confused her with his reluctance to kiss her lips. "You'd best go, else you'll miss the start."

He held up the kerchief. "I'd better. And thank you—this will bring me luck, I am certain."

Sean watched her disappear around the stable wall while clenching his jaw. He either needed to have a somber discussion with her brother, or rein himself in. And given his present state of affairs, he should do the latter. MacDougalls didn't marry Campbells, not since the time of Robert the Bruce when the MacDougalls had lost over half of their holdings—some of which were unfairly dispatched to the Campbell Clan. Many a man loyal to his father still harbored deep resentment for the Campbells.

The ram's horn sounded, announcing the race would soon begin. Sean shook his head and headed off. He hadn't come to the games to make merry with Gyllis. He'd come to earn the respect of his countrymen—to win these games and ensure MacDougall continued to be a feared name throughout the Highlands.

Nearly fifty contestants formed a queue at the edge of Loch Etive whilst Lorn's clerk launched into a proclamation of the rules. "There will be no backstabbing and no weapons of any kind…"

Sean chuckled to himself. A Highland race wasn't without its share of backstabbers. It didn't surprise him to see Alan MacCoul halfway down the line leering at him like a venomed snake.

Duncan trotted up beside Sean. "I nearly missed it."

Sean arched an eyebrow. "Is anything amiss? 'Tis not like you to be late to a contest of any sort."

"A missive came from the king."

"Aye? What did it say?"

Duncan patted his doublet. "Dunno—haven't opened it yet. If I had, I would have missed the start. Besides, a missive can wait a bit even if it is from his grace."

"Remind me to tell the king you said that the next time we're at court."

Duncan smirked. "Should such a foul rumor come my way, I would deny it emphatically."

The clerk finished his oration and the ram's horn sounded. Sprinting, Sean sped ahead to ensure he positioned himself at the front of the pack. And in an eight-mile race, he'd keep pace behind the leader until the very end.

Duncan had the same idea and bloody MacCoul wasn't far behind. Sean wouldn't concern himself with that blackguard. He'd drop off soon enough.

Everything proceeded in respectable civility until Sean and the leaders rounded a farmhouse at the halfway point. Two brigands wearing chausses and shirts sprang from nowhere, barreling straight toward Sean. Startled by the movement of the first attacker, Sean's instincts took over. Ducking, he flung the bastard over his back. When the second one hit, he wasn't so lucky. Walloped in the side of the head, he stagger-stepped sideways until he crashed to the ground.

It was bad enough to have the contestants fighting each other, but now hoodlums had been planted? Someone must have a very large wager indeed.

Sean scrambled to his feet, fists at the ready. Out of the corner of his eye, he saw Duncan throw a boot into number one's gut. Sean eyed the second man and aimed a blow at the hinge of his jaw. Hitting his mark, teeth cracked. The bastard's hands flew to his face before he collided with the dirt.

Duncan beckoned him. "Hurry."

Sean ran beside his friend. "Who were those swine?"

"No idea." Duncan took in a deep inhale. "But I'm certain they were waiting for you. They darted straight for you without a mind to the others."

Sean sped his pace. "We can still win if we push."

Duncan waved him on. "This is your sport. Go."

Sean sprinted for the leaders, more intent than ever to win. Someone had set a trap for him—knew he was the man to beat.

***

Most of the spectators lined the outer bailey wall-walk on the Loch Etive side of the castle, all straining for a glimpse of the leaders in the footrace. Gyllis stood beside Helen, barely able to contain her excitement.

Yes, Sean had appeared a tad despondent when she'd given him her kerchief, but after all, he was preparing for a race. If they hadn't been interrupted last eve, she would have given it to him then. But she didn't want to think about that now. The weather was fine and Sean would sit with her during the feast just as they'd planned. She needn't consider a thing beyond that at the moment.

"There they are," someone yelled.

Gyllis cast her gaze toward the wood. Four runners barreled out of the trees, racing for the castle. The second man shoved the leader, who swung back his elbow. The closer they came to the finish line, the more the runners pushed with fists swinging.

"How can they stay ahead of the pack when they're fighting like that?" Helen asked.

"The fighting has most likely just begun," said a man behind them.

A fifth man darted from the forest. Gyllis made out Sean's long stride, close behind the fighting leaders.

Alice shook her finger. "Look! Alan MacCoul is winning."

Unable to believe it, Gyllis leaned further over the crenel notch. Sure enough, Alan had shoved his way into the lead. "But Sir Sean's speeding around them."

Shouts from the crowd grew louder.

Gyllis hopped in place and clapped her hands. "Faster, Sir Sean!"

Alice shook her fists in the air. "Run like the wind, Mr. MacCoul."

Gyllis gave her sister a firm whack on the shoulder. "Excuse me. How can you cheer for that blackguard after he threatened Sir Sean with his dirk last eve?"

Alice stopped hopping up and down. "He did?"

"Aye." With a well-founded nod, Gyllis returned her attention to the race. Sean indeed was moving closer to the lead, now one or two paces behind Alan. Her gaze darted to the finish line. *I don't think he can make it. Heavens, if Alan wins, it will upset everything.*

Sean closed the gap. Alan struck out with his right. Sean clutched his arm and stumbled over the finish line right behind that blasted MacCoul. Within the blink of an eye, the Lord of Lorn's officials surrounded Sean.

"He's been cut!" someone yelled from below.

Gasping, Gyllis started for the stairwell.

"You shall remain up here, young lady." Mother grasped her shoulder.

"But Sir Sean's been hurt."

Mother rolled her eyes with a tsk of her tongue. "I assure you, simply sparring with your brother has caused Sir Sean injuries much worse than a wee cut on the arm."

Gyllis huffed and resumed her place in front of the crenel notch. She couldn't see *anything*. Sean was surrounded by any number of men and Alan was nowhere to be seen.

"It appears you were right about Mr. MacCoul," Alice said. "He definitely acts like he's a bastard."

"Pardon me?" Mother stepped between them. "Mind your vulgar tongue."

Gyllis inched away until she was out of Ma's grasp. Not knowing how badly Sean was injured twisted her stomach in knots. She could stand there no longer. "I'm heading out to see what I can do to help."

"Gyllis," Mother called.

She didn't stop. If nothing else, she had to ensure Sean was all right. She dashed down the narrow spiral steps, pushing past people dawdling about, and ran out through the gate. Stopping in her tracks, Gyllis suddenly couldn't breathe. The crowd had thinned and Sean stood with a woman wrapped in his embrace. The woman's face was blocked by her wimple, but there was no mistaking it, Sean had his arms around the lass for a good long time.

Dumbfounded, Gyllis stood and stared. Her hands shook. She wanted to scream, but could form no words through the tightening of her throat.

A man walked past and brushed her shoulder. "I beg your pardon."

Gyllis blinked, but was still too stunned to acknowledge the man. She backed into the tunnel of the barbican and drew her hand to her chest. *I'm a fool, a stupid romantic who will never find a husband because my family locks me away in a castle and hardly ever allows me to visit court. Beltane was my chance—and now if that mutton-head dares to come sit on my plaid this eve, I'll tell him exactly what I think of him. Mayhap he's double-crossed Mr. MacCoul—mayhap that's why Alan lashes out at Sean at every opportunity.*

***

Da? Dead? Sean had gone completely numb. He couldn't feel the wee cut to his arm, nor did he care. When Angus and Jinny approached with the news, he'd fallen into Jinny's outstretched arms, hardly able to inhale.

"It has only been two days. He told me he was fine." Sean coughed to choke back the tears welling in his eyes.

"Aye," said Jinny, the MacDougall Clan's healer. "We all thought it was a passing cold, but last eve he took a turn. 'Twas the sweating sickness for certain."

Sean glared at Angus, his father's man-at-arms. "Why did no one fetch me last eve?"

"He didn't complain at all. We had no idea how bad it was until this morn when Sarah took him his porridge." Angus looked him in the eye. "By then he was gone. 'Tis now up to you to lead the clan, m'laird."

Sean stood dumbfounded. For the love of God, he was now the Chieftain of Dunollie? Yes, he'd always known he'd succeed his father, but not like this, not now.

Angus inclined his head toward the horses. "We must away."

Jinny grasped Sean's arm and shoved up his blood-soaked sleeve. "I'll need to wrap this first. Angus, I've a rolled bandage in the satchel. Fetch it for me."

Sean tugged his arm away. "Nay. It can wait."

"'Tis too deep to ignore." She took the bandage from Angus. "You're as pig-headed as your father. It won't take but a moment, unless you want to grow weak in the head by the time you reach Dunollie."

With a groan, Sean held out his arm and nodded to Angus. "Who else knows about this?"

"We kept it quiet—didn't want word to slip out without informing you first."

"Good. I shall pen a formal proclamation after we reach Dunollie."

Jinny tied off the bandage. "'Tis only fitting it should come from you."

Sean pushed down his sleeve and strode toward his horse. At least Angus had been smart enough to gather his things and have his horse saddled and ready to ride as soon as he crossed the finish line.

"Where are you off to?" The Lord of Lorn rushed up to him, his black mantle billowing with the wind. "The swimming competition is anon—and MacCoul was disqualified for using a blade. You're our victor. You cannot—"

Sean gripped his uncle's shoulder and placed his lips to his ear. "Da's dead. Keep it to yourself until I have the keep in order. I must muster my men. Word like this gets out when our enemies ken I've been away, God knows what they'll do." Dread snaked up Sean's neck. Aye, he needed to grieve his father's death, but it was more important for him to take care of the clan. Once he had control, he'd issue an appropriate decree to be read by the criers.

"I shall make your excuses." Lorn pursed his lips. "Do what you must. I'll keep your confidence. But do not wait too long, else a scandal could erupt with your reputation sullied. People will think you've something to hide."

"It shan't be but a day, two at most." Sean mounted his horse. "Besides, this news would serve to put a damper on your festivities. You wouldn't want that." He dug in his heels and cantered south to Dunollie. Thank God he was only four miles away. If he'd still been on the borders it would have taken him a week to travel home—and even longer for Angus to find him.

Chapter Five

Gyllis sat in her saddle with her back hunched and stared at her gelding's withers. She'd been furious when Sean didn't bother to present himself at all during last night's Beltane festival. She couldn't decide what hurt worse, seeing him in the arms of another woman, or having been completely disregarded as if her invitation meant nothing. Her heart ached—felt like Sean had taken his dagger and cut it out.

Duncan had been right. Sean MacDougall was not good enough for her or any of the Campbell sisters. He was a womanizer of the worst sort.

Worse, Gyllis had not accomplished a one of her goals on their trip to Dunstaffnage and now she and her sisters were headed back to Kilchurn Castle to be tucked away until Lord knew when. Her entire body hurt. Her throat was sore—probably from crying herself to sleep—her eyelids were heavy and her head hurt so much, she could have sworn someone clamped it between a pair of smithy's tongs.

At least she'd be protected from the cruel world cloistered within Kilchurn Castle's curtain walls. If she never saw Sean MacDougall again, it would be too soon. She stuck out her tongue and spat. *And to consider I kissed*

*his filthy mouth. I wish I could curl up in my chamber and never
come out.*

Her sisters were riding just behind Mother with Gyllis
taking up the rear. Of course, they were accompanied by a
heavily-armed guard of sixteen men in four-point
diamond formation. When they traveled, Duncan always
ensured they had a well-armed retinue to protect them
against outlaws.

Gyllis looked over her shoulder and realized her
brother wasn't with them. "Where *is* Duncan?"

Mother turned in her saddle. "He received a dire
missive from the king. He left for court at first light.
Enforcers business."

*What is it about the Highland Enforcers? They are always here
and gone. Sean's most likely traveled with him—not that I care
about his whereabouts in the slightest.*

"Lady Meg will not like it when she discovers he's off
to court again," Helen said.

Alice tapped her mare's rump with her riding crop.
"Heaven's stars, Duncan's wife awaits him with two wee
bairns and he's off on yet another *inordinately* important
errand."

"It is not our place to question your brother. He's the
Lord of Glenorchy," Mother said. Gyllis could swear Ma
would defend Duncan with her last breath.

Helen smoothed a hand over her veil. "Aye, but not
everyone is made of iron, Ma. I have no idea how you
lasted for seven years while Da was fighting in the
Crusades."

"That which you cannot change must be endured. I
coped quite nicely—and the Glenorchy coffers grew
healthier as a result. If you are faced with adversity, you
must meet it head-on and make the best of your lot."
Mother twisted round and shook her finger at the lasses.
"Eventually you will gain reward from your efforts."

Slumping further in her saddle, Gyllis presently cared not to think of being strong and industrious. She was not the lady of a keep, nor did she have any prospects of becoming one…unless Duncan was at court arranging a betrothal with some unsuspecting noble. *Aye? That will never happen.*

Swooning with a wave of nausea, she moved her hand over her mouth. Her throat burned with an awful taste oozing over her tongue. Quickly, she leaned away from her gelding and retched with a gagging croak.

If it hadn't been for her knee hooked in the top pommel of her sidesaddle, she would have fallen on her face, curled into a ball and waited for death to claim her right there on the trail.

"Halt!" Mother shouted. A circle of horses surrounded Gyllis. "Are you ill, child?"

"I think I am." Gyllis's mouth filled with saliva while her head pounded even more relentlessly than before. "Initially I thought I was upset, but I'm perspiring and shaking. Everything aches."

Mother pointed eastward. "Mevan, you must speed our pace."

"Very well, m'lady." The man-at-arms circled his hand over his head. "You heard her ladyship. Onward."

Gyllis had no choice but to persevere, growing sicker by the moment. By the time they reached Kilchurn Castle, she could no longer sit. She slumped over her horse's neck, eyes closed, holding on and hoping the gelding would remain on course with the others. Her entire body felt as if pins had been jabbed into her flesh. Every step the horse made jostled her bones like she would shatter at any moment.

Maintaining a fast trot, Mevan led them into the inner courtyard. Unassisted, Mother hopped from her mount and addressed her man-at-arms. "We must see her above stairs straight away." She then pointed to Marion and Alice. "Quickly, fetch Lady Meg. Tell her Gyllis's illness came on suddenly. She'll know what to do."

Mevan stepped beside the gelding and reached up. "Fall into my arms, Miss Gyllis, I'll see you're right comfortable in no time."

It took all her strength to slip her knee from the top pommel and ease off the saddle.

Mevan's grip clamped too tight, like knives gouging her flesh. "You're afire, lass."

The rumble of his voice caused her head to throb with unbearable pain. Gyllis shook uncontrollably. Her teeth chattered. "I'm so c-cold."

"I've no doubt you're fevered," he said, whisking her into the keep and straight up the tower stairs.

Gyllis clutched her arms close to her body, praying the jostling would soon stop so she could collapse in the folds of her bed. The whole castle was drafty—made her teeth chatter. With no fire lit in her chamber, it was as frigid as it had been outside. She crawled under the bedclothes and shivered while her head pounded mercilessly.

***

Angels wept from the dreary skies while Sean stood at the graveside beside Kilbride Church on Dunollie lands. The priest droned in an endless monotone, chanting the Latin burial mass. The Tenth Chieftain of Dunollie's death mask had been hastily made. Sean had arranged for the most skilled stonemason to carve the effigy that would complete the tomb, but presently his father's body lay wrapped in linen, hands still holding his bejeweled sword, awaiting internment into the granite crypt that would house his body through eternity.

Sean's mother had died of consumption five years past. Her death had been a somber time in his life, but did not compare to the hollow void now filling his heart.

Da had been a powerful and decisive man. His father led the clan, facing the brutal realities of life, yet he had a gentle streak—one Sean didn't always understand. But from his first memories, he'd looked up to his father— aspired to be like him. A tickle of doubt needled at the back of his neck. How in God's name would he fill his father's shoes?

The clanswomen lamented and sniffled around him. Yet he couldn't weep. The Eleventh Chieftain of Dunollie could not demonstrate weakness. Sean's jaw clenched as he endured the morose tones from the seemingly endless mass.

When at last the priest was silent, he nodded to Evanna, Jinny and Angus's daughter. The lass stepped forward, wiped her eyes, inhaled deeply and began to sing a ghostly tune.

Watchin' yon hills of the heather,
On the shores of the deep blue sea,
A bonnie young lassie sat singin' her sone,
Wi' dew on her plaid an' a tear in her e'e.
She swayed wi' a galley a'sail and aw'ee,
An' aye as it lessen'd she sigh'd an' she sung,
Fareweel to the lad I'll ne'er again see
I'll nay forget ye. Alas, yer mem'ry 'll alway' be wi' me…

Evanna's voice sang clear as a curlew soaring above a loch on a misty dawn. The purity of her tone made chills spread across Sean's back. She repeated the sad verse twice while wails from the women rose.

When the song ended, an eerie pall cast a heavy blanket atop the gathering of MacDougall clansmen and women. The only sounds were sniffles and rainwater dripping from the leaves. Sean had not the inclination to move. He stared at his father's body. Everyone did. He'd always known this time would come, but had been so busy adventuring throughout Scotland, he had never considered it would come so soon. But it wasn't unusual for any man to meet the Lord at eight and fifty.

If only I had spent more time with him. Now I'll nay have a chance.

Angus stepped forward and bowed. He then retrieved the sword from Da's body and strode directly to Sean. "In the name of King James, you are the rightful heir. Carry the chieftain's sword with pride." The henchman held the two-handed sword out. "*Buaidh no bàs.*"

"*Buaidh no bàs!*" the clan chorused with the Gaelic MacDougall motto, victory or death.

Clenching his teeth, Sean grasped the sword and drew it from its scabbard. "I will carry this with pride and the MacDougall Clan will grow and prosper." He held the blade over his head. "*Buaidh no bàs!*"

He slid the sword back into its sheath, secured it in his belt and set out. Thunder cracked overhead as he led the clan down the path to Dunollie Castle.

Behind him, hurried footsteps slapped the mud.

The hackles on Sean's neck prickled.

Before he could turn, Da's sword was yanked from his belt. "I should be Chieftain of Dunollie, not a miserable piss-swilling maggot!"

Drawing his dirk, Sean whipped around and crouched. Alan MacCoul moved fast as a fox. With teeth bared, he hacked down in a deadly challenge. Sean jumped back as the blade hissed through the air, just missing his flank. Circling, Sean eyed his nemesis. At last the bastard had given him the opportunity to end their feud once and for all.

Eyeing his target, he waited for Alan to strike—to give him a flicker of an opportunity, and Sean would attack. "Make your move," he growled.

A thud sounded like a stick of wood hitting a tree. Alan's arms dropped with the sword, his face stunned. He plummeted to his knees then fell to his face.

Angus stood behind him, holding a branch as big around as a man's calf.

Sean picked up his father's sword. "Why did you not let me finish it?"

Alan writhed and groaned.

Angus grasped the cur under the arm and tugged him to his feet. "I've no stomach for another funeral this day."

Sean sauntered forward and slid the blade under MacCoul's chin. "In honor of my father I'll spare you. Take your galley and be gone. I'll have no more of your backstabbing. You are banned from Dunollie lands forever."

Spitting, Alan struggled in Angus's grasp. "He was nay merely your father."

"Aye, we're all hurting." Angus pulled him toward the embankment where the clan's galleys were moored.

"Angus," Sean hollered. "I'll need to see you in my solar forthwith."

***

Sean sat and stared at his goblet of whisky. His jaw twitched and his gut churned. This was a black day. He may as well make it blacker.

A rap resounded on the door.

Sean raised his goblet and sipped. He'd swirled the fiery liquid around his mouth before swallowing. He knew who'd knocked and it served the varlet right to wait. After one more sip, he placed the goblet on the table. "Come."

Angus stepped inside with his bonnet in hand. "MacCoul has sailed with his galley, m'laird."

After staring at him without blinking, Sean grasped his armrests and squeezed. "I'd have finished him if you hadn't stepped in."

"Aye."

"You ken more than anyone, MacCoul has been a thorn in my side since the day I was born."

"Aye."

"Have you nothing else to say for yourself?" Sean leaned forward. "My father protected that bastard. Do you now see yourself taking up MacCoul's mantle?"

Angus let out a labored sigh and glanced sideways, high color flushing his face. "Nay."

"Then why did you stop me?" Sean slammed his fist on the table.

The older man jolted at the sudden noise then spread his palms. "I-I just reacted. Mayhap 'twas your father's voice in my head."

"It'll nay happen again." Sean shoved back and stood with his palms flat on the table. "Do you ken how your actions made me look in front of the clan?"

"Aye, but you were distraught."

"Damn it, man, I was defending myself from attack." Sean paced then kicked a chair. "I respect you as my father's henchman, but you will never make me look the fool again."

"Apologies." Angus bobbed his head. "Agreed. I acted without thought. You've every right to be upset with me."

Sean shook his finger. "I do and I am." He flicked his wrist. "Go fetch the factor. I want an accounting of the coffers—everything from crofters rents, to notes outstanding, to the size of our herds."

"Aye, m'laird."

Sean held up his hand. "A moment."

Angus raised his brows expectantly.

"Have we any eminent threats?" He didn't know of any, but he'd been away so much the question needed asking.

"Aside from the errant cattle thief and outlaws in the wood west of Black Lochs, things have been at relative peace for the past five years."

"What have you done to rid the forest of the outlaws?"

Angus's Adam's apple bobbed. "Whenever we run them off, 'tis a matter of time afore they're replaced by another unsavory lot."

Sean nodded. "I aim for Dunollie to remain at peace and free from attack. After I've met with the factor, I want a detailed account of skirmishes as far back as you can remember."

Angus bowed. "Very well, m'laird. I'll return with Master Murdach momentarily."

Chapter Six

Alan MacCoul didn't sail far—it wasn't even a league to the miserable Isle of Kerrera his father had granted him in hopes he'd till the soil or raise sheep and live a quiet life away from the scrutiny of society. But Alan had no yen for the life of a farmer. He was a warrior, a leader of men.

Even his father would be proud to see the army he'd amassed. The nobleman had been embarrassed by Alan his entire life—did everything to hide his bastard from the world, but that only served to make Alan more determined to prove his worth. He'd spent a few years on the borders, helping the reivers steal sheep and cattle from the English—and each other in lean times. Alan had grown strong and his sword was valued there—as was his coin. All he need do was send word and he'd have five score of Lowlander fighting men, not to mention another score of deposed MacDougalls in addition to Campbells who couldn't stomach the Earl of Argyll's tyranny.

He kept things quiet on Kerrera, however—at least until all was in place to declare his superiority. If he moved too soon, he might lose his income stream, and that most certainly wouldn't do.

He seethed. He'd been standing alone at the stern of his galley, jaw set. Being exiled by Sean MacDougall was almost more than he could bear. *I will make that sniveling magpie pay and I'll laugh as I watch him suffer.*

Alan's mother had made sure he had a place in the MacDougall Clan. After all, it was her clan too, though she had passed years ago.

His most trusted men, Brus and Trevor, came up on either side of him as the galley neared the shore. Brus placed a foot on the bench. "You're nay planning to roll over and take your exile like a dog are you?"

Alan lashed out with a fisted backhand. "Watch your bloody mouth."

Brus stumbled into the hull and wiped his jaw.

Alan leered at him and then Trevor. "How many times do I have to tell you we must wait—seize the opportunity when the time is right?"

"Aye, but with recent events, I'll wager it'll be soon."

Alan grinned. "I've some games planned for the new Chieftain of Dunollie to keep him occupied whilst we prepare."

Trevor nodded. "I like the sound of that."

"First we'll need to ensure our galley is hidden from the mainland. No need for passersby to spot my boat—especially MacDougall men."

"Easily done," Trevor said.

"Good, call the men together. We shall set things in motion this eve." When the galley eased to a stop upon the smooth rocks, Alan looked toward the shore. "Have you found a smithy? We need to keep building our cache of weapons."

Brus pointed toward the cave. "I can hear the iron clanging—but he's nay happy with his accommodations."

"Bloody hell, most smithies sleep on the hard floors in their shops—what kind of milk-livered…"

The blacksmith stepped out of the cave and held a sword up to the sunlight. Wearing a leather apron, the man must have weighed eighteen stone. His forearms alone were as thick as the galley's mast. The corner of Alan's mouth ticked up. "See to it he has first pick of the wenches next time the whores visit from the village. I could use muscle like that fifty times over."

After Alan hopped over the rail, he strode directly to the smithy and held out his hand. "Welcome. Alan MacCoul here."

The man offered a firm shake and a suspecting eye. "Walter, m'lord."

"I'm no man's lord." Alan smirked. "At least not as of yet. Tell me, is everything on Kerrera to your liking?"

The big man rubbed his backside. "Aye, but I could use a bit more hay for my pallet."

"Consider it done." Alan clapped the smithy's beefy shoulder. "I aim to ensure everyone shares in my success and I only ask for one thing in return."

"What would that be?"

"Loyalty." He uttered the word slowly to ensure there'd be no misunderstanding.

***

Gyllis lay on the bed and listened to Mother and Meg discuss her failing health. They likely thought she couldn't hear them. Though she could barely move, her ears and eyes had not been affected by the illness that plagued her.

"It has been over a week and she continues to decline." Across the room, Meg wrung her hands. "And now she's showing signs of paralysis. Her joints are stiff. I'm afraid her condition has gone beyond my abilities."

Mother cast a worried glance toward Gyllis. "This morn she could scarcely swallow her willow tea."

Meg crossed herself. "May God have mercy on our dear sister."

If Gyllis could have screamed, she would have. But presently her voice was but a garbled whisper, her throat raw and sore. She had no intention of dying. She couldn't. There were too many things she had yet to do in this life, bless it. Her head pounded and she closed her eyes, willing the pain away.

"I wish Duncan were here." Mother covered her mouth with her palm. "Last eve I sent for John."

Though Gyllis's head throbbed, her heart squeezed at the idea of seeing her closest brother. John had joined the priesthood and now was the prior at Ardchattan. Gyllis rarely had the chance to see him, but enjoyed it immensely when she did. *If only he could make me better.*

"As a man of the cloth, I do believe he may be a better brother than Duncan. He'll know what to do for certain," Meg said. She'd always been pious, and though Gyllis adored her, she was growing rather tired of Duncan's wife voicing her fears of doom.

"Mother," Gyllis said, her voice croaking like a toad from the loch.

Ma hastened to her bedside and grasped her hand. "Aye, my sweeting?"

"When will John arrive?"

She cast a worried glance to Meg. "Soon—as soon as he can spirit away from the priory, I'll ensure he comes straight up to see you."

Gyllis tried to swallow and coughed. "I want to see him."

"'Tis a good sign." Mother patted her hand. "Drink some more tea whilst we wait."

Meg reached for the cup while Mother helped Gyllis sit up. She could barely move her hands to grasp it. Meg helped her by tilting it back, but when the bitter brew hit her mouth, she erupted in a coughing fit. The tea spewed across the bedclothes and down the front of Mother's apron.

Wheezing, Gyllis hung her head and tried to swipe her brow with her hand, but couldn't lift the trembling appendage. "I'm sorry."

Mother helped her recline and brushed at the wet spot. "You mustn't worry. We should have used the spoon."

Tears stung Gyllis's eyes. "I hate this."

"I know sweetheart. Do not worry overmuch, John will be here soon." Mother patted her cheek. "You should rest until he arrives."

With heavy eyelids, Gyllis nodded. "What is wrong with me?"

"I wish we knew," said Meg. She brushed her fingers of her good hand over Gyllis's hair. Meg had a cleft hand she called *the claw* that she tried to keep hidden for the most part. "One thing I do ken—you are a fighter, just like your father. You will not allow this illness to overcome you. Of that I am certain."

Gyllis shivered and sank into the mountain of pillows the women had layered behind her back. If only this horrid sickness would pass, she could focus on regaining her strength. Mother and Meg headed toward the door, their voices muffled in hushed tones. Gyllis wanted to listen, but the effort was more than she could manage.

After the door closed, Meg pattered across the floor and sat on the bed, picking up Gyllis's hand. "I've sent to the physician's council in Edinburgh and requested information on your symptoms. I'm not sure what my appeal will turn up, but I'll leave no stone unturned. Until then, the priory is the best place for you. The monks will be able to provide the care you need."

Gyllis licked her dry lips. "I do not want to go to Ardchattan. I'll be away from you and Helen."

"I ken." Meg lightly brushed her fingertips over the back of Gyllis's hand. "Helen told me things didn't go well for you at the Beltane festival."

"The first night, Sir Sean was so charming." A lump caught in her throat. "I cannot bring myself to speak of the rest."

"Well, if Sean MacDougall isn't the man for you, I'm sure we shall find another gallant knight who will adore you completely. Let us see to your recovery and then I will make it my duty to ensure Duncan has a line of suitors queued up to offer for your hand."

"*If* I ever do recover." The lump in her throat grew.

"Do not say that. Your illness may have knocked you about, but between John, the monks and what I can find, we shall see you set to rights."

"Thank you." Gyllis weakly brushed her thumb over Meg's finger. "Has Duncan returned from court?"

"Not as of yet," she sighed.

"I am sorry."

"No need. He shall be home as soon as the king's business is settled else we shall need to build a home in Stirling as well."

Gyllis emitted a rueful chuckle and then yawned. "If you want Elizabeth and Colin to know who their father is, that may be your best option."

Meg leaned forward and kissed her forehead. "Sleep my dear. We shall wake you when John arrives."

***

"Gyllis?" a deep voice called her name. He spoke so softly, the tone soothed her. If only she could hear it again, but then she would have to wake. "Gyllis, lass," it came again.

She stirred. "Sean MacDougall, is that you calling my name?" She'd welcome a dream even of Sean to while away the body aches and sickness—for her dreams were the only place she'd ever again see him.

"Nay, 'tis your brother, John."

Gyllis opened her eyes, a faint smile splitting her upper lip with a sharp sting. "You came."

"And you still have your heart set on that MacDougall roustabout."

She attempted to raise her hand, but it was too heavy. "'Tis good to see you."

Dressed in black robes, John looked ever so serious— a far cry from the lad who used to show her how to climb trees and net fish in Loch Awe. He tugged the bedclothes down slightly and grasped her shoulders. "What's ailing you?"

"It started with the sweat and shakes, and now my limbs ache so much I can hardly move."

He took one arm and massaged it between his large hands. "Does this feel good?"

"Aye."

He took each arm and rested them by her sides. "Now see if you can lift them."

With all her effort, Gyllis clenched her muscles and tried to raise her arms, but only the one John had rubbed rose off the bed."

John's brow creased. "Is that all the better you can do?"

Gyllis closed her eyes and bore down, trying to force her arms to rise.

John patted her shoulder. "'Tis a fine effort. I do not want you to overexert yourself."

"Have you ever seen this before? Do you have any idea what's wrong with me?"

He frowned and brushed a wisp of hair from her face. "You've paralysis for certain."

A cry caught in her throat. "Is there a cure?" she whispered, dread filling her voice.

"I've seen it in the infirmary at the priory. It seems to attack its victims and linger." He scratched his chin and hummed. "If anyone can recover from this, 'tis you, but it will not be easy. God gave you a willful spirit for a reason."

He pulled the bedclothes up to her chin and gave her a pat. "I'll need to take you to Ardchattan Priory. The monks can care for you far better than Lady Meg—nothing against Duncan's wife, but you need more care than one person can give."

A tear slipped from Gyllis's eye. "Oh John, why has this happened to me? One day I was happy and gay and the next, I became so ill I was certain I would die."

"Only God knows the reason one person is afflicted and another is not." He stood and clasped his hands as if he were praying. "As his sheep, our role is to take our lot in life and make the best of it—be strong and trust in God to lead us through the dark shadows."

She wanted to wipe the tears from her eyes, but had not the strength to put forth the effort. "When did you become so wise?"

He offered a faint smile. "If only it were thus. Rest. I shall arrange a transport forthwith."

Chapter Seven

Sean and his men rode west toward Fearnoch Forest. Cattle thieving had begun before the effigy had been placed on his father's grave. *If the outlaws think they can cross me, they've another thing coming. And why did Da not send for me when I was on the borders? Every time the MacDougall drove out the vermin they were replaced by others? I've been battling lawlessness since I reached my majority. Now's the time to end it on my own lands.*

If the thieves thought they could take advantage of the MacDougalls because they were in mourning, they were sorely mistaken. "Did anyone see the backstabbing tinkers?"

Slapping his reins like he was beating a drum, Angus struggled to keep pace. "Nay."

"Six cattle thieved without a sign?" *I find that hard to believe.* A lot of things hadn't sat well with Sean since he started diving into the estate's affairs. And all had not been smooth whilst his father lived either. Small coin and livestock disappeared from the ledgers with a stroke of a pen. With each little adjustment Sean uncovered, his suspicion grew. That he had a traitor in his midst was certain. Who...was yet to be discovered.

"A rider approaches from the south," bellowed a sentry at the rear of the retinue.

Sean held up his hand and slowed his horse. Circling around, Fraser galloped toward them. Of all the MacDougall clansmen, Sean trusted him the most. They had been boyhood friends and Fraser often rode with him when carrying out Highland Enforcer tasks for the Lord of Glenorchy and the king.

"Another five head missing by the southern border."

Sean gaped. "Any sign of the thieves?"

"No, m'laird."

"That makes no sense at all—if the outlaws are holing up in Fearnoch Forest to the west, how are they slipping unseen to the south...and where are they driving *my* cattle?"

Angus rode in beside him and pulled up. "The two crimes could be unrelated."

Fraser's horse snorted and stomped its right front. "I reckon someone's testing your verve—trying to see what they can take from the new chieftain afore they get caught."

"They'll be caught and the risk is nay worth the gain." Sean looked up and watched a hawk circle overhead. "I've plenty of enemies, but only one comes to mind who'd go to so much trouble." He eyed Angus.

The older man's shoulder ticked up. "I do not think Alan MacCoul would stoop so low, besides, he sailed off in his sea galley a fortnight ago."

Sean smirked. "I could never trust that bastard." He raised his voice and eyed all his men. "Where did MacCoul sail after he left Dunollie lands?"

No one said a word. He dug in his heels and walked his horse along the line of men. "We'll rid the wood of outlaws, but moreover, I want a scout on MacCoul's trail." He spun his horse and started back the other way. Right now there weren't many men he could trust—or who had the necessary skills to follow a cold trail. "Hell,

I'll find him myself. I'm the best damn tracker in the Highlands."

"That you are," Fraser said.

"Do you think it wise to leave your lands so soon after you've taken up your father's mantle?" Angus asked. "There are a great many affairs needing your attention."

Sean had always trusted his father's henchman, but presently he questioned the man's loyalty.

"MacDougall!" A rider galloped from the direction of Dunollie. "I've a missive from the Lord of Lorn."

Sean threw up his hands. "Does everyone ken our whereabouts?"

"I didn't think it was a secret," Angus said.

Sean pointed at the laggard's sternum. "We need a sober discussion, you and I." He beckoned the messenger. "Come."

Sean took the missive and ran his finger under his uncle's red-wax seal and read.

"What is it?" Angus asked.

"My uncle…ah…has requested a meeting." He wasn't about to say where or when—not to Angus and most definitely not in front of all his men when there could be a backstabber about. He needed to learn whom he could trust and whom he couldn't and fast. Unfortunately, his uncle's summons changed Sean's plans.

He stuffed the missive in his doublet. "Angus, take the men and drive out any outlaws in the wood. Fraser, find out where MacCoul sailed after he left the clan. Better yet, find out where he's holing up and report back. I want to see you at Dunollie within a fortnight." He grasped his friend's shoulder and squeezed. "Do not fail me."

"On my way, m'laird."

***

"Trevor's galley approaches, sir," Brus hollered from the cave entrance.

With two more rutting thrusts, Alan ground his teeth with a grunt and finished swiving the whore he had shoved up against the cave's wall. Pulling up his trews, he shook himself off, revived at the relief of tension the quick hump had brought.

He expected good news. Hiding out on this God-forsaken island didn't suit him. The damp made his bones ache and his temperament border on the verge of tyrannical—not that intimidation was a problem. It was a tactic he used even when he wasn't feeling like an ogre.

Brus caught the mooring rope while the galley ran aground on the beach.

Followed by his men, Trevor hopped over the side, a daft grin spread across his face.

"Well?" Alan asked, leaving the whore in a tousled heap.

"Easier than taking a Sunday stroll with my ma," Trevor boasted.

"Out with it, man. I want details."

"Two bands thieved cattle. One to the west and the other to the south—exactly as you said." He dug in his purse. "I sold the beasts to a transport headed to Glasgow—Eleven marks, one for each head, less payment for me and the men."

Alan snatched the coin and counted it. Trevor had taken the agreed quarter. He didn't like that his men had taken their share first—but if he challenged the brigands with coin in their pockets, their loyalty would wane. "Did you see any trouble?"

"Nay—could thieve the laird's cattle every day, I'd reckon."

Alan was no fool. "If you tried tomorrow, you'd be caught for certain."

"I beg your pardon?"

"The alarm's raised by now. It will not be half as easy next time—besides how much torture could any one of your men take if caught?" Alan adjusted his crotch. "We shall lay low for a time—travel to visit our allies in the Lowlands where we do not have to hide in a cave."

The men nodded in agreement.

"Walter," Alan hollered over his shoulder.

The smithy stepped out from the cave's shadows. "Aye?"

"While we're away I want you to fashion irons for a man."

"You mean you're not taking me with you?"

"You heard me."

The blacksmith knuckled his head and glanced at the woman Alan had just discarded. "You'll leave the whore?"

"Very well."

"All right, then, but I'll need measurements."

Alan gestured to his body. "My size, but a hand taller."

Walter shook his head. "'Tis nay that easy—"

"Just see it done. I'll hear no more from naysayers." Alan turned to Trevor and Brus. "We sail at dawn."

***

Propped up with pillows, Gyllis closed her eyes and yielded to the monk's gentle ministrations. She'd been in the cell at Ardchattan Priory for a month now and, though the sickness had passed, the paralysis still plagued her. Even her breathing had become shallow and labored. She closed her eyes. Dark thoughts of a life as a cripple blackened her mind. She'd be a burden to her family—or to the priory unless by some miracle, God saw fit to give her the strength to walk again.

"I'll wager things are not as comfortable here for you as they are at Kilchurn Castle," Brother Wesley said in his ever-soothing voice. He had a sallow complexion with grey eyes, black hair, and his front teeth were large and crooked. It was difficult not to stare at them on the rare occasion he smiled.

How different and ever so mundane things were cloistered behind the priory walls. Nothing exciting ever happened—she never heard a voice raised or the clanging of swords when the guard sparred as she'd heard daily at Kilchurn Castle. The dangers of the world seemed a hundred miles away.

Gyllis glanced at the stark walls with a single wooden cross nailed above her head—aside from the bed, the only piece of furniture was a wooden stool. Brother Wesley looked at her expectantly.

"Aye, my chamber is five times the size of this cell," she answered. "And the bed is far softer than this cot." Indeed, she'd prefer to be home now.

He pressed the heel of his hand into her thigh and rubbed with a circular motion. Had he not taken an oath of celibacy, Gyllis could never have permitted him to care for her. "With God's grace, we shall have you up in no time. I'm sure you are anxious to return to your kin."

"If I could spring from this bed this moment, I would."

"You must take one thing at a time. 'Tis a long process to recover from a disease like paralysis." He patted her leg then resituated her skirts. "Let us see how your arms are faring today."

Her fingers twitched and she closed her eyes. Clamping her teeth and scrunching her face with effort, she forced herself to lift them from the bed. Sucking in a gasp, the worthless limbs dropped back down. She glared at Brother Wesley. "They're useless."

He lifted her hand and held it in his palm, offering a serene smile as if he had not a care. "You raised them twice as far as yesterday. I am impressed with your progress."

If only Gyllis could share in his subdued exuberance. If Brother Wesley were to raise one of his thick eyebrows, it would be an untoward display of emotion. "I most certainly am not pleased. Do you have any idea how miserable it is to lie on this cot hour upon hour unable to move?" And now she'd begun to suffer from bed sores.

"It must be very monotonous indeed."

"'Tis unbearable."

The monk frowned. "I shall continue to pray for you, Miss Gyllis."

That's all she'd heard since arriving at this miserable priory. "Praying? What good will that do? I cannot even feed myself—and the indignity of being changed like a bairn." She turned her face toward the wall and groaned.

"I am sorry—I shall continue to try to help, though my efforts have not met with your satisfaction."

Gyllis cringed. She'd just insulted the kindest, gentlest person she'd ever met. Devil's bones, this illness turned her into a curmudgeon. "Apologies, I did not mean to imply your ministrations have not been met with my sincerest gratitude." She took in a deep breath and willed the air to fill her limbs right through her fingers. With her exhale, her hands rose at least six inches. She chuckled and glanced at Brother Wesley.

"Praise be to God, Miss Gyllis." He stood and clapped his palms together. "I do believe the Lord's strength just showed the greatness of its power right through the tips of your fingers."

Her heart skipped a beat. "Let me try again." She closed her eyes. *Please, please, please.* Once more her hands rose from the bed. They trembled a bit, but she'd done it. No matter how small the win, it was something. She splayed her fingers. Without telling Brother Wesley, she tried to wiggle her toes. Possibly the toes on the right foot moved. She couldn't be certain.

The door opened and John stepped inside, holding a lute and a parcel. He grimaced at Brother Wesley and bowed his head. "Have I interrupted you?"

"I was just finishing." The monk straightened and smiled. "Miss Gyllis lifted her arms further than ever before."

John smiled. "Very good news."

"Indeed." Wesley bowed. "I should prepare for vespers."

"I shall be in the nave shortly." John sat on the stool beside her bed. "Mother sent a few things."

Gyllis eyed the lute in his hands, her spirits again sinking. "I doubt I'll ever have the wherewithal to play that again."

The cell was so small, he simply leaned back to place the instrument in the corner across from the bed. "We'll keep it here until you are ready." He reached inside the satchel and pulled out a book. "You might start with this first. We can prop you up and I'll wager you'll be able to turn the pages since you can raise your arms a bit."

Gyllis squinted at the title. *The Wedding of Sir Gawain and Dame Ragnelle & other Romantic Tales.* "My heavens, 'tis not the Holy Bible?"

John smoothed his palm over the leather binding—with light dun hair, her brother posed a handsome man. "I suppose Mother thought you'd prefer something lighter, though I'd be more than happy to replace this with a Bible from my own library."

Gyllis's fingers twitched, if only she could snatch the book from his hands and cradle it to her chest. She may never find romance for herself, but she certainly could live it through the text on the page. She'd read *The Legend of King Arthur* over and over until she could recite lengthy passages. "Please, can I start now?"

"Very well." He glanced around the tiny cell. "Perhaps you'll be able to read if I rest it in your lap." He opened the book to the first page then lifted Gyllis's arms and placed them across her lap.

Instantly she was transported by the mystical knight, Sir Gromer Somer Joure as he challenged King Arthur to discover what women desire most. Anxious to turn the page, her fingers twitched, her arm moved spasmodically and knocked the book from its perch.

John slid it back in place, but kept it open to the page she'd already read.

Grinding her teeth, Gyllis concentrated, focusing on the simple task of turning the page. When at last her feeble hand grasped the velum, her motion jerked, and the cursed book clattered to the stone floor. A cry caught in her throat. "Bless it, I am completely useless."

"I'll fetch it." He retrieved the book and again set it on her lap.

Gyllis shook her head. "No. What use is it if I cannot turn the pages myself?" She looked at the ceiling and wailed. She couldn't even clench her miserable fists. "My God, why has this happened to me? What did I do to deserve a life in purgatory?"

John placed his hand on her arm. "There, there. You mustn't fret."

"But I can do nothing without help." A tear spilled down her cheek. "It would have been better if God had taken my life than to have left me paralyzed with no prospects of recovery."

"I wouldn't say that. You've made progress."

"D-do you honestly believe that, John?" Uncontrollable sobs racked her body. It had been ages and ages since she fell ill—and she hated every moment of her confinement. "I am the most worthless lass who ever lived. I cannot even hold a miserable book. I'll never walk again. I'll never be courted by a dashing knight. I'll never bear children." She wiped her miserable nose on her shoulder because she couldn't—possibly never would be able to—use a worthless kerchief. "I am nothing."

Chapter Eight

Sean couldn't remember the last time he'd been to Ardchattan Priory, but he was looking forward to the prospect of seeing John Campbell, the prior. After the untimely death of John and Duncan's father, the younger son had left the Highland Enforcers to become a priest. Sean hated to see him go. He was a fine knight and a better friend.

He raised the blackened iron knocker on the cloister gate and rapped it twice.

Not long and a monk slid open the viewing panel. "Yes?"

"Sean MacDougall here, Chieftain of Dunollie. I've come to meet the Lord of Lorn, has he arrived as of yet?"

"Afraid not." The monk moved to shut the screen.

Sean thrust the hilt of his dirk into the opening before it closed. "Then perhaps I may have a word with the prior. John Campbell and I were boyhood friends."

A single eye peered through the gap. "I shall inquire if he is able to receive visitors."

The monk slid the panel closed. To Sean's surprise, the hinges on the big black gate creaked. When the door opened, the monk gestured to a bench in the cloister, walled on one side, hedged by a row of trimmed holly on the other. "Wait here."

Sean sat as directed. He crossed and uncrossed his legs, folded his arms, whistled a tune and then he stood. Not one to be idle, he paced. Behind the hedge someone chuckled. *A woman's voice.*

He peered over the shrubbery but saw no one. Only a few steps from the courtyard entrance, he walked to the break in the hedge and peeked around. A woman wrapped in blankets sat on a bench directly opposite from where Sean had been sitting. She wore a plain white veil atop her head and was looking down—in fact she was reading.

The book must have been interesting because her shoulders shook as if she might be laughing. If only he could see the joy upon her face, he'd enjoy a good laugh himself.

The woman's hands trembled and she slowly reached to turn the page—as if she were very old—though her fine-boned hands appeared smooth and ageless. Her shoulders tensed as she struggled to grasp the vellum. Sean cringed at her effort.

What illness afflicts the lass?

When she finally had the page turned, the blasted thing flipped back the other way.

"Argh." The agony in her voice clawed at Sean's heart.

He strode forward and plucked the book from her fingers. "Please. Allow me."

The woman gasped as if she'd been accosted.

Sean glanced at her face and froze. In that instant, his heart stopped, his mouth dried and his stomach plummeted to his toes.

He knew her. Cared for her. But something was terribly wrong. In that moment, she appeared so vexed and more so, stricken by horror. Christ, she was so skeletally thin, but he could never mistake the pair of mossy green eyes encircled by rings of navy blue.

He swallowed. "Gyllis?" he asked, his voice filled with disbelief.

She quickly averted her face. "Go away."

"It *is* you." Sean knelt beside her. "My God, what happened?"

Her shoulders tensed and she moved a trembling hand to block her face, seemingly afraid of catching a disease from him.

He wanted to place his palm upon her shoulder, but stopped himself by clutching the book tighter. "You're so frail and thin." He cast his mind back. "Yet a mere two months have passed since Beltane…"

"Please, return my book and leave me be."

Why was she being so despondent? They were friends—more than friends, for the love of God. "Will you not look at me—tell me what ails you?"

She snapped her head around, tears welling in her eyes. Unimaginable pain and anguish stretched her features. "Must you taunt me?"

The words came out as if she'd slapped him. "I would never do that." He knelt beside her. "Tell me what happened…why are you here?"

The fire that flashed through her eyes was akin to hate. What suffering had caused such bitterness? "As if you would care about me, Sean MacDougall. I'll not have you make a mockery of me, not ever again." Her voice choked. "Go. Live your life and forget I ever existed."

Sean reached for her hand and squeezed. *A mockery? Not ever again? She couldn't possibly mean that?* He'd always adored Gyllis, always thought of her as his… He blinked successively. Why was she acting thus? "Please—"

"Sir Sean." A monk hastened toward him, brown robes billowing. "The Lord of Lorn has arrived. He's asked to meet with you at once."

"I must go." Sean regarded Gyllis and placed the book on her lap. "I'd like to visit you again."

She stared at the volume. "'Tis best if you did not."

Sean's heart twisted with her every bitter word. Never had she been discourteous toward him. Why did Lorn have to be in such a damned hurry? He would have liked to find out more, but presently the lass proved none too eager to talk.

He pursed his lips and grasped her hand. Bowing his head, he pondered at the frailty of the fingers in his palm, whilst he savored her sweet fragrance. It had always captivated him. Closing his eyes, he pictured the Gyllis he knew—the lass with the free spirit and easy laugh. He placed a gentle kiss on her hand and straightened. "Until we meet again, Miss Gyllis."

The monk beckoned him. "This way. Prior John said he would attend you after."

Walking away, Sean cast one last glimpse over his shoulder. Gyllis watched him out of the corner of her eye. That something dreadful had happened was a certainty. What, he intended to find out before he left.

***

Gyllis stared at the book in her hands, except she couldn't see it through the tears filling her eyes. If she could have curled into a ball and died she would have. How long had Sir Sean been watching before she attempted to turn the page?

She never wanted anyone to see her feebly try to accomplish something she'd done with ease only months ago. Tears ran down her cheeks. She sucked in a deep breath to stifle her weeping, but it only served to heighten her remorse.

Had he any idea how much it tore her apart to see him again? And he made no mention of why he'd broken his promise to sit on her plaid. Aye, it was a simple matter, but it had been a savage cut to her heart. *Why, I mightn't have become so ill if it weren't for my broken heart.*

Her nose was running and it streamed over her lips, spreading an unwelcome, salty taste in her mouth. She opened and closed her fist. Blast it to hell. In one determined motion, she raised her hand and swiped it across her face. She blinked rapidly and stared at her fingers.

"Heaven's stars."

She raised the trembling hand again, but this time she missed her face altogether. That she'd first connected with her head at all must have been accidental.

Groaning, she cast her gaze to the clouds above. Everything about Sean MacDougall reminded her of the fool she'd been. Happiness was only a fleeting speck given the duration of one's life. How could she have ever expected to live happily? She smirked at the book on her lap—the pages were full of fairytales—events that could never come true.

At least now she had no illusions. With life came pain and humiliation. She could not even visit the privy closet without assistance. *How much worse can things become?*

Forced to succumb to the monk's ministrations like a bairn still in swaddling clothes, she hated being dependent on someone for her every need. Everyone around her shot pitying glances her way. She didn't want pity, she wanted freedom.

This situation is untenable. She clenched her fists. *I will walk again.* With effort, she folded her hands and closed her eyes. *God in heaven, give me strength to overcome this illness.*

Pushing the book aside, she bore down and swung her legs over the side of the bench. Her head swooning with the effort, she took in a deep breath. Sliding to the edge, she placed her slippered feet on the ground, just as she'd done many times with the assistance of Brother Wesley.

But this time she was far more determined.

With her palms flush against the bench, she shifted her weight onto her legs and pushed up. Wobbling with exertion, standing was excruciatingly slow. Her heart fluttered when, for the first time in two months, she stood unassisted.

Her legs shuddering, Gyllis eyed the grass before her. *One step.*

Swallowing, she inched her foot forward.

Her knee buckled. Gyllis cried out. Before she could fling her arms forward, she landed face-first in the moist grass.

"Miss Gyllis," Brother Wesley cried as he hastened to her side. "Whatever are you doing?"

Her nose throbbed and she stretched her jaw to the side only to be met with a sharp pain. "My, that hurt." Dear Brother Wesley, always rushing to her aid. If only she didn't need his charity. He was a selfless and giving monk, and right now Gyllis needed him far more than she wanted to admit.

"You mustn't do that again—not without assistance." He gathered her in his beefy arms. "Let us see you back inside."

She looked him in the eye. "Mark me—I *will* walk again and show Sir Sean MacDougall I can overcome anything."

Concern creased Brother Wesley's brow. "Did he upset you?"

***

The monk led Sean beyond the cloister walls to the stables where the Lord of Lorn waited with his men. Sean held out his hand in greeting. "Uncle, I must say I'm eager to hear what you have brewing, given the secrecy."

With a grin, Lorn offered a firm handshake. "And I'm all too eager to share it with you." He inclined his head to a path leading into the wood. "Come, walk with me—away from prying ears."

Sean cast a sideways glance to Lorn's men. Could the earl not trust his inner circle? *I suppose I shall find out.*

Together they walked into the wood along a well-kept path, one obviously used by the priory monks on a regular basis.

Lorn plucked a maple leaf and twirled it between his fingers. "How have you been coping since your father's death?"

"Well enough." Sean shrugged. "A few head of cattle have gone missing, but nothing too alarming."

"How many head have disappeared?"

"Ten or so—two different raids."

"You must stop all insurgence, else you'll have an uprising you cannot control."

"No need to worry overmuch about me." They came to a split in the trail and Sean chose the wider, more traveled path—though he'd rather have taken the overgrown one had he not been accompanied by the older man. "I reckon we're far enough away from the others. What is so important to make you opt to meet here?"

"One can never know whom they can trust." Lorn eyed him. "Especially a young chieftain who's only come into his title."

Sean gaped. "You no longer trust me?"

"'Tis not you, but rather your men. To prove my point, you just said yourself Dunollie's suffering from raids."

Sean opened his mouth for a rebuttal, but Lorn held up his hand. "'Tis always the way when a new pup rises to power. Someone feels thwarted and wants to test your grit. Deal with reivers firmly. In a few months, things will again settle."

Sean didn't want to admit he had a few misgivings about the loyalties of some of his father's men. However, this conversation cemented his decisions. He must weed out the conspirators quickly. "You've no cause for alarm."

"That is what I like to hear." Lorn plucked another leaf—a birch this time. "I wanted to meet with you in secret because I've given it a great deal of thought and have decided to act on your suggestion."

Sean looked toward the clouds, rifling through his memory of the last time he'd seen Lorn—*Beltane*. What the devil had they talked about? "I beg your pardon?"

"Must I spell it out?"

With no idea, Sean shrugged.

"Since May I've given it ample thought and come up with no other option. I'm to wed Dugald's mother."

Sean grinned. Now he remembered the conversation. And that had been the first time in his life he'd realized that at nine and twenty, he was aging. Had his uncle finally come to his senses? "At last you will make your son legitimate?"

"Aye." Lorn glanced over his shoulder as if he feared someone was following. "But you must keep it quiet, lest my enemies learn of my plans—especially Argyll and the Campbell lot."

"Heavens, Uncle, the Campbell Clan could be your greatest allies—especially the Glenorchy sect."

Lorn flicked his leaf into the brush. "Mayhap, however, I'd prefer if you kept it between us."

"Very well." Sean stepped around a mud puddle. "What do you need from me?"

Lorn stopped and craned his neck to face him. "Protection. I need your army to provide ample guard during the ceremony and the feast."

Sean remembered well the lands Lorn had bequeathed him when he reached his majority. The gift was given on the promise a call to arms would be forthcoming whenever needed. "You'll have my sword and my men. Have you set a date as of yet?"

"Autumn—when the leaves start to turn."

"Why wait?" Sean asked. "You should have brought Mary MacLaren to the priory and had John Campbell marry you this day."

Lorn waved his hands. "No, no, that will not do. There are formalities to arrange—the first being a visit to King James to ensure his blessing."

Sean was no stranger to the dealings of court. "And his sanction of lands."

"Of course. The only reason I'm proceeding with the marriage at my advanced age is to ensure my title remains with my line."

Sean chuckled. "And the Earl of Argyll doesn't inherit the Lordship of Lorn."

"Exactly."

Sean glanced toward a raven squawking at them from a tree limb above. "You are aware, the king's enforcers could add iron-clad protection for you and your bride." He didn't want to use the moniker Highland Enforcers. That had originally been the label used by Black Colin Campbell and it had stuck. Everyone knew there was no force in the Highlands that could match the well-trained group of knights led by Lord Duncan Campbell, but Lorn would never admit dependence.

The older man clapped Sean on the shoulder and headed back toward the priory. "Let us keep this quiet for now. The fewer people who know my plans, the less likely my enemies will cross me."

"Agreed."

"In the interim, you need to see to it you weed out all backstabbers from your clan."

Sean balled his fists. "No one wants that more than I."

"'Tis good to hear."

***

After seeing the Lord of Lorn off, Sean returned to the garden, but Gyllis was no longer there. He looked at the sundial. The afternoon was growing late and soon the monks would head to the nave for vespers. He turned full circle. Could Gyllis be staying in the dormitory? It wasn't usual for monks to take in the sick, but he had no idea if Ardchattan had an infirmary.

One thing he knew for certain, he wouldn't find her whilst turning circles in the garden. When he headed toward the cloisters, John stepped around the corner.

Sean opened his arms. "Just the man I was looking for."

"Sean MacDougall." With a hearty laugh, John pulled him into an embrace. "Bless it, 'tis good to see you."

"Bloody oath." Sean stepped away and took in the telltale black robes. "How long has it been?"

"Years." John gestured for him to continue walking. "Word has it you're the Chieftain of Dunollie now."

"Aye. Da passed two months ago."

"I am sorry." John bowed his head. "I shall pray for his eternal soul."

"My thanks." Sean grasped John's sleeve and rubbed it between his fingers. "So you've attained the exalted rank of prior in record time, I see."

"Aye, I've found my calling—no more armor and swords for me."

"Or women."

John frowned.

Sean shook his head. "Bloody waste of a fine knight."

"You sound like my brother."

"Apologies." He clapped the priest on the back. "I should be offering congratulations."

"No need. We live a life of humility here, void of pride."

That certainly was the man Sean knew. John Campbell never could be accused of suffering from the sin of pride—something Sean envied in his friend. *Envy, yet another sin.* But he had something of a more serious nature to discuss. "I saw Miss Gyllis when I first arrived."

"Aye, she mentioned as much." John frowned.

But Sean didn't let the dour face dissuade him. "What happened to her?"

"Paralysis."

Sean gulped. "'Tis worse than I thought. She looks so frail. When did she become afflicted?"

"She fell ill on the journey home from the May Day festival."

"That long ago? What are her chances of recovery?"

John steepled his fingers. "Who knows? The longer she goes without being able to walk, the less likely she will ever find her legs."

"My God." Sean pushed his hands through his hair. "I must help her."

"What do you think you can do?" John stopped outside the chapel doors and faced him. "She was very upset after she saw you—refused to eat—I couldn't even get her to take a sip of mead."

His mind swimming, Sean barely listened. "But we've been close ever since we were young. I always thought…" He couldn't say it, not to her brother. "I want to see her."

"I'm not certain 'tis a good idea." John grasped the latch. "Whatever happened between you two?"

"Pardon me? We've always been…" He almost said sweethearts, but that wouldn't sound right confessing to a priest, or to her brother, no less. "Good friends."

"Something about your visit upset her. What did you say?"

"Me? Nothing at all." Sean grasped John's elbow. "Please, I want to see Gyllis again."

John sighed and looked to the sky. "I should not agree, but you seem emphatic—and I do not approve of leaving things on a sour note. Give her a sennight or two. She's so frail. Any upset could ruin her progress."

"Must I wait that long? I'd prefer to return on the morrow."

"Please, I ask you to heed me in this." John placed his hand on Sean's shoulder. "For Gyllis's sake."

"Very well, if your request is for her benefit." Sean clenched his teeth—Gyllis was exactly who he had been thinking of, but good sense told him not to argue, else he could be banned. "My thanks."

"No need for gratitude." John held up a finger. "If she has an adverse reaction on your next visit, I shall have no recourse but to request that you stay away."

***

Mounted on his warhorse, Sean puzzled while he rode the six miles back to Dunollie Castle. Beltane seemed like it had happened years ago, yet it had only been a couple months. At the feast, he'd danced with Gyllis. She'd never looked so radiant—healthy and lively on her feet. How quickly the paralysis must have come on.

He chuckled, remembering how delightfully forward she'd been. Ah yes, and the kiss he'd stolen in the garden had been sublime. That she had never been properly kissed was a certainty and it made his blood thrum to think he'd been the first gentleman to claim her lips. His grin stretched wider.

She invited me to sit on her plaid—and then Angus and Jinny came to tell me Da had died.

Sean pulled his horse to a stop and slapped his forehead.

God's teeth, I neglected to send my apologies. Has anyone informed her as to why I'd been called away?

Chapter Nine

Gyllis sat sideways on her bed, reclining into a mountain of pillows propped against the wall. John massaged the sole of her foot—the feeling must have been returning because it caused a mildly painful sensation of pin pricks.

She squeezed her eyes shut. A picture formed of Sir Sean and how horrified his face had looked when he first saw her in the garden. Every time she thought about Sean MacDougall, Gyllis shook her head and forced her mind to focus on anything else. Presently, the story of how Sir Gawain had opted to allow Dame Ragnelle to choose whether or not she would be cursed by ugliness during the day or at night replaced imaginings of Sean's azure eyes. Gyllis loved how Sir Gawain's selflessness resulted in breaking the spell and thus turned Dame Ragnelle into a beauty forever. If only such chivalry existed.

She sighed.

If only Sir Sean could do something to break the miserable spell that plagues me. She tsked her tongue. *Curses, there I go again, finding any way to allow that lusty laddie into my thoughts.*

"Push the sole of your foot against my hand," said John, seated upon the stool beside her bed. He had been helping her more as of late, and for the past week, Brother Wesley had been away on an errand to Iona.

Gyllis grasped the bedclothes and squeezed. Though the dexterity in her hands had not fully returned, in the past fortnight she'd become adept at turning the pages of her book. Threading a needle was yet to be accomplished. She grimaced and tried to push against John's hand with all her might. Though her forehead perspired, he seemed not to be putting forth any effort at all. Gyllis let out a puff of air. "Blast it."

"Keep trying."

She wanted to scream. "I *am*."

"Good." John grinned—he could calm an entire room of grumblers with his smile. "Now just a bit harder."

Gyllis pushed. "Och, you are killing me."

"Simply trying to make you stronger." He rubbed his knuckles into the sole of her foot. "You made a good effort."

"Thank you." She watched him while he lifted her other foot and started in massaging her leg. He was so different compared to Duncan. Her older brother was a commander of men, a warlord and chieftain. Somehow, John had inherited all the traits to make him Duncan's opposite. Though they both had inherited the Campbell good looks.

"What do you aspire to, John?"

"Me?" He chuckled. "I suppose to spread the word of God and tend wee lasses like you who come to the priory in need of care." It was typical of him to respond with something vague.

Gyllis persisted. "Do you ever miss riding with the Highland Enforcers?"

"Not really. I enjoyed the companionship, but I never could stomach living by the sword."

She adjusted her shoulders against the pillows for added comfort. "I suppose it would be unsettling to ride into battle knowing it could be your last day on this earth."

"It wasn't my death I was worried about so much as worry for others. Even vile men who've committed crimes have souls. I never believed I had a right to take a life—not ever."

Gyllis admired his handsome face, now framed by dun-colored locks with the top of his head shaven. "You would have made a fine husband."

"And you talk too much." He kneaded his fingers into her thigh. "What about you? You should be thinking about marriage soon."

She rolled her eyes to the cross on the wall above her head. "Oh, you are full of practicality—all lassies stricken with paralysis leap from their beds and proceed to the altar."

"I'm serious. You are beautiful and charming." John looked up and narrowed his gaze. "Why only a fortnight or so ago, Sir Sean MacDougall inquired about you—he showed genuine concern."

Gyllis harrumphed. "Sir Sean is the last person I'd marry. Besides, he's the type to take his vows and the following day ride off with Duncan and never look back."

"I suppose he has an adventuresome spirit—though I've not met a more trustworthy friend."

"I cannot fill my head with thoughts about that man. He's vile." Her voice trailed off and she swallowed. If only she could actually *void* her heart of her feelings for Sir Sean. Before she'd fallen ill, he had thwarted her. How would he treat her now that she was a cripple? "Let us talk about something else."

"Very well." John reverted to long languid strokes that made Gyllis's leg tingle. "I've been thinking. When you return to Kilchurn, we could move your things to the first floor solar."

Gyllis shook her head. "When I return to Kilchurn, I will be walking and able to climb the tower stairs."

John stopped rubbing and looked up. Sadness filled his eyes. "What if…"

"Do not say it. I…I am making progress." Gyllis strained to pull her foot from his grasp. "I will walk again, whether God sees fit to help me or I am forced to do it on my own."

"I appreciate your fighting spirit, but…."

"But what?"

"As humans we are only flesh and blood. Sometimes we can picture our bodies doing things they're incapable of."

"Enough!" Gyllis scooted to the edge of the bed and inched her feet onto the floor.

John stood and held out his hands. "Let me help you."

"No. I'll do it myself."

His lips formed a thin line, but he took a step back.

She leaned forward until her chin was over her knees. Giving herself a healthy shove, Gyllis attempted to stand. Her legs faltered. With a startled gasp, her weight shifted too far forward. Having given too much of a push, she teetered then fell straight into John's outstretched arms.

A wail caught in her throat. She balled her fists and pounded them into her brother's chest. "Curses, curses, curses to paralysis! Why did this happen to me? Why can I not walk away from this damnable bed? I hate this. I hate it, I tell you!" Gyllis had been sick for so long, she couldn't take it anymore—couldn't face her miserable life. She was hopeless, useless and without a single prospect.

When she burst into tears, John lifted her into his arms and sat on the cot. Oh his lap he cradled her for what seemed like an eternity, patiently rocking back and forth while she bawled like a bairn. "There, there, Gyllis.

Everything will be all right." His soothing voice calmed until sleep took away her pain.

***

Swaying in his saddle, Murdach, pointed. "There she is, m'laird."

Sean had never been so happy to see the ominous outline of the Dunollie battlements looming against a sultry summer sky. They had spent the last fortnight visiting every crofter who paid rents. True, Sean relished being on the trail, but this excursion with his factor had no adventure. And though this mission had been extremely important to renewing and securing loyalty, he was relieved it was at an end.

Chatting with clansmen about the rents wasn't at the top of his list of entertaining subjects. If a crofter's rents were up to date, the conversation turned to more interesting pursuits. But more often the people who made a living off his lands had fallen behind, and thus it was necessary to sit down and discuss a plan to set their accounts back to rights.

Murdach had been some help, but the aging factor proved to prefer his quill over his tongue.

Sean grinned at the portly man, then turned round to face his guard. "Let us make haste and we shall enjoy Dunollie whisky tonight." He dug his heels into his horse's barrel and led the canter along the shoreline to the castle.

Once inside the gates, he led them to the stables and dismounted.

Murdach hopped off his gelding with a grunt. "Will you be needing me for anything else, m'laird?"

"Nay. Put the ledgers in my solar and then go home to your lady wife."

"My thanks."

Sean gave his reins to his squire and sighed. Even the air at Dunollie smelled fresher than it did outside her walls.

"M'laird." The man's voice came from behind.

Sean whipped around and a grin spread across his face. "Fraser!" He embraced his friend and slapped him on the back. "I was wondering what had happened to you."

The warrior's eyebrows drew together and he inclined his head away from the guard. "May I have a word in confidence?"

"Of course." Sean led him to the rear of the stables. "Did you find Alan?"

"Aye, at least where he'd been hiding."

Sean rolled his hands in anticipation of more.

"An eyewitness reported he was holding up on Kerrera."

Sean drummed his fingers to his lips. "That island is chartered MacDougall land."

"Aye, but Alan told her it was his."

"Her—a woman?"

"A whore named Osla."

Sean smirked. "Credible source."

"She wasn't the most refined of women even for a whore, but she described him well enough—described his men, too." Fraser frowned, his gaze darting left then right. He leaned in. "She said he's amassing quite an army."

Sean didn't believe it. "I ken he's got a following of roustabouts, but an *army*? She must have been jesting."

"I'm nay so certain. She kent a number of names— and clans. Said he's not only got disgruntled MacDougalls, he's drawn in some lowlife Campbells and it gets worse."

"Aye?"

"Lowlanders—hundreds of them. Osla said that's where he is now."

"In the Lowlands?"

"Aye—training for a reckoning."

Sean studied the concern on Fraser's face then swiped his hand over his mouth. "It sounds like the old hen grasped ahold of your ear and gave it a good tug."

"I ken, it sounds farfetched, but Alan is a snake. I wouldn't put it past him to be scheming something."

"True, but I doubt he has the coin or the gumption to command an army. A handful of vagrants, I'd believe but no more."

Fraser scratched his beard and glanced away. "I'm sure you're right, but why not let me track him to the Lowlands—see for myself if the whore's claims have any merit."

Sean glanced over his shoulder to ensure no one was eavesdropping. "I'd rather have you by my side as henchman. I trust you more than any other in the Clan MacDougall. You're the best with a sword, too."

"Thank you, m'laird, but my gut is telling me Alan MacCoul is up to something. I wouldn't feel content to leave things unresolved with that man and his *army*."

Sean reflected on Lorn's advice. There had been raids and any threat must be investigated no matter how absurd. "Very well, but I do not want you traveling to the Lowlands alone. Choose two guards with whom to ride and I'll expect to see you return in a month—two at the most."

***

When Sean retired to his solar, he poured himself a well-deserved glass of whisky. He stood at the window for a moment and gazed out over the Firth of Lorn. A sultry breeze caressed his face and he sighed. Summer had always been his favorite season. The gardens were alive with greens and colorful flowers and the sea yielded an abundant harvest.

Sean sipped his whisky and savored the oaken flavor as it slid over his tongue. Every moment he'd been away, he had thought about Gyllis. *I shall set out for the priory at first light.* He turned and looked at the ledgers spread out on the table. *But first I must make some sense of Murdach's chicken scratch.*

With a sigh, he placed a quill and inkwell on the table and sat in his upholstered chair. He spread a sheet of vellum to his right, opened a ledger and began to record sums, listing them in an orderly fashion as he deciphered the random splotches of ink made by his factor.

Two pages in, Sean had no doubt Murdach was blind. *That's bloody wonderful—how the devil hadn't Da noticed all the errors?*

A breeze blew in from the window and mussed the parchment. Sean glanced toward the sound of the roaring sea. Oh to be shed of responsibility and walking along the shore at sunset. *Holding Gyllis's hand.* Warmth spread through him. *Paralysis? I want to be the one massaging her thighs, not some recalcitrant monk.*

But will she accept my help? She told me to stay away. How can I possibly do that? I've cared for her since... He thought back to all the times he and Gyllis had danced or talked or shared a meal together during his fostering. *I've been such a dolt all these years. I should have asked her father for her hand whilst he was still alive. If only I'd had the sense to do so.*

And now she's...

He shook his head and stopped himself.

Ballocks. I need to see her.

After inking his quill, he calculated the sum of his figures. He then compared it to the balance written on the ledger. *Short by five crowns.*

The hour was growing late, but he couldn't rest before he rechecked the numbers. After deciphering Murdach's entries a second time, Sean again came up with a five-crown shortfall. It wasn't a huge amount in comparison to his vast holdings, but over the course of a year, such losses would add up. He rested the quill in the silver holder and reached for his whisky.

Shall I confront Murdach first thing in the morning or head to the priory to see Gyllis? His mind made up, Sean closed the ledgers, rolled the vellum of sums and secured it inside his doublet.

Chapter Ten

If there was anything Sean hated, it was waiting. How difficult was it for a priest to announce his arrival? Was Gyllis having a bath? He continued pacing. *If John doesn't return by the count of ten, I shall go looking for him—or Gyllis, whomever I find first.*

When he reached nine, John stepped into the cloister, looking stern. "I'm sorry. Gyllis refuses to see you."

"What?" Sean spread his arms to his sides. "I will not leave until I gain an audience with her. At the very least, she must give me a chance to explain why I hastened to away from the fete last May. I'd agreed to sit on her plaid, but before the feast I received word of my father's death."

Opening his arms, John strode toward him. "Is that why she's so upset with you?"

"I can think of no other reason."

John grasped the cross hanging around his neck. "I do not believe—"

Sean pushed past him and marched ahead. "Where is she?"

John hastened to keep pace. "She is vulnerable."

"Do you not think I ken?" Sean barreled around the corner and opened the first door. "I'll find her if I must open every door in the priory."

John skirted in front of him. "Please. She needs more time—she's incredibly frail."

Sean again pushed past and flung open another door. "That is exactly why I must see her now." Sean slammed it, grinding his back molars. "Damn it all, tell me where she is."

John's gaze shifted along the corridor to a door at the far end. "Perhaps I could deliver a missive on your behalf."

Sean turned in the direction of John's stare. "There's no time for that." He strode directly to the door at the end.

"Please." The priest scuffled after him. "I have parchment and a quill in my quarters."

Sean ignored John's plea and yanked open the door.

Gyllis gasped, her eyes horrorstruck, she clapped a hand over her mouth. A monk had her skirts up around her thighs, his fingers clear up to her...

"Unhand her!"

Shoving her kirtle down, Gyllis scooted back.

Sean grabbed the lecherous monk by his collar and yanked him up. Before the man could raise his arms, Sean slammed his fist into the sniveling maggot's pasty face. With a high-pitched wail, the monk toppled to the floor. Sean advanced.

"No!" Gyllis shrieked.

John darted between Sean and the monk, seizing Sean's shoulders. "Have you lost your mind?"

Enraged, Sean broke from John's grasp. "Did you not see him? He had her skirts hiked up so far I could see—"

"Miss Gyllis requires stimulating massage several times per day. I assure you, Brother Wesley has taken an oath of celibacy."

Sean glanced at the monk now sitting on the floor, rubbing his jaw.

"Are you all right, brother?" Gyllis asked.

The monk nodded. "Aye." He stood, giving Sean a wide berth.

"How could you barge into my chamber and accost a man of the cloth?" Gyllis moved slowly, but folded her arms, her face redder than a boiled lobster.

"Apologies, Miss Gyllis." Sean couldn't have made things any worse with his bravado, storming into her chamber like a jealous cur. "I did not think."

Gyllis pursed her lips—God, her face was still as lovely as sunrise. "No, you did not."

"Miss Gyllis, please," Sean pleaded. "Allow me a moment of your time, 'tis all I ask."

John grasped Sean's elbow and squeezed. "If I must resort to force to make you leave, I will."

If anyone in this God-forsaken priory could pose a challenge, it was John Campbell. He'd been a damned good knight before he became a priest, but Sean doubted he'd sparred much as of late. He steeled himself for a fight.

"I will hear him." Gyllis held up a trembling hand. "Leave us." She looked to John. "Brother Wesley will be standing directly outside the door should I require his assistance."

Sean tried not to grin.

The bumbling monk, bowed. "Very well, Miss Gyllis. We can keep the door ajar if you wish."

Gyllis met Sean's gaze and then looked down as if she were embarrassed. "That should not be necessary." The high color in her cheeks betrayed her unease.

"A quarter hour. 'Tis all I will allow—even for you," John said. "And the door shall remain ajar."

"My thanks." Sean ushered the two holy men out of the small cell and pushed the door until only a sliver of light shone through. When he turned to face Gyllis, he swallowed, completely at a loss for words. "Uh." He shifted his feet. God, her face was aglow with fury—and something pained. He guessed he'd hurt her deeply by not sending his regrets at Beltane.

She inclined her head toward the stool. "Will you sit? Looking up at you is making my neck sore."

She obviously had no intention of making things easy for him. But moving toward the seat gave him a moment to gather his thoughts. He may as well start from where they'd left things in May. "Were you aware my father passed?"

Slowly, she covered her mouth with her dainty hand. "Oh my, I hadn't heard. When?"

"Beltane. My kin were waiting with the news at the footrace finish line."

Her delicate eyebrows drew together. "Your kin?"

"Aye, Jinny the healer and her husband, Angus."

Her hand slid to her cheek. "The woman you embraced is married?"

Sean bit the corner of his lip and grimaced. "You saw that, too?"

"Aye." Gyllis blushed scarlet. "After Alan slashed you with the blade, I hastened from the curtain wall to see if I could be of assistance." She cringed. "When I found you in another woman's arms...I...I..." She blinked in rapid succession. "And then you didn't come to the feast nor did you send word."

He reached out and held his hand steady for a moment, then took a chance and grasped her palm. Her fingers were cold. "I must ask your forgiveness. I was distraught with the news. Then things fell into mayhem and I was gallivanting around the countryside chasing after thieves and visiting crofters to ensure their loyalty."

She stared at their interlaced fingers. "It sounds as if you've had a difficult time."

Touching her calmed the thrumming beneath his skin. "Nowhere near as troublesome as things have been for you."

Gyllis tugged her hand away and rubbed it, refusing to meet his gaze.

Sean's fingers throbbed where her hand had been. He wanted to reclaim it and declare his undying love, but that would be nonsensical. If only he could pull her into his arms and make her well again. "I want to help you."

She smirked. "What on earth do you think you can do that the monks have not already attempted?"

He didn't have an answer. "What treatments have they tried?"

"Massage mostly, and tinctures that never seem to work."

"But your hands have more dexterity than since I last saw you. What about your legs?"

She harrumphed. "No good whatsoever. I still cannot take a step without falling."

"Can you stand?"

"For a moment."

"'Tis a good sign."

She looked up. "How do you ken?" The pain in her moss-green eyes was unmistakable.

Sean's heart squeezed. He was no healer. "I just do. Besides, you promised me dancing lessons."

"Please." She covered her face with her hands, her long tresses dropping forward. "You are completely daft if you think I shall ever be able to dance again."

"Pardon me for being so bold to think you will." Sean scooted the bench away and kneeled before her. Again he grasped her hand and rubbed it between his warm palms. "Are your hands always this cold?"

"I suppose, aye."

"Please allow me to warm them." The corner of his mouth ticked up.

Using her shoulder, she shyly moved a lock of hair from her face. Though the gesture was innocent, it was unbelievably seductive. Had she not appeared so frail, he would have wrapped her in his arms and kissed her lips—ravished them as he'd done in the garden at Beltane.

Moistening his lips, he lifted her hand and kissed it. *Her scent's more heavenly than a field of heather.* "If it would bring you a modicum of comfort, Miss Gyllis, it would be an honor to see you again."

She held his gaze for a moment, her bottom lip slipping beneath her top teeth. "Please do not tease me."

He drew his eyebrows together. "I would never do anything of the sort."

"You are a chieftain now. You said yourself you've a great many affairs to attend. The last person you should concern yourself with is a silly cripple."

A lump took up residence in his chest. "Do not say that. You are as beautiful today as you were at the festival."

She tried to pull her hand away, but he held fast.

"I want to see you again. Will you please allow it?"

She drew in a sharp inhale and hesitated for a long moment. "Aye," she whispered.

Sean could have picked her up and swung her in a circle. "Thank you." Restraining his exuberance, he kissed her hand again rather than risk breaking her bones. "Now, would you like to show me how you stand?"

Cringing, she leaned away. "Oh no, it would cause too much embarrassment."

That damned lump stretched over his heart again. "Why? Are you afraid I will laugh?"

"Nay." She looked down.

He lifted her chin with the crook of his finger until her lovely green eyes met his. Ah yes, the irises were still circled with navy blue. He could lose himself in those eyes forever. "Then why?"

"I am afraid you will never come back." Her voice trembled.

Without thought he slid his hands to her shoulders. "Ah, Miss Gyllis. Nothing could keep me away. Spending time with you is as natural as breathing." He kissed the top of her head.

"Honestly?" She focused her gaze on his chest.

"Aye. I love you. Always have." He heard the words bubble from his mouth before his mind realized what he'd said. Sean's tongue went dry. He did love Gyllis. He'd just never admitted it to himself.

Before she looked up, she gasped.

When her gaze met his, her eyes were filled with life. They were as bright and clear as they'd been when he'd watched her dance at Beltane. "You'd best not be teasing a poor, crippled lass, Sir Sean MacDougall."

Chapter Eleven

The following morning, Sean sat in his solar with Murdach and Angus, but he looked directly at the factor. "Please explain how five crowns went missing from your figures."

Holding his palms out, Murdach appeared to be completely flummoxed. "Five crowns, m'laird? Are you certain?"

Sean snatched the ledger and slapped in down in front of the fool. "Aye I'm bloody certain. I lost a good amount of sleep over it as well."

Murdach looked across the table at Angus. Blast it, Sean could have sworn the pair was in collusion.

He shoved back his chair and paced in front of the hearth. "Ballocks! You are two of my most trusted men."

"We've done nothing to incite your ire, m'laird," said Angus.

Sean whipped around and slapped his palms on the table. "No? Why are both of you sending silent messages across the table at one another?"

Angus sat back and shook his head. "We are doing no such thing."

"Then where are my five crowns? How long has this been going on? Must I call in others to replace you?" He'd already decided to ask Angus to retire when Fraser returned. Murdach as well—the man could scarcely see past his nose.

"This was my fault. Do not blame Angus," Murdach said. "I must have made a recording error. Please, if you must punish someone I am guilty as charged."

Sean threw up his hands. "How long were you my father's factor?"

"Near thirty years, m'laird."

"And how old are you now?"

"Eight and fifty."

Sean resumed his pacing, this time gripping his hands behind his back. "You provided satisfactory service to my father for thirty years?"

"Aye."

"And how often did he catch your errors?"

"Rarely." The man scratched his chin. "As a matter of fact, I do not believe he ever complained of errors or my loyalty."

Most likely because he couldn't read a damn thing you scrawled on a sheet of parchment. Sean waved a hand in front of Murdach's face. "How is your eyesight?"

The factor grasped the lapels of his doublet, perspiration beading above his lip. "Not as good as it once was, but I still manage."

Sean sat in his chair and groaned. "I have decided 'tis time for you to retire."

"But sir—"

Sean held up a hand. "I've made my decision. You will receive a pension and continue to live out your days in the cottage with your missus."

Murdach stared across the table at Angus, a frown pulling down his jowls. "As you wish, m'laird."

Sean regarded his henchman who should be seeking retirement as well. However, with Fraser away, it was best to leave things with Angus alone for the time being.

A rap came at the door. "A missive from the Lord of Lorn, m'laird."

Sean eyed the two men. "I'll return momentarily." He crossed the floor and opened the door. Stepping into the passageway, he accepted the note. "Thank you," he said rather loudly. "Come with me whilst I fetch that for him."

The messenger looked puzzled, but Sean grasped him by the elbow and inclined his head toward the man's ear. "This way."

He clomped his feet on the floorboards, making a show of walking toward the stairwell, then released the messenger's arm and whispered, "Go to the kitchens and get something to eat. I shall prepare Lorn a reply anon."

"Very well, sir."

Sean quietly returned to the solar and stood outside the door. He opened the missive from Lorn. King James had given consent and the wedding was still on track for autumn—fortunately news which didn't require Sean's immediate attention.

"You should tell him," Angus's deep voice rumbled through the wall.

"But that is not what Alan declared."

Sean held his breath. *Alan?*

"I cannot renege on his final request," Murdach continued.

Sean released a whoosh of air. At first he'd thought they were referring to MacCoul, but his father's name had been Alan as well. He leaned closer to the door.

"Aye, but he cannot run his affairs from the grave," Angus argued.

"If he'd set aside a provision, we wouldn't be in this situation."

"Well, if 'tis a case between proving my loyalty and support for the living and honor for the dead, I'll choose the living. Sir Sean deserves our fealty now."

"You are right as always, Angus."

"Then we're agreed. Regardless of what the chieftain requested from his deathbed, it stops today."

"Aye."

Sean leaned against the wall. He could hang them both for what he'd just heard. But then they had been acting upon a promise to his father—something Da wanted to keep hidden. Whatever it was, they had called an end to it. Content that the men within his chamber were not trying to swindle him, he opened the door and stepped inside.

Angus and Murdach looked up expectantly. What Sean had earlier interpreted as collusion now looked like faces torn. He hoped to God his hunch was right.

He grinned and strode to the sideboard. "I believe we should toast to Murdach's retirement."

***

Gyllis studied Brother Wesley while he circled his knuckles into her calf. "Have you taken a vow of silence in the past few days?"

He looked at her with pinched brows and shook his head.

"You've scarcely said a word since Sir Sean was here."

"Have I not?" He set her leg down and started on the other.

Gyllis cringed. Had she been insensitive? After all, Sean did give him a good wallop. "How is your jaw?"

He opened his mouth and stretched it to the side. "'Tis coming good."

"I am sorry he hit you."

Brother Wesley grumbled, "As am I."

"Honestly, Sir Sean MacDougall is a nice man. He never would have struck out if he hadn't thought I was in danger."

"It might save him some trouble if he learned to ask questions before he started swinging his fists."

Gyllis smoothed her hands over her kirtle. "You abhor violence, do you not?"

"Aye, 'tis why I joined the order."

"I shall ask Sir Sean to apologize as soon as he returns."

"*If* he comes again." Wesley stopped rubbing. "Besides, there is no need. As you said, he thought he was protecting you."

When Gyllis looked into the monk's troubled eyes, she could tell the topic of Sir Sean did not sit well with him. "You should forgive him."

"I have. 'Tis a vice to hold a grudge."

Gyllis folded her hands. "But I sense you do not care to talk about him."

"'Tis because he likes you."

She laughed. Sean *loved* her, and thinking about it had tickled her insides with joy for the past few days. Though she wasn't about to lose her head over it. She had no doubt he loved her as a fostered sister—but still it was enough to make her heart soar. "Is that such a bad thing?"

Wesley grew quiet again. He pulled down her skirts and patted her knee. "I should prepare for vespers."

"But I haven't practiced walking yet today."

"Perhaps we can do that on the morrow." He stood and bowed. "If you will excuse me."

Gyllis watched the monk take his leave. It didn't take a seer to discern something bothered him and she had no doubt it had everything to do with Sir Sean. She couldn't understand Brother Wesley's recalcitrance. Since the young chieftain's visit, she'd actually been happy. She'd also made marked progress. Presently she could stand on

her own without wobbling and, if she leaned on Brother
Wesley's hands, she could take a step.

Gyllis was so close to being able to walk, she was
anxious to keep practicing. She flexed her feet, yet another
thing she'd recently been able to accomplish. She leaned
forward and placed her hands on the stool. Perhaps if she
supported herself on it, she could practice walking around
it and wouldn't fall. If she wasn't careful, she could end
up on the floor in her chamber alone for hours.

She placed her feet flush with the floor and took her
weight on her hands. Once sure she was balanced, she
sidestepped. She closed her eyes and pretended she was
dancing. *Step together, step together around the stool.*

After she'd made two circles, she grew more
confident. With an inhale, she released her grip and
straightened. Her knees quivered a bit. She held out her
hands to gain balance and stood still for a moment. She
sidestepped just as she'd done when holding onto the
stool. Drawing her feet together, she decided she could do
it again. Taking the smallest of steps, Gyllis managed to
make it completely around the stool without falling. She
clapped her hands and squealed with delight.

Excited to do more, she boldly stepped away from the
stool. Her knee buckled. With her heart flying to her
throat, Gyllis flung her hands forward to break her fall.
Collapsed in a heap on the floor, she waited for the pain
to come. When it didn't, she moved her arms and rolled
to her bottom. She straightened her right leg, then the left.
She chuckled—thank heavens she wasn't hurt in the
slightest.

But the best thing? She had actually shuffled her feet
around the stool without help.

Gyllis threw back her head and laughed out loud. Her
skin tingled, her belly muscles tightened and she laughed
some more. Heavens, it was good to laugh for a change.

She'd done so much crying since she'd arrived, Gyllis never thought she'd find the will to laugh again.

She covered her mouth with a gasp when the door swung open.

Before she could blink, Sean dashed inside and scooped her into his arms. "My God, Miss Gyllis. Are you hurt?"

She sucked in a few stuttered breaths. "I-I am quite well. Just had a wee tumble." After he set her on the bed, she grinned broadly. "I took my first unassisted steps today. The only problem is no one was here to see me."

"Wonderful news...but you shouldn't have been so bold without someone to assist you."

She jutted out her bottom lip. "Please, since I arrived a monk has had to help me with every bodily purpose imaginable. I stepped around the stool on my own."

"That is exciting to hear." He sat beside her and clasped her hand. "'Tis quite an impressive feat. You shall soon be dancing."

The touch of his rugged fingers made her blood rush hot beneath her skin. "I imagined myself dancing around the stool." Gyllis couldn't stop smiling.

Sean smiled back. Bless it, he was handsome. His eyes sparkled with the ray of light beaming from the window. He'd combed his dark locks away from his face and his chin was shaved clean. Gyllis brushed her fingers along it.

His eyes grew dark, intense. He moistened his lips with a slow lap of his tongue. "I shaved close this morn."

She looked closer—not a hint of dark stubble. "I do not believe I can remember ever seeing your chin so smooth." *Or your lips so kissable.* Sean's upper lip was slightly fuller than his lower. But together they reminded her of a ship with two sails—a very sensuous ship that perhaps might take them away to a place where paralysis did not exist.

He grinned—a lazy grin that made her desire a wee kiss all the more. "I took extra care with the sharpening leather."

Raising her chin, she pursed her lips.

But rather than kiss her, Sean stood and paraded in a grand circle, his arm stretching out before him. Finishing the turn he bowed deeply. "May I have this dance?"

She covered her mouth and giggled. "I said I scooted around a stool, silly."

He straightened and stepped closer. "In my arms you shall not falter, m'lady."

Gyllis blinked. "You mean to—"

Before she could finish, he swept her into his embrace and swung her in a circle. Sean's melodic voice hummed a bard's ballad as he swayed. Gyllis latched her arms around his neck and held as tightly as she could. *Mm.* He smelled of cedar and spice.

After her initial shock, Gyllis relaxed into him, closed her eyes and smiled. The way her body pressed against his was scandalous, but who would know? His powerful arms supporting her made her bubble inside.

She laughed and laughed while he swayed and twirled her in circles until her head swooned. "My, I'm dizzy."

He stopped turning when they reached the wall. "Then we must promenade." He hummed a slower tune and when he stepped forward, his thigh moved hers back. A tingling sensation swirled up her leg and intensified in her nether parts. How she wished she could wrap her legs around his body and cling to him throughout eternity.

Stopping in the center of the room, he stood still, gazing down at her face. His expression had grown serious, hungry.

"Why did you stop?" Gyllis whispered, breathless.

"I-I do not remember the rest of the tune."

"Has anyone ever told you that you have a beautiful singing voice?"

Sean didn't say a word, the look of hunger intensified in his eyes. He lowered his lashes and shifted his gaze to her lips. Gyllis's heart thundered so forcefully, she was sure it was pummeling Sean's chest right through her bodice. Ever so slowly he inclined his head.

Please, kiss me now.

Gyllis lifted her chin and met him halfway. His lips parted with a quick inhale of air. Blinking, his gaze dipped to her mouth. Her entire body came alive with swirling want. With one more quick lick of his lips, he covered her mouth with bone-melting fervor. The intensity and passion behind his kiss sent her mind whirling in a cyclone of rapture. She closed her eyes and melted into him. Aye, kissing at the Beltane festival had been amazing, but now Sean ravished her mouth with unexpected hunger. Together with his woodsy scent, Gyllis's entire body ignited with fire. She returned his smoldering kiss with vigor. Thank the heavens her tongue had not been affected by paralysis.

When he paused, he drew in a ragged breath. "Forgive me. I must not take advantage."

The door swung open. "What, in the name of all that is holy, are you doing with my sister in your arms?"

Holding her tight, Sean spun around and faced the prior. "John." His voice cracked. "'Tis good to see you."

John hastened inside and shut the door. "I wish I could say the same."

"We were dancing," Gyllis explained.

Sean assisted her to ease onto the bed. "Apologies. I took liberties."

John scowled. "I ought to—"

Gyllis held up her palms. "We must have been overcome. I walked all by myself today, a-and Sir Sean and I danced to celebrate my success."

John glared at Sean. "You danced?"

Sean nodded. "Aye."

"He supported me in his arms was all." *And he kissed me.* She brushed her fingers across her lips. *The most wonderful kiss imaginable.*

John shifted his glare to Gyllis. "What would Duncan and Ma say if they knew Sean MacDougall had been unchaperoned in this cell with you in his arms?"

Gyllis sat erect and raised her chin. "Pardon me, but there's no need to tell them anything except that I'm making progress."

Sean folded his arms. "John is right, 'tis not proper for me to attend you in your cell. Upon my next visit we should converse in the gardens."

Gyllis clapped a hand over her heart. *Sean is coming back!* "I hope you will return soon."

He smiled, the warmth of his grin making her heart flutter all the more. "Things at Dunollie require my attention, but I plan to visit two days hence."

John opened the door. "I shall see you out."

"Very well." Sean grasped Gyllis's hand and pressed pillow-soft lips against it. "I'll see you soon."

"And I will await your return with rapt anticipation, Sir Sean."

Gyllis watched him until the door closed. With a loud sigh, she clapped her hands to her chest. Perhaps God *had* intended for her to contract paralysis.

Chapter Twelve

In the following week, Sean visited Gyllis every
morning. Riding his horse at a fast trot, he easily traversed
the six miles to Ardchattan Priory in under an hour.
Today he was especially excited to see the bonny lass
because he had something to give her.

When he arrived, Gyllis was in the courtyard working
with Brother Wesley. Seated on the bench, the monk held
her hands and helped her stand. When he nodded, she sat.

Deep down, Sean was glad he'd hit the monk the first
time he'd seen him. Brother Wesley may have taken an
oath of celibacy, but he was a man all the same. He was
completely unable to hide his adoration for Gyllis, and the
piss-swilling swine fed his lust by having his hands all over
her limbs throughout each day. John considered it
improper for Sean to be alone with Gyllis? He should take
a look at his own men and deem the same.

"Sir Sean, I am surprised to see you this day." Gyllis
beamed radiantly as always.

Sean shifted his angry stare from Brother Wesley and
smiled at Gyllis. He held up the crutches in his hand. "I
commissioned the carpenter to fashion these for you.
When I arrived home yesterday, they were awaiting me."
He placed them under his arm, took her hand and kissed

it. "I could not wait until the morrow to see you use them."

She blessed him with a delightfully dimpled grin. "How so very kind of you."

Brother Wesley cleared his throat. "I was planning to make you a pair myself." He eyed her and held up his finger. "When you are ready, Miss Gyllis."

Sean arched an eyebrow at the errant monk. "I believe the lass is ready now."

"I think not." Wesley shook his head, black curls jostling. "'Tis still too soon."

"And what makes you an expert on the matter?" Sean tapped his foot.

The little monk managed to draw upon enough cods to puff out his chest. "I'll tell you, Miss Gyllis is the second patient with paralysis I've tended, and—"

"Enough." Gyllis reached out for the crutches. "I want to try them."

Sean shouldered past the monk and held the pegs out to her.

The sext bell rang.

"You'd best go pray," Sean said over his shoulder.

Brother Wesley pressed his palms together. "If she falls, it will be on your conscience."

"That it will." Sean returned his attention to Gyllis and grinned. "Are you ready?"

"Aye." She batted her eyelashes. "But you weren't very nice to Brother Wesley."

"Nay? Well, how would you like it if a nun had her hands all over me day and night?"

"Oh, please. 'Tis not like that."

"You think not? I ken a lustful man when I see one."

Gyllis glanced back toward the church. "Honestly?"

"Aye." Sean balanced the crutches. "Come, grasp the posts and see if you can pull yourself up."

She bit her bottom lip and looked at the crutches like she was about to mount an untrained horse. Wrapping her fingers around them, she launched her body forward and up. Sean's arms quivered a tad while he held the pegs steady.

Once Gyllis had gained her balance, he nodded to the armrests. "Now slide them under your arms."

When they were properly in place, she blew out a breath.

"How do they feel?" he asked.

"Good."

He gestured forward. "Well then, give it a try."

The look on her face reminded him of a young lad concentrating on firing a bow and arrow for the first time, but she moved the crutches forward and shuffled up to them. Then she chuckled, a rapt grin spreading across her face. Sean stepped back to encourage her to do more.

In no time, she had moved a quarter of the way across the courtyard.

He hastened beside her. "You're doing well."

"Thank you."

"Do you think you'll be able to use these to gain a modicum of freedom?"

"Aye." She took in a deep breath. "But I've grown tired so quickly."

Sean pointed to the bench. "Can you make it back?"

She nodded and awkwardly crisscrossed the crutches until she had herself turned around. Sean resisted his urge to help, but he followed her with his hands out, ready to catch her at any moment. When Gyllis arrived at the bench, he placed his arm around her waist to give support and helped her sit. He leaned in and inhaled the scent of heaven and heather. He squeezed his arm a little tighter, savoring her supple hip as it molded against his.

"Goodness," she chuckled.

Pushing away his lustful urges, he sat beside her and crossed his legs. "I think you did quite well for your first try."

She rubbed under her arms. "It might take me a while to get used to them."

"Did they cause you pain?"

"A wee bit under my arms."

He held up a crutch and examined the wooden armrest. "I'd bet we could sew some sheep's wool around these and make them a mite more comfortable."

She ran her hand over the hickory. "No need to bother. The carpenter has done a fine job of sanding them smooth."

"I like to bother—and nothing gives me more pleasure than watching you battle to overcome your illness. I'll take these with me and they'll have a cushion of wool when I next return."

A blush blossomed across her cheeks. "My thanks. You are ever so kind."

Sean ran his finger over her skin. "Rose petals." He used the crook of his finger to turn her head to face him. "The problem with the priory is there is no privacy."

She inhaled a stuttered breath. "I think 'tis designed that way."

After placing his hands on her shoulders, he glanced left, right and then focused on her lips. "Presently they're all praying." His voice trailed off.

Her pink tongue snuck out and moistened her lips. "How fortuitous." As she pronounced the words, her lips reminded him of rosebuds, better yet, she smelled more heavenly than a basin filled with petals.

Inclining his head, he could no sooner resist those roses than he could stop breathing. She raised her chin, enticing him further—begging him to steal a wee kiss. So fierce the memory of her passion when he last kissed her, his blood thrummed with fire. Closing the distance, he first plied her mouth gently, slipping his tongue inside and tasting her sweetness. Her fingers slid around his neck and drew him ever closer. Then her gentle moan rumbled through his body. Hot and raw, he could never totally control himself when within Gyllis's arms.

Exploring the silky smooth recesses of her mouth, his entire body craved her, could have devoured her. He cared not if they were on holy ground. The desire flooding his senses was nothing if not sacred. He clutched his arms around her, afraid to let go. God, he wanted to hold her forever—protect her from all the evils of the world.

Heaven help him, he could have lost Gyllis without even being aware of her illness. It was only by a stroke of luck when Lorn had asked him to meet at Ardchattan Priory. Never again did he want to see her sick and in pain. He would do anything to keep the lass safe for the rest of their days.

She pulled back and stared into his eyes. Oh, how Gyllis could control him with her sultry stare, especially when her lips were rouged from a passionate kiss. "What will happen…?" She looked away.

He circled his hand on her back. "Is something weighing on you, lass?"

She shook her head. "I cannot say it."

"Please. How can I know what is troubling you until you speak your mind?"

She bit her bottom lip and exhaled. "What will happen when I return to Kilchurn Castle?" She placed her hand over his heart. "What will happen to us?"

"Nothing will change—but that day is far off."

"I am not so certain. John thinks I'll be able to return home soon, especially if Mother puts my bed in the first floor solar."

Sean didn't care for that idea. She'd be further away from Dunollie and then he would have Duncan's ire to contend with. "I shall speak to John about insuring you're fully capable of climbing stairs. The solar? 'Tis no place for a highborn lass to sleep. And after dark there are drunken guardsmen everywhere below stairs."

The doors to the chapel creaked open and the resounding chant from the processing monks filled the courtyard. Sean slid his hands to Gyllis's shoulders. Closing his eyes, he inhaled her sweet scent once more while placing a tender kiss upon her forehead.

***

Sean left the priory later than he'd intended, something which was becoming a habit. Too many things demanded his attention at Dunollie, yet he continually found excuses to visit Gyllis.

He'd ridden about halfway to the castle when prickles at the back of his neck told him he wasn't alone. Over the years Sean had developed an uncanny sense, one respected and valued by Duncan and the Highland Enforcers. He'd tracked and eluded many men in his past. Easing off on the reins, he cocked his head and listened. Damn, they were close—riding through the trees off to the right. He palmed his dirk while glancing over his shoulder. A flicker of metal caught the sunlight.

Too close. My senses must be addled.

Sean dug in his heels, spurring his warhorse into a gallop. From the pummeling of the earth behind, at least four outlaws made chase. He pulled on the reins slightly—just enough to give the leader a chance to gain some ground.

Peering over his shoulder, the blackguard wore a great helm covering his entire head, as did the bastard behind him.

Too cowardly to show their faces.

Sean listened and from the corner of his eye, he watched as he allowed the leader to approach. As the man reached Sean's shoulder, the Chieftain of Dunollie threw a backhand with his dirk. Grunting, the outlaw shirked from the blade and swung a mace. Sean jerked aside, but not far enough. The spike on the iron ball caught Sean's upper arm, knocking him aside. He squeezed his legs around his horse's barrel, latched his fingers under his pommel and pulled himself up. His arm throbbed, but he had no time to think of pain.

Still holding the knife, he countered with an undercut and knocked the helm from the scoundrel's head. The man gaped, blood running down his cheek where the dirk had slashed.

Sean recognized the face and his gut squeezed.

Hoof beats thundered. The others had gained ground. Sean dug in his heels with a bellow. Faster than a Highland wildcat, his stallion launched into a thundering gallop. Relentless, Sean urged his horse faster while the beast took in steady snorts of air through enormous nostrils. When they cleared the forest, Sean glanced behind. The brigands had dropped speed—smart enough to know if they chased him all the way to Dunollie, they'd be dead men for certain.

Haste, you bastards.

He slowed his horse to a canter as the castle loomed on the horizon. He'd seen the outlaw before, and by the shocked expression when he exposed the brigand's face, Sean had no doubt the man knew who he was—perhaps even feared him. Sean rifled through his memory—yes, he'd seen that ugly face at Beltane. He was one of the bastards who'd attacked him during the footrace. The man wasn't a MacDougall and Sean hadn't recalled seeing him in Lorn's retinue a few sennights past. Was the ugly boar a Campbell? He didn't want to come to conclusions, but needed to find out what the hell was afoot. Were these petty thieves, or was something more sinister stirring?

Clomping across the wooden bridge, he raced his mount through the barbican gates and rode straight to the keep.

Angus met him with a groom on his heels. "What the devil, m'laird? You rode in here like you were being chased by Satan."

Sean dismounted and glared at him. "Perhaps I was."

Angus gaped at the blood dripping from Sean's sleeve. "Lord Almighty, what happened to your arm?"

Sean handed the reins to the groom. "A sniveling maggot and his helmed accomplices thought they'd bludgeon me with a mace."

Angus examined Sean's arm, his shirt thick with blood. "I'll bring Jinny up to you at once."

"Nay. First send out the guard to track the bastards— they attacked two miles from here on the path to Ardchattan Priory."

"Ardchattan? Is that where you've been off to?"

"Bloody hell, you're worse than an old woman." Sean dismissed him with a flick of his wrist. "Send the men after them before the trail grows cold."

Once inside his chamber, Sean strode directly to the table and poured himself a cup of whisky. He tossed back a gulp and waited until the fire flowed down his gullet and pooled in his empty stomach. It took only a moment for the calming spirit to spread through his blood. He yanked his shirt off and examined the gash in his arm. The cut was jagged and a purple bruise swelled around it.

I'll send every last one of them to hell.

As master of Dunollie lands, it was Sean's responsibility to ensure the safety of his clan—a responsibility that had taken second place as of late—a

folly. He'd been spending too much time doting over
Gyllis. Worse, every time he went to the priory, he ended
up staying far longer than he planned. He was a chieftain,
damn it all.

He took another sip of whisky and winced. By God,
he needed to stop acting like a lovesick fool. Aye, he'd
win Gyllis's hand in time, but he could no longer shirk his
duties. He crossed to the ewer and bowl and poured in
water. Splashing water over the gash, he hissed at the
stinging burn.

*I must limit my visits to Ardchattan to Sundays and
Wednesdays.* He reached for a drying cloth and clamped it
over his arm. He hated the thought of waiting to see her.
At least today was Friday. He need only make it through
tomorrow and he could again be with the lassie. *If only I
could meet with her alone.*

"M'laird?" A rap came at the door.

"Come."

Jinny bustled into the chamber with Angus on her
heels. "I came as soon as I received word." She set her
basket on the table and gestured to a chair. "You'd best sit
and let me have a look."

Sean frowned at Angus. "Is the guard away?"

"Yes, m'laird."

"Why are you not with them?"

"I felt it best to bring Jinny up here to tend your
wound." He peered around for a look. "Good Lord, we
must bandage that straight away."

"Aye." Jinny placed her fingers on either side of the
cut and cringed. "'Tis a nasty gash. We'd best put some
leeches on it while you're still bleeding. Then I'll have to
sew you up."

Sean took another draw on his whisky. "Do what you
must. I've no time to be waylaid by a wound of the flesh."

Angus grumbled under his breath. "Do you ken who attacked?"

"Nay. They wore bucket helms. I managed to knock one off—thought I recognized the brigand from the fete—one of the snakes who attacked me during the footrace."

The man-at-arms combed his fingers through his unruly grey hair. "You mustn't keep leaving without a guard. 'Tis dangerous for any man, especially a man of property such as yourself."

Sean didn't care to be lectured by someone who'd been withholding secrets. "And whom do you think attacked me?"

"I've no idea, m'laird."

"Nay? For all I know you had a hand in it."

Jinny stopped with a leech held in her fingers. "Angus would never do anything—"

"What are you saying?" Angus held up his hand to stifle Jinny's rebuttal. "Are you accusing me?"

"I heard you talking to Murdach in my solar. I ken there was no error when *my* coin went missing." Sean batted Jinny's hand away. "I ken an ugly deception has taken root under my own roof."

Angus stammered and spread his palms.

Sean stood. "Tell me I am wrong."

The older man hung his head. "I made a promise to your father I would never reveal his secret."

Sean smashed the cup of whisky and sent it flying into the hearth. "Bloody secrets!" he bellowed. "Are they what nearly got me killed?"

"N-no, m'laird."

Sean drew his dirk. "My father had secrets that he could not relay to me, his only son?"

Angus pulled down his collar and offered his throat. "I made a promise to a dying man." His Adam's apple bobbed. "His son has my fealty and I will gladly lay down my life for him, but I will not renege upon his father's wishes."

"Merciful Lord." Jinny crossed herself while her voice trembled. "Please, m'laird."

Sean watched the blue vein in Angus's neck pulse. If he sliced his blade across it, the henchman would bleed out before his face hit the floor. "I will tolerate no backstabbing in my clan."

"Nor will I, m'laird."

Jinny tugged on Sean's arm. "Please sit. You've had a terrible ordeal."

"Quiet, woman." Sean narrowed his eyes at Angus. "Because my father requested your silence upon his death bed, I shall make this one allowance. But moving forward, there must be no secrets between us. If I discover one more deception, you will be hanged, make no bones about it."

Angus released his collar and bowed his head. "Yes, m'laird."

Glancing between the two, Sean frowned and took his seat.

Without a word, Jinny applied the leeches while Angus stood at attention. Sean studied the man he'd known all his life. As before, he didn't believe him a traitor, but something wasn't right. By God, he would tolerate no deception within the clan. Sooner or later, someone would make a mistake. That's when Sean would attack and heaven help anyone caught. They would not be long for this world.

Unrest twisted in his gut. He would not sit idle while the Dunollie guard chased his attackers. "Make haste, woman. Angus and I shall follow the guard at once."

Chapter Thirteen

Gyllis was a tad disappointed when Sean didn't pay a visit the next day. Brother Wesley had kindly propped her up on the pillows for the afternoon, where she leafed through John's Bible. After having read her storybook a dozen times, she relented and gave in to her brother's urging to read something to enrich her soul.

She looked up when her door opened, her stomach fluttering in hopes that it would be Sean, but Helen's radiant smile brightened the cell. Gyllis put down her book and opened her arms. "Praise the heavens. I'd thought you'd forgotten me."

Helen wrapped her in a warm embrace. "Not at all. Have you not received the missives we wrote?"

"Aye, I have, but 'tis not like seeing you."

"I ken." Helen sat on the stool beside the bed. "Unfortunately there aren't any inns nearby, or I'd spend an entire sennight with you."

Gyllis adjusted her shoulders so she wouldn't have to twist her neck. "How long will you be able to stay?"

"Just the afternoon and Mother sent an entire army to escort me across Loch Etive and home again."

Gyllis laughed. "At least you are in the company of a retinue of brawny knights."

Helen twisted a lock of her dun hair around her finger—the color always reminded Gyllis of honey. "I suppose so." She lowered her gaze along with her frown.

"Whatever is wrong?" Gyllis hadn't seen that woeful visage on her sister's face often.

"Nothing, really." Helen smiled. "'Tis just Ma didn't send any noble knights along—just the same old dreary guards from Kilchurn Castle."

Gyllis laughed. "You mean Sir Eoin MacGregor isn't with you?"

She unwound her hair. "Afraid not."

"Why, how utterly heartless of him."

Helen sighed. "Honestly, I haven't seen Sir Eoin in some time."

"Where has he been?"

"How should I know? No one tells us lassies anything."

"Some things do not change." Gyllis chuckled and placed her hand atop Helen's. "My, 'tis good to see you."

Helen smiled, but it wasn't her usual sweet grin. It was guarded. "And how are you, my dearest?"

Gyllis bit her lip. Though she and Helen could always tell each other their deepest secrets, a tickle at the back of her mind told her not to talk about Sir Sean. Things were only beginning to blossom between them and, presently, she didn't know if his attentions were because they had been dear friends and he felt sorry for her. Yes, she'd sensed his genuine fondness and delightful kisses, but things were so different now. She had an illness that very well could leave her a cripple for life. No man would ever want to marry a cripple. No. She would keep her meetings with Sir Sean to herself. She'd lock away any happiness that he imparted and, for the first time in her life, would refrain from thinking about the future.

She ventured to look at her legs, covered by a blanket. "I've gained a bit of use of my hands, but my legs are generally worthless."

"That is awful." Helen folded her hands in her lap. "Do you think the monk's treatments are helping?"

"Gradually—but not fast enough for me." Gyllis clapped. "I would prefer not to talk about me. How are things at home? Mother?"

"Mother is worried half to death about you, but recently she's been busy running the keep. Duncan took Lady Meg to Edinburgh to spend midsummer at court with King James. It seems the king always requires something from our brother."

"Aye, and his wife could no longer bear for them to be separated, I'm sure."

"I'd agree. Being apart makes it rather difficult for them to produce…ah…more bairns."

Gyllis burst out with laughter and cupped her hand over her mouth. "You do surprise me at times, Helen."

"Well, 'tis the truth." She smiled—now a warm, genuine smile. Gyllis realized all her sisters were rather pretty—funny she hadn't thought much about it before. "Alice and Marion are the same, still at that age where they're driving Mother mad with their silly remarks and back talking."

"Aye, I remember when we were ten and six." Gyllis chuckled. "We were hellions."

"We were for certain. God bless Ma, she lived through it." Helen glanced to the corner where John had rested the lute sennights ago. "Have you been playing?"

Gyllis held up her hands. "I'm afraid my fingers have not yet found the dexterity they once had."

"Perhaps it would be soothing if I played for you?" Helen's eyebrows raised, as if asking for permission.

"Please do."

Easing into the pillows, Gyllis closed her eyes and listened to Helen's magical fingers. Of all her sisters, Helen was definitely the most talented with the lute. She plucked the strings with such lithe grace, the music came alive. And when she sang, it was as if larks had joined together in a heavenly chorus. The music moved Gyllis, sent tingles up her spine. She had missed Helen's company, though she wasn't yet ready to return home. Besides being an invalid, she'd rarely see Sir Sean if she went back to Kilchurn Castle.

Mid-strum, John entered with Mevan, Kilchurn Castle's man-at-arms. Helen rested the lute on the bed and greeted John with a warm embrace. After they'd exchanged pleasantries, John gestured to the guard. "'Tis time to away home. I've arranged for your transport to ferry you across Loch Etive giving Fearnoch Forest a wide berth."

"Has something happened in the forest?" Gyllis asked.

John gave her a stern look as if she hadn't the right to ask her question. The intensity in his eyes made her shoulders rigid. Something had happened for certain.

Helen bent down and embraced her. "Next time I'll see if we can stay longer."

Gyllis kept her eyes on John. "I'd like that." She held her tongue until Helen's footsteps echoed down the passageway. Thank heavens John didn't leave her to fret alone in her cell. "Tell me what happened."

"We received word of an outlaw attack in the forest."

He was going to force her to draw it out of him, but she had to ask. The gooseflesh rising on her skin was warning enough. "Is Sir Sean all right?" Gyllis nearly choked on the words.

John let out a long breath. "He escaped with only minor injuries. The crier stopped by to warn us of the danger. Dunollie men are after the culprits now. If I ken Sir Sean MacDougall, they will be brought to justice before this week is through." John pulled the latch.

"But—" Before she could finish, John closed the door. Gyllis stared for a moment, hating her damned legs. What on earth could she do to help? Balling her fists, she pounded her useless thighs. There she sat, incarcerated within the walls of a priory while Sean rode into unimaginable danger.

She smoothed her hand over the Bible in her lap and closed her eyes, offering a silent prayer for his well-being. What did John mean by *minor* injuries? And when would she see Sir Sean again? *Please, dear God, watch over your servant Sean MacDougall, and lead him home to safety.*

***

Sean wasn't one to let a few stitches and a bruised arm set him back. Besides, spending a night tracking was what he needed to cement his priorities. He'd not taken the cattle thieving seriously enough and the brigands had the gall to attack *him*. It was the slap in the face he needed.

With the dawn, Sean and Angus lay on their bellies, staring down at the outlaw's camp.

"Only four," Angus said.

"If I'd just attacked the Chieftain of Dunollie, I'd be a bit less conspicuous," Sean growled.

Obviously they didn't expect retaliation. The bastards were sloppy. Nestled within a glen, their morning fire was like a beacon flickering through the light mist. For the past half mile, Sean could practically smell the roasting meat. The MacDougalls had them surrounded. All Sean needed do was give the signal. But he was more cautious than that. Were they stupid or were they luring Sean and his men into a trap?

Only four men. Regardless, they do not stand a chance.

Sean slid back and mounted his horse. Drawing his sword, he gave the signal by holding it straight up above his head. Bellows erupted from the men charging down the hillside. The bastards barely had time to draw their weapons and face the onslaught. Fifty to four were unbeatable odds.

Sean called a halt before the fighting began. "Throw down now."

The leader faced him. "Throw down so you can run us through? I'd rather you gave me a fighting chance."

Once again, he recognized the man's face—aye, he was sure of it now. This was the same man who'd attacked him during the footrace. "I'd be running you through this day regardless." Sean dismounted and Angus followed suit, sword at the ready.

The man's gaze darted to the right. Sean followed that gaze, straight to a MacDougall guard—Gawen was his name. Sean gave the guard a stern stare to let him know he'd not missed the interchange, then he focused on his prisoner. "Why did you attack me in the forest?"

The scoundrel spread his palms and smirked. "I see a man with a horse as finely outfitted as yours and I ken he has some coin in his purse."

The smug look on the bastard's face made Sean's blood boil. He closed his fist. With a roar, he slammed it across the animal's face. The man careened to his arse, blood streaming from the corner of his mouth. He swiped an arm across his lips and eyed Sean. With a bellow, he jumped up, brandishing his sword. Sean skittered aside and disarmed him. The laggard was no match for Sean's years of training. The other mongrels dropped their weapons. A mangy lot of mutts they were. Sean yanked the bastard's arm and spun him into a hold with his sword leveled against his neck.

"I'll be paid my due respect the next time you address me," Sean growled. "I've seen you afore. Now tell me why you attacked me during the footrace at Dunstaffnage."

The man spat blood, squirming in a futile attempt to break free. "Don't kill me."

"I need to know. Why?"

"He paid us a crown."

Sean pushed the blade until it drew blood. "Who?"

"Jesus Christ." The man's fear stank like a steaming pile of cow dung. "I don't ken his name. Black hair—an ugly bastard—wore leather breeks."

Sean nodded to Angus. "Tie them up. We'll take them back to Dunollie and hang the lot at dawn on the morrow. Give them a chance to atone to the maker for all their evil deeds."

"Please, m'laird, have mercy on a poor beggar," the miserable leader whined.

Sean threw him to the ground. "Would you have been merciful had your mace knocked me from my mount last eve?" A guard wrapped a rope around the man's wrists and Sean sheathed his weapon. "I think not."

***

By the time the Dunollie guard arrived at the castle, the sun had set. As a warrior, Sean had gone days without sleep before, but his limbs were heavy with exhaustion. His shoulder throbbed—hurt like the devil. "Take the prisoners to the dungeon," he bellowed, then he pulled Angus aside. "Do not allow Gawen anywhere near the prisoners. If he tries to visit the dungeon, throw him inside and he'll hang with the others."

"Gawen, m'laird?"

"You heard me."

Pushing into the keep, he yelled louder, "Jinny, I need your salve and a flagon of whisky in my chamber. Now."

He loosened his sword belt as he climbed the stairs. When in God's name had he aged? He strode into his chamber and tossed his weapons on the bed. Life had been a mite easier before he'd become a chieftain. Chasing a mob of thieves provided good sport, but digging into the Dunollie coffers and acting the part of lord-high executioner soured his stomach.

Jinny dashed in with her basket. "Do not tell me you've torn your stitches, m'laird."

"What would you do if I had?" He pulled off his doublet and shirt and sat in the chair in front of the hearth.

She set her basket on the table and crossed her arms. "Don't you be patronizing me, m'laird. You may be lord of this keep, but 'tis my duty to see you do not succumb to the fever or worse."

Groaning, Sean leaned back. "'Tis but a scratch, woman."

"Aye? You should have let my Angus track down the brigands. Look at you, you've purple bags under your eyes," she hissed. "Goodness, oh my goodness. Your shoulder is a sight."

Sean glanced down at the swollen mass of purple flesh. "Quit your bellyaching and slap some salve on it— you ken, the concoction that eases the pain."

She fished in her basket and pulled out a pot. "You need to rest your blessed shoulder." She leaned forward and sniffed. "At least it is not putrid—yet."

"Did you bring up the whisky?"

"Aye." She swabbed on a glop of smelly goo.

"Well, are you planning to keep it to yourself? A man could die of thirst whilst you dawdle."

She reached into her basket and pulled out a flagon. "Here, since you cannot wait."

"You're a good matron. A swipe of your ointment and a few strong tots of MacDougall whisky, and I'll be fit to fight on the morrow." He pulled the stopper and took a long drink.

"Bloody men," Jinny whispered under her breath.

"Aye, that's too right. Where would the lassies be without men to look after them?" The whisky hit his empty stomach and burned.

Jinny finished rubbing and examined her work. "You're going to have a nasty scar."

"Good." He took another healthy swig. "The lassies like scars."

"Oh do they now? I thought you might be done with your womanizing." Jinny stoppered her pot. "And what about Miss Gyllis Campbell?"

Sean's eyes flew open. "What about her?" If Jinny had been a man, Sean would have jumped to his feet, fists ready for a fight.

But Jinny chuckled. "Look at you, you big bear of a man. You're smitten. You used to be quite free with the lassies, but I haven't seen a one catch your eye in months." The matron looked mighty proud of herself. "And I'd reckon all those trips to Ardchattan have had something to do with it."

He grumbled into the flagon and drowned his next words. So what if he liked her? Christ, he'd already said he loved her. But did he love her like that? Sean glanced up at Jinny. The damned woman looked like she'd just swallowed the best plum duff ever made. "So? Gyllis needs me." Her crutches were leaning against his clothing trunk with the sheepskin pads around the armrests. Thank God something was working as it should.

"Aye?" Jinny didn't let it rest. "And how is she recuperating? You ken, some folks are never the same again after a bout of paralysis."

"Gyllis will come good, mark me." He flicked his hand toward the door. "Off with you now."

***

The next morning, Sean couldn't say what throbbed more, his head or his blasted shoulder. But he wasn't about to call Jinny and ask for another application of her salve. Listening to her bloody opinions was worse than the pain. Besides, he had an ugly duty to perform and he might as well be in a foul mood for it.

He grimaced as he pulled on his shirt. He could scarcely lift his left arm. He reached for the flagon, but he'd drunk the damn thing dry. The chambermaid brought in a tray. "Angus said they'll be ready once you've broken your fast, m'laird."

"Is everyone looking after my health?"

"Aye. Everyone kens you didn't eat a thing all day yesterday and your shoulder is on the verge of turning putrid, and if you do not take care of it you're going to end up like your da and we'll not have a chieftain to replace you."

Sean stared at the lass. Now a skinny wisp of a girl was spewing the same rubbish he'd heard from Jinny?

She handed him a spoon and curtsied. "For your porridge, m'laird."

He snatched it from her and pointed to the door. "Go. Tell Angus I'll be down momentarily."

Sean had half a mind to leave the food, but it smelled too good. His stomach rumbled. Cook hadn't missed a thing, porridge, eggs, bacon and haggis. Suddenly ravenous, he ate every bite and then headed down to face his duty.

By the time Sean walked into the courtyard, Angus had the prisoners lined up on the gallows with their hands bound and nooses around their necks. The man-at-arms had carried out his duty efficiently, without a qualm.

Sean surveyed the faces of his men, all standing as witness to the hanging. Gawen stood away from the others on the far end. "Gawen, how do you know these men?" Sean asked.

The lad looked up as if shocked the chieftain knew his name. "Pardon, m'laird?"

"You heard me." Sean scowled. "Come forward and tell us about these scoundrels."

"I-I do not know them."

"Very well. Then you'll have no qualms kicking the stools out from under these outlaws' feet?"

The lad blanched. "N-no, m'laird."

Sean nodded at Angus who grasped Gawen by the arm and led him up the gallows' steps.

The cleric stepped forward and opened a scroll. "For the crime of attack on Sir Sean MacDougall, Chieftain of Dunollie with intent to do harm, you are sentenced to hang by the neck until dead. May God have mercy on your soul."

Gawen hesitated at the first stool. The lad glanced at Sean over his shoulder with fear in his eyes. Sean gave him a thin-lipped nod. Turning slowly, Gawen kicked the stool, followed by a clatter, a twang of the rope and a crack, breaking the man's neck. Death was never a pretty sight, even when it was done to rid the world of murderers—men who placed no value on human life. Sean had no idea how many people these men had killed or how many women they might have raped.

In the somber moment of the misty dawn only one thing was certain. Not one would live to pillage another day.

Chapter Fourteen

Sean mounted his horse and drove the beast like he was running from the devil. Aye, he'd attended hangings before, but he'd never presided over one as Chieftain of Dunollie. The image of the men swinging from their nooses, their feet kicking like beheaded chickens would be seared on his memory forever. Would he pass such severe punishment if again faced with the same circumstances? Yes. There would be no question. If not dealt with relentlessly, lawlessness would pervade Dunollie lands and his clan would suffer the consequences.

He rode full tilt all the way to Ardchattan Priory. When he pounded the knocker, the monk who answered didn't even ask him his purpose—one look at Sean's face and the man opened the door. "Miss Gyllis is in her cell."

"My thanks," Sean mumbled, carrying the crutches as he strode past.

Though he wanted to rush in and gather her in his arms, hold her for hours and ask her to take away the agony caused by hanging four brigands, he stood at the door and watched. She worked the embroidery needle, making painstakingly small stitches—something he knew would be difficult for her. The concentration on her face made his heart squeeze, but it wouldn't be right to try to help. She was a determined lass and would regain her strength as a result.

Something in her determination, her concentration soothed him. When he watched Gyllis, the evils of the world faded as if they no longer mattered. With Gyllis, his soul sailed to an island of peace.

When Sean rested the crutches against the wall, she looked up. "Sean!" She cast her sewing aside. "Thank heavens you're safe."

The corner of his mouth ticked up. "You heard?" He had hoped she would have been spared the burden.

"I've been so worried, I could scarcely think of anything else." Gyllis reached for his hand. "John reported you had injuries."

He kissed her hand and sat on the stool. "Just a bruise to the shoulder." He kept her palm in his. The softness of her skin soothed him as did the depth of the concern reflected in her eyes. The tension in his neck eased. "I hanged four outlaws today."

"My God." Gasping, she clapped her free hand over her mouth. "How awful."

"I hope 'tis not something I have to do often. I'd much rather fight a man than tie his hands and hang him—even if he is a scoundrel."

"But you risk injury by fighting."

Sean said nothing. Painfully aware of the open door behind him, all he could do was stare into those eyes. Gyllis could caress his soul with a single look. And from her expression, he could read so much. She cared as deeply for him as he did her. So intense was the current holding their stares, he could not bring himself to look away.

Gyllis smiled, her dimples melting the tension from his shoulders to the base of his spine. "And what are you thinking about, sir knight?"

Sean grinned. "Why, the winsome maiden seated before me, miss." With her tiny gasp, his blood rushed like a white-capped river.

He raised her hand to his lips, closed his eyes and kissed. There in that room with monks wandering about the halls, he was completely and utterly entranced with this woman. He'd never met anyone who could calm his deepest agony with a look. Her pulse thrummed a steady rhythm beneath his lips. If only they could be alone.

Long lashes shuttered those green eyes and for a brief moment, Sean felt lost.

"I know not what to say," she whispered, a blush spreading across her cheeks.

He raised her chin with the crook of his finger. "Sometimes more is said with a look than with words." He gestured to the wall behind. "I've returned your crutches complete with sheepskin armrests."

She looked past him and beamed. "They are marvelous, and I'm certain I've grown stronger since your last visit."

"Do you think you can make it out to the garden?"

"I'm sure I can." She clapped her hands. "If I could use those things to walk outside the cloistered walls I would. I've felt so cosseted, what I wouldn't do to sit a horse with the wind in my hair."

Sean fetched the crutches. "Well, let us start by taking a stroll out into the sunshine." He chuckled. The Gyllis he'd grown up with had gradually returned and gone was the skeletal, bitter lass. She'd put on a wee bit of weight and maneuvered her crutches with lip-biting determination. Aye, she indeed was a woman to be admired.

***

Though Sean hadn't been able to visit the priory as often in the past few sennights, Gyllis's heart swelled every time she saw him stride through the cloisters. Long legged, tall, and incredibly handsome, her problems faded into oblivion when the young chieftain came to call.

And on account of his generosity, in the past fortnight she had become more adept with her crutches. How wonderful it was to regain a modicum of freedom and tend to her most personal needs without a monk's aid.

Today she and Brother Wesley were working in her tiny chamber due to a bout of morning drizzle. After John and Sean had their disagreement, her brother required the monk to keep the door ajar when he ministered to her within. Gyllis pulled her woolen mantle around her shoulders. "'Tis difficult to believe only yesterday the sun provided a balmy day."

"Are you cold?" Brother Wesley asked. His voice always sounded so serene, it calmed her directly.

She tried not to shiver. "A wee bit."

"Shall I light the brazier?"

"Oh no, 'tis early yet, I'm sure the day will warm. Mother always says 'tis a waste of peat to burn it during the summer months."

"Your mother is a wise woman."

Gyllis reflected. Ma had a way of running an efficient keep for certain. "I suppose she is."

"I have no doubt of her wisdom. Your brother is still young and is already a prior." He stopped massaging and arched his eyebrows. "Then there's Lord Duncan. He's one of the most powerful men in the Highlands—both men raised by *your* mother."

Gyllis smiled, though her heart squeezed. "Do not forget our father was Black Colin of Rome. He had something to do with our rearing for certain and his legacy alone will transcend generations."

Wesley grinned. "That it will."

"Good morrow," a deep voice came from the corridor.

Gyllis's heart leapt. "Sir Sean, what a pleasant surprise."

The good-looking laird strode inside, barely acknowledging Brother Wesley. "I have a surprise for you, m'lady." He grinned, his teeth flashing white, framed by the shadow of his beard. The chieftain's dark features and crystal blue eyes could stop her heart.

Her cheeks grew hot. She loved it when he referred to her as m'lady, though as a baron's daughter, her proper title was miss. Perhaps one day she would be able to again hope to marry into nobility. Gyllis's insides fluttered with anticipation. "Do tell me what it is."

Sean held out a lady's riding crop. "I'll wager you are well enough to sit a horse."

Gyllis clapped her hands. "Oh my, I'd love to ride again."

Brother Wesley stood. "You cannot possibly be serious."

"Why ever not?" Gyllis asked.

Spreading his palms to his sides, the monk looked incredulous. "Do you realize how dangerous it is? What if the horse rears and you were to fall? Besides, it takes strength of arm to ride."

Sean's fists snapped to his hips. "I assure you, we will exercise the utmost care."

"My arms have nearly made a full recovery." Gyllis grasped the crop. "Besides, it isn't as if I've never ridden before."

"But 'tis raining," Wesley persisted. "You could catch your death."

"Hardly a drop fell from the sky during my ride from Dunollie." Sean collected the crutches from where they were propped against the wall. "Come, Miss Gyllis. Your gelding awaits."

With a huff, Brother Wesley strode toward the door. "Do not complain to me if riding a horse sets you back sennights and ruins all my work."

Gyllis watched the monk walk away, mumbling something akin to "ungrateful lass". But his uncharacteristic chagrin didn't dissuade her. She smiled up at Sean. "That's the first time I've ever seen him irritated. I'm afraid he's none too happy about your idea."

Sean offered his hand. "If it were up to that pasty monk, you'd still be abed so he could run his fingers along your thighs through eternity."

Gyllis placed her palm in his and allowed Sean to pull her up. "Oh please, Brother Wesley wants to see me well just as you do. He just doesn't have an adventurous spirit like yours."

Sean kissed her hand before giving her a crutch. "I doubt that."

"You are insufferable." She grasped it.

"How so?"

"You think that poor monk ogles me at his every chance."

"I don't think it." Sean slid the second crutch under her arm. "I ken he does."

Gyllis giggled. "Take me to this horse before I'm forced to wallop you with one of these crutches."

He bent down and nuzzled into her ear. Goodness, he smelled fresher than a pine forest. "A fine lady like you wouldn't do a thing like that."

Tickles flitted all the way up her neck. If only her confidence would return, she might steal a wee kiss. "I cannot wait for you to spirit me away."

Performing an exaggerated bow, he gestured toward the passageway and pulled her cloak from the peg on the wall. "Very well, m'lady."

When they reached the stables, Sean's man, Angus, led an old gelding up to them. Holding her hand to his nose, Gyllis let the horse smell her and then ran her fingers through his sorrel mane. "You're a kind fella, are you not?"

Sean placed his warm palm on her waist. "If you'll pass Angus your crutches, I'll give you a lift."

Her insides jumped like a swarm of butterflies had taken to flight. Leaning into him, Gyllis relinquished her crutches and held up her arms.

"Are you ready?" he asked.

She swallowed down her excitement. "Aye." Sean's large hands squeezed ever so gently as he lifted her into the sidesaddle. The tang of pine and rugged male curled through her nostrils, making her head swoon. The horse sidestepped, bringing her back to earth. Once situated, Gyllis tried to raise her knee over the upper pommel, but she couldn't raise the miserable appendage high enough. She cringed.

Sean closed his fingers around her thigh. "Allow me to help."

Even through her skirts, his simple gesture made her shudder. A jolt of pleasure and need spread through her entire body. His touch was so different than Brother Wesley's, so much more rugged, yet reassuring...and exciting.

Not trusting her voice to speak, she nodded.

He grasped her ankle and grinned. Oh how incredibly handsome he was when he smiled. His azure eyes narrowed slightly with a wee crinkle at the corners, and his teeth gleamed healthy and white. Sean's gaze darkened as if he had a secret he wanted to share. Hot, raw energy passed between them while he took his time bending her knee and lifting it over the pommel. All the while, his fingers plied her thigh.

Gyllis caught her breath on a gasp and fanned her heated cheeks. "I think you rather enjoyed that."

He patted her knee. "I did." If his grin could grow more devilish, it did.

"You are bold."

When he leaned within a hand's breadth of her chin, his smile stretching his features, it was all she could do not to clasp his face between her palms and kiss him. But Sean's retinue of guards surrounded them. Gyllis sat upright and adjusted her skirts while watching him from the corner of her eye. Aye, she'd enjoyed the few kisses they'd shared, but she wouldn't lose her head. Things had grown so different. At one time she'd been awash with confidence, but her illness had stripped that away too. A lead ball suddenly sank in her stomach. She would never be able to bear it if Sean rejected her.

Of course ages ago, he'd said he loved her—words Gyllis would never forget. It wasn't as if he'd said it again, though. Yes, he did kiss her rather passionately. His love couldn't exactly be compared to brotherly love, but she was too clumsy for it to be real man and woman love. *Is there such a thing as kissing friends love?* She didn't know, and right now she didn't want to think beyond spending the afternoon with Sean.

He brushed her nose with the back of his knuckle. "Is boldness such a bad thing?"

A fire inflamed her cheeks and she fixated on the reins. "Nay," she admitted in a whisper.

"Exactly what are you doing?" John marched into the stable.

Gyllis lifted her reins. "Sir Sean is taking me riding."

John crossed his arms and glared at the chieftain. "Not through Fearnoch Forest, 'tis not safe."

Sean faced him. "I assure you my men have cleansed the forest of all outlaws."

"Are you certain? You suffered attack yourself. Have you caught the culprits since we last spoke?"

"Four men hanged." Sean placed his palm on John's shoulder. "Has it been so long since we rode together you have forgotten our oath of brotherhood? You may have become a priest, but our bond of kinship will endure for a lifetime."

John stopped and stared, then his shoulders dropped. "You are right. I would trust you not only with my life, but the lives of every soul in Ardchattan Priory."

The two men grasped each other at the elbows—a sign of Highland kinship. Sean held firm. "I'll have her back before compline."

"I'd expect no less."

Once Sean had mounted his stallion, they rode straight out the gates. The rocking motion of the horse beneath her gave Gyllis an enormous sense of freedom. "'Tis wonderful to ride again."

Sean walked his horse alongside hers. "I thought you'd enjoy a jaunt away from the cloistered halls of the priory."

A breeze picked up the hood of her cloak. "I couldn't have thought of anything more invigorating myself."

Thunder clapped overhead. Sean arched his brow and gave her a sideways glance. "I'd hoped to picnic beside the babbly burn at Glen Nant."

Gyllis peered at the sky, swirling with grey clouds. *Please withhold the rain, if only for a little while.* She grinned. "What a lovely idea."

Thunder rolled and Sean cringed. "I'm not so certain. I wouldn't want to see you end up with the sweat or worse."

"Perhaps if we increase our speed to a fast trot, we shall arrive sooner." She glanced back toward the priory. The grey stone walls were as foreboding as a prison. In no way did she have any intension of turning around.

He stared at her for a long moment and then clicked his tongue. The entire retinue sped the pace to a trot. Droplets started falling, but this was Scotland. It always rained, but rarely did they have a lasting downpour.

"Thank you," Gyllis said.

"A faster pace is going against my better judgment." He flashed a wicked smile that tickled her insides. "But from the excitement in your eyes, I'd wager it would be too much of a disappointment not to give it a go."

She giggled and slapped her riding crop, demanding a canter.

"Gyllis." Sean hastened after her. "You could fall."

She shot him a challenging grin. "Sean MacDougall, I swear you are the most adventurous man I know. Do you honestly want to amble along when there's a picnic to be had?"

His eyebrows waggled with his grin. "Since you put it that way..." His stallion lurched ahead.

Gyllis laughed. This was the wild lad she'd admired whilst she was growing up. She slapped her crop and loosened her reins, giving her horse his head. Together they rode at a moderate canter for miles, Gyllis unable to stop giggling. Though she knew Sean could ride much harder, she dared not try to push more. As it was, her legs bounced with the motion of the horse. One errant move and she might be flung from her saddle.

A sloppy raindrop splashed her face.

Lightning streaked and lit up the sky.

Sean slowed and Gyllis pulled up beside him, the sentries circling around. "A storm's coming for certain."

"Dunollie's only a mile away. 'Tis the closest shelter," said Angus.

Sean frowned as if he didn't care for the idea, but then he nodded. "I hope you do not feel it improper, seeing you are unaccompanied."

Gyllis scanned the staring faces. "You've an entire retinue of men." She slapped her crop and headed west as the skies opened up and doused them with a torrent.

***

When at last they rode through Dunollie's gates, Gyllis was soaked clean through and shaking like a sapling in the wind. Sean drove the horses past the stable, straight to the keep's huge, oaken doors. After dismounting, he strode directly to Gyllis's horse, his face awash with rainwater. Pushed away from his face, droplets splashed from his dark hair, soaking his cloak and linen shirt beneath. Her gaze dipped to the laces of his collar. Curls of hair peeked through the opening, the wet fabric plastered to his chest. God help her, she wanted to tug open the laces and gaze upon the treasure beneath. Raising his arms, his cloak opened, revealing more. The linen hugged every curve of his rigid chest—chiseled as if carved in stone. Dropping her gaze further, the cloth clung to undulating abdominal muscles akin to those hammered into the iron breastplate of a Roman god.

Before she could blink, he placed a hand upon her waist. "Come, we must see you warmed by the hearth."

Teeth chattering, she braced her hands on his shoulder while he slipped an arm beneath her knees and carried her up the stairs. Once inside, Sean turned full circle. "Light the fire in my mother's chamber," he bellowed.

"Straight away," said Angus. "But it will take some time to warm the chill from the air."

Sean tightened his grip. "'Tis summer, blast it all."

A matron pattered across the hall. "You're soaked to the bone, m'laird."

"Miss Gyllis needs a change of clothes. Can you arrange a kirtle and shift?"

The woman wrung her hands. "Perhaps I can find something suitable."

"Good. Have them sent up to my chamber forthwith."

She clapped a hand to her chest whilst her eyes bulged. "*Your* chamber, m'laird?"

"Aye, Jinny," Sean barked. "'Tis presently the only room without a draft. Angus, follow us with the basket. I'll not be returning the lady to Ardchattan with even a hint of fever."

Gyllis sneezed.

"Quickly!" Sean hastened toward the stairwell.

"Apologies." She tried not to shiver and snuggled into him. Dripping wet, he was still as warm as a brazier. "I'm feeling well, honestly."

"I'll take no chances." Skipping two steps at a time, at the first landing Sean proceeded through the passageway and pushed through the door. He carried Gyllis to a chair beside the hearth and gently set her down. She shivered when he pulled away—the warmth of his body no longer soothing her. But the smell of the chamber washed over her in a delicious fragrance of pine and musky male. *Sean's scent.*

"The coals are still smoldering. I'll just toss on a few sticks of wood and you'll be toasty warm in no time."

"Th-thank you." Her teeth again chattered as she glanced back at the enormous four-poster bed across the room. Festooned with a green satin comforter and canopy, she wondered if Sean's favorite color was green. She hoped so.

Sean brushed her cheek with the back of his finger. "Your cheeks are rosy."

She clapped her hands to them. "Are they?"

"Aye." His voice grew deeper. "I like them with a bit of color."

When he turned and reached for the wood, a rap sounded at the door. Angus walked in, a basket slung from his elbow while he held a bundle of clothing at arm's length so not to get it wet. "Jinny sent these up for the lady, m'laird."

Sean tossed another stick of wood with a thump and straightened. "Where the devil is your wife?"

Angus shifted his weight between his feet, with water squishing out his boots. "Called to Morag's cottage. The bairn is coming."

A clap of thunder sounded beyond the stone walls, so loud the castle shook. Gyllis shuddered.

Sean gestured toward the bed. "Of all the miserable times for a woman to birth a wee one. Please set the things on the bed and go dry yourself."

"Aye, m'laird." Angus did as told and gave Gyllis an apologetic look. "Will you be needing anything else?"

Sean brushed off his hands. "Nay. I reckon all the womenfolk are at Morag's?"

Angus nodded. "I guess I'll leave you be, then." But the old henchman didn't make a move until Sean showed him to the door.

"No need to worry. I've managed far more difficult tasks."

The corner of Angus's mouth turned up. "You reckon?"

Gyllis knew what the henchman meant. It wasn't easy for a cripple to dress. She pulled the wet hood from her head.

Sean clapped his back. "Off with you. Put something warm in your belly to stave off the cold."

"I've just the vintage of whisky—"

Sean closed the door behind Angus and turned. Gyllis rubbed the outside of her arms, her teeth chattering.

"We must warm you."

"I am c-coming good. The fire is crackling." *If only the hearth were emitting a modicum of warmth.*

Sean gestured to the bed. "I should leave you to change."

Gyllis glanced toward the pile of clothes all the way over on the bed and then the door. "I d-don't think I can."

"Pardon?" His eyes trailed down to her shoes, then he hit his head with the heel of his hand. "Forgive me. I'll fetch them for you."

A slow exhale whistled past Gyllis's lips. "My thanks."

He set the bundle on the small table beside her. "I had hoped Jinny would've come up to help you dress." He shifted his feet. "Is there anything else I can do to help?"

"I think not. I should be able to manage."

"Very well. I shall be right outside the door if you should need me."

Gyllis bobbed her head in time to her chattering teeth.

Sean sidestepped to the door. "You're certain you'll be all right?"

"A-a-aye." She clapped a hand over her mouth and sneezed.

"Bloody hell, Gyllis, you best not be coming down with a fever."

She flicked her hand through the air. "Would you be off? I'll catch my death with your dawdling."

He grasped the latch. "Apologies."

She waited until the door clicked shut. Then the realization that she was alone sunk in. No one had brought her crutches above stairs. Gyllis studied the pile of clothes. Once the dexterity of her fingers had returned, she'd been able to do most everything herself—aside from anything that required her to stand. She wiggled her bottom and tested the chair. It was indeed sturdy.

After shrugging out of her cloak and loosening the laces of her kirtle and shift, she had an easy enough time gathering her skirts and pulling them up to her hips. She planted her feet firmly on the floor and bore down while using her hands to lift herself with the armrests. Once up, she released one hand and grasped her skirts. Her legs shuddered under the strain and cold. The damp cloth stuck to her skin and the harder she tugged the more it seemed to stick.

With a grunt, the muscles in her thighs gave out and she collapsed back into the chair with her kirtle up past her knees. Gyllis took a deep breath. *I've been pulling myself to a stand and walking with crutches. Surely it will be easier if I stood. I've the chair to lean on if need be. Goodness, 'tis more difficult trying to brace myself in a crouch.*

Again she grasped the armrests. With one deep inhale, she pushed herself up. Once certain her legs would support her weight, she released her hands and tugged the kirtle over her head. Knees wobbling a bit, she gathered up her damp shift. After she pulled it off, the warmth from the hearth radiated across her skin and her teeth ceased their chattering.

Enlivened by her ability to stand unassisted, Gyllis faced the table and reached for the dry linen shift. The kirtle tumbled to the floor, revealing a set of modern stays. She hadn't worn stays since she'd come down with paralysis. There'd been no need. But she would look so much prettier with her bosoms supported with fashionable wooden slats.

Stepping forward, she reached her hand out to brush her fingers across the feminine garment. The table teetered. Her knees buckled. Before she could fling her arms out, she crumpled to the floor with a shriek.

"Curses." She cringed at the throbbing pain in her hip. *I shall never be able to fend for myself.*

The door burst open. "God's teeth, are you hurt?" Sean dashed across the floor.

Gyllis clutched the shift atop her breasts and hastened to cover her nether parts. "I had a wee fall. Leave me." She turned her face to hide from him. There was nowhere to run even if she could spring up. Dear Lord, why must she bear this humiliation in front of Sean?

Without moving, he gaped at her, his eyes huge. This wasn't like having a monk help her with necessities. Without a stitch of clothing aside from the garment in her arms, Sean could see every inch of her naked flesh. Yes, concern stretched the features of his face, but something deeper smoldered in his eyes.

Revulsion came to mind.

Gyllis wanted to curl into a ball and crawl under the bed. How utterly devastating to have Sean see her in a state of complete undress, totally helpless, sprawled on the floor. Her spine curled. "Please do not draw out my humiliation. As soon as I am covered you can return me to Ardchattan."

He stepped closer. "Why would I do that?"

"How can you possibly want to keep company with the likes of me?" She turned her face away. "I am a useless cripple."

"Nay." He kneeled beside her. Why he wouldn't flee the chamber and leave her in wretched peace, Gyllis couldn't fathom. "When I look at you I see an extraordinary woman who was stricken by infirmity. A beautiful lass who has the strength to fight, who will not remain abed and give up."

She grimaced, clutching the shift tighter to her body. "How can you stand the sight of me—an enfeebled, worthless lass? You are strong and full of life. You are brave."

"You think I'm brave? My courage is nothing compared to yours. Before me I see a woman who will not be cut down by a devastating illness, who will look it in the face, grasp it with both hands and fight. Not only today, but you continue to fight, to work through your pain and agony so one day this will be behind you."

A tear slipped from her eye and dribbled down her face until it dropped from her chin and splashed her chest. "You cannot possibly mean that. I'm hideous."

"Look at me," he whispered in her ear.

She shook her head. "I cannot." She was wretchedly naked for heaven's sake.

"Please." He placed his fingers on her far cheek and lightly kissed the other. "Look into my eyes, Gyllis."

Oh heavens how she wanted to, but if she gazed into his crystal blue eyes, he'd see the fear in her own.

Thunder clapped outside and the rain slapped against the stone outer walls.

Sean leaned forward until Gyllis could no longer hide her face. He smelled of wood smoke and fresh pine. Her lips trembled as she slowly raised her lids. Though her vision was distorted by tears, she'd never seen a more beautiful sight.

"Why do you think I've been to visit you so often?" he asked.

"I don't know…"

He arched a single brow. "I think you do."

Gyllis wouldn't succumb to his handsome face. She was wretched—helpless. "We were childhood friends. You feel sorry for me." That's what she'd told herself over and over.

He brushed a wisp of hair from her face. "I love you, Gyllis Marietta Campbell. I said it before and I meant it."

Oh God in heaven, she wanted to believe it. "How can you? I am despicable." Streams of tears dribbled down both cheeks. Yes, she wanted to believe him, but she couldn't. "I cannot even manage to pull a shift over my head." She again turned her face away. *By the stars, I love him more than life itself and want nothing more than to pledge my love, but not here. Not like this.*

"Allow me to assist you." His voice was softer than a kitten's purr.

Chapter Fifteen

Sean clasped his hand over Gyllis's fist. She had it clamped so tightly around the shift, he wondered if she'd ever be able to let go. Truth be told, he was damn cold himself, but Gyllis came first. In no way would he be the cause of a setback to her health. She'd come so far in the past month, he couldn't bear to think of a relapse or worse. "Let us pull the shift over your head. Once you are covered, I'll lift you back to the chair."

She pursed her pouty lips. "I can do it."

"Are you certain? I promise to uphold the laws of chivalry." Though it would most likely kill him to do so.

She smiled for the first time since he'd entered the chamber. "Avert your eyes please."

Heaven help him, she could melt a heart of stone with her dimples. But Sean obediently stood and faced the hearth. "I am your servant, m'lady."

A muffled giggle came from her direction. Sean heaved a sigh. Thank heavens she wasn't completely devastated that he'd barged into the chamber whilst she curled up naked on the floor. A fire flared in his groin. Once he'd realized she wasn't hurt, it was all he could do to keep from scooping her into his arms and carrying her to the bed. Blast his hot-blooded urges. Did she have no idea how alluring she was? He cared not about her illness. Gyllis's charm grew every time he laid eyes on her.

Sean's gaze darted toward a flicker. He forced himself to choke back his gasp. Her reflection in the mirror caught him completely unaware. The cloth rustled behind him, but across the room, he had a delectable view of creamy white skin. Her breasts were round and pert, tipped by buds of rose. He licked his lips and stretched his fingers. Desire shot through him so strongly, he swayed in place. *Damn it all, control yourself.* No matter how much he wanted to collect the lass in his arms and shower her with adoration, he must refrain. He was a knight, a man of honor. In no way could he show Gyllis disrespect. She was an angel from God, her body a temple.

The shift dropped over her head and concealed her breasts while she worked to push her arms through the sleeves. Before her head popped through the neckline, Sean averted his gaze from the mirror and rubbed his eyes. He shouldn't have allowed himself to look, but the lass was too beautiful for any mortal man to resist.

He shivered, suddenly remembering he, too, was soaked through. Stepping closer to the flame, he held out his hands and savored the warmth.

"If you'd be so kind as to help me up," she said in a voice smoother than honeyed mead.

Sean turned. Gyllis had not only pulled the shift on, she wore the kirtle atop, laced as if she were ready for Sunday mass. She glanced toward the stays on the table and bit her bottom lip. "I nearly have everything in order."

She needn't apologize. He remembered seeing her at Beltane. She'd been cosseted by one of those newfangled contraptions. He hadn't thought much of it at the time, but holy mother, why would she want to crush her breasts now? And why had Jinny sent the miserable garment up?

He couldn't help his lopsided grin. "I prefer you without the stays."

In the blink of an eye, her face turned scarlet. "'Tis said they keep a woman's bosoms from sagging."

He chuckled. "Oh do they now?" If only he could tell her how perfectly round her breasts were, but then she'd know he'd stolen a peek. Instead, he knelt. "Shall I lift you?"

Gyllis pinched the sleeve of his shirt and rubbed it between her fingers. "You're so wet, you might soak me through again. Are you not cold?"

An involuntary shiver shuddered across his chest. "I am a bit." He straightened, pulled off his shirt and cast it aside. "That's better."

Gyllis gulped, her eyes blinking. "I-I-I. Oh my goodness."

Afraid he had a leech attached to his belly, Sean glanced down but saw nothing but muscle. "Is something amiss?"

She clapped a hand to her chest. "Nay, but it has been a long time since I saw you sparring in the courtyard without your shirt."

He liked her reaction. It made him want to beat his chest and bellow. The look on her face was perfect. Rosy cheeks, red lips and green eyes as round as gold sovereigns, Sean could have scooped her into his arms and ravished her. Instead, he grinned dumbly. "Shall I lift you now?"

She smoothed her hands over her skirts and looked up with a coy grin. "Weren't we planning to picnic?"

He glanced at the basket on the bed. "Aye."

"Why not eat here in front of the hearth? Then your breeks can dry as well." She fanned her face as if she'd had an errant thought. Sean hoped she had—thoughts akin to his own.

"Wonderful idea." He jumped up and fetched the basket. "I've some wine to warm our insides."

She clasped her hands. "Splendid."

Sean moved to the sideboard and poured two goblets of wine from the ewer, thanking his stars the master brewer had brought him a new vintage only the day before. When he returned to the hearth, Gyllis lifted the cloth from the basket. "And what did Cook prepare for us?"

Sean set the goblets on the floor and sat on the plaid rug beside her. He peered inside the basket, not sure. "Looks like sliced mutton, bread and cheese."

She reached in and pulled out a sprig of red grapes, pulled one off and popped it in her mouth. Her eyes widened as she chewed. "Mm, a burst of tartness."

Sean glanced at the fruit in her hand. As if she read his thoughts, she plucked the plumpest grape and held it to his lips. "You must taste."

The fire in his groin inflamed while she placed it on his tongue. Then the vixen kept her finger on his lip as he closed his mouth. She giggled and ran her finger across his bottom lip. Christ almighty, did she know how seductive she looked?

Biting down, tart juice spurted throughout his mouth, tickling the underside of his jaw. "Delicious."

She leaned closer. "I want to taste it too."

Sean needed no more encouragement. He slid his hand behind her neck and cradled her head. She smelled sweeter than the grape he held in his mouth and the closer her lips neared, the hotter the flame beneath his breeks grew. He hardly noticed the damp wool—for all he could tell, it had already dried. God knew his flesh was hot enough to singe it.

When their lips met, Gyllis's gentle moan vibrated through his chest. Her cool fingers smoothed up his abdomen and around his back as she entwined her tongue with his.

The lass learns quickly. "Do you ken what that does to me?"

Her inhale stuttered. "Nay, but if it makes heat flare deep inside your body, I've some idea." Her voice grew breathless.

No stranger to the temptations of the bedchamber, Sean tightened every muscle in his body to bring his lustful urges under control. He would not take advantage of Gyllis, not ever. She was as fragile as a glass ornament, to be put on a pedestal and admired.

"You are the most beautiful man I've ever seen."

Holy Christ. He took a deep breath. *I must resist.* Then he looked into her eyes—moss encircled by dark blue. She smoothed her delicate fingers back and forth over his chest. With each feathery caress, his nipples grew harder, sending shocks of heat straight to his cock—now as rigid as an iron pole. In one motion, Sean pulled her onto his lap and covered her mouth with a smothering, claiming kiss. He wanted Gyllis like he wanted no other woman in the world and now her supple bottom cradled his ravenous cock.

She moved her hips, rubbing along his length. He hadn't been with a woman in so long, he'd lose control with one more shift of her hips. But he could not bring himself to stop kissing her. Gradually, he lowered her to the floor and lay her down. His hand slid from her waist and cupped her breast. In unison they moaned. Round and full, he kneaded her all the while joining with her mouth.

Trailing his fingers to her kirtle laces, he tugged the bow free and slipped his fingers beneath her neckline. Pushing it aside, he exposed her rounded flesh. With one more tug, the succulent nipple he'd seen in the mirror stood erect for him.

He barely noticed the rumbling thunder outside.

Gyllis gasped. "I cannot resist you."

"Why would you want to do that?" Sean flicked out his tongue and tasted the sweet rosebud standing proud before him. He took her fullness into his mouth and savored her taste. Heaven help him, his cock jutted against her hip, ready to burst with a single stroke.

Gyllis writhed beneath him, mewling like a virgin goddess. "This is the most diverting picnic I have ever attended."

Sean swirled his tongue around her blessed nipple. "I must agree with you there."

A rap came from the door. "M'laird?" It was Angus's voice.

"A moment." Sean helped Gyllis resituate her shift and kirtle then crossed the floor and opened the door.

Angus stood with Gyllis's crutches in hand, his expression grave. "The burn's flooded. Worse, the keep's surrounded by water. There's no way out."

"So quickly?"

"You've been up here for ages and all the while the rain's been coming down in sheets."

Sean glanced back at Gyllis.

"Is everything well?" she asked.

He told her about the rain. "'Tis looking as if you may need to stay at Dunollie."

She clapped a hand over her mouth and looked toward the window. "Oh heavens. John will be furious."

"He'd be a might angrier if we tried to cross a flooding river in a downpour."

Angus handed him the crutches. "The lassie's chamber is warm and ready." He glanced sidewise and leaned in. "It might be best for her reputation if you moved her straight away."

"Are the men talking? Already?"

"Cook's served the evening meal—aye, the rumblings started when you didn't come down, m'laird."

By the looming grey sky beyond the narrow window, Sean couldn't tell what time of day it was. "I'd best inspect the extent of the flooding."

"'Tis grave, m'laird. There'll be a number of crofters in need of help for certain."

Sean started to close the door. "I shall meet you in the great hall after I have Miss Gyllis settled in her chamber."

"I'll inform the guard."

"My thanks." Crutches in hand, Sean faced the lady. He hated to put an end to their picnic, but it was for the best. In no way could he sully her reputation. "We'd best see you to the guest chamber, or we'll nay avoid a scandal."

"Oh dear." She slipped her fingers to her well-kissed mouth. "I'm afraid I was so overcome, I considered not the consequences."

"I should have thought of it." He ambled toward her. "'Tis my responsibility. But fear not, I'll ensure no ill befalls you on account of my folly."

He knelt beside her and gestured to the crutches in his hand. "Would you prefer to use these, or should I carry you?"

"As much as I'd prefer to be in your arms, I fear someone may see us."

"Och, aye. That would help your reputation not at all." He winked. "But there's a secret door that adjoins the lady's chamber to mine."

"Truly? A secret passage akin to one in a storybook?"

Sean pointed. "'Tis behind the tapestry."

She stroked her chin. "Do the servants ken about it?"

"Not likely. I only discovered it when I moved into the chamber after Da passed."

"How scandalous." She giggled. "Do you think your parents used it?"

"Perhaps." He'd never really considered it, and as an only son, he now wondered if his parents had a happy marriage. His mother was an Irish lass, married to Sean's da by an arrangement, as marriages often are. Presently there was no time to ponder it. He stooped to help her up. "Though I doubt we'll see a soul in the passageway, let us make a show of walking to the outer door."

She held on to his arm with one hand and reached for a crutch. "Very well, but I shall miss you."

"I'm afraid there won't be much to entertain you whilst I'm making the rounds."

"Have you anything to read?"

He looked at the leather-bound Bible on the sideboard and pointed. "Only scripture."

She smiled. "'Tis better than doing nothing."

Once he retrieved the book, they proceeded to the lady's chamber. Sean hated to leave her alone, but he had a clan to look after. He opened the door. "I'll have Cook bring you a tray."

She'd become quite adept with her crutches and easily moved inside. "Thank you." Gyllis regarded him over her shoulder, her tongue sneaking to the corner of her mouth. "Will you check on me when you return?"

"Not sure. I'm afraid it will be too late." Besides, if he came to her later, he might not be able to control himself. Indeed, Lusty Laddie could rear his lovesick head and Duncan would be fully within his rights to chop it off. Sean fingered a lock of her chestnut hair. "I wish I could stay, but my clan must come first."

"I ken." She nimbly turned and stepped up to him, her face a hand's breadth away. "I like kissing you, Sir Sean."

She placed a palm on his cheek and turned up her mouth. Thank God they'd seen no one else in the passageway because there was no way in heaven Sean would be able to resist those succulent lips. He paused and drew in a ragged breath. Then he slowly lowered his lips until they met hers. Sliding his fingers around her waist, he didn't want to hurry. With languid licks of his tongue, he savored her, enjoying the lingering tartness from the grapes. She melted into him, her pliable breasts caressing his chest, bringing on another torturous erection. If only he could take her inside and explore every inch of her silken flesh with his tongue.

He forced his hand to stray to the latch. "I shall see you on the morrow."

Chapter Sixteen

Gyllis smoothed her fingers over the page. Randomly she'd opened the Bible to II Samuel and read about how King David watched Bathsheba bathe. Doubtless, she couldn't have opened it to the Book of Job. Sean had held her in his clutches and she'd needed no constricting stays to swoon in his arms. Who knows what would have happened had Angus not come to the door when he did. As it was, she'd allowed Sean to bare her breasts and fondle them. Her nipples still tingled at his heavenly touch.

As sure as she'd opened the Holy Book to King David's sin, God would punish her severely for enjoying Sean's touch so much. And now she craved it. Worse, reading about King David's lust served to further ignite the flames smoldering at such depths of her body, she'd never imagined so powerful an emotion.

She set the Bible beside her on the bed and reclined against the lush pillows. Appointed with a large four-poster bed, the lady's chamber was twice the size of her rooms at Kilchurn. Across the floor, a fire crackled in the hearth. They had even drawn the furs across the window to keep out the chill.

Gyllis let out a long sigh and trailed her fingers over her breast. It still tingled as if Sean's lips continued to suckle her. How on earth would she ever forget this day? That she didn't want to forget was a certainty—nor had she wanted it to end. *I am a wanton woman. God will strike me down for this.*

She rolled onto her side and covered her face with her hands. *Why does sin feel so good if it is a terrible thing? A person should feel awful if they sin—like I do when I tell a fib or something akin to that.*

Watching the crackling fire, she was well aware the hour had grown late. Ages ago, a serving boy had brought up a tray of food. But sleep eluded her like a rainbow's end. *How can I sleep when so many thoughts fill my head? Heaven help me, my entire body is tingling with happiness for the first time in ever so long.*

A door slammed. She sat upright. The candle beside her bed had nearly burned to a nub. Footsteps came from behind her headboard. *Sean's chamber.* Gyllis held very still and listened. Something clattered to the floor that made her jolt. She held her breath. Rustling, perhaps cloth, followed by footsteps.

She couldn't mistake the sound of the bed creaking. Gyllis swallowed and clutched the bedclothes to her chin. The image of Sean in his bed did unholy things to her mind. *Does he wear a nightshirt? Does he keep his dirk under his pillow? What does his face look like when he's sleeping? Is it as beautiful as when he's alert? Does he sleep on his back or otherwise?*

The bed creaked—louder this time. Still clutching the bedclothes, Gyllis scooted to the edge of her bed. Heavy footsteps clapped the floorboards followed by a hiss. She inclined her ear toward the wall. *Is he dancing?* The floor groaned as if he were moving in a rhythmic pattern. *I do not recall a rocking chair in his chamber.*

Gyllis reached for her crutches. As quietly as she could, she slid behind the tapestry and felt for the latch. When it clicked, she gasped and froze in place. Something hissed through the air, followed by more footsteps. But the sound wasn't up close. It came from across the chamber, near the hearth. After opening the door far enough to slip inside, she maneuvered the crutches out from behind Sean's tapestry and popped her head out from beneath it.

In the blink of an eye, she couldn't breathe, and the thrumming of her heart consumed her entire body. Now she knew exactly how King David felt when he gazed down upon Bathsheba. The great Chieftain of Dunollie wore not a thread of clothing.

Sean swung his sword in an arc over his head, lunging into a crouch where he stopped, the sword and his arm forming perfectly parallel lines.

Lit by a candelabra and the fire from the hearth, the room glowed amber and smelled of beeswax and wood smoke. The flickering light cast a dreamy shroud over the chamber and filled it with dark shadows, but nothing appeared more surreal than Sean's naked body flexing with his every move.

Gyllis's hands trembled as she stared at Sean's chiseled back. He mustn't have heard her, because he held the crouched position like a statue. His dark, wavy locks brushed broad shoulders, rounded by thick muscle. He straightened slowly, the undulating muscles in his back contracting until he stood straight. His waist narrowed, supported by hips that appeared chiseled from pure marble. His rounded buttocks dimpled at the sides and curved down to long, slender thighs, peppered with dark hair.

He lunged to the right, the big sword hissing through the air. But this time he thrust his weapon as if defending himself from attack. On and on he fought the demons, slashing, thrusting and spinning with his blade. When he next straightened, he faced her holding the sword high above his head.

Gyllis had seen his chest only that evening, but the muscles rippling over his abdomen appeared even more defined in the glowing light. A line of black hair trailed from his navel, pulling her eyes lower. That a man had a splay of curls over his sex as she did surprised her, as did the alabaster length of this manhood at his apex. Aye, she'd seen animals mate, and was aware men were different, but never guessed they were so amazingly so. She had never gazed upon pure beauty before this moment.

Clapping a hand over her mouth, Gyllis tried to muffle her gasp.

Sean's gaze snapped to her face. Before she could blink, he bellowed an inhuman roar and barreled toward her. In one motion, he spun her around. The crutches clattered to the floor as he leveled the sword against her neck. "I'll not tolerate a spy."

"I-I heard…I-I did not—"

"Gyllis?" Immediately he dropped the sword with a resounding racket and released his hold. "I'm sor—"

She tried to pull away but crumpled to the floor. "Forgive me." Tears welled in her eyes as she shook with mortification. "I did not mean to intrude. I was awake and heard…"

"Nay, nay, nay." Sean dropped to his knee beside her. Gyllis tried to avert her gaze, but he was so amazingly naked. He lifted her into his arms as if she weighed nothing and ran kisses along her cheek and neck. "I am the one who must ask for forgiveness. I've no idea what I was thinking. I saw movement and assumed someone had spirited inside."

Gyllis looked into his eyes and began to tremble. It was as if he hadn't recognized her, as if he were in some sort of trance. "You were like a madman for a moment."

"Apologies. I was concentrating—not thinking straight. No one has ever entered my chamber when I've been—ah—sparring with the devil." He nuzzled into her tresses. "You ken I would never do anything to hurt you." Still cradling her to his bare chest, he stood and walked to the bed. Gently he set her on the mattress then kneeled before her, holding her hands between his palms.

Filled with concern, his eyes flickered gold, reflecting the fire from the hearth. Her overwhelming curiosity had led her straight into the fabled lion's den. And now the gentle beast had lured her under his spell of beauty. *My stars, he even smells as wild as a pine forest.* Gyllis stared for a long while, then moistened her lips and nodded once, never breaking their gaze. That he was naked before her seemed as natural as breathing, except for the tight yearning that ached so badly, she had to steal at least one more kiss. Even her breasts were afire. He'd kissed them earlier and it had been sinfully delectable.

Will God forgive me as he had his servant King David?

Continuing to hold his gaze, she slipped her hands from his and untied her shift's bow—just as he'd done earlier. She took in a staccato breath, aware of what she was doing, but not fearing the consequences. Sean watched motionless as she slipped the linen from one shoulder and then the other. Then he reached up and tugged the cloth down to her waist, fully exposing her breasts.

A feral growl rumbled from his throat. "God help me, you are the most beautiful woman on earth."

His features were shrouded by the dim light, but the darkness made the world seem like a dream. With a low moan, Sean cupped her breast and joined his mouth with hers. Gyllis kissed him back with all the passion she could muster, allowing him to guide her. She grew bolder and lightly suckled his tongue while he swirled it deeper in her mouth.

As he eased the kiss, Sean trailed his lips down her neck. Gyllis sank her fingers into the thick bands of flesh on his shoulder while he continued lower. Met with jagged flesh, the wound he'd sustained when attacked in Fearnoch Forest was no scratch. Rather than spoil the moment with a gasp, Gyllis inclined her head and ran kisses along his puckered flesh. "I shall ease your pain."

"I feel no pain when I am with you."

She gasped when his tongue circled the tip of her breast. So sensitive, a flame burst inside as if it were fanned by a blacksmith's bellows. Gyllis threw back her head and moaned as he kneaded her breasts and plied them with his tongue. "Your wiles seduce me to the point of madness," she managed a breathless whisper.

"'Tis only a sampling of what is to come."

Gyllis ran her fingers through Sean's hair, wanting more of something she knew nothing about. When she could take no more she pulled his face to hers and kissed him. Showed him how the passionate urges churned within her. And now she'd seen him bare, she wanted to know what it was like to be taken by not just a man, but by Sean MacDougall, the man she'd adored all her life. "I want to lie with you, Sean."

"Sweeter words I have never before heard." Again his lips trailed down the length of her neck, but this time he didn't stop at her breasts. No, Sean's feather-light kisses continued down her flesh. Gooseflesh rose across her skin when he swirled his tongue in her navel. Then he grinned and glanced up at her, his white teeth glowing through the dim light.

With a devilish chuckle, he pulled the pillows behind her. "Ease back and I will take you to heaven."

"What…"

"Wheesht." He placed his palm on her shoulder and encouraged her to lie against the pillows. "Are you comfortable?"

"Aye." Though her breasts were exposed, her flesh tingled everywhere.

Sean tugged up her shift.

"No." Gyllis shoved her hands down. "Sean."

He eased her fingers away. "I cannot take you to heaven without kissing the treasure between your legs."

Gyllis sat up. "You're planning to do what?" She squeezed her knees together. "Is that done?"

"Not often." He grinned again, looking like a temptation on a silver platter. "But I guarantee you will be begging me for more." He kissed her mouth and eased her back into the cushions. The length of his naked body pressed against her. His warm chest molded into her breasts, but that was nowhere near as shocking as the length of his manhood filling the crux of her body. Moaning, she rocked her hips, seeking more friction. Agony that good absolutely had to be sinful.

But Sean didn't remain atop her for long. Again, he slid down to his knees and tugged up her shift. This time Gyllis didn't fight him. Cool air caressed her womanhood. Sean's deep, rumbling sigh made dampness pool between her legs. "Your scent is so bonny, it will bring me undone." He placed a palm on her abdomen and spread her legs wider with his shoulders.

Gyllis had never felt so wicked. She grasped the bedclothes on either side. When his tongue stroked her, a shrill gasp erupted from her throat. Holy Mother Mary, she'd never experienced anything so erotic in her life.

Again he licked her. Gyllis bucked. *Yes, more. Please, more.* Sean complied with swirls of his tongue.

He slid his finger down and circled it below—yet another action that sent her mind into a maelstrom of hot, driving need. His finger slid in and out while his tongue performed pure magic. Gyllis could no sooner pull away than she could run a mile. With uncontrollable shuddering, her voice made high-pitched noises while she succumbed to his touch. Suddenly her entire body went taught. A cry caught in the back of her throat. Sean rumbled a groan that spread tremors through her body. With a shocking gasp, the entire world shattered into pulsing bursts of euphoria.

By the time Gyllis recovered her senses, Sean had pulled her shift down over her knees. He stood and grinned. "Was it good for you lass?"

"Good?" she asked. "There are no words…"

"I ken." He grinned—the devilish one that made her heart leap.

When Gyllis's gaze slid down to his erection, Sean almost lost his seed. Her face was so seductive, yet innocent. Her wide-eyes made him want to roar like a lion, climb between her legs and make his conquest. But Gyllis was no alehouse tart who could warm his bed at night and be forgotten by morning.

Though it did unholy things to him to have her watch him, he would be no kind of knight if he took advantage.

Her lips parted almost as if she were planning to place her mouth on him. Sean's knees buckled.

"But you are not satisfied?" she asked, her voice filled with wonder.

He cleared his throat so as not to expose his lust. "I cannot take your innocence, lass."

"I do not understand." She crossed her arms over her breasts, shielding them from him. "I give you my maidenhead. There is no other man on earth I wish to possess it."

'Twas a bold statement, even coming from Gyllis. "'Tis a gift I cannot take lightly."

"I do not give it lightly."

His mouth dried as if he'd been a week without water. "Do you ken what you're saying?"

"Aye." Her gaze drifted to his manhood again, then she did something completely unexpected. Without his bidding, she wrapped her lithe fingers around his shaft. "Show me."

God save him, no mortal man could resist the tug of her hand. He threw back his head and leaned his hips into her. "You will drive me to the brink of madness."

She had the gall to chuckle. "Like you did me?" She smoothed her fingers down and then back up. Where on earth did she learn to do that? "Come, I'm not completely unwise. I've seen a guard hidden in the shadows with a serving maid. Please, Sean. Show me."

He couldn't think with her hand milking his cock. With a feral growl, he nudged her deeper onto the bed and climbed between her legs.

She cupped his face in her hands. "Who were you sparring with?"

"My inner demons."

"I've never seen a more beautiful sight."

Sean chuckled. "You are the beautiful one, lass, and I'll nay let you forget it." He slid his member up the crux of her legs, allowing her moisture to spread over him. She shuddered. He lowered his head and kissed her. "Can you taste yourself on my lips? 'Tis the scent that attracts me every time I'm within arm's reach of you."

"You are a lusty laddie, are you not?" She rocked her hips beneath him, mewling softly. "Show me how lusty you are."

Her hips arched up and caught the tip of his cock. Sean held his breath. Hot moisture brimmed around him. God, he could come right now, but he wanted to make this good for her. Show her exactly what she'd been missing all these years. "I'll try to be gentle."

She nodded, her hips continuing their seductive rhythm. Christ, he was supposed to be the one seducing Gyllis, but without a lick of schooling she'd proven an expert. Slowly, he pushed inside. She sucked in a shocked gasp.

Sean froze. "Am I hurting you?" He started to pull away. "If you want to stop…"

Her fingers clamped into his buttocks. "No." With a firm tug, she urged him deeper. God, he loved this woman. Gradually he slid the length of her, and when he reached a wall he gazed into her sultry eyes. Even in the dim light he could see the moss encircled by dark blue. "Are you all right?"

She wriggled beneath him. "Heavenly."

"Once I start, I'll not be able to stop myself."

"There's more?"

"Aye lass."

Her fingers again dug into his buttocks. "I want to experience it all."

Sean tried to be gentle at first, but with Gyllis's hands kneading his backside, he soon lost all sense. Her breathing sped. Her scent ensnared him. Stars flashed across his vision and his ballocks packed so taut, he thought he'd go mad before he released his seed.

Faster and faster he thrust. Gyllis cried out, holding on to him for dear life. And now that she'd reached her peak, he was free to drive hard and fast. His breathing sped, his heart hammered, and all at once the peak of ecstasy flooded through his blood. A heartbeat before his seed released, he pulled out and spilled into the bedclothes.

He hated the unsatisfactory finish to his release, but he would not sire a bastard, even though he fully intended to make Gyllis his wife. He had not yet proposed—something he'd need to do soon.

He held himself over her with his elbow, careful not to crush her. God, she defined beauty, her intoxicating green eyes staring up at him as if they were the only two people in Scotland. He trailed kisses down her neck. "Was it good for you, lass?"

A wee giggle tickled his ear. "Aye. I cannot believe how good."

"You are the world to me." Breathing deeply to catch his breath, he rolled to his back and pulled Gyllis atop him. "You ken I love you, always will."

She rested her head on his chest. "I love you, too. 'Tis as if God intended for our souls to be joined."

He ran his fingers through her hair and cherished the silkiness of it. The woman in his arms filled his nostrils with fragrance from heaven. Even a bed of rose petals would not smell as sweet. He could lay there all night with Gyllis entwined in his embrace. And he fully intended to lose himself in her wiles until the sun rose on the morrow.

Chapter Seventeen

A ray of light streamed in from the window. The rain had stopped. Sean blinked several times in succession and rubbed his eyes. Gyllis slept cradled in the crook of his arm, her long tresses spread across his bare chest. Her breathing rhythmic, she was as radiant as an angel. Dipping his chin, he nuzzled into her hair and inhaled. *Mm.* As sweet as a meadow of wildflowers, he could breathe her in for an eternity.

Last night she'd taken him soaring to the moon. He almost regretted the sun had decided to make an appearance this day. He wasn't one to laze about, but spending an entire day making love to Gyllis tempted him.

The crutches sprawled on the floor caught his eye and his stomach twisted. She was yet to complete her treatment at the priory. He closed his eyes tightly. *Dear God in heaven, please do not let me be the cause of any setback.*

She moaned and moved in his arms. A more beautiful creature could not exist. In slumber she embodied the meadow nymph dreaming in the morning's sun. Mahogany tresses tangled around them both, her dark lashes shuttering those eyes he adored. Her lips slightly parted and she sighed. If only he could be there with her in such a soothing dream.

Sean hadn't intended to take advantage of her. It had happened. She'd been right when she said their souls were meant to be together. He knew that now, but he couldn't stand in the way of the progress she was making toward recovery. And then he had his uncle's wedding hanging over his head. Though Lorn had the king's approval, the neighboring clans would not be happy, especially the Campbells of Argyll. Gyllis's sect, the Campbells of Glenorchy paid fealty to Argyll. Relations could become strained, even between Sean and Duncan. He hated feuds.

He'd need to wait until news of the wedding had passed, especially since he would be the one providing protection for the Lord of Lorn.

Gyllis cleared her throat and stirred.

Sean grinned. "Good morrow, my love."

She rose up on her elbow and covered her mouth with a dainty hand. "Blessed be the stars. Last eve was real?"

He brushed away a lock of hair covering her eye. "Aye." Kissing her forehead, he inhaled. In an instant he was hard again. "Every passionate moment was real, *mo leannan*."

Snuggling into him, she slid her hand across his chest. He moaned with the tingling her deft fingers brought. "I wish we could remain in this bed forever. I cannot remember ever being so happy."

"Aye, but time will nay stand still. I promised your brother I'd return you to Ardchattan before compline last eve."

"Surely he will understand," she said with a wee yawn. "No one could have traveled in that torrential rain."

Sean twirled strands of her hair around his finger. No matter how much he wanted to lie abed with Gyllis in his arms, he needed to return her to the priory quickly. The weather had been a good excuse to have her spend the night at Dunollie, but to keep her after the weather cleared would be unacceptable. It could lead to the lass's ruination. As it was, if word of their indiscretion were to become known, Duncan Campbell would be after Sean's head. "We must make haste to return else there could be a scandal—even if everyone believes you slept in the lady's chamber. One night due to the weather might be permissible, but if we delay, a scandal will erupt for certain."

She flopped onto her back. "Ugh. I've been imprisoned in that tiny cell for so long, I'd forgotten how wonderful things could be outside."

"Aye, though you have come so far, you must continue your treatment. Why, you're so strong, I wouldn't be surprised to see you make a full recovery."

She clapped her hands over her face. "I'd be too embarrassed to have anyone other than you see me."

"Why? You are beautiful."

"I am a cripple. For some reason, you have chosen to see beyond that, but in society I will be seen as a monster."

"I don't think anyone could believe that."

She chuckled. "Sometimes I wonder if you are not blind. You've been to the fetes, people treat cripples like lepers."

Sean clenched his jaw. "If anyone dare taunt you, they'd have to answer to me."

She rolled to her side and again draped her arm across his chest. "If only I could stay in this bed forever. Then every night you would return, and one day the witch who cursed me with this illness would be satisfied with my unbounded dedication to you and cure me."

"You read too many fantastical tales." He lifted her chin and kissed her lips. "I shall take you back to Ardchattan. I have a duty to perform for my uncle. After things have settled, I will gain an audience with your brother and ask for your hand."

Gyllis didn't seem to pay attention to the duty part, for her face beamed. "Do you mean that, Sean? I will become the lady of your keep?"

"I can think of no other woman more perfect for the role."

The passion in her kiss nearly kept them abed for another hour.

***

Sean helped Gyllis dismount. She loved how easily he could lift her. He showed no strain in his face and only set her down when Angus came up with the crutches. He rapped the big knocker on the priory door.

The knocker was so loud up close, Gyllis touched a hand to her ear. "I hope John isn't angry."

"I cannot see how he could be. Now, if we'd had Noah's ark last eve, we might have made it back.

She inclined her lips toward his ear and whispered. "I'm glad we didn't."

He winked. "Me as well."

A monk slid aside the viewing panel. "Miss Gyllis? We were about to send a search party."

"The burn flooded. There was no way to ferry her back safely," Sean said.

The monk frowned and ushered Gyllis behind him. "We will see to her safety from here." Before Sean could say a word, the monk closed the door.

"Pardon me, but that was rather abrupt." Sean's voice resounded through the door. "I haven't even said goodbye."

The monk slid the panel open. "She bids you good day."

"I shall see you again soon, Miss Gyllis," Sean called past the pushy old monk.

"Thank you for your kindness, Sir Sean."

Gyllis gave the monk a heated look, just to let him know she didn't appreciate his impertinence. Yes, she had been away longer than Sean had promised, but for good reason. She turned and proceeded through the cloisters. She wouldn't allow the monk's sourpuss attitude to diminish her good spirits. She had a semblance of a spring in her step—at least as much as the crutches would allow. Strength radiated through her limbs and she nearly cast the supports aside. Her breast filled with joy, she could not believe her fortune. Last May, she'd gone to the fete seeking to impress Sean MacDougall and had returned home dejected, downtrodden and ill. Only after she'd suffered through the worst of paralysis, had he come to her like a gallant knight and wooed her. Ravished her. And she'd savored every moment in his arms.

Nothing could make Gyllis give up now. She would focus on her treatments more diligently than ever before. Soon she would be walking without assistance. The next time Sean visited Ardchattan, she would be stronger. Every time he would come, she would surprise him with her improvement.

Gyllis leaned on her crutches and opened the door to her cell.

Her smile instantly dropped.

Dressed in black priest's robes as customary, John faced her, crossed his arms and frowned. It wasn't his usual frown. His eyes grew dark—almost hateful. "Where the devil have you been for the past day?"

Gyllis's first thought was to cower—beg for forgiveness. Her face burned, but she straightened, refusing to allow her brother to intimidate her. "The burn flooded. It was impossible to return."

He stepped closer. "Where did you stay the night?"

"Sir Sean graciously provided me with a chamber at Dunollie."

"Gracious?" John spread his palms to his sides. "You forget I am quite familiar with Sean MacDougall and his gallant womanizing."

A lump the size of her fist blocked Gyllis's throat. Heat prickled her skin. Did John speak true? Were Sean's actions a ruse to take advantage of a cripple?

No. I will not believe it.

"If he laid a hand on you, the Campbells will not rest until he is brought to justice."

"Nay." She clapped a hand to her chest, trying not to heave. In no way could she be the cause of a clan feud. "You are stretching the truth."

"Me? Lie?" John threw up his hands and paced in a circle. "He has compromised you, has he not?"

Trembling, Gyllis clamped her lips and refused to answer. Sean would ask Duncan for her hand. It had been she who had gone to *his* chamber, not the other way around. If she hadn't heard him practicing and grown curious, her virtue would still be intact. She glared at her brother as hotly as he glared at her.

John grasped her shoulders and shook, his eyes bulging. "I can tell by your reluctance to speak."

"Please, John. Stop." She stamped her foot. "We are to be married."

"MacDougall?" he yelled. "The man's a superb tracker, but he's aligned with the Stewarts. You cannot be serious."

She tightened her grip on her crutches. "I love him."

"You stupid lass." He shoved his hand over the shaven part of his head. "You will spend the rest of this day repenting in your cell. At first light on the morrow, the monks will take you back to Kilchurn."

"No, please." The crutches tapped the floor as she pattered toward him. "I have only started to respond to Brother Wesley's treatment."

He glared with a disdainful scowl. "Your treatment has ended. 'Tis time you return home."

"Will you...?" She couldn't say it, but she knew full well John had the power to ruin her.

He stopped pacing. "I shall pen a missive to Duncan and you'd best pray my ire cools before I touch my quill." He stormed past her and slammed the door.

As her crutches dropped, Gyllis staggered to the bed and dropped face down. Just when she thought her luck had changed, everything came crashing down and crumbled at her feet.

***

Silently, Gyllis rode with an escort of guards and monks. John hadn't joined them, nor had he seen her off. Brother Wesley hadn't come to say goodbye either. She felt filthy like a fallen woman—a leper who was too diseased even to be tended by the faithful.

Her own brother had cast her from his priory. What treatment could she expect from her family? *Will they lock me in my chamber? Will they fear me? And what rueful words did John impart in his missive to Duncan?*

When the grey stone curtain walls of Kilchurn Castle loomed ahead, Gyllis's stomach clenched into a tight ball. Upon the battlements, the ram's horn sounded, indicating the Campbell guard had seen them. Mother, Duncan— everyone would now know they were approaching. *Dear Lord, please make everything all right.*

The gate was open and the retinue rode straight through the barbican and into the courtyard. The reins slid in Gyllis's sweaty fingers. From the keep's great doorway, Duncan, Lady Meg, Mother and her sisters all stared at her. Was that fear Gyllis read on their wide-eyed visages?

The lead guard dismounted, drew a missive from his doublet and handed it to Duncan. "This is for you from the prior, m'lord."

Gyllis nearly fell off her horse. If only she could have read its contents first, she'd at least know what to expect. Would Duncan take the strap to her? He was fully within his rights if he chose to do so.

When Duncan slipped the missive into his doublet, she breathed a sigh of relief. She would have died if he'd stood in the courtyard and read it aloud as if it were a proclamation.

Mother pushed past him, followed by the lassies. "Praise the good Lord, Gyllis has returned to us."

Mevan, Mother's most trusted man-at-arms stepped beside her mount and reached up. "Welcome home, Miss Gyllis. Can I assist you?"

"My thanks." She hesitated and searched for the monk bearing her crutches. When she saw he'd already dismounted, she braced her hands on Mevan's shoulders and let the old guard help her down. "How is your wife?" she tried to make conversation as if her world weren't falling apart.

"She is well, thank you."

Gyllis took the crutches from the monk and faced her family. Mother's eyes were red and welled with tears. "At last you have come home." She pulled her into an embrace.

Mother always smelled of sweet lavender. And her hug was soft and warm and welcoming. Gyllis closed her eyes while her own tears welled.

Perhaps the family would not fear her.

Before she knew it, she was surrounded by her sisters, all chatting and hugging, laughing and crying. Gyllis looked to Meg with Elizabeth in her arms. "You've returned from court?" She grinned at the babe. "My, the bairn has grown so much. I cannot believe it."

Meg beamed, her blue eyes twinkling with the sunlight. "Aye, she's a healthy lass." She inclined her head to the nursemaid behind holding the other redheaded twin. "Colin as well."

"A moment," Duncan boomed.

Gyllis could have fainted. *Has he read John's missive already?*

Mother stood aside. Duncan grasped Gyllis's shoulders and hugged her. "Welcome home, sister."

Her resultant sigh of relief nearly made her swoon. "'Tis good to be amongst you once again. Though the monks did so very much to help me, not a day passed where I didn't miss you."

Mother straightened Gyllis's veil. "I am surprised John sent you back so soon. From his last missive, I assumed you'd remain in his care through autumn."

Gyllis tried not to cringe, though her cheeks burned. "We agreed I could complete the remainder of my training at home," she hedged and looked toward Helen and Meg. "After all, I have three sisters and a sister-in-law who can help." If only she could have read what John had scribed in that missive before she opened her mouth.

Meg grinned. "I think we might try a new treatment when you're ready."

"I for one am happy you're here." Helen placed her hand on Gyllis's shoulder. "I've much to tell you." Helen's expression appeared strained.

Unusual. Something is wrong.

Gyllis arched her brow. "I cannot wait." She moved toward the keep, painfully aware that everyone watched how she managed with her crutches, praying that no one asked how she acquired them.

"Can you climb stairs with those?" Mother asked.

"Aye. I can do almost everything." Gyllis winked at Helen. She seemed to need a lift of spirits. "And I intend to be walking without them soon."

"You mustn't push yourself, dear," Mother said.

Gyllis looked to the sky. If Ma wasn't telling someone what to do, she wouldn't be happy. "It has been a long ride. I'd like to retire to my chamber until the evening meal."

Helen walked beside her. "I'll escort you." Her tone was too chipper. Something was afoot for certain.

Together they left the others staring after them.

Gyllis had surmounted the first hurdle. She had no doubt she'd face Duncan later, but for now she and Helen would have an afternoon to themselves. And it seemed they both needed to talk. If there was one person on earth Gyllis could confide in it was she. When they were but young lasses they had made a pact that anything spoken in confidence could never be repeated.

"You move along very well with those," Helen said as she led Gyllis up the stairwell.

"Sir Sean made them for me," she whispered.

Helen stopped. "Are you jesting?"

Gyllis inclined her head toward the landing. "I'll not utter another word until we are behind closed doors."

"At least you've had some fun?" she asked, waggling her brows.

"That's the first time I've ever heard anyone call paralysis fun."

Helen opened the door. "You ken what I mean."

Gyllis hobbled into her chamber and sighed. She'd never really appreciated the grandeur of her rooms. Her four-poster bed had yellow drapes embroidered with wildflowers. She'd forgotten how pretty they looked. Heading toward the overstuffed couch in front of the hearth, she inhaled. The chamber smelled of rose oil. A ray of sunlight shone in through the narrow window with a breeze fluttering the yellow canopy above her bed.

She plopped onto the couch and rested her crutches on the floor. "Come. Tell me what is afoot."

Helen plodded across the floor and sat with a huff. "'Tis not fair."

"What?"

"Remember when I told you Duncan and Meg went to court whilst you were away?"

"Aye, I was surprised to see them in the courtyard." Gyllis reclined against the padded backrest, wishing Duncan and Meg were still at court, and would remain there for the next fifty years.

Helen heaved an enormous sigh. "It appears Lady Meg decided it was up to her to play matchmaker."

Gyllis leaned forward, eyebrows drawn together. "Have you ever mentioned to her your affinity for Eoin MacGregor?"

"Wheesht." Helen glanced over her shoulder as if someone would burst into the chamber. "Of course not."

Gyllis cringed. "Oh, dear."

Helen grasped Gyllis's hand and squeezed. "Duncan would never allow a MacGregor to marry one of us. He believes them beneath the Campbells."

"They pay fealty to our clan. That makes them no better or worse."

"Aye." Helen again glanced around as if she expected spies in every corner. "Well 'tis too late for any of that now. If you had arrived a sennight hence, you would have missed me altogether."

"Pardon?"

"In two days Mother will be escorting me to Ardnamurchan where I will marry Sir Aleck MacIain, Seventh Chieftain of Ardnamurchan."

Gyllis could scarcely swallow. She'd only arrived home and now her dearest, most beloved sister was leaving—not only leaving, but wedding someone Gyllis knew nothing about. "You are to be married?"

"Two days hence."

"Oh my heavens." Gyllis couldn't believe it. Helen could not possibly leave now. Not when she—they both—needed an ally. "H-have you met Sir Aleck?"

"I've never seen him. Meg tells me he's agreeable and Duncan says our marriage will make a necessary alliance with the MacIain Clan."

"He's chosen your husband to make an alliance? I ken that's the way of things but, Helen, ages ago we agreed we'd never settle for an arranged marriage—we shall marry for love."

Helen coughed out a rueful laugh. "'Tis easy for you to say. If you hadn't come down with paralysis, it would be *you* heading to Ardnamurchan."

Gyllis clapped a hand over her mouth. Helen was right, she *would* have been the one to suffer marriage to a complete stranger had she not been away ill. "This cannot be so."

"Would I jest about something so grave?"

"My God." Gyllis cringed at her blasphemy and moreover, her failure to be there in support of her sister. "I feel responsible."

Helen spread her palms and shook her head. "At first I blamed you…but then when I thought about it, I realized I'd rather marry a chieftain, and help the family strengthen relations with the northern clans than be in your predicament. Oh Gyllis, is it so wrong of me to think that way?"

"Of course not." Her stomach twisted in knots. If only she'd come home sooner. Poor Helen would never have been able to stand up to Duncan with Gyllis away.

Gyllis had always been the stalwart spokesperson between them. "Why did you not refuse?"

Wringing her hands, Helen hunched forward. "What should I have done? I am soon to be twenty with no other offers, no other prospects."

"What of Eoin?"

Helen smirked. "I've admired him from the battlements, but now he's off patrolling the borders or carrying out some other inordinately important task for Duncan and the king. I'll most likely never see him again."

"I cannot believe this." Gyllis pounded her fist on the couch. "Why are you not fighting?"

"And go against Duncan, Mother, and what is best for the clan?" She clapped her palms to her cheeks. "It is my duty."

The guilt encircling Gyllis's neck couldn't have closed her throat any tighter. She scooted closer and placed her arm around Helen's shoulders. "You are right. It should have been me making this sacrifice."

"Aye." Helen threw up her hands. "And you had to go contract paralysis."

Gyllis bit her bottom lip. Never in her life did she think she'd feel guilty for her ailment. Already twisted inside for her indiscretions with Sir Sean, the wretched lump in her throat returned. "I suppose I did."

"If 'tis Sean MacDougall you want, he'd best propose soon, else you'll be wed to some old chieftain aiming to make a Campbell alliance."

Gyllis slid her arm from Helen's shoulder. Given her sister's sacrifice, she couldn't allow her happiness to bubble over.

She must have looked shamefaced because Helen knit her brows. "I thought you'd sworn off Sir Sean after his deplorable actions at Beltane."

Gyllis couldn't meet her sister's gaze. She stared at her hands. "I did, until I learned the reason for his disappearance. His father died that day. 'Twas the healer who embraced him after she and her husband told Sir Sean the news."

"How awful." Helen leaned closer. "And then he visited you at the priory?"

"Aye." Gyllis would not admit to anything else.

"Oh no, you're not pursing your lips. Sir Sean gave you the crutches? How often did he visit you?"

Gyllis clapped her hand over her mouth to hide her grin, but Helen pulled it away. "Very well..." She divulged all except the night she'd spent at Dunollie. She'd speak of that to no one.

Helen pressed her fingers to her lips and smiled. "If anyone deserves to be happy after all you've endured, 'tis you." She held up a finger. "However, I meant what I said. Sean had best have a serious conversation with Duncan, and soon."

Gyllis wouldn't let on how much the butterflies flitted around her stomach. Two things worried her...How long would it be before Sean discovered she'd returned home? And what was written in that meddlesome missive from John?

Chapter Eighteen

Alan MacCoul lunged, thrusting his sword. Missing his mark, he threw his head back and cackled. If his sparring partner hadn't been fast, he'd be dead. Though Alan needed well-trained men, poor fighters would be culled. He advanced on the sentry, hacking his two-handed blade left and right, giving no quarter. Wearing his partner down renewed his strength. Lust for blood pulsed through his veins, the stench of fear bled through his sparring partner's pores.

"M'lord." The booming voice behind him registered, but Alan didn't stop.

His opponent tripped and fell on his backside. Alan pounced, pointing his blade against the coward's neck.

The man held up his hands then pointed. "Y-you'd best turn around m'lord."

If this was a trick to draw attention away, he'd skewer the miserable sop.

"M'lord," the gravelly voice behind came again.

"This had better be good." Alan looked over his shoulder and grinned.

Brus dragged a prisoner into the clearing, leading him by a rope tied around his wrists. The man's face was purple and swollen. Blood streamed from his nose, and from the red soaked into his shirt, his nose wasn't the only thing that had been bleeding. Even though the prisoner looked like shite, Alan still recognized him.

Fraser.

Before he turned completely away, Alan grazed his blade up his sparring partner's cheek, opening up a stream of blood. "Learn to fight before you spar with me again, else it will be your last match." He smirked at Brus. "Where'd you find this pox-ridden whoreson?"

"Spying for MacDougall—looking for us. His two accomplices are already dead." Brus tugged the bastard forward. "But I thought you might want a word with this one before I ran him through."

Alan examined his prisoner with an evil chuckle. Snot ran from Fraser's bloodied and broken nose. Brus hadn't been kind. From the dirt and grass covering his body, he'd not only been beaten, he'd been dragged. One eye was swollen shut and a cut at his temple still streamed red. "You've shown him our hospitality, I see."

Fraser spat, hitting Alan in the chest.

Clenching his fist tight around the hilt of his sword, Alan thumped him in the jaw. "You always were a sniveling maggot."

Blood trickled from the corner of the miserable wretch's mouth.

"Did Sean send you?"

Fraser spat blood on the ground this time. "I kent you were causing the mischief at Dunollie. Why must you always be a bastard?"

"I'm asking the questions. If you hadn't noticed, your life is mine to take." Alan recoiled and slammed his fist into Fraser's gut.

With a grunt, the Dunollie guard doubled over, his spittle spraying the dirt.

"I'm the lord and master here. You are but a rodent caught in my snare."

The rat had the nerve to glance about. "It looks as if you're preparing for war," he growled through clenched teeth.

Alan threw back his head and roared with laughter. "My force is rather large. Perhaps I'll take the crown."

"You're mad."

"I'm a man looking to claim my rightful place. I've been ignored and shunned all my life and I'm weary of it. I've no choice but to take that which should have gone to me."

Blood oozed from the corner of the prisoner's mouth and his head hung forward. "What the devil are you raving about?"

Alan sauntered up to him and pulled his head up by the hair. "You'll not be around to find out." Gnashing his teeth, Alan sliced his blade across Fraser's exposed jugular and watched the errant guard drop to his knees as his lifeblood drained into the ground.

MacCoul leered at Brus. "Deliver the body to Dunollie. I'm sure young Sean will be worried about his spy."

"Straight away," Brus sniffed. "I'll leave at dawn."

Alan glanced at the sky. It was afternoon, but he supposed it didn't matter if his man-at-arms left on the morrow. After all, Fraser was dead. He'd just smell that much worse when he arrived at the castle.

Alan's messenger rode into the clearing. "A missive, m'lord."

He marched over and snatched the parchment from his hand. *The Lord of Lorn's seal, addressed to that sniveling maggot, MacDougall.* "Where did you find this?"

"Intercepted it from Lorn's runner."

"What did you do with the body?"

The man threw his thumb over his shoulder. "He's at the bottom of Loch Etive with a rock in his belly."

Alan grinned. "Good man. Help yourself to an extra ration of whisky."

"Thank you, m'lord."

Brus stepped in. "What does it say?"

Alan ran his finger under the red wax seal and read, a wicked smile spreading across his face. "'Tis the invitation we've been waiting for."

***

Sitting in his solar, Sean poured over the ledgers now kept by his new factor, a cleric. If he couldn't trust a holy man to keep accurate accounts, there'd be no hope. Fortunately, thus far the man had proved to be precise.

To be honest, Sean was happy to have found a competent factor. Recently he'd had some difficulty concentrating. He hadn't been pleased with the way he'd been forced to leave Gyllis at the priory gates. The monks had never kept the doors closed to him before. At his earliest opportunity he'd make a trip to Ardchattan and ensure John hadn't made errant assumptions due to Gyllis's absence. A rational man would understand there had been no choice.

Sean cradled his head in his hand. He'd lived up to his philandering reputation for certain. Any errant assumptions John may have made would have been spot on.

Though thoughts of the lovely lass consumed his mind, he should have waited until they were wed. God, had he no self-control whatsoever? He loved her—kept her on a pedestal. In his eyes, she was an angel, a goddess to be worshiped. Blast his MacDougall hot blood. The moniker "Lusty Laddie" had been well-earned and had plagued him for years.

He chuckled to think he'd been hooked by Duncan's sister. Duncan was the very man who'd given him the label, but truth be told, nary a lass in Scotland matched Gyllis's beauty.

When the ram's horn sounded, Sean's gut clenched. An internal warning made the hairs on his arms stand on end.

It wasn't unusual to receive a visitor. But it was odd for him to be uneasy about it. He'd also earned the nickname of "Ghost" from his service in the Highland Enforcers. He'd developed a perceptive ability rare to most men, a sensation honed by years of knighthood.

Moving with the speed of a cat, he fastened the top button of his quilted doublet and pulled his heavy hauberk over his head. He would not be stepping into the courtyard without the protection of chainmail or his arms. After buckling his sword belt in place and testing the daggers in his sleeves, he headed out.

Angus met him at the keep's doors. At the far side of the courtyard, the portcullis creaked as the gate rose with its blackened iron fangs pointing downward.

Sean squinted through the dank guardhouse. "Who is it?"

"Not sure," Angus said.

A lone horse galloped through the gate. Eric, the stable hand raced in with his palms held high. "Easy boy."

Sean's heart lurched.

A body draped across the steed's back. Blinking, Sean recognized the horse, the tack, and the backside of the rider. Revulsion was the only word to describe the icy tension clamping every muscle in his body. Bile bit the back of his throat with an acrid burn.

War had been declared, a line drawn.

"My God. 'Tis Fraser." Angus unsheathed his dirk.

The lad brought the horse under control and led him to Sean. He pointed to the dead man. "His throat's been cut."

"MacCoul," Sean growled through clenched teeth.

Angus pointed. "What's this?" He snatched a note secured in Fraser's belt and handed it to Sean. "Addressed to you, m'laird."

"It's been opened." He slid his finger under the compromised wax. "Lorn's seal."

Angus leaned in and studied the crumpled velum. "The bloody bastard."

Sean arched his eyebrow while his gut twisted. "I thought you had a soft spot for him."

A shadow crossed the old man's face. "Not on your life."

A twinge of relief clicked at the back of Sean's mind. He'd been keeping his henchman at arms-length. Not doubting his loyalty to the clan, but questioning his affinity for MacCoul. Something wasn't right when it came to that sniveling maggot and Fraser's death marked the last severed thread. If MacCoul wanted a feud, he'd just purchased one. His friend would be avenged.

Sean eyed Eric. "Take Fraser's body to the priest. He'll ken what to do." Then he flicked open the note and read. "God's bones. Lorn's wedding is only two weeks away—set for the feast of Michaelmas."

"And our enemies know about it," Angus said.

"Aye." Sean folded the missive. "Word was MacCoul's been in the Lowlands training an army."

"Jesus Christ." Angus pressed the heels of his hands to his temples. "Alan isn't daft enough to attack the Lord of Lorn. 'Tis you he's insanely jealous of."

Sean agreed, but that didn't mean Alan wouldn't stage something rash—especially a demonstration to make Sean look bad. He cast his gaze to the MacDougall guard, who were watching him from the battlements above. The men would be riled by Fraser's death and looking for blood. The MacDougalls were good fighting men, but against an army? He needed to call in some overdue favors. "You must ride to Glen Strae with a missive for Eoin MacGregor. I'll head to Glen Orchy straight away and solicit help from Lord Duncan."

Angus gaped. "Campbell? But he's aligned with Argyll—Stewart's enemy—the reason Lorn is proceeding with this marriage is so Argyll cannot claim the title for himself."

"Aye, and he's my closest friend. Given the gravity of MacCoul's message, Duncan will stand beside me. I have no doubt." Sean marched toward the keep. "Come, I've a missive to pen."

***

Lady Meg was anxious to try her new treatment for Gyllis and presently her chamber was half full of chambermaids and buckets of hot water. Gyllis stood with crutches under her arms and her shift knotted up over her thighs while the lasses wrapped warm cloths around her legs.

"Word came all the way from France that warm wraps assist in speeding the recovery of paralysis," Meg said, standing as tall as she could, looking pleased with herself. Her bright-red, curly locks stuck out from under her veil in every direction as if she'd been boiling water in the kitchen for hours.

Gyllis sighed, wondering where on earth Meg gained information all the way from France. *A wives' tale, most likely.* "I suppose I'll try anything if it helps." *And return me to Sir Sean MacDougall's arms sooner.* She needed to find a way to send a message to Sean and advise him that she'd returned home. Not only was it improper for an unwed lassie to send a missive to a man, it bore too much of a risk. If Duncan received word of it, she'd doubtless be locked in her chamber for life.

Meg moved in front of Gyllis and held her hands firmly. "Lassies, pull the crutches from under her arms."

Afraid she'd fall, Gyllis clamped her fingers around Meg's wrists. "I need those."

"Do as I say," Meg said in an authoritative voice—rather pushy for such a petite woman. She gave Gyllis a stern look. "Were the warm cloths stimulating?"

Gyllis flexed her muscles. "Aye. I think mayhap they were."

"Good, then take a step toward me."

She did as told, then took another while Meg slowly backed away. After they'd crossed the floor, Meg pulled her around. "Now do it without holding my hands."

Gyllis held fast to her grip. "Oh no, more than a couple of steps and I'll fall for certain. I always do."

Meg gave her a stern look that meant she wouldn't be accepting no for an answer. "I'll keep my hands out for you. Grasp them at your first weakness."

Gyllis took two unsteady steps and gasped. She'd nearly fallen—but she hadn't. *Oh blessed be the saints.*

"Again," Meg said with the most reassuring smile Gyllis had ever seen.

Concentrating very hard, she took another step, followed by another. Gyllis laughed. "My knees are scarcely wobbling."

Meg backed further. "Try again."

Gyllis stepped forward. Her knee buckled and she listed to the side. Meg clamped onto her shoulders. "Easy lass. You've done well." She turned her attention to the line of chambermaids. "From now on we shall include warm compresses to Miss Gyllis's treatments of massage."

Gyllis could have jumped for joy. "I shall be walking again in no time." *And Sean will be so happy.*

"'Tis what I like to hear." Her sister-in-law patted her cheek. "If you keep telling yourself you can, you *will*. Only the naysayer lies abed and allows herself to waste away."

"Did you have this many monks tending you at Ardchattan?" Duncan's deep voice resounded from the doorway.

A chambermaid slid the crutches under Gyllis's arms as she shot a shocked glance at her brother. He rarely ever paid a visit to her chamber. "Not by half."

Duncan clapped his hands. "Leave us. I need a word with my sister."

Gyllis watched the lassies file out of her chamber and wished she could follow them. John's missive had caught up to her for certain.

Meg brushed his arm as she walked past. "I shall be in the nursery with Elizabeth and Colin should you need me." Duncan grinned with a daft look on his face—one he only affected when Lady Meg was present.

After the door closed, Duncan gestured to the couch. "Let us sit."

Gyllis's legs were noticeably stronger as she moved and took a seat. She leaned her crutches against the table and bit down on her lip to calm her nerves. "How have things been at Kilchurn whilst I've been away?" Her high-pitched voice had a tremor. She clenched her fists until her fingernails bit into her palms. Whatever was coming, showing nervousness to Duncan would make him all the more suspicious.

"John advised you were recovering well and that the priory can no longer handle you." He took a seat beside her and leaned over, eyebrows slanted inward—definitely not a happy stare. "What the devil did he mean by that?"

"Ah..." Gyllis stared at her hands, her entire body growing hot as a boiling pot. *Stop it Gyllis. He mentioned nothing about Sean. Surely Duncan would have brought him up first had John revealed the night at Dunollie.* "Ah...I-I believe one of the monks became infatuated with me." It was the best she could do on the spur of the moment.

Duncan sprang to his feet and slammed his fist against the backrest. "I knew it. Did he touch you?" He pounded his fist again. "I'll kill the bastard. Tell me his name and I'll see to it he never again looks at another lass."

Gyllis waved her hands across her body in rapid succession. "Please no. 'Twas an innocent fascination. He did nothing untoward."

"No?" Duncan paced. "Then why did John send you home—using a pair of pegs no less?"

"They're crutches and they help me move around quite nicely." Seizing the opportunity to steer the conversation away from her indiscretion, Gyllis pointed to the buckets. "Besides, your wife found a new treatment the monks hadn't used. Already this morning I took seven steps on my own."

Duncan sat again and frowned.

"After today's treatment, I have no doubt I'll be walking again soon." She clapped a hand over her heart. "I give you my vow I'll not become a burden to the family."

"Ah, Gyllis." He draped an arm around her and squeezed her shoulder. "Is that what you think? You'll be a burden?" He snorted. "You're kin. Even if you'd remained bedridden I'd have taken care of you. You ken that do you not?"

"Aye." Yet another tear stung her eye. She'd honestly believed Duncan would send her to a nunnery if she didn't recover. "Thank you." She allowed herself to exhale. Thank God for John. He hadn't betrayed her confidence after all. She owed him a debt of gratitude.

Now to focus all her energy on her recovery—and finding a way to see Sir Sean as soon as possible.

Chapter Nineteen

Sean followed the sentry into the keep. How odd to be escorted. He practically knew Kilchurn Castle better than he did Dunollie. God knew he'd spent more time there. The irony was the woman he couldn't clear from his thoughts was elsewhere. Though Fraser's death and the blatant message he'd received from MacCoul weighed heavily on his conscience, he couldn't ride to Kilchurn without thinking of Gyllis.

He'd decided to keep his intentions to marry the lass quiet for now. First he needed to see Lorn wed, and deal with MacCoul before he approached Duncan for her hand. *I should have hanged the bastard when I had him in my grasp. If it hadn't been the day of my father's funeral, I never would have allowed Angus to step in. And now look. My failure has caused the death of one of my closest friends.*

The guard knocked on the door to Duncan's solar—a place where Sean had spent many hours debating Highland Enforcers' affairs. Though he didn't realize it at the time, life had been far simpler before he'd inherited his father's mantle.

"Sir Sean MacDougall of Dunollie," the guard announced, as if Sean needed an introduction.

Duncan shoved his chair back with a grin. He marched forward and clasped Sean at the elbow and held firm—a more personal greeting than a handshake—the one used by the enforcers. "By God, 'tis good to see you."

Sean couldn't bring himself to smile. "You as well."

"Too much time has passed." Duncan gestured to a seat. "Are you ready to rejoin the enforcers? Tension with England is mounting."

"I wish I were." He sat and leaned back with his knees wide. "Being Chieftain of Dunollie has brought on a host of problems."

Duncan moved to the sideboard and pulled the stopper out of a flagon. "I'd agree there. I never had an appreciation for my father's responsibilities until I stepped into his shoes." He set a cup in front of Sean and raised the one remaining in his hand. "Let us toast to our clans as well as long health."

Sean held up his whisky. "*Slàinte*." He sipped and swilled the oaken flavor across his tongue. One thing was always a certainty when he visited Kilchurn. There was no finer whisky in all of Scotland than that from Campbell's still.

Duncan took his seat at the head of the table. "So, if you're not itching to head back to the borders, what brings you to Kilchurn?"

Sean watched the whisky while he swirled it in his cup. He needed to choose his words carefully, else he'd come across as an incompetent boob. "I've some grave news…"

Looking Duncan square in the eye, he leaned forward on his elbow and started with Alan MacCoul's banishment from Dunollie lands, the cattle thieving, Fraser's mission and the return of his body—and the missive. "…now I've nay choice but to provide fealty service for Lorn's wedding."

Duncan thoughtfully rotated the cup in his fingers. "You're worried about a wedding?"

Sean tossed back the last of his whisky. "The last thing Fraser said was the whore told him MacCoul was amassing an army."

Duncan chuckled. "A bedraggled crew, no doubt. It sounds like a gang of renegades. They'd be no match for your trained men."

Sean wished he were as confident as his friend. "I'm not so certain. I think they're organized."

"What kind of men would follow a festering pustule like Alan MacCoul? What means has he?"

"I know not. But my father had an affinity for the bastard."

"Well, you've put a damper on your da's former misguided affections." Duncan rested his elbows on the table. "My bet is he'll be a thorn in your side until you lure him back to MacDougall land and arrest him—string him up like you should have done after he attacked you. Christ, he challenged you right after you were declared chieftain?"

"Aye, I ken what I *should* have done. But now I cannot take a chance on him causing mischief for the Lord of Lorn." Sean sat taller. "I need your help, Duncan."

"'Tis a wedding, no?" The Lord of Glenorchy smirked.

"Aye, at Dunstaffnage Chapel."

"MacCoul would be an idiot to attack you on the king's lands. Besides, you'll have your army as well as Lorn's. Surely you can handle a wee skirmish."

"But I won't have the stealth of the enforcers. I want to establish an impenetrable barrier for my uncle."

Duncan sat back and spread his arms to his sides. "'Tis a wedding for Christ's sake. Worse, it's John Stewart, Lord of Lorn's wedding. If I'm there and something does happen, the Stewart Clan will be blaming me."

God, the man made Sean's worries sound daft. But Sean persisted, "You ken I'd vouch for you."

"Aye, after the dust settles."

"What about sending in a dozen of your best men? They can wear my colors."

"All but a handful are on the borders. Wouldn't get them back here in time." Duncan shook his head. "Nay, I'd be daft to call them away from the king's business to stand watch during a wedding."

Sean bit the inside of his cheek. "Bloody hell, Duncan. You're the closest thing to a brother I have."

The lord tapped his finger against his cup. "I ken."

"Can you not put aside your fealty for Argyll for a wedding and provide some weapons?"

"That's just it." He ground his finger into the board. "'Tis a miserable wedding—hardly something we need an army for. Christ, man, you've at least fifty skilled men in Dunollie's guard. In my opinion, you are overreacting to Fraser's death. He rode into the wrong camp is all. You know that as well as I."

Sean groaned. "When you say it like that, I feel the fool for having traveled so far to gain your audience."

"Not at all. I'm always glad to share a tot with you." Duncan stood and grabbed the flagon from the sideboard. "If you have more trouble with MacCoul's thugs thieving your cattle, the enforcers will be able to help you. That's our motto—to support the king and maintain order."

Sean watched him fill his cup with another shot of whisky. Had he overreacted? What would his father have done in his stead? He puzzled. The MacDougalls always had their enemies, but Duncan was right. The Dunollie guard posed a force to be reckoned with. Had Sean lost confidence because of his lack of trust? Angus had proved his loyalty. So had the others for the most part. Even Gawen had proved his loyalty when he kicked the stools at the hanging. It was time for Sean to cast his misgivings aside and lean on his own men for support. Besides, Angus might have better luck soliciting help from Eoin MacGregor.

Sean raised his cup. "I hope I do not have to take you up on that offer. I intend to squash MacCoul the first time he shows his beastly face."

Duncan grinned. Sean hadn't noticed it before, but the Lord of Glenorchy's smile was dimpled like Gyllis's. He sipped the fiery liquid. If Duncan had any idea how often he'd seen Gyllis in the past few months, he'd run him out of Argyllshire. *I'd best stick with my plan and leave the topic of marriage alone this trip. Duncan is likely to blow hot steam through his ears—just like old times.*

Duncan shoved his chair back. "Of course you'll stay for the evening meal—head back on the morrow?"

"I will, thank you. 'Tis a long ride."

"Mayhap we can get in a sparring session afore the meal is served."

Sean swirled his fingers over the basket-weave pattern on his sword's hilt. "I'd welcome a healthy round. No one's given me a good run since you left me on the borders."

Duncan clapped him on the shoulder. "'Tis time you groomed a champion. A chieftain should not be the best sword—'tis not healthy for the longevity of the clan."

"Oh?" Sean scoffed. "And why have I not seen any Campbell guard best you?"

The Lord of Glenorchy winked. "I'm working on it."

***

Gyllis sat in the embrasure of her window and stared out over Loch Awe. September was always her favorite month. The warmth of summer lingered, though something in the air warned the nice weather wouldn't last. It made her anxious to enjoy it all the more. This season it also made her anxious to shed her crutches. She'd been suffering paralysis for so long, she yearned for the days without constant care, when she was free to run and dance.

The chamber door opened and Helen stepped inside carrying a missive. "Have you a moment?"

"Meg and her retinue of lasses have come and gone." Gyllis beckoned her. "What is that?"

Helen skipped over and sat on the padded bench opposite. "I've received a letter from Sir Aleck MacIain."

"Honestly?" Hopefully this was a pleasant surprise. Gyllis waggled her eyebrows. "What does it say?"

"He wrote me a poem and said some nice things."

Gyllis rolled her hand. "I'm sure you didn't come in here to talk about the lovely weather we're having. Read it to me."

Gyllis listened to the love letter. The chieftain's prose put Helen on a pedestal, reassuring her that all would be well, reinforcing she was needed as the lady of the keep in Ardnamurchan posthaste, and Aleck awaited her arrival with fond anticipation. He even signed it "your servant". When Helen finished reading, she folded the velum and stared at it with a long sigh.

"He sounds very nice."

She nodded her dun locks and pursed her delicate mouth. Gyllis had always considered Helen a bit frailer. Though now stricken with paralysis, Gyllis figured the tides may have changed in that regard. In so many ways over the past months, Gyllis had doubted herself, feared she would be a burden and hated every moment of her dependence.

But her sister needed reassurance now more than Gyllis did. "Surely, Sir Aleck's letter has eased your mind."

"Aye." Helen looked up and smiled—a sad smile all the same. "I believe he has a good heart at least."

Gyllis leaned forward and patted her hand. "'Tis a start."

Her sister stood and moved to the window, gazing out over the loch. "I shall miss this place."

Gyllis scooted along the bench and grasped her hand. "And I shall miss you."

"I'm ever so anxious." She glanced at the crutches. "Would you be up to a stroll?"

"Aye—let us venture to the battlements."

Helen's gaze dropped to Gyllis's legs. "Are you able to climb that many steps?"

"I will not know until I try." She slid back and plucked her crutches from the floor. "I nearly made it across the chamber without these today."

"That is wonderful news, but I'm not certain you should be climbing all the way to the battlements. What if you fall?"

The more Helen balked, the more Gyllis wanted to cast the blasted crutches aside and race her to the top of the stairwell. *If only I could.* Mayhap they'd be able to race the next time they were together. "Come. If I fall, I'll have a wee bruise. If 'tis too far, we shall turn around."

Helen giggled. "I suppose I could always ask a young guard to carry you back to your chamber."

Gyllis pulled herself to a stand and started toward the door. "Now that's the best idea you've had in ages."

"I thought you were head over heels for Sir Sean."

"I am. But I'm not dead."

Helen followed her into the passageway. "You're still incorrigible."

"And you are still a prude."

Giggling, they made their way up through the narrow stone stairwell winding like a spiral to the wall-walk. At the top, Gyllis leaned against the stone battlements to catch her breath. "I cannot believe I used to run up those stairs."

Helen fanned her face. "I cannot believe you've suffered paralysis and climbed all the way up here with a set of crutches. You are truly amazing."

Gyllis chuckled and took in a deep breath. The deep blue water shimmering on the loch caught her eye. She could see for miles. Even the purple heather on the surrounding hills was in bloom. Violets and lavenders climbed for miles up the slopes of Ben Cruachan, the sight was enough to take her breath away. A breeze caressed her face and summer's fragrance filled her with renewed energy. "This view made our effort worthwhile."

Behind them iron clanged. Gyllis snapped her head around and headed across the stone walk to a crenel notch. "Remember when we used to watch Eoin and Sean spar from this very spot?" She poked her head through the gap. Only two men sparred in the courtyard. She instantly made out her brother, but her heart leapt when she recognized the man with his back to her. Only one man on earth could make her heart stutter an arrhythmic beat—make her knees turn into boneless limbs, and most of all, heat pool in the most sacred place of all.

Tall, wavy, dark hair brushing his nape, built like a prized bull from his broad shoulders to his sturdy hips. "Sean," Gyllis whispered.

"Oh, my." Helen pushed in beside her. "Do you know why he's here?"

She gaped at him. "I haven't a clue."

Helen fanned her face. "But he is."

Gyllis sighed. "Aye." Her body went from trembling recognition to floating. Her mind drifted to the night she'd seen him sparring with an imaginary partner completely nude. Sean moved like a cat. His movements so fast, his sword and limbs blurred. His lunges deep, his

spins precise, calculated. Duncan kept up, but her brother
could hardly match the younger chieftain.

She could watch Sean forever, her mind's eye
picturing the bulging muscles beneath his linen shirt. The
men circled. She could see Sean's face now. His hawk-like
eyes focused on Duncan as if nothing around them could
draw his attention away. With the laces of his shirt spread
open, his chest glistened with perspiration. Even from
five-stories up, Gyllis could see the sheen, and all too well
she was familiar with the bands of sinew taut beneath.

Heat spread throughout her body. Her breasts swelled
against her stays. From such distance she could smell his
spicy musk soaring up to her with the breeze, as if
begging her to float down to his arms. Her lips parted
with her stuttered breaths.

"Och aye, you are smitten." Helen nudged her. "You
should see your face."

Gyllis clapped her hands to her cheeks. "'Tis that
obvious?"

Helen laughed. "You may as well hold up a placard
that says 'marry me'."

"Oh please, how utterly unheard of." Gyllis
straightened, though she couldn't bring herself to pull her
gaze from the Adonis down below.

"Come, I ken what we should do." Helen hastened
toward the stairwell.

Gyllis hobbled after her as fast as she could, her
blasted crutches clicking the flagstone.
"What are you on about?"

The dun-haired lass had never looked like she was up
to so much mischief as she did when she stopped at the
entrance to the stairwell and grinned. "We've not much
time to make you look as bonny as a queen."

Gyllis's insides flipped upside down. "I think the idea
of matrimony becomes you. You're not half as dull as you

were when we rode onto the Dunstaffnage foregrounds for Beltane."

Helen slapped her hand through the air. "Hogwash. I'm as passionate as you. I just do not let everyone know about it as you do."

Gyllis tried to keep up with Helen's fast pace. "Honeyed cryspes? You would have rather sought out food than stroll past a gathering of brawny knights."

Helen stopped and faced her. "Ah, but you forget even knighted lads enjoy sweets. Mother doesn't pay a mind to us if we're seeking out a treat, silly. I'm not half as dull as you may think."

Gyllis covered her smirk with the tips of her fingers and snorted out her nose. Evidently her sister was a master at pretenses. Perhaps she should pay more attention in the future.

Chapter Twenty

Standing at the well, Sean splashed his face with water and ran his fingers through his hair, shoving it from his eyes. He didn't have a comb in his kit, so a quick brush with his fingers would have to do. He straightened his sword belt and headed into the keep. He wasn't enamored with the idea of spending the night, but it would be folly to head home in the dark. Not only would he have to travel through Fearnoch Forest, the delivery of Fraser's body broadcast loud and clear that Sean's problems were far from over. Traveling home at first light was his only option.

Once inside the great hall, he strode through the crowd to the dais. Duncan sat in the lord's chair at the center of the table with Lady Meg on his right and his mother, Lady Margaret, on his left. If anyone had entered the keep wondering who was lord and master, there would be nary a question. The trio looked as regal as the king's retinue at court.

Duncan stood. "Sir Sean, please take the seat at the end. I've no doubt my sisters will enjoy your conversation."

Sean gulped. Duncan never wanted him to take a wee gander at his sisters. *Hmm. Perhaps he believed there was no threat with Gyllis away at the priory.*

"How are you Sir Sean?" Lady Meg asked holding out her hand. "It has been ever so long since we've seen you."

"I'm well." Sean strode around the table, took her hand and kissed it. "My dear lady, you are bonnier than ever. And how are the twins?"

"Elizabeth's almost as beautiful as her mother," Duncan said. "And Colin is a lad who would make my father proud."

"Congratulations to you both." Sean then bowed to Lady Margaret. "And how are you m'lady?"

"Very well," the woman who'd been a second mother dipped her head. "Please accept my condolences for the loss of your father. He was a good man."

"That he was."

Sean took his seat, but no sooner had he done so, a hush dampened the banter in the hall. Lady Margaret clapped a hand to her chest and sat forward. Sean followed her gaze.

Gyllis stood at the foot of the stairwell wearing a crimson mantle. Both the over and under gowns were a work of art. Low cut, Gyllis's breasts swelled above the sealskin-trimmed neckline, her flesh more perfect than pure white calla lilies. Her tresses were held away from her face under a matching French hood, also trimmed by sealskin. Looking directly at him, she offered a lovely smile before she handed her crutches to Helen.

She's not?

She did.

With her first step, the gold satin underdress caught the glow of the candlelight and shimmered. Sean scarcely noticed Helen walking closely behind with one hand out. Gyllis grinned at him, her face alive and filled with joy.

She took another step and another.

Sean wanted to dash from the dais and gather her into his arms, but in no way would he wish to detract from her performance.

Duncan stood, as if he'd had the same thought.

Lady Margaret sat transfixed, her hand covering her mouth. "Praise God."

"'Tis a miracle," said Lady Meg.

Sean grasped his armrests. He couldn't allow her to cross the entire hall unassisted, no matter how much she wanted to impress her family. When he slid his chair back, Gyllis stumbled forward. Helen squealed and reached for her, but the lovely lass tumbled beyond her sister's grasp. Benches scraped across the floor as Gyllis collapsed into a heap.

Sean didn't remember his feet touching ground as he dashed to her side. "Miss Gyllis!" He dropped to his knees before her. "Are you all right?"

"Blast." She smacked the floorboards with her fist. "I wanted to impress you, and I had to go and fall on my face like a cripple."

"You are a cripple," Alice said from behind the small gathering of people. Sometimes little sisters could be so maddening.

"No. She is not." Sean gathered her in his arms. "Miss Gyllis may have suffered from a bout of paralysis, but I've never seen anyone with more courage and determination."

Frail and light in his arms, he stood with ease.

She buried her face in his chest and a tear moistened his shirt. "I'm so embarrassed. I wanted to show you how much I've improved."

"Are you jesting? You *walked*, Gyllis. You practically strode across the entire hall without a lick of help. I've never been so impressed by anything in my life as much as I witnessed in that moment. I know how hard you've worked. You are truly amazing."

She met his gaze with a joyous bleary-eyed smile adorned by delightful dimples—so much more enchanting than Duncan's. "Lady Meg started applying warm compresses. I think they've helped a great deal."

"Aye? I'd wager your pure determination has done as much or more than a handful of warm rags." He proceeded to the dais, met with Duncan's angry glare. But before Sean neared close enough for the baron to hear, he pressed his lips to Gyllis's ear. "You've never looked as radiant as you do this night."

Why she was there and not at the priory he'd uncover later.

Duncan planted his fists on his hips. "Was it necessary to carry my sister all the way to the dais?"

If Sean weren't cradling Gyllis in his arms he'd challenge Duncan on the spot, friend or no. She'd had the courage to attempt to cross the entire great hall unassisted and when her frail legs had given out, the bastard hadn't rushed to her aid. "I believe it was. Only a few sennights ago, Miss Gyllis had just started to walk with crutches."

Duncan crossed his arms and tipped his chin up. "It seems you know an awful lot about my sister's ailment."

Sean pushed past him and climbed onto the dais. "I've had dealings at Ardchattan and chanced to visit with Miss Gyllis a time or two." He set her on the chair beside his. "Are you all right now my...lo...ah...Miss Gyllis?"

"I am, thanks to you, sir." She cast a heated stare in her brother's direction.

Sean took her hand and bowed deeply over it. "'Tis my pleasure to be of assistance." Her lithe fingers smelled of rose oil and he could have hovered there forever. Watching her eyes, he kissed her hand. "Is there anything further I can do to help?"

Gyllis smiled, her gaze trailing down the length of his body. A bold move for a somewhat innocent maid, but a gesture telling him she desired more than a kiss on her hand. "I would be honored if the gallant knight who rescued me would be so kind as to sit beside me during the meal."

Duncan stepped behind them. "Do not make me challenge you MacDougall. I suggest you take your seat and stop carrying on like a wet-eared lad."

"I thought he was rather chivalrous," Helen said, taking the seat on Gyllis's other side.

"He's being a fair bit too familiar if you ask me," Duncan groused.

"Stop," Mother said. "I find Sir Sean's actions endearing. Besides, you didn't spring across the room and dash to assist your sister. If not you, I can think of no one more suitable. Sean is practically family. Why, the pair has known each other since childhood."

Sean leaned toward Gyllis's ear. "I could talk to him now…um…you know."

She held a finger to her lips. "Nay. Let me speak to Mother first. Perhaps she can build a bridge."

Sean glanced toward Duncan. He'd resumed his seat and poured himself a tankard of ale. Slipping his hand under the table, Sean grasped Gyllis's fingers. "Why are you here? I thought you'd remain at the priory for another month at least."

"John was waiting for me in my cell after you brought me back from Dunollie. He said if I was well enough to stay out all night, I could return home." Gyllis squeezed his hand tight. "He even guessed that we…"

Sean choked on his ale and froth spewed across the table. "Oh no."

Gyllis bit her lip and dropped her lids. "He did."

Sean rubbed the back of his neck and flicked his gaze toward the Lord of Glenorchy. "Duncan isn't aware."

Gyllis gave him the most perplexed look. "How did you…?"

"He hasn't tried to hang me—yet."

Gyllis muffled her giggle with her free hand. "And you, why are you at Kilchurn?"

Sean couldn't bring himself to tell her about all the problems with Alan MacCoul. The last thing Gyllis needed right now was to worry about an ornery varlet who would soon be brought to justice. "I had dealings with your brother."

Her face reddened. "Clearly those dealings did not include me," she whispered so softly, Sean scarcely caught every word.

"Not yet, my love." Sean pressed his lips to her ear. "Speak to your mother. Then I will approach Duncan after the Michaelmas feast and the Lord of Lorn's wedding."

She picked up a piece of bread and took the tiniest bite. "Only speak to him if you truly want to. I know I'm not—"

Sean tightened his fingers around her hand. "Cease. There is no question of my love or devotion for you."

Duncan pounded the hilt of his eating knife on the table. "The two of you have had your heads together since you sat down. What is so surreptitious you cannot share it with all the table?"

What was it about Duncan Campbell that brought out Sean's urge to hit something—namely the arrogant lord's face. God's teeth, he'd been friends with Duncan forever, but that didn't mean he'd take his shite. Gyllis must have sensed Sean's building ire because she squeezed his arm with surprising strength.

But Sean met the baron's glare. "If you must know, after seeing Miss Gyllis struggling at the priory, I had my carpenter fashion a pair of crutches for her." He pointed. "Those she attempted to cross the hall *without* today. She was simply informing me of her progress." Sean glared back, just as intensely as the Lord of Glenorchy. Duncan may be his senior peer, but Sean was a chieftain. A man to be reckoned with. And he would win the bastard's favor regardless of any past indiscretions. "I happened to be quite amazed with her attempt to walk the length of the hall. I trust you were equally so."

Lady Margaret leaned forward, blocking the intense current between the two men, though the matron's eyes focused on the hand Gyllis had on Sean's arm. "I could scarcely believe my eyes. It appears Lady Meg's treatments have been overwhelmingly helpful."

Gyllis released her grip and folded her hands in her lap. "Aye. I never would have thought hot compresses could make such a difference to the monk's treatments."

Mother's gaze slipped to Sean. "Perhaps we should have kept you at Kilchurn."

Sean knew Lady Margaret to be a shrewd woman. His exuberant display of concern for Gyllis wouldn't have gone unnoticed. Sean only hoped Gyllis's mother would be an ally when it came time to ask for the lass's hand.

Sean and Duncan had spent too much time swilling whisky in alehouses with buxom wenches when they were lads. Aye, they'd both acted like rogues, but Duncan had changed after he'd met his wife—sworn off alehouse tarts. If only the lord could realize more than one man could do the same. Sean hadn't thought of another woman since…since…*in a bloody long time for certain.*

***

Sean didn't balk when Lady Meg offered him a bed in a guest chamber above stairs—though he'd intended on bedding down in the stable. The soft mattress did nothing to soothe his unease. He needed this business with Lorn's wedding to be over. Though Duncan's argument made sense—Alan MacCoul's quarrel was with Sean and not with the Lord of Lorn. If the bastard was foolish enough to try an attack, it would be a siege on the fortress of Dunollie, not the wedding party and not a castle being part of the crown's holdings. Sean considered sending a missive to Lorn and asking him to change the date or the venue, but doing so would admit weakness.

Sean closed his eyes and slung his arm over his face. A picture of Gyllis immediately came to mind. She'd been so radiant this eve, he could have swept her into his arms and stole her away like a Viking from ages past. The thought of taking Gyllis to his galley and sailing to a distant shore tempted—but only for a moment. He was a chieftain, by God, and his plan was solid. He'd see out his duty and then Gyllis would be his. Not even Duncan Campbell would be able to stand in his way.

Gyllis was his. They may not have pledged their love before God, but she was his woman—always had been. Duncan would not arrange her marriage to any other. Sean would not stand for it. The idea of her marrying any other man made his blood pulse icily through his veins. Hell, if another man looked at Gyllis he turned into a raving lunatic.

The door opened and quickly closed. Sean sat up, the bedclothes dropping to his waist. Gyllis stood against the door, holding a candle, using only one crutch. She wore a dressing gown belted at the waist. Staring at him, the whites of her eyes grew enormous.

"Gyllis?" Sean reached for a plaid and circled it around his hips as he slid out of bed. "What are you doing in here?"

She drew in a sharp gasp. "I cannot sleep."

"Nor can I, but 'tis not proper for you to be in my chamber." He tucked the plaid at his hip and hastened across the floor. "You could be ruined." Not to mention Duncan would sever Sean's cods if the lord of the keep found them together.

She handed him the candle then placed her hand on his bare chest. His breath caught at her touch. Heaven help him, he could not resist but a single fingertip's caress. The tingling of flesh on flesh stirred molten fire from his chest all the way through the tip of his cock.

She trailed her finger from his heart to the edge of the plaid with a seductive chuckle. "I am already ruined thanks to you."

Sean had no control over his body's reaction. In the blink of an eye, his cock lengthened and stretched taut against the woolen fabric. "I would never see you ruined."

"Mm, mm." She didn't miss his reaction and ran her fingertips along the inside of the plaid perched precariously on his hips.

He took a step back and grasped her shoulder. "We mustn't."

"Why?" she purred.

He squared his jaw. "I should march straight to Duncan's chamber and ask for your hand."

"I do like that idea, however…" She chuckled like a wanton. "He's most likely making another bairn with Lady Meg."

She stepped closer, again toying with the plaid. Sean stepped away and placed the candle on the table. He needed both hands to control the lassie's advances, no matter how much he wanted her, damn it all.

"When is Lorn's wedding?" she asked.

"A fortnight."

The crutch clicked the floorboards as she moved further into the chamber. "'Tis soon. I shall await your return with great anticipation." Her scent made Sean's knees waver, yet Gyllis moved forward unaware of the spell she'd cast over him. "Mother has always been fond of you—but I shall never understand Duncan. You're his best friend, and yet he cannot bear to see you place a hand upon me." She reached out her finger and stroked it across his lips.

Damn, the wavering of his knees rocketed up his thighs, spread through the ache in his groin, and continued to his chest.

Sean forced himself not to tug her into his arms and devour her. God's bones, Duncan's chamber was directly above theirs. If he heard Gyllis's crutch tap the floorboards, the lord would charge in like a raging bull. Sean swallowed, lightheaded from his growing erection. "'Tis difficult for a man to see his friends take an interest in his sister. You ken we've talked about it."

"Aye." Gyllis's voice grew husky. "'Tis why mother must make him understand." She grasped the plaid and tugged.

Sean held her wrist. "We mustn't."

She met his gaze with an arched brow, but she released her fingers from the wool. "No one saw me. No one will know."

Helpless to turn her away, Sean followed while Gyllis moved to the foot of the bed, placed her crutch on the floor then grasped the bedpost with one hand. Reaching out with the other, she again closed her fingers around his plaid. Her eyes flashed wide and a sultry laugh spilled from her throat as she pulled off Sean's plaid. His cock bounced out and pointed directly at her. He was harder than an oak broomstick and more aroused than a lad staring at a pair of breasts for the first time. Christ, he needed release.

Gyllis didn't help matters. Her pink tongue slipped to the corner of her mouth as her gaze undulated down his body and stopped at his cock. "I-I've wanted you ever since..." She untied the sash around her waist and let the dressing gown drop to the floor.

God save him, she wore not a stich of clothing. Every shred of self-control fled. His mind consumed with the tantalizing woman before him. Somehow she was even more beautiful now than he'd remembered. The candlelight flickered amber across her skin. Chestnut tresses slid over her shoulder, framing two perfectly formed breasts, tipped by rose.

Sean licked his lips, those delectable rosebuds would be his second stop. In two strides, he wrapped her in his arms and crushed his body against hers. "For all that is holy, you have claimed my soul, my flesh and my mind."

He covered her mouth with his, her minty taste flooding his senses. Claiming her for his own, he forced his tongue inside her mouth. She matched the ferocious swirling of his tongue. No, Gyllis wasn't one to shy away from anything life threw her way. She was strong and wild and seductive, and he loved her to the depths of his core. His cock slid across her stomach and he moaned.

In an act of unbridled trust, she released her hold on the bedpost and clamped her arms around his shoulders. Their mouths joined, she thrust her hips against him. "I want you."

He needed no more encouragement. Sean swept her into his arms and placed her on the bed. His mind consumed with desire, his senses overpowered by her smell, her seductive way she rocked her hips in anticipation of receiving him, and the deft fingers plying the muscles in his back, he was powerless to resist.

He trailed kisses down her neck while kneading her breast. Her soft moan made his seed dribble from the tip of his cock. Christ almighty, he needed her and soon, else she'd unman him just by the sultry tenor of her voice.

He clamped his mouth over her breast and teased her delectable nipple with the swirling of his tongue. Her body quivered as she arched her back and mewled. "I cannot take much more."

Sean looked into those alluring green eyes and chuckled. "You taste like ambrosia from the Gods."

A slow grin spread across her lips and she tugged on his shoulders. "'Tis my turn to taste you."

"Nay."

She tugged harder. "If you haven't realized it yet, I am seducing you, not the other way around."

God, he loved this woman. Sean slid alongside her and gestured to his body, his muscles as taut as they were after he'd been an hour or more in the sparring ring. "I am at your service m'lady." A groan of desire rumbled from his chest.

She ran her tongue over her teeth, sweeping her gaze down his body. The way she looked at him set his cock on fire. The woman was a lioness in the bedchamber, her innocence and eagerness more arousing than anything he'd ever experienced. She rolled atop him and kissed his cheeks, his forehead, his chin.

Sean grasped her shoulders and tried to claim her mouth, but she held up a finger. "You must allow me to seduce you."

"I fear you already have me in your clutches." His voice came out deep and hoarse. He hardly recognized it. He'd been with countless women, but they all paled to the one in his arms. With but a look she could do unholy, rapturous things to his body. He could think of nothing but Gyllis—how much he wanted her in his bed—how much he wanted his cock inside her right now.

But she slid her mouth downward and covered his nipple. Christ his cock spurted another dribble of seed. It felt so damn good, he wouldn't last long. And then she trailed her kisses lower. Sean clenched his bum cheeks so tight his muscles cramped. When she took him into her mouth, he muffled his gasp by draping his elbow across his mouth. Never in his life would he expect Gyllis to taste him, but by God, he was about to explode for the rush of urgency she built up with every sweep of her tongue.

At the ragged edge, his buttocks burning, shaking with frenzy, he grasped her shoulders and tugged her up. When his fingers found her hips, he raised her high enough to impale her on his erection.

She gaped at him, eyes wide. "I can be on top?"

He stirred himself within her warm core. "Aye, lass. You can and you are."

She followed his lead and together they found a rhythm that sped with the intensity of their breathing. Their bodies quivered with the strain, thrusting, swirling, mounting the precipice of no return until, all at once, together they reached their peak, clinging to each other with silent screams of ecstasy.

She collapsed atop him, their bodies joined, their souls joined. Neither spoke. Even their breathing matched. With her in his arms he was whole. For the first time in his life he knew what it meant to be a man—not just a warrior or a chieftain, but a man who loved a woman so much it hurt. He wanted a family he could protect and cherish, and Gyllis would be the center of his world.

As she rested in Sean's arms, her breathing took on the slow cadence of sleep. No matter how much Sean wanted her to remain in his arms throughout the night, he couldn't risk being discovered. Not only would it ruin Gyllis, it would validate all Duncan's unfounded misgivings—the reason Sean tried to stop her when she'd first slipped into his chamber. The moniker "Lusty Laddie" rang in his head.

"I must take you back."

"Must you?" Gyllis rose up on her elbow. "Why not take me to Kilbride Church and marry me this night?"

He pressed his lips to her forehead. "Because I want to do this right."

Chapter Twenty-One

"If you don't stop smiling, Mother and Duncan will suspect you're hiding something," Helen said while she placed her looking glass in the trunk between the folds of her clothing. She closed the lid. "You'd best pay heed to me. Ever since Sir Sean arrived, you've been flitting around as if you've been touched in the head by a fairy."

Gyllis reached in and fastened the hasp. "Perhaps I have."

"You are hopeless." Helen gave her a prying stare. "It makes me suspect he may have spirted you to the garden and stolen a kiss."

"My lips are sealed." Though she tried, Gyllis couldn't stifle her giggle and it blew through her nose. "Though I must admit, he is very good at kissing." She could never tell Helen what had transpired—heaven strike her dead, she'd actually gone to Sean's chamber and seduced *him*. She hadn't ceased spinning her rosary around in her pocket, reciting Hail Mary's at all hours—while throwing in praises of thanksgiving every now and again.

Helen placed her hand on Gyllis's arm. "I'm happy for you, but tell me, when is he planning to speak to Duncan?"

"As soon as the marriage business is finished with the Lord of Lorn, and after Mother returns from your wedding. I need Ma's support if Duncan launches into one of his rages."

Helen rubbed her palms together. "I could mention something to Ma on the journey to Ardnamurchan. At least it will give us something interesting to talk about."

Gyllis thought for a moment. She hadn't said anything to Mother about Sean because she couldn't decide how to broach the subject. But if Helen planted a seed, it might make her task all the easier. "Perhaps if you mention that Sir Sean gave me the crutches and paid a visit or two to Ardchattan during my confinement."

"Exactly my thoughts, too. Besides Mother isn't blind. She knows you admire him."

Gyllis cringed. "She just doesn't know how much."

A rap came at the door and in walked two groomsmen. "We're here to take your trunks to the wagon. Are you ready, Miss Helen?"

Her poor sister turned as white as bed linen. She cast a worried glance at Gyllis then gestured to her things. "I'm all packed. I shall be down in a moment."

The sisters stood and watched the men haul away the first trunk while Gyllis couldn't stop thinking it should be she who was traveling west to meet and marry a strange man. Her throat grew thick and her palms moist. "I wish you didn't have to go," she whispered.

Helen straightened. "It will be fine. 'Tis time for me to marry and Mother will be there to ensure all progresses well."

The remnants of Gyllis's euphoria sank to the bottom of her toes. "You will write as soon as you are able?"

"Of course, and you will send word when your wedding date is announced?"

"I will." She forced a smile. "And I'll expect you to be there."

"I wouldn't miss it for the world."

"'Tis settled then." Gyllis tried to hold in her tears, but one dribbled from her eye anyway. She tugged Helen into an embrace. "Hug me now whilst no one can see me weep."

Her sister's body shuddered as a woeful wail burst through her lips. "I...I..."

Gyllis couldn't hold it in. She patted Helen's back and tried to regain control. "Everything will be all right."

With a stuttered inhale, Helen clung tighter.

"A wedding is a happy occasion and you shall be lady of the keep, just as you've always wished."

Helen pulled away, her eyes and nose red. She drew in a staccato breath and nodded while she dabbed her face with a kerchief. "I'd best be off before my tears set the bed afloat."

Gyllis also dried her eyes. "Come. I'll see you off."

***

Sean had no opportunity to visit Gyllis again before the day of Lorn's wedding arrived. Earlier that morning, he and his men, reinforced by a dozen MacGregors, fanned out through the forest surrounding Dunstaffnage Chapel and found nothing out of place. Things were also quiet in the village surrounding the castle.

The locals had a healthy respect for the Lord of Lorn. As the king's emissary, he provided them with land to till or graze.

The boats moored in Loch Etive were all owned either by local fishermen, or were part of Lorn's retinue, having sailed down from Lorn's Castle Stalker to the north. Angus reported no sign of Alan MacCoul or any of the foul men who followed him. Nonetheless, Sean did not don his ceremonial armor. He met the Lord of Lorn in the king's chamber wearing battle armor.

Lorn, who was wearing an ornate coat of blackened ceremonial armor, gave Sean a quizzical look. "Are you expecting a fight?"

Sean bowed. "I figured it best to be prepared for anything, uncle."

Lorn patted his shoulder. "You're a good lad."

A long breath whistled through Sean's lips. He didn't expect anything to go awry, but Fraser's death weighed heavily on his conscience. "Sentries are posted atop the battlements as usual and I have a contingent of fifty men surrounding the chapel."

"You did take me seriously," Lorn chuckled. "You've a mob of brigands guarding the chapel? What will my guests think?"

"They're hardly brigands." Sean pulled his helm over his head and pushed up the visor. "Would you rather not be well guarded?"

Lorn studied himself in the looking glass. "I asked you to provide security for my wedding, not to invite an army to it."

Perhaps Sean had overreacted. "Shall I have them stand down?"

Lorn squinted. "You say you've scoured the forest?"

"Aye."

"And the pier?"

"Not a galley moored that isn't accounted for."

The old man batted his hand through the air. "Then there's little for which to be concerned. Send your army home and keep a few steadfast guards."

Sean knew better than to abandon all security. Aye, most of their work had been done, but to send the guard back to Dunollie would be folly. "You must be jesting. How am I to insure your safety?"

"You're the best man with a blade I know." Lorn appeared too relaxed—perhaps indulged in a tad too much whisky before donning his armor. "I do not want a cohort of men surrounding the chapel—it will look more like we're attending a hanging than a wedding."

Sean didn't like it. Bloody hell, the man first asked him to provide security and then told him to send his men away. *Ballocks to that.*

Sean excused himself and found Angus in the great hall. "Lorn wants the guard hidden."

"Pardon?" The man-at-arms nearly spat out his teeth with the force of his P.

"You heard me. He said to send our men home, but we didn't scour the forest to walk away and let our enemies move into place." Sean lowered his voice. "I've not informed him about Fraser."

Angus held up his hands. "So what do you want me to do?"

"Tell the men to pull back—stay out of sight, all except a few. I want two guards at the chapel doors and escorts for Lorn and his bride along the path from the castle."

Angus scratched his head. "Sounds like a lot of work for nothing. Where do you want me?"

"Lead the men in the forest. Remain mounted. If you hear the ram's horn, you'll ken what to do."

"Aye, I bloody well ken what to do—ring Lorn's neck. 'Tis a dangerous game he plays."

"I do not like it either, but he's our lord and master."

"Aye and soon his daft son, Dugald, will be lording over us."

Sean clamped his gauntleted hand on Angus's shoulder. "Dugald Stewart is Lorn's flesh and blood. 'Tis past time he was given his due."

Angus's expression grew dark. "He's a bastard, just like..." He pursed his lips and shook his head. "Och, bugger it."

Sean puzzled while he watched his henchman march out the doors. Though a fine warrior, Angus allowed himself to grow emotional about things that shouldn't concern him. So Lorn wanted to legitimize his only son? As far as Sean was concerned, the Stewart lord should have done it sooner.

After Sean rejoined the wedding party, they started for the castle with a small, but respectable assembly of knights. "Where is Dugald, m'lord?" Sean asked.

"He's already at the chapel with his mother." Lorn's eyes sparked with pride. "I thought it would be best if he stood up for her."

"Good thinking." Sean gestured toward the door. "Shall we proceed?"

Once they exited the barbican bridge, the hair on Sean's nape stood on end. His gaze shifted across the scene. He'd been a warrior too long to ignore the familiar warning. As they neared the chapel, sweat burned his underarms, a prickling sensation skittering across his skin. Sean grasped the hilt of his sword.

The townspeople lined the path, shaded by birch and oak trees. An anxious hum filled the air, akin to a beehive. All were eager to see the Lord of Lorn in his regalia. They placed flowers and flung rose petals before him, shouting congratulations and good tidings.

But still, that damned prickling needled at Sean's neck.

Everything slowed. He looked right, then left. His steady breathing rushed in his ears. The sound of Lorn's voice registered, but Sean couldn't make out the words. Due to the clamminess of his skin, for a moment he thought he might have contracted an illness.

When the chapel door came into view, Sean stared at the guards posted outside it. They wore MacDougall colors with hauberks beneath and great helms atop their heads. He squinted—true, a number of his men possessed bucket-shaped helms, but Angus would have instructed them to remove them for this wedding duty. Such helms were worn on the battlefield alone.

"Did you hear me?" Lorn asked.

"Pardon, m'lord." Sean blinked and shook his head. "I was assessing my men."

"Me as well." He pointed at the guards. "I daresay you are frightening my guests with this display of mettle."

Sean ground his back molars. "Apologies. I'll have them remove their helms after you've moved inside."

"Aye? I'm sure that will make a fine impression once everyone is out of sight." Lorn's sarcasm was palpable.

"At least you will be wed knowing you are safe. I did not take your request lightly." A bead of sweat drained into Sean's eye.

Two paces before they reached the door, the guard nearest Sean shifted his battleax across his body—a defensive pose. Sean squinted at the eyes flickering under the concealing helm—eyes filled with hate. His gut clamped into a solid ball as he drew his sword. The guard advanced. Stepping in front of Lorn, Sean shielded the earl with his body and deflected a downward blow. Those eyes still glared at him with evil intent.

Sean's attacker moved with lightning speed. With a swing of his sword, he met the battleax midair, slicing it in two. From his sleeves, the guard pulled two knives and advanced with the screech of a madman. Swinging his blade in an arc, Sean defended the attack, protecting Lorn's right flank. He prayed to God, someone had the earl's left. Around them, grunts of the fight escalated. Iron clanged to the rear and to his sides. Unable to avert his gaze, Sean defended the attack as knives slashed at his face.

Beside him, Lorn dropped, a hideous scream ripping through the air. Bellowing like a warrior, Sean swung his blade in an arc, cutting through the neck sinews of his attacker. The helm flew from the young man's head. *Gawen. A traitor after all.*

Afforded a heartbeat to assess the battle, what Sean had seen through his side vision was confirmed. The Lord of Lorn clutched at his gut, blood streaming through his fingers.

"Sound the alarm!" Sean bellowed while he watched his men as they were cut down by an army that appeared from nowhere.

"Bring the priest. I will be wed before I draw my last breath," Lorn wheezed.

Sean raced for the doors as a blow came from his right. Slamming the pommel of his dirk into his attacker's skull, he continued on. The priest opened the door with Lorn's bride. Her face contorted with fear as she looked past the holy man's shoulder.

"I've killed the tyrant lord and now MacDougall will be mine!" From behind, MacCoul's rasping voice attacked Sean's every nerve.

His worst fears confirmed—the bastard had warned him with Fraser's gruesome delivery.

"Recite the vows now. My son will be my heir!" Lorn shouted.

Sean spun to face the scourge who had plagued his every waking hour. The bastard who cared only for ruination, for destruction.

The priest's Latin chants rang above the maelstrom, but Sean couldn't stop. For an instant, Sean caught sight of MacCoul's beady eyes glaring at him beneath the eye slits in the hideous helm. The bastard raised his sword and advanced on the bleeding and wounded lord.

Clenching his teeth, Sean launched himself at MacCoul, slamming his feet into his chest, knocking him from completing a blow intended to sever Lorn's head.

The blackguard skittered backward, but Sean didn't hesitate. Rage propelling him forward, he advanced with relentless hacks of his blade.

Alan defended each blow, weakening with every strike. Sean would show no quarter this time. The menace would pay with his life. Alan fell to his backside. Sean pounced, pulling his blade up for the killing thrust.

A crack blasted in his ears, reverberating in his helm. The world shattered. Sean's eyes rolled back as bitter bile burned his throat. His failing arms worked to continue with his strike, but his knees buckled before his blade connected with MacCoul's neck.

As he hit ground, everything grew peaceful, quiet and black.

***

Alan MacCoul laughed out loud when Sean MacDougall dropped to the earth. Most of the guests stood around them, cowering with looks of horror on their faces. The pummeling of horse hooves shook the ground.

Alan's gaze darted to the miserable Lord of Lorn, surrounded by guardsmen, taking his vows. *One plan thwarted. At least the maggot won't see out the night. I'll deal with his sniveling offspring later.*

"Riders," Brus yelled, his voice echoing from beneath his great helm.

Trevor sprinted up, leading the horses. "Make haste."

Alan grasped MacDougall under the arms. "Help me heft him."

Brus kicked the Dunollie chieftain. "Do you think he's dead?"

Alan strained with Sean's weight. "I'll take no chances." He picked up MacDougall's sword and secured it in his belt.

Together the three men draped MacDougall's body over a horse. "Quickly. They'll be upon us before we can blink."

Alan and his band of renegades mounted and raced for Dunstaffnage's barbican.

Behind them, Angus urged his men faster.

Alan clutched MacDougall's reins tightly in his fist. *The miserable bastard had best not be dead. He hasn't suffered enough.*

He buried his spurs deep into his horse's barrel demanding more speed. Glancing over his shoulder, his gut clenched. Angus and the MacDougall army were gaining. Alan squinted against the wind whistling through his eye slits. The iron teeth of the portcullis loomed ahead, but if it didn't close quickly, they'd have another battle on their hands. He could make it. "Lower the gate," he bellowed. "Now!"

While he surged forward, he pulled the trailing horse alongside him. MacDougall's body bounced and listed sideways. The cogs of the portcullis groaned and creaked to life as the teeth of the deadly gate inched downward. Alan dug in his heels and plastered his body against his mount's neck. An iron spike scraped the back plate of his armor with a screech.

Once they cleared, the guardsmen let the gate drop with a resounding boom. Alan looked back. Angus and the MacDougall guards reined their horses to a halt. Alan motioned to an archer on the battlements.

The guard pointed his bow high and let his arrow soar. Alan grinned. Then his laugh thundered in his helm. His plan had been executed flawlessly—except for Lorn. But Alan would solve that minor detail at a later date. At least Dugald Stewart was a sniveling maggot who deserved to be a bastard.

All in all, he had won. While the miserable wedding party processed, his men had slipped in and taken Dunstaffnage Castle from under MacDougall's nose. Soon all would know the truth and Alan would become the rightful Chieftain of Dunollie. *And once Dugald has been dispatched, the king will grant me the Lordship of Lorn.*

Alan's men dismounted in Dunstaffnage's inner bailey and removed their helms. Shoving them in the air, the cry of victory echoed between the old castle walls.

Alan's throat tightened, though he forced a frown. He dismounted. "We're not finished yet. Is the blacksmith ready?"

"Aye, m'lord," said Trevor, bowing deeply.

"Brus, you're in charge of the siege until my return. Trevor, bring two strong men and come with me. MacDougall weighs more than a pregnant heifer."

A burly warrior stepped forward. "I'll carry him, m'lord."

Alan smirked and assessed the man's form. "I like a man with ambition. Follow me."

Heading toward the last phase of his coup, Alan led a small group of men as they slipped out a long forgotten sea gate and into a waiting *birlinn*.

Chapter Twenty-Two

Sean's head throbbed as if his skull had been bludgeoned on the inside. He tried to open his eyes, but the slightest movement tortured him with relentless pounding. Everything hurt. Points of his flesh ached like he was resting on a bed of iron rivets. He shivered against the cold. The air smelled of dirt and rotting seaweed. Water dripped in the distance.

Am I in a dungeon?

The thought made his head throb so badly, his stomach churned. Sean swallowed, another movement that made him wish for death. If the banging inside his head grew any worse, it would kill him for certain.

Though the air was dank, his lips were chapped, his mouth dry. *How long have I been unconscious?*

A light flashed and a vision of a battle passed through Sean's mind. The last he remembered, he'd been in a cutthroat fight to save Lorn. *The earl was stabbed, but called for the priest.*

A drop of water splashed on Sean's nose. Sniffing, he tried to move his hand, but his arm hit cold iron. His eyes flashed open. Iron bars blocked his view. He again tried to move his arm—turn his head, but he couldn't move. Even his legs were encased in irons. Nervous sweat oozed across his skin. *My God, wake me from this nightmare.*

A contemptible laugh echoed off the walls and increased the pounding in Sean's head. His skin crawled. Only one man had such a distasteful, grating rasp to his voice. *Alan MacCoul.*

"I wondered if you would give me the satisfaction of waking."

Sean's jaw tightened as he focused his glare on the dark figure sitting across from him.

"It would have been rather disappointing if you had died before I had my say."

"You'll hang for this," Sean growled through clenched teeth, his vision blurring with every throb of his skull.

Alan smirked. "I think not."

"You've murdered the Lord of Lorn."

"Aye." Alan looked at his fingernails. "But not before he managed to make that miserable lout his heir."

"Dugald was his firstborn."

Alan sniffed. "Och aye, how valiant of John Stewart to recognize his bastard son before he drew his last breath."

Sean clenched his fist—at least the irons provided enough room for one simple motion. So, Alan had been successful with his attempt to kill the earl? Evidently the slimy maggot had more than one score to settle. Sean forced down his urge to heave and shifted his eyes to scan his surroundings. This was not a dungeon, it was a bloody cave. "Where are we?"

"On my father's miserable island. The place where he wanted me to settle and raise a flock of sheep. Kerrera."

"Your father?" *He kens who his father is?* Sean's mind engaged. "But Kerrera is Dunollie land."

"Aye, and unofficially given to me by *our* father. The louse couldn't even bother to make a grant of land legal."

Sean closed his eyes and tried to shake his head, only to be met with cold iron rivets stabbing his temples. "Did you say *our*?"

"You miserable wretch." Alan prodded Sean in the ribs with a stick. "Our father never recognized me as the firstborn son. For years I stood by and watched him mollycoddle you, give you the best of everything whilst I was doled out the scraps. The bastard was even too embarrassed to recognize my birthright on his deathbed."

"I didn't—"

"Of course you didn't. You were always too wrapped up in your own spoilt self to give a damn about anything or anyone. I stood by and watched you learn to ride the finest horses whilst I was given a nag. You had the finest clothes, the finest weapons, and I received a bent sword thrown out by one of Father's guards." Alan held up the Chieftain of Dunollie's sword. "But this one I shall keep for myself."

Sean swallowed. He had a brother? But Alan had gone too far, blood kin or nay. He attempted to move his arms, but was held back by riveted irons digging into his flesh. "Why did you not tell me?"

An ugly chuckle resounded between the cave walls bringing back Sean's headache full force. "Me? Tell you we're kin? Oh no. You need to pay for all your years of tyranny—all of Father's favors—every last farthing in the Dunollie coffers." Alan poked him again. Sean's ribs throbbed. How long had MacCoul been jabbing him with that stick? "When you cut off my funds, you tore away the last shred of my...ah...*affection*."

Sean closed his eyes and grimaced. *Angus and Murdach knew.* But something was still amiss. Alan had attacked him before Sean uncovered the missing coin. "You are the lowest of whoresons. I cannot believe Angus and Murdach conspired with you."

The bastard had the gall to laugh again. "You're jesting. Those miserable sops wouldn't assuage their loyalty to Dunollie for all the coin in Scotland."

So they were protecting Father. "How did you slip past the Dunollie guard?"

Alan smirked. "Your pitiful guard." He threw his head back and howled. "I've a loyal man or two within your ranks."

"Gawen."

"Aye," he chuckled. "Wearing great helms and your colors, not even Angus knew the difference." Alan raised his damned stick, but hesitated. "I'd have been able to take Dunstaffnage much more easily if Angus wasn't such a loyal prick."

In a burst of rage, Sean rattled the irons with all his strength. "You traitor!" he roared. "You've taken Dunstaffnage?" If only he could grab that stick and shove it down the bastard's throat. What more was this monster accountable for? *I'll hang every single backstabber in my ranks.*

"Aye and next I'll take Dunollie." Alan leaned over, his nose so close, the man's foul breath seeped across Sean's face. "Once word of the lands denied me reaches his royal highness, he'll have no recourse but to name me Chieftain of Dunollie and Lord of Lorn."

Coughing against the stench, Sean glared. "You've gone completely mad." *King James will never grant lands to a bastard—especially one who used force to seize the king's property.*

Alan probed with the stick—harder this time. "Angry as hell, but not mad, brother."

Sean closed his eyes and swallowed his urge to bellow. MacCoul had not only proven he was a raving lunatic, he was capable of the most heinous crimes imaginable. Sean's back sunk into cold iron rivets. Though unable to move his head, he knew the trickles sliding down his skin were blood. "So 'tis the death of a lowlife for me, then?"

Sean kept his voice steady, but inside he wanted to bellow, wring the cur's neck and tell him exactly what he thought of his miserable coup.

"'Tis what you deserve." The cold stare in MacCoul's black eyes made Sean shudder.

If there was one thing he couldn't stand, it was being cosseted—a mummy wrapped in iron. Again he shuddered. A blend of sweat and blood oozed from his temple to his mouth. He had to get out. He clenched every muscle in his body and stared. He hated to utter kind words to a madman, but it was Sean's last hope. "Release me now and together we will rule Dunollie lands." He forced a smile. "Think on it. Together we'll be more powerful than our ancestors. We'll take back the Lordship of the Isles and rule the Highlands."

Alan smirked. "I've an army of two hundred, and every day more fighting men frustrated with our weakling king come to me begging for a place in my guard."

Christ, things grew worse with Alan's every word. Sean clenched his teeth against the throbbing pain and strained with all his might to break the irons. God in heaven, he needed to ring Alan's bloody neck. "You'll never get away with this," he seethed.

When Alan stood, Sean focused on the sword in Alan's belt—the same one he was given at their father's funeral. "Well, little brother." The bastard whacked the stick over the top of Sean's head, splintering it on the irons. "You won't be around to witness my success. Everyone saw me spirit your body into Dunstaffnage Castle. Little did they know I uncovered an ancient sea gate on the firth side."

Stars clouding his vision, his heart could have exploded. The bastard intended to leave him for a rat's feast? Sean strained his arms against the welded irons encasing them. He fought and jerked his entire body, but the welds held firm.

Alan stood back and crossed his arms. "Fight all you like. The smithy made your cage impenetrable. You *will* die here." He set a cup of water beyond Sean's reach. "Be it from thirst or starvation, I do not much care, as long as your death is a painful one."

Ice pulsed through Sean's veins. Death gibbeted by irons was the most torturous demise imaginable. Buzzards would peck out his eyes before he succumbed, rats would feast upon his flesh. "You wouldn't," he hissed through clenched teeth.

Alan threw the broken stick against the cave wall and strode away, the rumble of his laugh crawling up Sean's skin.

He drew in gasps of breath while he turned his head side to side, inhibited by strips of iron. God on the cross, even Alan wouldn't stoop so low. "Give me a knight's death! Please brother, if you have a soul, you will not leave me to face the vilest coward's death!"

Sean strained with all his might but the irons budged not an inch. Sweat streamed into his eyes and across his flesh. His lips trembled with every sharp inhale. He fought again, this time, the rivets stabbing him with unyielding bites.

"You cannot leave me here!"

***

Gyllis responded so well to Meg's warm compresses that two days ago she'd started walking without assistance. She'd taken to forcing herself to climb the tower steps to the wall-walk and pacing around the battlements. The ascent was strenuous, but every day the effort grew a wee bit easier. From the top of Kilchurn's walls, Gyllis could see for miles, spotting riders by land or boats approaching down the long and narrow Loch Awe.

She'd hoped Sean would have paid a visit at least one more time before the Lord of Lorn's wedding, but she understood how a chieftain must attend his responsibilities. She clapped her hands together and held her fingers to her lips with a smile. He'd be so impressed with her progress. She had a horrible limp, but one day she would grow so strong no one would ever know she'd suffered paralysis.

Amid one of her daily walks, Gyllis strode along the back of the castle wall-walk, which had a glorious view of Loch Awe. When the ram's horn sounded, she snapped her head toward the lead guard positioned on the wall across the courtyard, but she couldn't see beyond the stone battlements. Running her hand over the merlon notches, she hastened her pace. By the time she reached the front of the castle, she gasped to catch her breath.

Patting her chest with her hand, she peered down the long path that led from the west to the castle. *Sean!* Horses cantered with haste, flying the Dunollie pennant. Gyllis couldn't make out the riders, but there was no need. Sean had come at last.

She raced for the stairwell. Her toe caught on a raised edge of stone. Flinging her arms out, Gyllis grabbed the craggy stone to stop her momentum. Her fingers latched onto the battlement ledge while her body flailed midair. Clenching her teeth, she prepared herself for the jarring impact.

An arm wrapped around her waist as thick chainmail cut into her back. "'Tis probably best not to try to run yet, lassie," a gruff voice said.

Firm hands gripped her shoulders and Gyllis glanced up. Sir Mevan smiled upon her with his careworn face. "My thanks."

He knit his thick eyebrows together. "Where are your crutches?"

"I've no longer a need for them."

He eyed her like a concerned father. "Then you must take care. It hasn't been all that long since I carried you to your chamber stricken with the first symptoms of paralysis."

She bowed her head and curtsied. "Thank you for reminding me. I shall exercise more care in the future." Her heart fluttered so fast, she hated to think of slowing her pace before she reached the bottom of the tower stairs. If only she could speed her recovery even more.

Mevan waved her away and Gyllis limped to the stairwell, using the wall for balance. When finally she arrived in the great hall, Duncan was escorting Angus and a few other Dunollie guardsmen into his solar. She knit her brows and stared at the keep's double doors. Surely Sean would be among them. Discounting her idea to go to the courtyard and look for Sean's horse, she hastened to the solar door.

The voices within were filled with muffled turmoil. She pressed her ear to the door to better hear them.

"'Tis grave indeed m'lord." Angus's weathered baritone was clearer now.

"The Lord of Lorn is murdered and the Chieftain of Dunollie captured?" Duncan's voice asked.

Gyllis clapped a hand over her mouth to muffle her gasp. *Sean captured? Lorn dead?* She couldn't breathe.

"Aye. All of Dunstaffnage is under siege."

My God, could it be worse?

"I never on my life thought MacCoul had the wherewithal to follow through with his threats," Duncan said. "The piss-swilling whoreson."

"Not even Sir Sean's father would have been able to turn a blind eye to Alan's treachery now."

"What say you?" Duncan asked. "Sean's complaints of his father turning a blind eye are founded?"

"Aye, m'lord."

"But why the devil did the old man allow it?"

"Laird Alan MacDougall swore me to secrecy with his last breath…Please m'lord, consider his given name. If you think on it, you cannot help but guess."

After a long moment of silence, Gyllis pressed her ear harder. Mother stepped beside her with an alarmed look and did the same.

"By God," Duncan said. "Alan MacDougall sired a bastard?"

"An elder bastard—one blind with rage and hell-bent on revenge." Footsteps clamored toward the door. "We've no time to waste. We must away to Dunstaffnage at once."

Gyllis clutched her arms around her midsection when the door opened, her eyes wide, the two women facing Duncan's grim stare. Her gaze darted from her brother to Angus. "W-where is Sir Sean?"

Duncan marched past them. "This doesn't concern you."

"Och aye, it does." Gyllis limped beside him with Mother right behind. "I love him. I-I must go to him at once."

Duncan pointed to Mevan. "Assemble the guard. We leave within the hour." Then he grasped Gyllis's shoulders. "You and I will have words about the source of your ill-grown feelings upon my return."

"You cannot leave me here." She pushed Duncan's hands away. "I must go."

"I ken you're not daft, sister. What good would a crippled woman be amongst an army of Campbell men?"

"But—"

"I said no," he bellowed. "Your place is here with your mother. Do not make me confine you to quarters."

Ma patted Gyllis's shoulder. "Come, dear, be reasonable. You must leave the fighting to the men."

Gyllis clapped a hand over her mouth. Locked in her chamber, she could be of no use to Sean. Worse, she'd be in the dark with no news of the siege. She threw a pleading glance at Angus. "Will Sir Sean be all right?"

The henchman shook his head, his eyes filled with fear. "I've no idea if he's even still alive, miss."

Gasping, Gyllis could have jumped out of her skin. Tears stung her eyes and rolled down her cheeks. Sean was in trouble and she was forbidden to go to him? Surely she could be of help. Somehow. No one could expect her to remain behind. "Duncan, please. I can cook, or mend or…or be a healer." Her head spun. "I've been tended to so much these past months, I've had a lifetime of education in the healing arts."

Mother grasped Gyllis's arm and pulled her toward the stairwell.

"This cannot be happening." She snapped her gaze to Ma's face. "If Alan captured Sean, he'll kill him."

She couldn't breathe. The room started spinning.

"Fetch Lady Meg," Mother shouted at a serving maid. "Tell her Gyllis needs a calming tincture."

"I do not!" Gyllis wrenched her arm away. Sobbing, she attempted to dash after Duncan, but her knees gave out and she fell, sprawling over the floorboards. "Blast my weakness!" The world was shattering around her and her miserable legs were too weak to withstand it.

Mother crouched beside Gyllis and patted her back. "I ken how worried you are, but Duncan is right. The men will face Alan MacCoul and rescue Sir Sean."

"But what if he's already *dead?*" The words caught in her throat as if placed there by Satan. An uncontrollable whimper seeped through her clenched teeth. Every extremity shook. This couldn't be happening. Sean had to be all right.

Offering her hand, Mother helped Gyllis up. "If Alan MacCoul kills Sir Sean, he is more of a fool than the lot of us believe. He'll have nothing with which to bargain."

"He may very well be a fool." Gyllis grasped her mother's arm and together the two women staggered up the stairs. "The man is consumed by hate."

Once inside her chamber, Gyllis still couldn't breathe. "How can you appear so calm? Sir Sean has been a part of this family for years."

Mother gestured to the settee. "It is not that I choose to do nothing. Our role is to wait and pray for not only the Chieftain of Dunollie's health, but for a quick victory by Duncan and our men so they all return home to their families." She sat. "Where is Meg with that tincture?"

Gyllis's limp became more pronounced as she paced. "I do not need a mind-numbing tonic." What she needed was to be on a horse heading west.

"Sit down before you fall," Mother ordered, her tone growing irritated. She patted the seat beside her. "Come. Let us read *The Wedding of Sir Gawain and Dame Ragnelle*. You've told me so much about it, I'm anxious to hear the story for myself."

Gyllis plopped beside Ma. "I cannot possibly read at a time like this."

"Perhaps if I read, the story will help calm you."

Gyllis clamped her mouth shut and nodded. She was about to jump out of her skin and Ma wanted to read?

"You are smitten with Sir Sean," Mother said, as if she'd just figured it out, but Gyllis knew better than to think her mother dim-witted. And the matron had only returned from Helen's wedding last eve. Helen had promised to hint at Gyllis's yen to marry Sean, but Ma was shrewd and Gyllis had best play along. Besides, the woman knew everything that went on under Kilchurn's eaves. If a pin dropped, Ma would know about it.

"I care for him. I always have." Since Sean had not approached Duncan about their engagement, she wouldn't make such a confession now.

"And he cares for you," Mother said. "I am still surprised to know he had your crutches made. I must speak to Duncan about..." her voice trailed off.

Gyllis chanced a glance in Mother's direction. "About?"

Ma batted her hand through the air. "'Tis nothing. This mess with Mr. MacCoul must be settled first. Come, read to me."

Before Gyllis opened the book, Meg rushed in, carrying a cup and pitcher. "My heavens. I came as soon as the twins were settled."

Gyllis held up her hands. "I do not need a tincture. Ma was overreacting."

"I should say not." Meg poured a cup of her potion. "You must be worried to death. Take this—you'll feel much better."

Gyllis took the cup and grimaced. "I honestly would prefer—"

"Drink it," Mother commanded. "We all could use a tot. The lot of us are worried half to death."

Chapter Twenty-Three

Gyllis had no idea what time it was when she woke. Meg's tincture had her dozing before she finished reading the first page of *The Wedding of Sir Gawain and Dame Ragnelle*. From her bed, she peered around her chamber. The others must have made it to their rooms because she was alone.

After lighting the candle, Gyllis slipped out of bed, her toes hitting cold floorboards. It didn't make a difference that they were in the midst of summer, night air still brought a chill. She gathered the plaid from the foot of her bed and lumbered toward the window embrasure. Pulling aside the furs, a moonbeam glistened blue-white on Loch Awe.

She strained for a glimpse of the eastern sky. From what she could tell, it was close to midnight. The sun wouldn't make an appearance for some time. Dropping the curtain, she rubbed her eyes to clear her head from the poppy juice or whatever it was Meg had drugged her with.

She clutched the plaid tighter around her body and faced the door.

Then a clammy sensation of dread spread across her skin, so powerful, it was as if a ghost had passed over her soul.

Gyllis froze.

"I will imprison you in irons and laugh while your body rots in a dank cave." The vow Alan swore when Sean defeated him at Beltane rang so clear in her mind, it was as if she'd heard the words spoken aloud right there in her bedchamber.

Had Alan been planning this even before Sean's father passed? She clenched her fists. *Will Duncan remember? I may limp, but I have a strong mind and I know of no one with a more determined will.*

But traveling alone during the day was dangerous. Who knew how much more perilous the twenty-mile trip would be at night...and for a woman.

At once she knew what must be done.

Gyllis hastened to her dressing table and quickly braided her hair. She could not allow anything to impede her determination this time or she'd never spirit past the gate.

After donning a pair of sturdy boots, she cast the plaid aside. Not even bothering to wrap herself in a dressing gown, she headed for Duncan's chamber.

Gyllis cracked open the door and peered inside. The room was so dim, she could scarcely make out the four poster bed, but she heard breathing. Since they'd been wed, Lady Meg had taken to staying in Duncan's chamber. They used the adjoining "lady's" bedchamber for a nursery.

Slipping inside, Gyllis held up her candle and stared at the bed, watching for any sign of movement. She didn't dare shut the door. A click of the hasp could ruin her plans. As quietly as she could, she tiptoed to the trunk where Duncan stowed his things, and set the candle on a nearby table.

The flame didn't cast much light and the contents of the trunk were dark as a dungeon. Sliding her hands over the clothing on top, then down the sides, grainy leather brushed her fingertips. *Breeks*. Her heart leapt as she tugged the trousers from beneath the pile. Holding them out, she stepped into the legs, shoving her shift through the waistband. When she released, the breeks slipped low around her hips. *Still too large.*

She turned toward the candle and examined the waistline. A cord swung, catching the light. *If only I had more experience with men's garments.* She found a matching cord on the other side and tied the breeks snugly around her waist. It felt awkward to have the bulk of her shift scrunched about her hips, but at least the linen filled up some of the extra space. She'd never realized how much larger Duncan was.

Her eyes adjusting to the dim light, she had an easier time locating a linen shirt—right on top. She pulled it over her head then tugged the laces closed and looked down. The shirt was large enough to hide her bosoms for the most part—and she couldn't spare the time to bind them. With one last dip into the trunk, she found one of Duncan's quilted doublets. By the musty smell, it had been well worn, but would help conceal her form. She shrugged into the oversized garment and rolled up the sleeves to her wrists.

Once assembled, she inspected her attire and pointed a toe to the side. *I think this will do. Now all I need is a hood.* She drummed her fingers against her lips. If only she'd kept her plaid. She'd never seen Duncan wear a hood. He either wore a feathered bonnet as a sign of his barony, or a helm. She picked up the candle and searched inside the trunk one more time, but found nothing resembling a hood.

Biting her lip, she turned toward the bed. Lady Meg lay on her side with the bedclothes pulled up to her chin.

All Gyllis needed to do was walk across the floor and pull the plaid from the footboard.

Easy enough.

Taking her first steps proved awkward. She'd never worn a pair of breeks before. The leather chafed her inner thighs. With her next footfall, her ankle twisted. She stumbled toward the bed, but caught herself before she fell. Had that happened a sennight ago, she would have fallen for certain.

Gyllis held her breath and peered at Lady Meg. By God's grace, the woman remained sound asleep. Drawing in a calming breath, Gyllis picked up the plaid, bundled it under her arm and headed for the passageway.

She'd nearly made it to the door when a floorboard creaked loud enough to wake the dead.

Behind her, the bed rattled and Meg gasped. "Who's there?" she clipped in a high-pitched voice.

Gyllis stopped and glanced back.

Sitting up, Meg had the bedclothes clutched under her chin. "Gyllis? What are you doing?"

"Nothing—go back to sleep."

"Why are you wearing breeks?"

Gyllis inched toward the door. "Please, just ignore me."

"Are those Duncan's?" Meg crawled across the bed. "What are you planning? I ken that look on your face."

With a groan, Gyllis shook out the plaid and draped it over her head. "I cannot sit in my chamber and wait for news of Sir Sean. The worry alone will kill me."

"You're not planning to spirit to Dunstaffnage by yourself?"

"What else can I do?"

Meg crossed her arms and affected a disapproving frown. "'Tis dangerous."

"If anyone in this entire household would understand, 'tis you. Goodness, I remember when you drugged your guard to help Duncan escape from Edinburgh gaol."

She tsked her tongue. "Aye, but that was different."

"Was it?" Gyllis spread her palm to her side. "How can you say that? Do you know how much I love Sean? Remaining in my chamber is torture. I've no idea if he's injured or…or, I can't say it. If I do nothing I will go completely mad."

Meg slid off the bed and walked toward her. "If you must go, you should take a guard."

"Why, so he can lock me in my chamber—listen to Duncan and Mother's every word?"

"Heaven's stars. You should look at yourself. You've been ill for so long." Her eyes dropped to Gyllis's legs. "You still have a limp—still weak."

Meg's words only served to cement Gyllis's determination. Everyone would cite her illness as reason for her to be cosseted in her chamber. No one would allow her the freedom she needed. She reached for Meg's deformed hand—*the claw*, she called it. "Of all others in this family who should be able to sympathize with me, 'tis you." Meg had been mollycoddled by her family and feared by society because of her hand.

Meg tugged her claw away and rubbed it. "Will you not wait until morning?"

"Nay. I cannot risk someone seeing me."

"Very well." Meg took Gyllis's candle and headed toward the garderobe. "Then I will go with you."

Gyllis hobbled after her. She wouldn't make it far without that candle. "What about the bairns? You cannot leave."

Meg stepped into a kirtle and began tying the laces. "It shan't be but for a few days. The nurse will look after Elizabeth and Colin. Besides, this gives me an excuse to see Duncan—he may need a healer—and he's been away ever so much during my confinement."

"Oh no, I cannot in good conscience approve of this. What if something happened to you? Duncan would never forgive me."

Meg pulled a cloak over her shoulders. "Either we go together or I raise the alarm now."

"You are wicked." Gyllis clapped a hand to her chest. "I'd die if you were hurt. How can I convince you to stay?"

"You cannot." Meg tugged another black cloak from a peg. "This is Duncan's. It'll be more concealing than that plaid you've got draped over your head. Put it on whilst I pen a missive to Lady Margaret. If we go without leaving word, she'll send all of Argyllshire after us."

Gyllis hadn't thought to leave a note, but she wondered if Mother wouldn't send an army to bring them back regardless. But then, Duncan was surrounded by his elite guard and Gyllis couldn't worry about Ma's reaction now. She would not return to Kilchurn until Sean was found.

On their way out, Meg insisted they stop by the kitchen and fill a satchel with oatcakes and fetch a flagon of watered wine. What they hadn't counted on was the guard watching them approach the stables.

"What are you doing up at this hour, m'lady?" he asked of Meg, crossing his arms.

Meg's intelligent eyes flashed toward Gyllis. Mayhap it was a blessing Duncan's spirited wife opted to come along. "Fetch Mevan. We've an urgent message for Lord Duncan and need an escort to Dunstaffnage this night."

The man didn't move. "Can you not send a messenger? 'Tis dangerous to travel at night."

"You heard me. I'll not tolerate your impertinence. You will fetch Mevan or I will be forced to do it myself, after which, I will assure you, I'll assign you to the very unsavory task of cleaning the middens."

The guard gave her a good stare and then dropped his arms to his sides. "I'll wake him, m'lady, but he will not be happy about it."

Gyllis waited until the man was out of earshot. "I thought we said no guards. Mevan is liable to wake Mother."

Meg grinned and held up her finger. "He won't if he is with us."

"Now I ken why Duncan says your spirit matches the color of your hair."

After they'd ventured into the stables, Mevan marched in, growling under his breath. "What is this, you need to take a message to Duncan? If you have something urgent to say, it would be best delivered by a messenger."

Lady Meg faced him with her fists on her hips. "I am the lady of this keep and when the lord is away, you will do my bidding. Miss Gyllis and I have business to attend at Dunstaffnage, and that is all you need to know."

The big knight pursed his lips. "Very well. If it cannot wait until morning, you ladies will need spirited horses—ones that can outrun an attack if need be."

Lady Meg bowed her head. "I will leave that to your wisdom. Please select horses you deem suitable."

Mevan looked a bit less grumpy after her acquiescence. But then he assessed Gyllis with a guffaw. "Might I suggest Miss Gyllis remain behind?"

She stepped toward him. "I will not. I can ride far better than I can walk."

Mevan frowned dubiously.

"She must come along," Meg argued. "Now let us saddle the horses."

Gyllis could have slammed her fist into the henchman's big nose. She'd been right to try to slip away without anyone knowing. If Meg weren't there she wouldn't have made it out of the stable. And how dare Mevan look at her as if she were an invalid, of no use whatsoever?

Mevan held up a dagger. "You'd best take this. If anyone makes a go for you, slam it into his wrist like this." He demonstrated with a downward strike.

Gyllis nodded and accepted the knife while Meg armed herself with a bow and quiver of arrows—though she had a crippled hand, Meg was an excellent markswoman, using her "claw" to pull back the bowstring.

Once mounted, Mevan took the lead, holding a torch. "We'll ride at a walk."

Gyllis's mount skittered sideways. The fine-boned colt couldn't be more than two. He whinnied and snorted through his big nostrils. "This fella wants to run."

"Rein him in and he'll follow my warhorse. With luck on our side, we'll disappoint the colt and arrive at Dunstaffnage without incident."

Gyllis kept the horse's head down, and as Mevan said, the colt followed his gelding. Though angry at their slow pace, at least they were on their way, and at this rate, she estimated they'd reach the castle about dawn. Thank heavens Sean had run the outlaws out of Fearnoch Forest. Their journey should be a smooth one.

***

The witching hour, they called it. Gyllis could barely keep her eyes open and the sway of the horse did nothing to help her stay awake. Ahead, Meg was hunched over and Gyllis suspected she was asleep. But Mevan sat tall in the saddle, still holding the torch to light their way.

Fortunately, the moon peeked through the wisps of clouds sailing above to help light the path. The eerie night shrouded the forest with dark blue hues.

He was a good man, Mevan. He'd been loyal to the Campbells for years. Mother never traveled without him. Regardless if he'd questioned Gyllis's abilities, he'd still done their bidding and she formed a new respect for the old henchman.

Something flickered out of the corner of her eye. Gyllis peered into the shadows and squinted. She saw it again—something shiny caught the light from Mevan's torch, perhaps twenty paces away. The more she stared, the clearer it became. Someone was following them. Someone clad in a breastplate with a very large sword.

"Outlaws!" she screeched, demanding a gallop from her horse.

Meg bolted upright and followed.

Mevan glanced back and cast the torch aside. "We'll outrun them," he bellowed.

In the blink of an eye, the trio sped through the wood with Gyllis in the lead. She hoped to God her horse knew the way, because the path was flying past so quickly, she couldn't be sure of each twist and turn.

"Faster!" Mevan bellowed from the rear.

Gyllis slapped her crop against the horse's rump. "Run for your life, you wee beasty!"

The forest thinned and the path became clearer in the moonlight. Gyllis dared a glance behind. Meg was close on her heels, the whites of her eyes round as silver coins. Mevan had replaced the torch with his sword, but Gyllis didn't see the outlaw. No matter, she didn't slow to give the blackguard an opportunity to catch up.

When Gyllis recognized the farmhouse on the outskirts of the village, she slowed her horse to a trot and Mevan rode in beside her. "'Tis safe now, lass."

The sky had turned violet with the coming dawn and the old guard smiled a weathered grin. Gyllis returned his grin. "Thank you, sir knight. Your assistance will not go unrewarded."

He tipped his head. "My reward is your safety, Miss Gyllis. I carried the pails of hot water on the day of your birth whilst your mother labored. You may not be aware of it, but you're as dear to me as my own children."

She stared at his back as he rode ahead and led them into the encampment. Yes, the old guard was a good man and now she knew why her mother trusted him with their lives.

***

After they found Duncan's tent and Meg announced their arrival, Gyllis's brother shoved the flap aside and glared at them both. Gyllis could have sworn a fire flickered in his dark eyes, his black hair mussed by sleep, all the while his face grew redder until his angry stare focused on Meg. "What the devil were you thinking? Why are you here? What about the twins? How could you have ridden all that way in the dark of night?"

Gyllis stammered. "I…we…" did he have to look so exceedingly angry?

"Are those *my* clothes?" Duncan snatched the hem of his—Gyllis's doublet. "Merciful holy Christ—"

"Stop." Meg held up her hands. "If you'd take a breath, I might gain a fleeting moment to explain."

He rolled his hand with a heated, yet expectant look.

"Firstly, the bairns will be fine in their nurse's arms for a few days, especially with your mother's constant doting. Besides, I can be of more use to you here—"

"We must find Sir Sean," Gyllis interrupted.

"Tell me something I do not already know." Duncan's steely gaze shifted her way. "Alan MacCoul has him in Dunstaffnage's dungeon."

Gyllis wrung her hands. "I do not believe so."

Duncan guffawed with his sneer. "So you think you know better than a dozen witnesses? Does wearing my clothing suddenly make you an expert?" He frowned, looking her over from head to toe. "Stay here. I'll fetch the guard to take you home." He started away and shook his finger. "But you'll be taking good men away from their posts."

"We are not leaving," Lady Meg called after him, but he proceeded on, marching like he was mad enough to kick a wounded dog.

Meg grasped Gyllis's arm. "You know something."

She drew in a ragged breath and nodded. "I remembered what Alan MacCoul said when he and Sean fought at Beltane—told him he would watch Sean die in irons whilst rotting in a cave."

"Why did you not tell Duncan?"

"If he'd given me a chance, I would have—but he wouldn't listen anyway. He never listens to me." Gyllis peered over her shoulder. "I must find Angus. He'll help me."

"Go. I'll set Duncan's priorities. Do what you must."

Gyllis caught her hand. "Thank you."

***

The morning's mist had begun to lift while Gyllis hastened through the camp, searching for the MacDougall pennant. She stumbled over an exposed tree root. Stutter-stepping, she tried to catch her balance, but her legs wouldn't work fast enough. With a yelp, she fell hands-first. Pain shot up through her wrists. Clenching her teeth, she rubbed them.

"Bloody Christmas, stumbling over a wee branch?" a deep voice cursed behind her. "Were you in your cups all night, lad?"

Gyllis blinked, remembering she looked more lad than lass. She tugged the hood lower over her forehead. "Nay.

The nasty thing caught the tip of my boot," she said in her deepest voice.

The man walked around front of her, but Gyllis kept her head low and stared at his feet. "You're just a lad. What is your business here? You could be hurt."

"I've a message for Angus, the MacDougall henchman."

"Oh do you now?" The man offered a weathered hand. "Then you best be telling me what it is."

"'Tis only for his ears." As she took his hand, Gyllis peered out from under her hood and gasped.

With a startled gasp, Angus tugged her up and stepped forward. "Miss Gyllis, what are you doing here? All matter of harm could befall you. This is an *army* camp—no place for a lady."

She stamped her foot. "That is why I'm dressed as a man."

"I'm afraid your disguise will not protect you for long. You're too bonny to mistake for a lad."

Gyllis swallowed her smile. She'd seen a bonny lad or two in her lifetime. Not that Sean looked feminine—but heaven help her, that he was bonny was not to be argued. She cupped a hand alongside her mouth so she'd not be overheard. It wouldn't be surprising if there were spies about. "Do you know of a cave nearby?"

"Aye, there are a few."

"Any that are secluded where a man wouldn't be found—perhaps on Dunollie land?"

Angus wrapped his fingers around his greying beard and tugged. "I don't ken…I seem to recall a cave on Kerrera—in the Firth of Lorn just south of the castle. On a clear day you can see it from the shore. But 'tis just an undeveloped island. There's nothing on it."

"Kerrera? That must be it." She grasped his arm and recited Alan MacCoul's threat.

Angus continued to scratch his beard. "Aye, but everyone saw Alan's men haul him into the castle."

"Did you see this as well?"

"Nay, I was patrolling the forest when the attack happened."

"Is it impossible for Alan to have spirited Sean to Kerrera?"

"Well, nothing's impossible, I suppose." Angus glanced in the direction of Duncan's tent. "But the Lord of Glenorchy is planning an attack soon, cannons should be arriving from Castle Stalker in a day. Once we storm the castle, we'll find the chieftain, I'm certain of it."

"Cannons?" Gyllis peered through the trees at the Dunstaffnage battlements. "Is that why we haven't driven them out yet?"

"We've tried." He pointed. "Every time we move within shooting distance, the bastards rain arrows upon us. Duncan also sent a missive to the Earl of Argyll requesting more targes to protect our men on the battering ram."

"When will the shields arrive?"

"Today, God willing."

"Please." Gyllis clasped her palms together. "All I ask is that we sail to Kerrera to look in the cave. You'll be back before Duncan even discovers you're missing."

"I'd like to help you, lass, but Sean MacDougall is shivering in Dunstaffnage's dungeon—not in the bloody cave on Kerrera. I can feel it in my bones." He grasped her elbow. "Come, I'll take you to your brother and he can organize an escort to take you home."

Chapter Twenty-Four

Two days. Sean licked his bleeding lips with a coarse and dry tongue. Another day without water and he'd be dead for certain. Everything ached. The rivets knifing into his flesh had already worn ulcers. His neck was stiff. Even the slightest movement of his chin caused a jabbing pain that made his teeth ache.

Immobile, the irons affixed to the cave wall, he had a sense of how Christ had suffered on the cross.

The ulcers and aches Sean could bear, but thirst consumed his mind. The cold and damp were but a minor inconvenience compared to his need for water. The ceaseless dripping behind him tortured his tongue to the point where Sean tried to lick moisture from the iron bar across his mouth.

Mucous drained from his nose, yet he was helpless to wipe it, helpless even to tend to his most basic needs. His skin chafed and the odor of his own piss mixed with the stench of rotting seaweed around him plagued his guts with the urge to heave.

Sean closed his eyes and willed himself to think of Gyllis. Her memory calmed him. Taking in a shaky breath, he pictured her long chestnut tresses when they caught the wind. His fingers could feel the silkiness of her hair, his cracked lips the pillow-softness of her mouth. If only he could travel back in time to the carefree days at Ardchattan when they would sit together in the garden.

Two miserable days had passed with nary a soul in sight. The only sounds were the surf and the damned water dripping and trickling under his feet.

If only he'd spent more time with Gyllis. If only he could hold her in his arms—one more time before he perished.

God on the cross, no wonder Alan MacCoul had killed Fraser. Sean would have been much better prepared if he'd known what his half-brother had planned. And by God, he should have been more forceful with Duncan. The Lord of Glenorchy had always respected Sean's intuition in the past. He should have stood his ground. Sean recounted his visit to Kilchurn over and over. He'd succumbed to his own foolish pride by not insisting Duncan and the enforcers attend Lorn's wedding. He'd played down the threats and the raids. Deep in his soul he'd known Alan MacCoul was behind it all. But he'd been too proud to admit it to Duncan—too proud to ask for the Lord of Glenorchy's help because he was a friend. If he'd been honest and presented the depth of his concerns, Duncan would have supported the MacDougalls without question. After all, he'd dedicated his life to Duncan and his father—served in the Highland Enforcers to maintain order for King James.

And now here he was, the feared knight, wrapped in irons, pinned to the wall, unable to wipe the snot from his face.

A water rat watched him from across the cave.

"Be gone with you." Sean's voice was so dry it painfully grated in his voice box.

The rat inched forward.

"Be gone," Sean bellowed, followed by a fit of dry coughs. The rat stopped and sat up on its haunches and stared at him, his nose twitching. Sean rattled the irons. "I'm not dead yet, you mongrel bastard!"

The rodent paced back and forth in front of Sean and his irons as if he knew Sean was helpless. The closer the creature came, the more Sean rattled his irons, the rivets digging into tender flesh.

When the rat stopped at Sean's feet, all he could do was cast his gaze downward. The first bite sunk into his shoe leathers. Stomach roiling with bile, Sean rattled his cage and slammed his foot against the unbending metal. The devil's spawn could feast all they liked after he was dead. Not before.

***

Gyllis should have known *a man* wouldn't listen to her. Men all took pity on her as if she were afflicted in the brain as well as in the legs. She snatched her arm away from Angus's grasp. "I am perfectly able to return to my brother's tent on my own. There is no need for you to assist me."

"Och, I'd be no kind of gentleman if I didn't see you delivered safely to his side. This camp is rife with young Highland lads who might get the wrong idea seeing a woman dressed in a pair of breeks."

Gyllis glanced toward the pier. It would be futile if she tried to run. Besides, she'd probably fall on her face like she'd done a hundred times before. Ahead, the camp started to stir, but the flutter of a blue mantle caught her eye. She smiled broadly—affecting her most innocent countenance. "There's Lady Meg. She accompanied me on the ride to Dunstaffnage. I'll join her. Duncan is arranging our transport home momentarily."

"Very well." He drew out his words slowly as if considering. "If the Lady of Glenorchy is here, I reckon I can leave you in her capable hands."

Gyllis continued to keep her voice low. She didn't want anyone else realizing she was female. "Thank you, sir. You have been most helpful."

Hastening her step, she caught up to Meg not far from a large tent and tapped her shoulder before her sister-in-law reached for the flap. "What are you doing?"

"Gyllis," Meg said in a loud whisper. "I should be asking you the same." She looked side to side. "Duncan could be here any moment.

"I need your help in creating a diversion."

A crease formed between the lady's red eyebrows. "Honestly, Gyllis. You should take Duncan's advice and return to Kilchurn. Things here are worse than I'd imagined."

A pained moan came from within the tent. Of course Meg would have already connived to see to the injured before she left. "And you're not?"

"They need a healer for the hospital."

"Please. Keep Duncan's attention diverted as long as possible—at least until I can...ah...slip away—tell him I've decided to stay so that I may assist you."

Meg frowned. "Have you gained more information? Where are you off to now?"

"I'd rather not say, lest Duncan intercept me." Gyllis balled her fists. "I will not be stopped."

Meg clasped her hand to her chest. "Promise me you will stay safe." She moved her lips close to Gyllis's ear. "Do not let on to anyone that you are a woman."

"I promise—just keep Duncan occupied. Can you do that?"

"I'll do my best, but you know your brother."

Gyllis jumped at a loud commotion booming from the direction of Duncan's tent. Hopefully the noise had nothing to do with her, but she didn't aim to stay around long enough to find out. "I'll see you upon my return."

Meg gave her hand a squeeze before she released it. "Go with God." She pulled the satchel with the oatcakes and watered wine from her shoulder. "Take this. You may need it more than I."

Slipping away, Gyllis again tugged the hood low over her forehead, but she wouldn't again make the mistake of greeting anyone she knew. She picked up a sturdy stick and hunched a bit so she'd be mistaken for an old man with a limp. Moving as quickly as she could, she headed for the pier.

One thing she knew for certain, the longer she remained in the foreground of Dunstaffnage, the greater the risk that Duncan would tie her to a horse and drag her home. Fortunately, all the fishermen must have set sail before dawn, because Gyllis saw not a soul. She hid behind a moored galley and held up the flap of the hood to better see. At the very end of the pier, a skiff bobbed in the water. It was exactly what she needed.

Before she set out, she peered over the galley's hull and looked toward the camp. A skirmish had erupted between the outlaws on the wall-walk and the soldiers below. Volleys of arrows traversed through the air while Duncan's men bellowed and slammed the pommels of their dirks against their targes. Gyllis crossed herself and offered a silent prayer for the good health of her brother and his men.

She hastened to the end of the deck, untied the skiff and carefully climbed into the tiny boat. She and her sisters often rowed a similar skiff across Loch Awe on summer days—but the Firth of Lorn was not a loch. It formed a major part of Scotland's sea trade and men sailed hearty galleys through her white-capped waves.

As she grasped the oars, she prayed the weather would hold while she pointed the boat south. Of all her problems, the greatest was that she had no idea where on

Kerrera the cave might be. Would she be able to see it from the water? How far away was the island? *Angus said you can see the island from Dunollie. How much further can it be?*

But asking for help had proven futile. Everyone was positive Sean was being held within the walls of Dunstaffnage Castle. Gyllis would have believed it herself if she hadn't heard Alan MacCoul's threat.

She heaved on the oars, dragging them through the swells. Doubtless, it would take a Herculean effort to row four miles to Dunollie and then only heaven knew how much further. Gyllis gritted her teeth. Nothing would stop her, no matter if she had to row all day and night.

By the time she reached Dunollie, the sun had traversed to the late morning sky. She'd been rowing for at least two hours and her arms were sore. Her back and neck punished her like she'd climbed the tower stairs on her hands more than fifty times.

Rowing a heavy wooden skiff was hard work. Though the current was running southwest, she fought the swells to keep from being pushed toward the mainland.

Blisters had begun to form on her palms and she changed positions frequently to shift the pressure to different points on her hands. When the castle came into view, she paused her rowing, shaded her eyes and searched. True to Angus's word, an island loomed off the coast—quite a bit further away than she'd hoped. Through the haziness, the shore sloped up into green hills, allowing no clear view of its size. But one thing was certain, she had quite a bit more rowing to do.

Her entire body ached. Even if she weren't recovering from a bout of paralysis, she'd be tired. She dared glance at her palms. Three big blisters on her right hand and two on her left. *How in God's name will I make it?* She pulled an oatcake from the satchel and washed it down with a gulp of watered wine.

Again, Alan MacCoul's damning words rang in her head. *"I will imprison you in irons and laugh while your body rots in a dank and musty cave."*

She blew on her palms and ground her teeth. "Damn you, Alan MacCoul!" she yelled at the top of her voice. Gyllis steeled her mind to the searing pain, and with each pull of the oars, sailed closer to Kerrera.

***

Working against the current, the passage across the sound took twice as long to traverse as it had taken to row from Dunstaffnage to Dunollie. When Gyllis finally glimpsed a clear view of Kerrera's northernmost point, her hands were completely raw, she could hardly move her arms and the muscles in her back and neck burned and tortured her with every pull of the oars.

She scanned the shore and beyond for any sign of a cave. A narrow, beach transitioned into grassy, rolling hills, filled with purple heather and spotted with trees. Gyllis wanted to scream. There wasn't one rocky outcropping that looked like it might house a cave. To the east, the surf was rougher, angered by wind and dark clouds. Whitecaps topped the waves coming across from the Isle of Mull. The westward current would be even stronger and all the more difficult to navigate.

She could scarcely drag the oars through the protected waters from Dunstaffnage to Dunollie. She gazed at the shore with desperate longing. If only her legs were strong enough to traverse the sandy beach or the craggy land beyond, she'd pull ashore and allow her hands a rest—but as sure as she breathed, the boat would be faster than walking. What would she do if she hiked away from the skiff and her legs failed? She didn't even have one crutch and she'd left the old stick on the pier at Dunstaffnage.

After blowing on her palms to cool the burn, she grasped the oars and gave them a solid pull. Crying out, she snatched her hand into her body and crouched over it. Searing pain shot through her palm. Blood dripped onto her breeks. Opening her trembling fingers, the blisters had rubbed raw. Blood oozed across her palm and dribbled into the hull.

Tears streamed down her cheeks while she clutched her arms to her body and rocked. Why couldn't someone have trusted her? Why did the men believe they were so damned right? More tears welled, blurring her vision and making dark splashes on the coarse leather. Wailing, her voice box grated. Gyllis looked up at the ominous sky. What if she was wrong? What if she'd come all this way and Sean wasn't there? How would she make it back with her hands blistered and bleeding? If only someone would have believed her—tried to help, but instead they all looked upon her as if she were an invalid—a burden no one wanted.

What if this God-forsaken island wasn't even Kerrera? A shrill scream pealed through her throat.

"Where is he?" She rocked in place clutching her hands to her body, tears streaming from her eyes, her nose running. Desperate for answers, she shook her fist at the sky. "Damn you! Where. Is. He?"

Exhaustion claimed her mind. She wanted to curl up in the bottom of the skiff and let it drift. Perhaps it might run aground someplace where people were nice and helpful. She tugged on the oars and shrieked with pain. Her hands could take no more. Slapped by the relentless waves, the boat had drifted further away from the island's beach.

"Sean, where are you?" she cried, slumping from the rowing bench into the hull. *I'm a complete and utter failure.* She gazed up at the black clouds and cursed at the heavens. "God in heaven, why will you not help me?"

Chapter Twenty-Five

"You think I'm brave? My courage is nothing compared to yours. Before me I see a woman who will not be cut down by a devastating illness, who will look it in the face, grasp it with both hands and fight. Not only today, but every day you continue to fight, to work through your pain and agony so one day this will be behind you."

Gyllis sat up with a start. She could have sworn she'd heard Sean's voice—or God's. More so, she remembered the words he'd spoken after she'd fallen at Dunollie. Only he believed in her strength. He believed she could overcome insurmountable odds.

But could she?

The boat teetered with the waves, the oars clicking in their locks. How long had she been wallowing in self-pity? How far had she drifted? She peered over the hull. The skiff had drifted toward the mainland, but a bit south, too. She could see the length of the island now—quite a long isle indeed.

But there was no time to think of that now.

Sean needed her.

While she drew in a stuttering breath, Gyllis stared at her shaking hands. Her pain did not matter. She would not allow anything to stop her. If the skin on her hands were to rub completely off, she would not stop. If the skies were to open with a deluge, she would not stop. If Duncan were to sail a fleet of galleys to find her, she would tell him to turn back because she would not stop until every last inch of Kerrera was searched for any sign of Sean.

Steeling her wits, Gyllis crawled back onto the rowing bench and wrapped her fingers around the oars. It stung, but she clenched her teeth and bore it. With every stroke of the oars, she grew bolder, pulled harder, worked though the aching agony in her limbs.

Thunder pealed from the west.

She ground her teeth and rowed.

A droplet of rain splashed her forehead and she threw her head back. "Bring forth your vengeance, oh God. I shall persevere like Job." She pulled again. *Why would God favor a man as evil as Alan MacCoul?*

She could think of no reason.

Another thunderclap resounded. Gyllis shifted her gaze to the darkening sky. "If you're listening to me, please help me find Sean. You may rain down on me with pellets of hail, but guide me to my love!"

Rain began to fall in sloppy droplets.

"Do you aim to forsake me?" she yelled at the top of her voice. "Is that why you turned me into a cripple?"

She scanned the shoreline. Still no sign of a cave.

On and on she continued to row until she rounded the southernmost point of the island. Once she crossed to the eastern shore, she'd be at the mercy of the storm and the stronger current.

Please. Help me.

The shoreline cut into a cove, exposing rocky cliffs—hidden both from the mainland and from the Isle of Mull to the east. Gyllis's heart fluttered. Her arms infused with renewed strength. Could she allow herself to hope? The skies opened with a deluge, the white-capped surf slapped against the skiff, making it bob precariously. Fighting, she rowed the little boat straight onto a sandy bank until it stopped.

She'd have to jump out into the water. But that didn't matter, she was already wet.

Cold water filled her boots as she splashed into the knee-deep surf. She wrapped the skiff's rope around her wrist and trudged onto the sandbank, pulling it with all her strength. The wooden hull was none too light, but it was her lifeline to the mainland. Who knew how long she'd be stranded if something happened to the skiff.

And what if I'm wrong?

With a heave, Gyllis dragged the boat out of the water and secured the rope around an enormous boulder, then slung the satchel over her shoulder.

Overhead, a buzzard squawked. Gyllis's shoulders tensed. Not but fifty paces away, an entire flock of the vile scavengers flew in a circular pattern.

Her heart flying to her throat, Gyllis stumbled toward the revolting birds. "No!" she gasped, trying to keep her footing on the slick ground. "I cannot be too late."

She reached the crest of a mound and saw it. Gaping like the mouth of a serpent, the cave could have passed for the entrance to Hades.

Oh God, oh God, oh God.

She bent down, picked up a rock and threw it at the buzzards. "Go away!"

A bolt of lightning streaked into three fingers overhead. The buzzards screeched and scattered while thunder boomed so loudly, Gyllis crouched and wrapped her arms around her head. Moving as fast as she could, she stumbled toward the cave whilst the rain came down in sheets.

When she stepped inside, she stood against the wall, shivering. With quick inhales, she rubbed the outsides of her arms and peered into the dark cavern. All she could see was blackness. She pushed against her eyes, willing them to adjust to the dim light. Slowly she crept in deeper, sliding her feet, bracing one hand against the stone wall.

"Sean?" Her voice warbled. "Are you here?"

She stood and listened, but the roar of the deluge outside resounded through the cave, so loud it was almost deafening. Reaching her free arm ahead, she continued on, sliding her feet over slick rocks.

The rain eased a bit.

"Sean?" she called, louder this time.

Through the dripping and splashing, Gyllis thought she heard a cough. She took another step. "Sean? Is that you?"

"Here," a faint voice rasped.

"God in heaven." Her stomach swarmed with fluttering butterflies. "'Tis you?"

Blinking, Gyllis focused on the source of the sound. She saw the outline of something bulky, immobile. *Is it?*

Hastening her step, she tried to run. Her toe caught on a rock and she stumbled forward. Straining to keep her balance, she crashed into the wall. "Blast it," she cursed, ignoring the pain radiating up her elbow, and again sliding her feet forward. *If I fall, I'll be no use to him at all.*

The cave brightened, as if there had been a break in the clouds. Then she saw him. Caged in irons like a criminal hanging from the Edinburgh Tolbooth. Stumbling, she made her way across the craggy ground while a sickly burn wrenched her insides.

Blessed Lord Jesus, what has Alan done? "I knew you were here." She grasped the iron bars and tugged…Nothing moved. The welds were immobile.

"Water," he rasped.

Sean's features were shrouded in blue shadows but the whites of his eyes were clear. They gazed at her like a starved and hunted fox. Quickly, Gyllis tugged the flagon from her satchel. "I've some watered wine."

She pulled out the cork and held it up and touched it to his lips through the bars. "I'll tip it now."

He opened his mouth and she eased the flagon up until she could hear him swallow. Then he sputtered and coughed.

She stoppered the flagon and set it down. "How can we free you from this contraption?"

"Bust…off the l-lock."

Heaven's stars, she'd never seen a man so weak. She rattled the cage and he groaned as if it caused unimaginable pain. "How?"

"Rock."

"But I could hurt you."

"Do it."

Gyllis found a good-sized rock and picked it up with both hands. She swallowed hard and faced him. The lock was a black, ugly thing. Her hands trembled as she lifted the stone and slammed it against the iron. The clang echoed throughout the cavern, but the lock held firm.

"Again," Sean growled.

She nodded and raised the stone. Hitting the lock over and over, Gyllis's exhausted arms burned. She cried out against the strain, but the blasted thing must have been hewn in the fires of hell. Stopping, she panted. "I-I will *not* fail."

"Easy lass." Sean moved a bit and rattled the irons. "Give me another tot afore you try again."

Gyllis winced when she reached for the flagon.

"Are you hurt?" he asked.

"'Tis nothing." She wasn't about to complain about her bleeding hands—not with Sean teetering on the brink of death. She held the flagon to his lips. "You mustn't drink too much, else your stomach might reject it."

He sipped without sputtering this time. "I'll be right."

She stoppered the flagon and picked up the rock. "Are you ready for me to give it another go?"

"Aye. Aim for the top of the loop. Any padlock will not withstand a direct blow."

She eyed the lock. "How did you know that?"

"I learned a thing or two serving in your father's enforcers." His voice sounded a wee bit better.

"You must tell me more soon." She raised the stone. "Where it bends, you say?"

"Hit it square."

Gyllis held her breath and smashed the rock downward. She let out a frustrated groan. "Damn this bloody thing to hell!" Roaring at the top of her lungs, she raised it over her head then slammed it atop the lock using her strength, her body and all the gut-wrenching fortitude she could muster. With a clang, the piece of metal dropped to the ground.

Squealing, Gyllis tugged on the grill. Though it was stiff, the hinges gave way with a screech. Sean fell to his knees, wrapping Gyllis in his arms and taking her down with him. "I've never been so weak." His hand covered his eyes. "I'm a bloody mess."

"How long has it been since you've had food or water?"

"Three days, I think." He swayed in her arms.

She smoothed her hand over his stubbled beard. "My God. 'Tis a wonder you're alive."

He leaned against her—his weight much heavier than she could have imagined. "I cannot believe you found me." He rocked back on his haunches and averted his face. "I am hideous."

Gyllis clasped his cheeks with the tips of her fingers and offered a trembling smile. "Nay, nay, nay. You are *alive*."

He focused on her eyes with an intense stare. "You are an angel sent from God," he whispered, his voice dead-level and heartfelt.

Gyllis gasped, holding back her urge to cry, pulled him close and clung to him for dear life. For the rest of her life she'd be atoning for all the cursing she did in the boat. "No one would listen to me, but Alan's bitter words replayed in my head over and over."

"When he threatened me at Beltane?"

"Aye, I'll never forget the hatred in his voice."

"Those words have haunted me these past days." Sean rested his head on her shoulder—as if he needed her. Gyllis's heart swelled. She'd been needy for so long, to have someone need her made gooseflesh spread across her skin. She ran her hand over his head, never wanting to release him.

"He's my brother."

She took in a quick inhale of air. "What?"

"MacCoul."

She gently ran a hand over his hair. "I always thought he was a bastard."

"He was…is. But he's my father's son. My father supported him all along but never revealed his secret." Sean reached for the flagon, his movement sluggish and awkward.

Gyllis pulled off the stopper. "So that's why Alan is so bitter."

"Aye." Sean guzzled the watered wine. "He not only thinks he should be Chieftain of Dunollie, he aims to claim the Lordship of Lorn for himself."

"No." She tensed. "He's insane."

"Insane with hate." He straightened and grasped her shoulder. "I must stop him."

"He's seized Dunstaffnage Castle. Duncan and the men are trying to attack, but Alan has amassed an army."

"I must hurry."

"You're on the ragged edge of death. How can you think about going after him now?"

Sean sat on his haunches. "With a bit of food and a few tots of whisky I'll come good." He pointed to her satchel. "Have you got anything to eat in there?"

"I've some oatcakes, but that's all."

"'Tis a start."

She reached for the bag and inclined her head toward the light. The rain had subsided, but droplets splashed down in rapid succession from the cave's entrance. "Let us move away from the stench."

"I'm afraid only a bath will help us there." He used the wall for balance and chuckled. "My legs are as wobbly as a newborn lamb's."

"I ken how that feels."

Both limping, she led him to a flat boulder where they'd be able to sit and she could see him better. When the light illuminated his skin, she clapped a hand over her mouth. "My God, where are your clothes?"

Sean grimaced. "I'm surprised the bastard left me braies and boots on."

She focused on the sores peppering his flesh. "What did he do?"

"Blacksmith's rivets bored holes through my skin. He not only wanted me to die, he wanted me to suffer as long as possible."

"The fiendish blackguard."

"Wheesht, Gyllis. I've never heard you use such a vulgar tongue."

She rubbed her aching arms. "Apologies. I'm a bit on edge. No one would listen to me about Alan's curse. Duncan tried to send me back to Kilchurn. Angus swore you were being held in the castle dungeon—not even he would listen to the reasoning of a crippled woman."

"How did you find me?"

"Angus mentioned Kerrera was part of the Dunollie lands. I took a skiff from the pier and refused to stop rowing until I found a cave. If I had to cover every square inch of Kerrera, I would have done it."

"My God, you are an amazing woman." He grasped her hand and kissed it. "You are my very own guardian angel." He slid his hand to her upper arm. "You rowed all the way from Dunstaffnage without assistance?"

She closed her eyes as his fingers kneaded her aching muscles. "I do not ken how I did it. If it weren't for my determination to find you, I would not have been able to continue past Dunollie."

His hand stopped. "Why are you wearing breeks?"

She chuckled and looked down. She'd forgotten about her clothing. Biting her bottom lip, she gave him a sheepish smile. "They're Duncan's. I couldn't very well slip away from Kilchurn in the dead of night dressed like a lass."

"You did?" He knitted his brows. "You could have been killed."

She reached inside the satchel and pulled out the remaining oatcakes. "You would have done the same for me."

"Aye, but I'm a man."

"So does that make me any less a person?"

"No, lass." He shoved a crunchy cake into his mouth. "You've proven that it most certainly does not."

Gyllis blew on her palms.

Sean leaned in and examined them. "Christ almighty, your skin is raw."

"I told you I wasn't about to stop."

He hissed. "Bloody hell. I still cannot believe you suffered so much for me."

"But I love you." She blinked back her tears. "I would have moved heaven and hell to save you."

He brushed his fingers along her cheek. "I believe you would have."

There was nothing Gyllis wanted more than to wrap him in her arms and smother him with kisses, but he was so weak and needed a bath. He'd require more than a few drops of watered wine and a handful of oatcakes. "Lady Meg is at Dunstaffnage. She can tend your wounds."

"Dunollie is closer. Jinny will set me to rights and I can gather my weapons and clean clothing."

"Weapons? You are not planning to fight…"

"Bloody oath I am. I'll not rest until Alan is brought to justice." He cradled his head in his hands as if it pained him. "If he'd told me he was my brother I would have honored my father's wishes and given him land and coin, but now there is no turning back for him."

"Aye, he must be caught and sent to the gallows, but let Duncan lead the charge."

"And lick my wounds like a miserable coward?" He tried to stand, but dropped back. "I will not sit idle while other men risk their lives for me."

Since he'd taken a wee bit of sustenance, a dangerous fire flickered in Sean's eyes.

Gyllis held his stare. She would not lose him. Not ever again. "But first you must promise we'll go to Dunollie and find your healer. I doubt you could raise your sword at the moment, let alone face Alan."

"Agreed. But I will regain my strength. Make no bones about it."

Chapter Twenty-Six

By the time they left the cave on Kerrera, the sun had begun to set. It would be dark before they reached Dunollie. Sean was almost relieved—almost. In no way would he allow Gyllis to row the skiff up the shore. Every fiber in his body ached. His mind was clouded by pain, starvation and thirst. God help him, he'd even swooned a time or two.

They'd filled the flagon with water from a spring, but his thirst would not be assuaged. His stomach rumbled. A few oatcakes made little impact and his fingers shook. Bloody hell, he could barely propel the boat in the seas, given the storm's effect and his trembling limbs.

Gyllis sat on the bench across from him, her eyes filled with adoration, even in his wretchedness. In no way could he fail her. She alone was the source of his motivation to continue on. The fascinating woman had singlehandedly overcome insurmountable odds to come to his rescue. He loved her before, but now his respect for her soared to a new level. He would love her through eternity. That her beauty outshone any lass in Scotland no longer mattered. If she were to turn grey with age on the morrow, he would love her no less.

When he at last moored the skiff at the embankment, he couldn't be certain who helped whom more, but somehow they managed to make it up the trail to the keep. The old guard, Cadan, ran to meet them, weapons clanking. "M'laird, you look as if you've been to hell and back."

Sean smirked. "I have." With Gyllis under his arm they hobbled toward the stairwell. "Send Jinny up with food and a salve." He stopped and regarded the guard over his shoulder. "Order a bath. I ride at dawn."

"Dawn, m'laird?" The guard stood dumbfounded. "In your condition?"

"Do as I say," Sean bellowed. "Make it quick. I cannot bear the stench of my own flesh."

Gyllis stumbled on a step, but held on. "I daresay Cadan may be right. 'Tis madness to ride when you're in such a state."

"Do not worry. After a good meal, a bath and a sleep, I'll be fit." His thighs burned with every step. Why in God's name did his chamber have to be on the third floor?

"We're nearly there," Gyllis said as if she'd heard his thoughts. "A meal will help us both I'd reckon."

After they pushed through the door, Gyllis didn't release him until she'd led him to the bed. "You'd best rest here until the healer comes."

He sat. "I hate weakness."

"As do I." She set to lighting a candle with the flint. "Now you have an inkling of what it was like to be confined with paralysis for months."

It wasn't that he hadn't thought about it, but her words hit a chord. How unconscionably difficult things must have been for her. Yes, he'd known she was suffering, but had no idea of the depth of that pain...until now. "Come here." He pulled her into him and wrapped his arms around her waist, pressing his ear to her breast. Her heart beat a steady rhythm "You are the strongest person I know—stronger than any man. If only I could have an iota of your strength."

She cradled his head in her hand. "You do. Can you not see it? If you had not inner strength, you would not have survived in that dank cave with all those lesions on your body."

The door opened and Sean swallowed down the lump in his throat. He would have preferred it if Jinny had taken a bit longer. Followed by a serving girl who was carrying a trencher of food, the healer walked to the bed with her medicine basket.

Sean begrudgingly released Gyllis's waist while Jinny set her things on the bedside table. "Thanks be to God, you are safe, m'laird." She glanced sidewise at Gyllis.

Sean gestured with his hand. "You remember Miss Gyllis Campbell. If it weren't for her, I would have perished this night in the Kerrera cave."

"Kerrera?" Jinny glanced between them. "But everyone thinks Alan MacCoul is holding you in the Dunstaffnage dungeon."

"Everyone but me," Gyllis said, nodding at the matron. "Pleased to make your acquaintance, matron."

Jinny remembered her manners and curtsied. "My thanks, miss." Then her eyes popped when she looked Sean head to toe. "Forgive me for saying so m'laird, but you look as if you're half dead."

"'Tis exactly how I feel."

She looked closely at Sean's lesions and then sniffed. "These have started to fester."

Gyllis blew on her palms. "The conditions in the cave were deplorable."

Jinny fished in her basket and pulled out a pot. "My salve will fix you up."

Sean jolted and hissed as she attacked the first sore. The woman's bloody ointment stung like a posy of nettles, but it worked—eventually. He clenched his fists and took the rest of her ministrations without any outward display of pain. He wouldn't be any sort of man showing weakness in front of Gyllis, not after she'd borne so much agony herself.

Jinny wiped her fingers on a cloth and stoppered her pot. "That ought to see you through to the morrow. Shall I bring up a tonic to help you sleep?"

"I should be fine with a tot or two of whisky." He reached for Gyllis's elbow and held up one of her hands. "The lady's palms could use a bit of your salve as well."

Jinny gasped. "My Lord, what on earth did you do?"

Gyllis shrugged and blushed. "I rowed a skiff from Dunstaffnage to the southern end of Kerrera."

"Blessed be the saints, and you being a noble lassie and all." She shot a concerned look at Sean. "Why did the men not help her?"

"They didn't believe me." Gyllis cleared her throat. Aye, the lass could speak for herself. "They tried to send me back to Kilchurn."

Jinny slipped the cork off the pot and dug in her fingers. "Is that why you're wearing a pair of men's breeks?"

The color in Gyllis's cheeks deepened. "Aye, matron." She pursed her lips and glanced at Sean, making it clear she didn't intend to relate the whole story. Sean figured she ought to because the tale alone proved how strong-willed and determined Gyllis was.

Cadan pushed through the door, carrying a wooden bath, followed by a pair of stable boys laden with buckets of water.

"Careful not to slosh on the floor," Sean said. Normally he wouldn't pay a rat's attention to whether they spilled a bit of water or not, but wet floorboards could be slippery for Gyllis.

Cadan placed the basin in front of the hearth. "Shall I light the fire, m'laird?"

"Aye, thank you."

Jinny frowned. "I suppose I'd best leave the salve here if you intend to wash it off."

Sean gave her a wink. "That's a good lass."

She didn't even try to feign a smile. "Miss Gyllis, you can come with me and we'll find you a proper bed."

Gyllis shot a panicked stare to Sean.

He stood with his fists on his hips. Heaven help him, he was still weak-kneed and dizzy. "I'll see Miss Gyllis to the lady's chamber. I've a word to have with her first."

By the way she crossed her arms and pursed her lips, Jinny didn't approve. "Pardon me for saying so, but you both need your rest."

Sean gave her his sternest look. "That will be all, Jinny."

She ticked up her chin. "Very well, m'laird. Do you require anything else?"

"I've a terrible thirst. Could you send up a ewer of ale?"

Jinny gestured to the table with the food. "The chambermaid brought one up with the trencher."

Sean spotted it and grinned. "That she did."

"Come, Cadan," Jinny said. "Let us leave our chieftain to his *rest* before he succumbs to exhaustion."

Sean waited until the door closed behind the servants. God he was tired, but he could smell Gyllis's allure from across the room. His mouth watered. He wasn't sure if it was hunger for her or hunger for food, but when his stomach growled he chose the latter. For now. "I ken I need a bath, but that food looks too good to pass by. If I do not get a good meal in my belly soon, I fear my strength will never return."

"Agreed, I'm famished." She looked at the door and twisted her mouth. "Your healer must think me a harlot."

"Do not worry about Jinny. I shall ensure her priorities are set straight at my next opportunity." Sean lumbered to the table and held the chair for Gyllis.

"My thanks, but I should be holding the chair for you. Jinny was right when she said you looked like you were on death's door. I've never seen anyone so pale."

Sean slid into the chair across from her, suddenly feeling twice his age, perhaps even thrice. He reached for a slice of roast lamb and shoved it in his mouth. "I'll be fit once I have something substantial in my belly."

She picked up the ewer and served his tankard first. "I'm sure food will help." She poured for herself. "But so will rest."

He raised his ale. "Then 'tis settled. We shall eat, bathe and then rest." He glanced at the bed, certain his idea of rest did not meet with Gyllis's, but he'd cross that bridge when he came to it.

"We shall eat, but you will bathe, not I."

"Only me?" He popped a grape in his mouth. The food must be helping because he grew more amorous by the moment. He inhaled deeply. "What the devil fragrance are you wearing? It's making the pulse thrum beneath my skin."

Her tongue shot out and she licked those delectable, pouty lips. "You must be mistaken. I've not applied a fragrance, especially dressed in men's clothing."

He reached across and ran his finger over the back of her hand. "Then it must be entirely your allure, m'lady."

She smiled, her dimples dipping into a lovely blush. "I should leave you to your bath. 'Tis not proper for me to remain in your chamber—especially when the servants are aware of my presence."

Sean puzzled at her shyness. "Do not think on Jinny's dour frown. 'Tis none of her concern what we do within this chamber."

"But rumors will spread—'tis different from the last time. Jinny had a bairn to deliver and I was appointed another chamber by Angus."

He reached across the table and cupped her face in his palm. "As long as you remain in Dunollie, your reputation is safe. I'll not stand for anyone sullying your name. Besides, as far as anyone is aware, you are staying in the lady's chamber."

Gyllis lowered her chin and looked up with the coyest of stares. "Very well—if you are certain."

He took a bite of cold roast lamb. "I am."

She raised her eyebrows and glanced toward the bath. "Then I should like to wash your back." Honest to God, what a change his promise had brought about.

Sean stopped mid-chew. His mind went blank. His hunger fled. His cock lengthened. And then he swallowed. "I would be bathed by no finer hands than yours, m'lady."

"I believe the fire has warmed the air enough for you not to catch a chill."

"Quite right." Not that chilly Scottish air ever bothered him. After shoving a bite of bread in his mouth, he stood and moved to the bath. Untying the braies, he let them drop to the floor. The heat of her gaze seared his back. He knew Gyllis as a passionate woman. Her earlier embarrassment had been a fear of gossip by the servants, not a fear of him. Sean wanted her to see him naked. He pivoted and faced her.

Her gaze raked down his body, lowering to his manhood, Gyllis gasped.

Even on the brink of exhaustion, his cock was hard.

He tapped his top lip with his tongue, anticipating her hands around his cock. Absently, his hand snuck down and he stroked himself. "I want you, lass."

Gyllis's green eyes sparkled as she inclined her head toward the tub and waited for him to climb in. She was right. He did need to bathe first. Unfortunately, the damned barrel wasn't large enough to pull her in. She removed her cloak and sauntered forward. Her limp hardly noticeable, she'd come so far since she was stricken.

Picking up the cake of soap with the tips of her fingers, she held it to her nose. "Mm. Rose."

Sean's flesh tingled with anticipation as she knelt beside the basin. His voice box was too thick to speak.

She dipped the soap in the water and with her first touch, Sean shuddered. He closed his eyes and moaned.

"Shall I cleanse your back first?"

"Aye," he rasped.

"I'll be careful to avoid your sores."

He'd scarcely felt the lesions when he'd slipped into the tepid water.

Gyllis smoothed a soapy hand over his shoulder.

Never in his life had he experienced a touch so ethereal. Her fingers plied his skin with light swirls, making his skin come to life and his blood pulse. Giving in to her heavenly ministrations, the tension shed from Sean's shoulders in concert with the water trickling down his chest and back.

Gyllis scooted forward, her face only inches from his. "Shall I cleanse the rest?"

Yes, for the love of everything holy, yes. "Aye," was all he could manage to utter.

Gyllis lathered the cake of soap. "I can be more careful when I use my fingers."

Sean needed those deft fingers plying him now. "Feels like heaven."

She tickled his chest and swirled her fingers around his nipples, leaning so close her wild, sensuous scent overpowered the rose in the soap. Sean's cock grew a mind of its own. It had been hovering just below the water, but it jutted through the surface, so hard it tapped his stomach.

A groan rumbled through his chest while Gyllis continued lower. He couldn't see her face, but he felt her eyes boring into his erection while her hands continued lower. Her touch became torturous as she bathed everything but his member, continuing to swirl her fingers around the sensitive skin on his inner thighs.

The further her hands got from his cock, the more he craved them to stroke it and free him from the hot, aching, yet exhilarating tension in his groin.

Sean realized he'd leaned his head back and closed his eyes, when she stopped.

Gyllis cleared her throat. "S-shall I wash you *there* too?" Her voice had taken on an erotically husky tone. The state of his arousal had affected her more than he'd realized, making his need all the more intense.

"Pleeeeease."

Slowly she lathered the soap between her fingers. Her braid swung around from her back. Sean grasped it and tugged off the thong at the end. Before she set the soap down, he had her hair released. The chestnut flickered with coppery highlights from the glow of the fire.

Their gazes collided as if steam erupted between them. Sean held his breath. Gyllis's lips parted and she released a stuttered exhale, her stare drifting down his body until it met with his cock.

Sean groaned before her slender fingers wrapped around him. She stroked him with such a feathery caress, he thought his heart would blast to the rafters. He realized he must have moaned when she asked him if she was hurting him.

"Nay," he managed through clenched teeth. "Grip harder."

With two more strokes, Sean could take no more. Either she would bring him undone or he would need to quell his burning desire and make this moment last. With a guttural growl he pulled her into the bath and smothered her mouth with his.

Holding her pliable body in his arms made his tension thrum to the surface. He devoured her mouth, claiming her face with his hands, probing his tongue deep inside with a bone melting fire that spread through his blood. Melting into his arms, she returned his fervor, matching his intensity with her own muffled mewls. Her kisses spread through his soul and claimed his heart, while gradually she took control and slowed their pace.

Gyllis licked his tongue like no one ever had before with languid brushes as if she'd been practiced in the art of kissing for a lifetime. Her lips wandered across his chin and down his neck—long, slow kisses that consumed his mind. Rather than releasing his tension, what he thought could not grow more intense compounded his need to possess her.

She clamped onto his shoulders and smoothed her hands down his arms, her sweet breath caressing his chest. "I want you." She gripped her fingers tighter. "I ken I should let you rest, but I cannot quell the longing in my soul."

After one last claiming kiss, Sean gathered her in his arms and stood, clenching his thighs to steady his weakened muscles. Dripping with water, he stepped out of the bath and set her on her feet beside the fire. "You're all wet," he said, his brogue taking on the most basal burr.

He stepped back to untie her laces and her gaze again floated down his body. He liked the way she looked at him with her eyes growing dark.

Then he pulled her shirt over her head and cast it aside. His breathing sped as he untied the cord around her waist and let the oversized breeks drop to the floorboards.

He couldn't help his chuckle as the hem of her shift dropped to the floor, the garment wrinkled. "I cannot believe you shoved your shift into your breeks."

"I was in a wee hurry." She crossed her arms over her chest. "Besides, it filled up the extra space inside."

He sauntered toward her and untied the frilly ribbon around the neckline. "Not to worry. A shift can easily be removed."

Gyllis's giggle was barely audible as she raised her arms. Sean needed no more encouragement. In one swift move he pulled the garment over her head and tossed it over the chair.

Her hands again crossed over her breasts. He grasped them with a gentle tug. "You've no reason to be bashful, lass. Allow me to gaze upon your beauty."

She let him pull her arms away. Light from the fire and candles radiated across her flawless skin—he'd never seen her in the light before. A gasp strained in his throat. He'd thought he'd seen perfection, but now without a doubt, he gazed on the most miraculously bonny woman in all the world. Not only was the face lovelier than a porcelain doll, Gyllis had a slender neck with graceful shoulders to match. But her breasts took his breath away. In the golden light, the lush handfuls of ivory flesh were tipped by pink buds that made his mouth water.

He cupped them in his hands and kneaded. Her moan rekindled the raging fire in his groin. He'd not last long, but first he had to taste her flesh. When he took her nipple into his mouth, she leaned into him with a shuttering moan. God, her voice alone could bring him undone. It spurred him into a frenzy as he plied her breasts with one hand and suckled with his tongue.

"Please," she begged. "Sean, I cannot take much more."

The pleading tone of her voice attacked his overwhelming need with such force, his cock pulsed. He couldn't take more either. Sweeping her into his arms, he pulled her into his chest and strode to the bed, droplets of water still streaming from his body.

When he set her down, she scooted against the pillows and spread her long legs, revealing the pink diamond of flesh he desired to enter with his ever fiber. She rocked her hips forward. "Please. I need you."

He climbed over her, his cock straining to take her. But he wanted to make it slow, see to her needs—if he rode her like an alehouse tart, he might come before she reached her release. No. He'd see to her satisfaction first. Bracing his body over her, he slid his hand down her belly and tickled the tufts of hair that concealed her secret treasure. When his finger slid over her tiny button, she arched her back and cried out. "Please!"

Sean covered her mouth with a languid kiss while he slid a finger inside her core. Her moan rumbled through his entire body. He had now taken control, but the movement of her hips circling around his finger brought on a renewed surge of blinding want. In and out he slid his finger while his thumb caressed her pearl. Her breathing sped. She was close. He wanted to peak with her.

But Sean continued on until she arched her back and clawed at him. "Sean, please."

With a growl, he grasped himself and slid inside.

Gyllis's eyes flew open. "All the way."

He moaned, so close to spilling, he didn't know if he could make it to her length. He clenched his muscles and pushed through her slick sheath. "My God, you are delectable."

Relentless, she sank her fingers into his buttocks and demanded he thrust. Her gasps of breath grew louder. Sean could control the pace no longer. Giving in to the thrill of their joining, he allowed her to dictate the tempo with her demanding fingers tugging his buttocks. She cried out, reaching her peak. The liquid heat gushing around him had him enraptured, the fire in his groin had never burned so hot. Over and over, he thrust deep inside her until stars crossed his vision. Shattering through the precipice of ecstasy, his seed burst.

Powerless to pull out this time, he filled her, and by God did he intend to claim her for his own. The woman beneath him would be his wife, even if he had to face every last Campbell in Argyllshire.

Chapter Twenty-Seven

After the most amazing experience of her life, Gyllis had fallen asleep cradled in Sean's arms. She'd thought nothing could top the last time they'd made love, but oh, how wrong she'd been. And how on earth was Sean able to be so virile after all he'd endured?

She, too, had been exhausted, yet exhilarated at the same time. She sensed the same raw passion in him, driving him to the point of release. Together nothing could stand in the way of their love. They were made to be together. Their souls were one.

Destiny had to be the only reason Sean had fallen in love with her—a cripple. It was almost as if he *needed* to protect her. He'd always handled her as if she were as fragile as a bird. Yet he made love to her with the sort of raw passion she'd seen from him when he sparred in the courtyard. Sean MacDougall would not be bested—not in the bedchamber—and not by the sword. He was solid Highlander through and through. Without an ounce of fat, his muscles were sculpted like the pictures of Greek statuary she'd seen in books. He was an Adonis and he was hers.

As Gyllis woke, she snuggled into the bedclothes and released a satisfied sigh. So satiated with love, she could spend the entire day abed. She moved her foot back to interlace it with Sean's leg, but was met with cold linens. Opening her eyes, she peered across the dim room and found herself alone.

She moved her hand over the spot where Sean had slept. *Cold.*

The bed rattled as she clutched the bedclothes under her chin and sat up. Sean was nowhere to be found, though a fire crackled in the hearth and her clothes were neatly stacked on the table beside last evening's meal.

She exhaled. At least the servants hadn't come in and found her in the chieftain's bed. *Goodness, I'd be mortified.* She wrapped herself in a blanket, crossed the floor and locked the door—Sean could knock when he returned.

Stretching, her entire body ached. She looked at her blistered palms, now crusty with scabs. Her arms and shoulders punished her most of all. She tried to raise them above her head and her muscles ached worse than they did at the height of her paralysis. But she knew rowing all that way would take its toll. Rubbing her neck, she vowed not to let a few sore muscles put a damper on her euphoria.

After pulling on her breeks and shirt, she splashed her face at the basin and used some mint to clean her teeth. She hissed at the pain when the water seeped over her palms. Last night she'd been too numb to notice the pain overmuch. A pair of leather gloves rested beside the basin, and she slid them on, stretching out the fingers. They were big, but the doeskin would protect her skin from further injury.

She moved to the window and pulled the furs aside, clammy chills coursed over her skin, and it hadn't been caused by the breeze. No longer dawn, the hour was later than she'd thought.

Sean's gone to face Alan.

As fast as her legs would allow, she dashed to the table, picked up the remaining bread and shoved it in her satchel.

Why did he not wake me? She pushed out the door and headed down the stairwell only to be met by Jinny.

"Good morrow, Miss Gyllis." The woman sounded chipper for someone who most likely thought her a harlot.

But Gyllis kept herself guarded. Scanning the great hall, her fears were confirmed. Sean was nowhere to be seen. She dipped her head respectfully. "Good morrow. Has Sir Sean left for Dunstaffnage?"

"Aye. He rode out before dawn."

"*Before?*" Gyllis clutched her satchel to her chest. "Bless it, he was on the brink of death."

She folded her hands at her waist. "There's no need to tell me how stubborn our chieftain is. He's been the same since he was a bairn."

"You knew him as a babe?"

"Aye, always the adventurer, that lad."

"Evidently some things never change." Gyllis headed toward the big double doors. "Since he did not wait for me, I must travel to the castle alone."

Jinny hastened beside her. "He mentioned you might not want to remain behind."

"Oh did he now?"

"Aye." The woman had the gall to wink. "And he told me you'll be the lady of the keep right here at Dunollie soon."

Gyllis stopped. "He said that?"

"Aye. Honestly, I'd never thought the lad would set his eyes on just one lass, but ever since he returned from the borders, I swear, he's not looked at another woman."

Gyllis knew Sean had a reputation for liking the lassies, but would have preferred if it were a little known secret. She cringed.

"Do not worry yourself." Jinny patted her hand. "When a woman catches a wandering man's heart, he's changed for good."

She nodded, preferring not to pursue the conversation further. There were many things that needed to be settled before Sean could make an official proposal, the first being he survives this day. "I need the lend of a horse."

"I'll send for Cadan. He'll escort you."

Gyllis spread her gloved palms to her sides. "You're not going to try to stop me?"

"Sir Sean told me to keep you occupied." Jinny grinned broadly. "But I kent a woman who'd recently suffered a bout of paralysis and practically rowed the whole coast of Argyllshire to singlehandedly rescue the Chieftain of Dunollie would not be content to stay behind and roll the dough for an apple tart."

A chill tickled Gyllis's shoulders. She'd found an ally right there at Dunollie—someone who understood her. She grasped Jinny's hands between her fingers. "Thank the Lord you understand. Please have Cadan meet me at the stables. I've already frittered away enough time."

***

Alan MacCoul sat in Dunstaffnage's second-floor solar alone and sipped a dram of whisky. The early hour could be damned—he needed a drink. He hated waiting, and the longer he waited, the testier his men grew. He'd promised them riches and knighthoods. The final seal of success was so near he could taste it. If only the king's reply would arrive, he could end this bloody siege and his power would be recognized. At last people would bow to him, honor him.

The standoff had intensified. More clan armies were arriving, and every day Alan's odds decreased. In addition to the daily volleys of arrows, Campbell's men had broken through the outer barbican walls. Now Alan held the inner courtyard, the towers and keep. But the person sitting in the king's solar had the power. *He* had the power. Stationed on the battlements, his men weren't forced to be spread out, a good vantage point to battle a larger army if it came to a fight. Alan was still in control. Besides, their numbers would be more effective from the inner curtain wall. But Alan didn't like being squeezed. And the bastards down below would pay with their heads when the king gave him due recognition.

Brus pushed through the door. "We'll be out of foodstuffs within two days."

That was another thing that had Alan on edge. The livestock were all housed in the outer barbican and beyond. His two hundred men were stuck with the rotting food in the cellar. Alan tossed back his whisky and gave the insolent cur a sneer. "Wheesht. This will be over before the stores run out." *By God, it had better be.*

Trevor filed in behind Brus. "By my account, we'll be out of arrows by morning."

Alan shoved back his chair and clapped his palms on the table. "You imbeciles. Can you not think for yourselves?" He leaned forward. "What about the arrows they're firing at us?"

"Most are hitting the wall and dropping. We're firing far more than we're reclaiming."

"*My lord*," Alan emphasized. "I *will* be shown my due respect."

The two men exchanged glances.

"I saw that." Alan barreled around the table and drew his dirk. "Do either of you question my rightful heritage? If you do, I'd gladly prove it here and now."

Trevor held up his hands. "N-no m'laird. Both of us have stood beside you through bad times and good."

"Aye," Brus agreed.

"But there's one more thing." Trevor took a step back. "Campbell's dragons are moving cannons through the outer barbican. They aim to blast the castle to hell."

Alan spun around and kicked over a chair. With all his strength, he slammed his dirk into the table. "The bastard thinks he can attack me with cannons?"

Trevor and Brus stared at him, both red in the face. They should be on bended knee, bowing their heads. Alan tried to yank the dirk from the table, but he'd slammed it so hard, the blasted thing held firm. With both hands, he bore down and wrested it out, then he turned and threw it at a portrait of King James.

"Where is that fool-born messenger? The king will approve my claim on Dunollie and name me the Lord of Lorn. *I alone* hold Dunstaffnage, Scotland's gateway to the Hebrides. I have held off the pompous Duncan Campbell and his cowardly Highland Enforcers. I have shown the king exactly who should be lord of these lands. I am the firstborn son of the great Alan MacDougall, not Sean. I am the true heir, descended directly from the sovereign Somerled, king and founder of this land."

"Aye, you are the heir." Brus bowed. "We're in your service. Of that you'll never need to question…ah…m'lord…if you'll excuse us, m'lord…"

Alan shook his finger. "My name shall be feared throughout the Highlands."

The men backed out of the door, but Alan followed them, his finger held high. "Now that I have disposed of the usurping Chieftain of Dunollie, the egotistical Lord of Glenorchy will bow to *me*!"

Chapter Twenty-Eight

Wearing a hood low over his brow and outfitted with his old weapons, Sean dismounted outside the tent flying the MacDougall pennant. Still early morning, the men in the camp had only begun to stir. Sean watched Angus push out the flap and hobble to a bush to relieve himself. More grunts and flatulence came from the old man than Sean had witnessed from the whole band of Highland Enforcers when they were on the trail.

Sean tugged his linen shirt away from his skin. The sores riddling his body were still raw, but he'd steel his mind to the pain. It wasn't the first time he'd ignored his wounds to face the devil. He doubted it would be his last.

Sean chuckled to himself and skirted around the tent. No use making an announcement of his presence. If he did, he'd lose the fabled *ghost* moniker, something he wasn't yet ready to part with.

He peered from the corner to find Angus still releasing his water. *Bloody hell, will the man go on all morning?* Silently, Sean slipped behind him and whispered in his ear. "We'll not allow my father's bastard to kick up his heels in the king's castle for one more day."

Blanching pure white, Angus's entire body convulsed as he dropped the hem of his surcoat and reached for his dirk.

Sean clamped ahold of Angus's wrist before the henchman did something rash. "Hold onto your braies, friend."

Angus sucked in a gasp. "M'laird? You escaped?"

"Kerrera, aye."

"Kerrera? But I thought...everyone thought."

"I ken what you group of bull-minded battlers thought, and if it hadn't been for Miss Gyllis's strong-willed determination, I'd be dead by now."

Angus shoved his dirk into its scabbard. "Jesus Christ, she asked for my assistance and I told her to go away home."

"Aye, just like her brother and every other miserable knight she asked for help."

Angus spread his hands to his sides. "I didn't intend—"

"I expect you to apologize to the lady later." Sean again tugged his shirt away from his skin to ease the burn from his lesions. "Where is Lord Duncan?"

Angus pointed toward the barbican. "We took the inner bailey. He's set up command in the guardhouse tower."

Sean shook his head. "I cannot believe we haven't yet driven them out."

"MacCoul has amassed quite an army. We estimate two hundred or more."

Sean headed toward the barbican gates. "How the hell did that scum-sucking weasel manage to find that many men to follow him?"

"Well." Angus twisted his mouth. "Between you, Campbell, and the king, I do not think it would be difficult."

Sean stopped and ran his palm over his dirk. "Pardon? Your words border on treason."

"Forgive me, m'laird." Angus bowed. "'Twas not my intent. I'll die defending you and Clan MacDougall, but all the outlaws we've evicted—all the work you and Lord Campbell have done in the name of the king—good deeds, mind you. But any time you take up the sword and enforce the law of the land, someone's going to feel slighted."

"Och aye, you're right there." Sean clapped him on the back. "Tell me, what else does Duncan have planned for my father's bastard?"

Angus cringed as if Sean's words had just sunk in. "Alan told you did he?"

"Aye. Had I known, all this mightn't have happened." Sean tugged on his hood to ensure his face was still hidden. "I would have at least tried to talk with him, give him his due."

"It seems the past has come to haunt me. I beg your forgiveness, m'laird. I made a promise to your father on his deathbed—vowed I would never reveal his secret." Angus stopped. "But there is one promise I broke."

"What's that?"

"When you figured out the coffers were being skimmed, I told Murdach I'd have no part in it. Your father wanted to keep his mistake a secret, but once you became chieftain, we had no right to continue sending MacCoul coin. Especially after you'd banished him."

"I ken." Sean continued on toward the gatehouse. "I overheard you saying as much to Murdach. 'Tis why your head's still attached to your neck."

Angus's Adam's apple bobbed as his hawk-like gaze met Sean's in silent thanks. They walked past the guard and ascended up the stairwell.

"Duncan's shipped the cannons down from Castle Stalker," Angus said loud enough to be heard over their echoing footsteps.

Sean exited on the first landing—he'd visited this guardhouse enough times to know where Duncan would be located. "Bloody hell," he mumbled under his breath. MacCoul had certainly dug himself in. *Let's see how long it will take to ferret him out.*

Duncan looked up from a map of the castle. His jaw dropped and he blanched as white as Angus had earlier. "By God, now I know you're a ghost."

Sean grinned. There was nothing more satisfying than confounding the leader of the Highland Enforcers. "Good to see you as well, m'lord."

"How the bloody hell did you get away? We haven't fired the cannons because I did not want to take a chance before we spirited you out." The corner of his mouth ticked up. "Not yet anyway."

Sean pulled up a chair and reclined with his knees wide. "Bloody MacCoul chained me in irons and left me to rot in a cave on Kerrera."

Duncan's jaw dropped. "My God, Gyllis was right."

Angus stepped behind Sean. "Exactly what I said m'lord."

Sean relayed the story of how Gyllis had found him on the brink of death—after receiving savage hospitality from his bastard brother. He held up his shirt. "No thanks to MacCoul's smithy."

Duncan hissed. "You should have Lady Meg see to that." Then his face went dark and his eyebrows knit together. "God's teeth, Gyllis was supposed to be assisting my wife this whole time." He cracked his knuckles. "When I get my hands on my wayward sister I'll—"

"You'll what?" Sean leaned forward. "No one would listen to Gyllis except your lady wife. If the lass had allowed you to ship her back to Kilchurn, the buzzards would be feasting on my eyeballs this morn."

"Jesus." Duncan plopped into his chair. "But witnesses saw him cart your body into the castle."

Sean reflected back to the cave. "He boasted about spiriting me out an old sea gate—said it was on the Firth of Lorn side of the castle."

"An old sea gate, you say?" Duncan studied the map then looked up. "Angus—dress two men in fishermen's garb and have them locate this gate."

Angus bowed and headed for the door. "Right away, m'lord."

Duncan pointed at the map. "We can attack from all sides—blast the cannons and end this siege."

Sean placed his palms on the table, fingers splayed. "I want Alan's head. He imprisoned me in irons without so much as a drop of water and left me for dead. I want to see the look in his eyes before I take his head."

"But you're—"

Sean held up his hand. "Let me slip through the sea gate."

"Perhaps not this time. What about your wounds?" Duncan frowned. "I can tell by looking at you, you're weakened from starvation."

Without moving, Sean eyed him. "I've fought while in worse condition."

Duncan stood and crossed to the sideboard then poured three tots of whisky. "'Tis a risk to go in there on your own."

"Aye," Sean agreed.

"I cannot allow it in daylight."

"Duncan, I can—"

The lord turned with a flagon in his hand. "I, more than any other, know what you are capable of. But I'm in charge of this standoff and I'll not have anyone recognizing you."

Sean bowed his head and accepted a cup from Duncan. "M'lord."

"A missive from the king," a messenger said from the doorway.

Sean kept his face averted.

"Thank you—report to the cook's tent and fill your belly." Duncan took it and ran his thumb under the wax seal and read. "My oath, the miserable sop has Herculean cods."

"What does it say?" Sean asked.

"It appears your bastard brother demanded the king grant him the Chieftainship of Dunollie *and* the Lordship of Lorn." Duncan tossed the missive on the table in front of Sean. "It seems there's been a premature announcement of your death as well."

Sean scanned the note then clenched it in his fists when he read the last line from the king: *Rid Scotland of this arrogant vermin. 'Tis why I hold ill favor for illegitimates. They oft do not know their place.*

Sean crumpled the velum. *It will be my pleasure.*

Duncan inclined his head in the direction of the camp. "How many people saw you?"

"Angus," Sean said, thinking back. "The guard down below. The camp was only beginning to stir when I arrived."

"Good. I want to keep your presence quiet." He pointed at Angus. "Go fetch Lady Meg. She can tend to Sean's lesions whilst we plan our attack."

***

It was a good thing Angus spotted her when she'd first arrived at Dunstaffnage, else Gyllis might have told the entire camp Sean was not only alive, she'd come to give him a piece of her mind. During the ride with Cadan, Gyllis had ample time to collect her conflicting thoughts.

And the more she pondered it, the more she didn't care to wake up alone in Sean's enormous four-poster bed.

He had no business taking up his sword so soon after she'd found him on the precipice of death only the day before. For heaven's sake, he'd hardly been able to climb the stairs last eve. Would he even be able to raise a heavy two-handed sword above his head? Aside from his foolishness, he'd up and left her alone at Dunollie. What if a chambermaid happened upon her sleeping in his bed? She shuddered. He could have at least had the decency to wake her before he took his leave. Who knew what kind of deleterious state he was in when he arose that morn?

Angus led her toward the gatehouse tower. "If anyone asks, tell them you're here to see your brother. Mind you, the chieftain's presence must be kept quiet."

"I understand." She tried not to limp and keep up with his fast pace. At least this time he hadn't told her to go home.

She followed the henchman up the stairs to the first floor of the tower until he stopped outside a closed door and turned to her. "Sir Sean told me it was you who found him in the cave. Please forgive me for not believing you, Miss Gyllis. If I had known you were planning to go after him alone, I would have assigned a guard to assist you."

Gyllis blinked. The man had been downright arrogant toward her. At the time, she sensed Angus considered her presence as irritating as a briar's thorn. But now was not the time to argue. She gestured toward her legs. "I hope you will disregard my limp and take me seriously the next time something important as your chieftain's life is in peril."

He turned scarlet and bowed his head. "Aye, miss."

When he opened the door, Gyllis clapped a hand to her chest. She'd expected to see Sean, but Duncan stood and glared at her. "Leave us, Angus."

"Very well, m'lord." The henchman shut the door and left Gyllis alone with her dragon-hearted brother. And from the look on his face, the dragon was awake and fiercely guarding his treasure of gold.

"You disobeyed me."

She moved her hands to her hips. "Pardon? As I see it, you *refused* to listen to me—even when your dearest friend's life was on the line."

He crossed his arms. "Let us not skirt the issue."

"Come again? The issue is—"

Duncan sliced his hand through the air. "I *told* you to ride home with the guard. And then my scheming wife convinced me you were helping her in the hospital tent. I ought to—"

"What?" Gyllis stamped her foot. "Send me to Ardchattan Priory to learn piety? Have you forgotten I've just returned from three months of their hospitality?" Oh no, Duncan wasn't about to quash her with: *I'm your brother and your lord so you'd better do as I say.* Gyllis balled her fists. Of all the pompous, bombastic, single-minded men she'd ever met, Duncan had to be the worst. She stomped up to him and glared. "When will you realize I am no longer a child?"

His eyes flashed with ire like they always did when she challenged him. "But 'tis my duty to protect you."

Though he could shoot daggers with his black-eyed glare, Gyllis wasn't about to back down. He always recited his *duty* as if it were more important than anything. "Mayhap, but 'tis not your burden to hogtie me and dismiss my every word as that of a daft cripple."

Blinking, Duncan stepped back. She'd caught him there. "I would never—"

"Oh no? And where would Sir Sean MacDougall be now if I had gone back to Kilchurn with my tail tucked between my legs? Tell me? Would you rather have his death on your hands?"

His face turned bright red. "But think of your reputation."

"My God, Duncan, is that all that consumes your mind?"

He pulled out his chair and plopped down, rapping his fist on the table. "Damn it all, you test me." He raked his fingers through his thick black hair. God, he looked like a dragon-fighter if there ever was one. "I've been friends with MacDougall since we were lads. We...we did things that young men do. I abhor the thought of my own sister—"

"Stop." Gyllis placed her hands on the back of a chair and leaned forward. "Do you think I have not heard the rumors? As I recall, you were considered as much a rogue as Sir Sean. Mayhap more so."

"That is different." Blinking rapidly, he swatted a dismissive hand through the air. "Lady Meg made me realize the error of my ways. Since she came into my life, I have put the single man's lifestyle behind me."

"And Sir Sean is incapable of changing as you did? Have you even discussed it with him, or did you draw your thick-headed line in the sand and make a decree that he would never be worthy of a Campbell lass?" Gyllis shoved the chair against the table with a clatter. "That's it, isn't it? Ever since the time of the Bruce, Campbells have deemed themselves superior, especially over the MacDougalls. After all, Sean's archaic ancestors supported the reprehensible King Edward of England. Sean and all MacDougalls should be punished throughout eternity for their ancestor's treachery and lack of vision."

Duncan stood. "Gyllis, you push me too far."

"Aye?" She straightened and folded her arms. "I did not come here to argue with you."

He swiped his hand across his mouth and looked away as if he were conjuring yet another dispute to dissuade her from loving Sean.

Whatever absurdity was about to spew from his mouth, Gyllis didn't want to hear it. "Where is he? When I found him yesterday, he was on the very precipice of death—so weak and pale. He shouldn't be here. He should be abed."

"Sir Sean is young and resilient. Besides, he's hell-bent on revenge. There'll be no stopping him."

Gyllis pursed her lips. "I ken, but I'll see him before he takes on Alan and his army, and you'll not stop me."

After a long stare, Duncan pointed toward the ceiling. "One floor up. Meg is tending his wounds. And the next time I see you, you had better be dressed as a proper noblewoman."

Chapter Twenty-Nine

Gyllis slipped into the chamber the next floor up. The guard tower wasn't built for comfort. The stairwell was extremely narrow and the stairs had been worn over years of use. Still sore and tired, she stumbled twice on her way up.

Fortunately, at each landing there was only one pie-shaped chamber. She caught her breath and pushed inside. Naked from the waist up, Sean sat in a wooden chair beside the hearth.

Meg stood beside him with a pot in her hand. She looked up and grinned. "Gyllis!"

A burning sensation spread throughout her chest. Limping, Gyllis marched across the floor and took the pot from Meg's grasp. "I should be tending his wounds."

The matron—Gyllis's closest friend—bowed her head and took a step back. "Of course. Apologies. Duncan sent me up. I was unaware you were here."

Gyllis glared at Sean. "Again it seems everyone wanted to cosset me in a tower whilst they solved the problems of all Christendom." She knew she was overreacting, but seeing Sean's bare chest in the presence of another woman with her eyes on him struck a nerve she could not control. "Must everyone take pity on me because I am a cripple?"

She shoved her fingers in the pot and filled them with gooey ointment.

Sean grabbed her wrist. "What are you saying? No one in this room has ever treated you any less because of your condition."

There. He'd said it—referred to her limp and slowness as a *condition*. "You do not need to say anything. Your actions give you away."

"How so? I, least of anyone, would pamper you because of a mild limp."

"You left me at Dunollie as if I could be of no help to you at all. And now you have my sister-in-law tending your wounds."

Sean's gaze darted to Meg. "That is because her husband ordered it."

Gyllis stammered. Hot blood pulsed beneath her skin. She wanted to scream. She wanted everyone to treat her as they had done before the paralysis. She hated being different—left in a big, comfortable bed to sleep whilst Sean rode into danger. How could he have frightened her like that?

"Do you think you are not wanted?" His voice grew softer.

Gyllis, too, looked at Meg. The lady curtsied and offered a gentle smile. "I should allow you two to talk. If you should need me I shall retire to the war room with Duncan for a bit."

After the door closed behind Meg, Sean stood and brushed his fingers over Gyllis's cheek. "*Mo leannan.* Look at yourself. You've come so far in such a short time. Everything you do amazes me."

Her lips quivered—not quite ready to forgive him. "Then why did you leave me behind? You didn't even tell me where you were going." She wiped her fingers off on his chest. Still mad, she needed to talk this through or she'd burst. "I did not row for miles to see you run through by Alan MacCoul's blade."

Sean stared at her, his dark features growing darker. "If I had told you, you would have tried to stop me."

She nodded vehemently. "As God is my witness, I would have."

"But this is something I must do."

"Why? Only yesterday, you were in purgatory, your body is weak. For heaven's sake, the color has not yet returned to your face." She gestured to his torso, riddled with seeping lesions. "How on earth do you expect to wear a hauberk over all those open sores?"

He grasped her palms between his hands. "I've fought injured before."

She jerked her hands away. "But you are too weak. Please. Let Duncan and the others—"

"Do you not understand? I will never be able to live with myself if I recline in my bed whilst others fight my battles. I *must* do this." He grasped her shoulders and held firm. "He imprisoned me in irons and left me for dead. His crimes are unconscionable."

"But I've seen him fight."

"He cannot best me. My entire life he has distained me. And now he is staking his claim on *my* title."

"I am not saying what he's doing is right, but I want you to live." Burning tears rimmed her eyes. How could she convince him not to fight? "Would you choose your will for revenge over me?"

His eyes narrowed. "What are you saying?"

"Am I to stand idly by while you march to your death?"

"Gyllis, do not do this. I love you. When this is over, I will talk to Duncan and we will be wed. Is that not what you want?"

She shoved her finger in the pot and smeared it across a line of lesions. "I want you to survive this siege. You are *wounded.*" She didn't wait for him to respond. If she didn't leave now, he'd twist her heart around his finger and she'd never be able to see reason.

How could he do this? How could he cast aside the sacrifice she'd made for him and the intense love they'd shared only the night before? Gyllis was so angry, she dashed down the stairs moving far too fast, but she needed air. She'd nearly made it down the two flights when one of her ankles twisted on an uneven step. Crying out, she flung her hands against the narrow walls to slow her momentum. But down she went with a crashing thud. Her buttocks hit the unforgiving stone first, followed by her back, then her head. The last thing she remembered was a man's voice hollering for the healer.

***

Gyllis clapped her hands over her eyes. She wasn't outside, but there was a blinding light surrounding her. "Where am I?"

Meg's face came into view right above hers. "You're awake." She inclined her head. "I had the guards carry you to Duncan's tent. It wouldn't have been proper to tend you in the hospital tent—too many men there. How are you feeling?"

Gyllis slid her hand to the back of her head and connected with a sizeable knot. "My head's throbbing."

"I'm sure it is. You had quite a tumble." Meg stuffed a pillow beneath Gyllis's shoulders. "I take it all didn't go well with Sir Sean earlier."

"I'll say." She closed her eyes and rubbed her temples. "He refused to listen to reason and he's about to get himself killed." Gyllis tried to sit up. "I must stop him."

"You must rest." Meg sat beside her and rubbed ointment on Gyllis's head. It had a potent, minty smell and made her eyes water. "This should help clear the cobwebs."

"What's in it?"

"My own concoction. Smelling salts blended with peppermint, valerian and whale oil."

Gyllis blinked to clear her tears. "'Tis potent."

"Aye." Meg wiped her fingers on a cloth. "You ken, Sir Sean is one of the most skilled knights in all of Scotland."

"Aye."

Meg let out a long breath. "If I were bound in irons and left to starve, I'd want justice."

Gyllis reached for Meg's cloth and wiped off the ointment, so foul it was clearing the cobwebs a bit too fast. "Would you seek vengeance yourself or would you allow others to do battle for you?"

"If I were a knight, there'd be no question. I would face my oppressor."

"Even if you were weakened by hunger and had lesions all over your body?"

"Aye, even then. When a man faces battle something potent overcomes him. I even got a sense of it when I helped Duncan escape from the Edinburgh gaol. It's as if fatigue no longer matters—as if your muscles are infused with superhuman power." Meg brushed a wisp of Gyllis's hair from her face. "Have you ever been stronger than you ever dreamed possible because you had no other option?"

She didn't have to ponder that question. "Aye. Only yesterday I rowed a skiff all the way to the southern end of Kerrera because I kent Sean was there. He needed me." Gyllis closed her eyes and swallowed. "I still do not know how I found the strength to row all that way from morning to late afternoon."

Meg drew a hand over her heart. "You rowed for miles and did not stop because you had to save the man you love?"

Gyllis gulped. "I did."

"Is it so different that he needs to take part in tonight's siege?"

"But he's not yet recovered."

"I've seen him better, for certain." Meg clasped Gyllis's hand. "Sometimes a man needs to prove he's a man—if not to others, to himself."

She bit her lip. "But I'm so frightened."

"Do you think I have no fear every time Duncan rides out with the enforcers?"

Gyllis pushed up on her elbow. "How do you face it? How can you bear to watch him leave?"

"I pray." Meg grasped her pot and stood. "And busy myself by helping others."

***

Sean hated upsetting Gyllis. On one hand, she was right. He'd need a few days of hearty meals before he regained all of his strength. But he doubted any woman would ever understand why he must face Alan.

At least he'd regained enough strength to overpower *that* scoundrel.

Sean looked at his hand. He closed his fist. *An eye for an eye. A tooth for a tooth.*

Angus burst through the door. "'Tis Gyllis." He drew in a sharp inhale and pointed. "She's fallen and hit her head. Lady Meg is tending her in Duncan's tent."

"My God." Sean shoved back his chair and bounded toward the door. "What happened?"

"Wait." Angus grasped his wrist. "You cannot be seen. Where's your cloak?"

"Ballocks, we must make haste." Sean snatched his mantle from the peg and threw it over his shoulders. He pulled the hood low over his head. "Is she hurt?"

"She was unconscious when we carried her from the tower."

Sean kicked himself for allowing her to run off. He knew she was angry and those uneven tower stairs were difficult for a soldier to negotiate. He'd been so wrapped up in his desire for vengeance, he'd not thought about her paralysis or the toll it must have taken on her body whilst she rowed for miles to his rescue. *No wonder she was so distressed.*

He flew down the steps with Angus right behind.

So controlled by hate, Sean hadn't thought to follow her. He just assumed she'd join Lady Meg with Duncan in the war room. He'd planned to give her time to cool off, but he should have escorted her. Christ, this was an army encampment filled with men, and he'd sat dumbly while the woman he loved fell, hit her head and lost consciousness.

His heart could have burst through his chest. His legs couldn't run fast enough. Jesus Christ, he wouldn't blame her if she never forgave him. He was the greatest fool who'd ever walked the shores of Dunollie.

"She slipped at the bottom of the stairwell." Angus panted, trying to keep up. "I h-heard her cry out. Lady Meg and I f-found her first."

"Bloody hell," Sean mumbled, running, clutching the damned hood low over his face.

He skidded to a stop outside the tent, grasped the flap and ducked inside. "Gyllis!" he said, running to her pallet. "Forgive me."

He dropped to his knees beside Lady Meg. "I never should have let you leave alone. I should have insisted someone escort you."

Thank God, she was awake and propped against the pillows. She reached for his hand. "Not to worry. I'll be fine."

"When Angus told me you were hurt, my heart seized." He held her fingers to his lips and kissed. "I don't know what I would have done if I had lost you."

"She has a nasty bump at the back of her head," Lady Meg said. "But she doesn't appear to have any latent effects—no forgetfulness, no vomiting."

That didn't ease Sean's racing heart. "As I ran the short distance from the tower to this tent, I realized there is nothing in the world more important than you. There is no one in the world I want more than you and there is no vengeance more important than your love."

A gasp caught in Gyllis's throat. Tears welled in her eyes.

Lady Meg stood. "I must go check on an arrow wound that has been festering. If you'll please excuse me."

Sean rose and bowed. "My lady, allow me." He escorted her and held the tent flap, then quickly returned to Gyllis's side, dipping to one knee. "Are you in pain?"

She squeezed his hand. "Aside from a wee headache, I'm well. 'Tis the problem with being an invalid, everyone thinks you're frail."

"But you *are* as fragile as a dove." She struggled to sit up and Sean pressed his hand to her shoulder. "You must rest."

"No." She pushed up, a crease forming between her eyebrows, those gorgeous green eyes flashing with ire. "I've had enough of everyone telling me what to do— treating me like I haven't a mind because of an illness."

Of all the things about Gyllis there were to love, he adored her spirit the most. "You're right, *mo leannan.* In my observation nothing can stop you from achieving anything you set your mind to."

She smiled and cupped his face with her palm. "You may be the only person who believes that."

Sean leaned into her hand then turned his lips into her palm and kissed it. "I meant what I said. You mean more to me than any other person in the entire world." His heart ached, but he had to say it. No matter what he wanted, Gyllis was more important. "If you do not wish for me to face Alan, I shall stay behind."

Never had he seen her smile so vibrant. That gift alone made up for the disappointment of watching another act in his stead. She wrapped her arms around his neck and pulled him onto the pallet beside her. "By the grace of God, I love you Sean MacDougall."

"And I you, Gyllis Campbell, with all my heart, my soul, my life, my riches. I give them all to you."

She threaded her fingers through his. "But I cannot allow you to step away from a task I know in my heart you must do."

Sean arched his brows, sure he'd misunderstood. "Pardon me?"

"If." She held up a finger. "If you were to face Alan MacCoul, would you promise to return to me unharmed?"

"That's a difficult promise to make." He scratched his head. "A man can be injured sparring with his guard in the keep's courtyard. Stepping in the midst of battle always bears a risk."

"I ken." She nodded and stared at their interlaced fingers. "If I give my consent and you join Duncan this night, will you promise to exercise every care so that you will return to my arms?"

He pulled her into his embrace and inhaled. Her hair smelled of home—exactly where his heart resided. Gyllis's fragrance from here out would remind him of home.

"You have my vow. It will make me stronger to face that demon knowing you are waiting with open arms."

"Then you must eat and rest, for you'll need as much strength as you can muster."

He grinned and ran his hand up the back of her head. "Are you sure that fall didn't do some damage?"

She gave him a playful smack to the ribs and they both laughed.

Gazing into her fathomless eyes, Sean grew serious. He'd always loved Gyllis, but in this moment, his love grew tenfold. Somehow, between when she left the tower to when she arrived in the tent, she had grown to understand him, understand what a man—a chieftain—must do to earn respect, and more so, to maintain his honor.

Aye, he would have stayed behind for Gyllis, but now he would never forget how she cast aside her conviction and stood by him. He would spend his life repaying her favor.

He closed his eyes and claimed her mouth, showing her the depth of his love. The woman in his arms would be his throughout eternity.

Chapter Thirty

After blackening their faces with soot, Sean boarded a skiff with the most elite warriors in the Highland Enforcers and together they rowed from the pier around to the sea gate. Sean sat astern, Eoin manned the oars and Duncan sat beside his cousin, Robert Struan at the bow.

They'd left the newest member of the enforcers in charge of the army. Iain Campbell, Duncan's youngest brother, had recently returned from his fostering with the Earl of Argyll. Better, the lad had acquired some training in the operation of the cannons Duncan's forces had aimed to blast through Dunstaffnage's walls.

But Sean planned to end the siege this night. Alan had been holed up, locked inside the castle for four days. Foodstuffs would be low and tempers flaring. Once MacCoul was subdued, his men would cross over, lest they all end up feeling the hangman's noose.

Sean slid his hands up his sleeves to ensure his daggers were secure, then he did the same to the knives hidden in his hose. He didn't have much time to slip in and find his quarry. When the chapel bell tolled the end of compline, Iain would fire a warning shot past Dunstaffnage's walls into the Firth of Lorn. That would be the signal for all to attack. There would be no turning back this time, no volley of arrows. Ladders for scaling the walls were readied, a tree had been felled and reinforced with an iron tip. The main gate would be rammed. Five hundred MacDougalls, Campbells, Stewarts and MacGregors stood at the ready to overthrow the usurper and Sean would see an end to it once and for all.

The boat lightly tapped the stone embankment above the sea gate.

"Ready?" Duncan whispered loudly.

Sean offered a nod. This was how he wanted it. No one was more elusive. Undertaking the king's business—the enforcer's business—Sean had slipped inside castles from England to the Orkneys and this was no different.

He thrived on danger.

Before Robert had the boat tied, Sean jumped over the rail and crouched on the narrow wall. He didn't look back at the others. They all knew the plan. They'd worked together so many years, there was no need to talk. If they didn't adhere to the plan, someone would be killed—a lesson not easily forgotten. The first Lord of Glenorchy, Duncan's father had been killed on a mission at Kildrummy Castle. They'd all followed the plan, but sometimes things happened that one couldn't predict. Another lesson which would never be forgotten. *Always expect the unexpected.*

Sean pressed his ear against the wooden gate. Faint footsteps paced on the other side. He'd need to be swift and deadly.

He slid his dirk from its scabbard and held up one finger to Duncan. There was one man for certain—two if Alan had another posted at the top of the incline, but they'd know soon enough. Sean levered the pin out from the top hinge while Duncan and Eoin steadied the door.

After he'd removed the bottom pin, Duncan gave the men a nod. As they pulled the door away, Sean reached in, grabbed the guard by the chin and snapped his neck.

"Sorry, you bastard. You might have lived if you'd not paid fealty to a blackguard."

With no movement ahead, Sean pulled the MacCoul guard through the hole while Duncan and Eoin slid the gate back into place.

Once he'd donned the man's helm and surcoat, Sean picked up the soldier's battleax and nodded to Duncan. "Ready."

"We'll cover the gate until we hear the signal. You'll not have a soul watching your back," Duncan warned.

Sean shoved the visor over his face. Why Campbell felt he had to say something was beyond him. Even the Lord of Glenorchy had tried to talk him into staying behind. *You look like shite*, Duncan had said. God's teeth. Sean had gone without food and sleep before—mayhap things had never been as bad as his last day in the cave, but he'd eaten three meals since he'd returned *and* he'd slept. How much fitter did Duncan expect him to be?

He had to do this alone. Not only was he the "Ghost", more than one newcomer would cause a stir amongst MacCoul's men. Even one was a risk, but Sean was a master at blending in. He took the torch from the wall and held it high.

He slipped up the incline from the sea gate, into a dark cavern, praying it led directly under the inner bailey and into the catacombs of the donjon. The dank tunnel dripped with water. A clammy sweat crawled down Sean's back as he was reminded of his recent hospitality on Kerrera. The lesions throbbed beneath his hauberk and infused his ire. He sped his pace.

Stopping at the door, he held his breath and listened. Once sure he would be met with no nasty surprises, he tugged the door open. The hinges screeched as if they'd been sealed shut for three hundred years. He slipped inside and palmed his dirk, ready for a fight. But no one came.

At the far side of the room, rats scurried away. Sean sniffed. It reeked of sewage. He strode across the dirt floor to the passageway. Dark in both directions, he continued to his left. If his bearings served him right, the tower stairwell was ahead.

He crept against the wall. At any moment, some unsuspecting bastard could venture down to the catacombs—though he doubted it. The bowels of a castle were akin to the path to Hades. And if Sean had them pegged right, this mob of outlaws would be a suspicious lot.

After he rounded the corner, dim light glowed from the stairwell. He'd chosen correctly. He doused his torch and snuck forward. Rumbles of voices from the great hall grew louder as he neared. He closed the visor of his helm. He'd need to cross through the great hall to get to the donjon—and Sean had no doubt MacCoul was biding his time in the second floor solar. It was where the king held court the infrequent times he was in residence—also where the Lord of Lorn had run his affairs. MacCoul would believe he was due such a chamber of opulence with its rich tapestries from France.

Sean's feet made not a sound as he ascended. Before the stairwell opened upon the great hall, he froze, his heartbeat pulsing in his ears. Conversation rumbling from the pillagers was gruff.

"Even more Campbell supporters have arrived—and still no missive from the king," a voice said. "Soon every army in Scotland will be here to drive us out."

"I think we should fight now—show them MacCoul's army is one to be reckoned with."

"Aye? If our leader doesn't move soon, we'll be the ones they're calling traitors."

Sean smirked. The lot of them were already traitors—and MacCoul would receive his missive from the king—in hell.

He slipped through the entrance and moved at a meandering pace, as if he'd just been relieved of guard duty. His breath turned to mist against the helm, the eye slits barely giving him the range of sight he needed to see if there were any eyes watching him with suspicion. But he resisted the urge to glance from side to side and kept his face forward.

Ten paces to the donjon stairwell, a man stepped in his path. "Why are you still wearing your helm?"

Sean rubbed his neck. "Just returned from duty."

Before he could stop him, the man flipped up Sean's visor and squinted. "I haven't seen you before."

Sean snapped his head back and the visor dropped. Thank God the fool hadn't recognized him. "I've been keeping to myself—guarding the rear." He didn't want to mention the sea gate. If this man put the pieces together, Duncan and the others could end up in a nasty fight. Sean tried to push past.

"Why are you in such a hurry?"

Christ, the bastard couldn't leave it alone. "I've a message for MacCoul."

The man grabbed his arm. "Have you a missive from the king?" he asked excitedly.

If Sean said yes, the entire hall would follow him above stairs. "Nay."

"Then what is it?" His pickled breath oozed through the helm's eye slits.

Sean wrenched his arm away. "'Tis of a sensitive nature." Jesus, the smelly varlet wouldn't let it be. "Follow me and I'll tell you."

That seemed to placate the cur because he chuckled and motioned toward the stairwell.

"After you." Sean bowed. "I take it MacCoul's in the solar as usual?"

Moving forward, at least the man wasn't smart enough to stay at Sean's rear. "Aye."

Good, that's all the information Sean needed from this maggot. At the first landing, he slipped one hand over the man's mouth, pulled him into the servant's closet and ran his dirk across the bastard's neck. He leaned the battleax against the wall. Sean preferred to fight with a sword and a dirk, not the clumsy axe of a novice.

He wiped his dirk on the man's chausses and then shoved it in his scabbard. "If you'd left me be, you'd still be alive." Then Sean dashed up to the next landing, not stopping until he heard voices coming from inside the king's solar.

Sean clenched his teeth. Alan was arguing with none other than that festering-pustule, Brus. Sean would recognize that backstabber's grating voice anywhere. Brus had always followed MacCoul around like a leech—had laughed in Sean's face before they'd left him to die.

Take your last breath, for hell is about to unleash its vengeance.

Sean silently lifted the latch and peered inside. Alan sat in the king's chair, with Brus leaning against the sideboard, arms and ankles crossed as if he owned the castle. Sean fingered the dagger up his left sleeve. In one fluid motion, he pushed through the door, flung the blade, hitting Brus in the neck, then drew his sword.

Thus far, not a shout had been uttered. Staring MacCoul in the eye, Sean closed the door behind him and bolted it.

Alan shoved back his chair and drew their father's sword. "You," he growled unable to hide the surprise in his voice.

Gurgling empty curses, Brus clutched at the knife and fell face first on the table.

Alan sidestepped, his eyes wide with fear. "Get thee from me, ghost. I left you for dead—no man could have lived this long."

"You are quite mistaken." Sean leveled his sword with Alan's heart. "Had you been honest with me from the outset, our feud wouldn't have ended this way."

"Oh?" he continued to circle around the table. "And I would have survived in my little brother's shadow?"

"You've lost that chance. Now you will die in it."

Alan lunged. "I think not."

Sean skittered aside, a chair toppling over. He nearly lost his balance as he deflected Alan's attack.

Alan advanced with relentless hacks of his blade. He'd grown stronger since Beltane.

And Sean had grown weaker.

Backing around the room, it was all he could do to deflect the onslaught of vicious strikes. Sean's muscles burned, barely able to wield the sword in his hands. Duncan had been right. Everyone had been right. Sean's strength was half what it should be, his movement slowed by sluggishness.

Gnashing his teeth, Alan lunged in for the kill. Sean raised his blade for the deflection, a hair's breadth before the sword sliced him across the neck. His helm flew from his head and clattered to the floor. Iron screeched with iron as their blades locked until they met at the cross guards. In a battle of strength, Sean could no longer control his muscles and he quaked mercilessly. Planting his left foot, he used his right to push MacCoul away and gain enough space to run.

He sped around the table to put some distance between them. Panting, he watched Alan swing his sword in an arc. The bastard laughed—taunted Sean. "I see my hospitality has turned you into a milksop."

Sean said nothing, sucking in deep breaths, willing the air to revive him.

Alan sauntered around the table. "After I kill you, I'll be Chieftain of Dunollie and I'll marry that Campbell bitch—something you never had the cods to do."

"You bleeding bastard. You'll not touch her!" Sean went on the attack, swinging his sword like a madman. He never allowed himself to lose control when in a fight, but rage gripped his chest like a vise. He couldn't stop. The thought of Alan claiming Gyllis for his own drove him to the brink of insanity.

A picture of Fraser's mutilated body sent him into a raving frenzy. "I will avenge Fraser's death."

"That spineless maggot?" MacCoul blocked Sean's strike and the next. On and on Sean advanced while the blackguard continued to back around the table. "I took great pleasure in gutting your asp-biting spy."

Rage infusing him with strength, Sean used both hands, spinning, aiming for the braggart's head. MacCoul ducked and came up, jabbing the pommel of his sword into Sean's gut. Wind whooshed from Sean's lungs. He gasped for air and steadied himself.

Never had he tired this easily.

A blast came from beyond the walls. The cannon's warning had been fired. MacCoul was already supposed to be dead.

Alan advanced. Sean deflected. Iron clanged. Sean erred with slips of the wrist and deadly mistakes. But he wasn't about to give up. Spinning, he hurled his blade. MacCoul met his strike with equal force. With jarring power reverberating up his arms, the sword flew from Sean's grip.

Before he could reach for his dirk, Alan slipped his blade against Sean's neck and laughed like Satan himself.

"I should have cut your throat at the cave and been done with it."

Sean spat. "You'll never succeed. The king will not recognize your claim."

Alan's eyes flashed wide and he pressed the blade harder. "I will be Chieftain of Dunollie and Lord of Lorn. It is my rightful place. My inheritance." The man's face grew red. Clearly, he couldn't bear to think he could possibly fail.

Pride is a great sin.

"What about Dugald?" Sean purchased time. "He's Lorn's heir."

"I killed Lorn," Alan gloated.

"But he didn't die before he took his vows." Sean dropped his arm and slid the dagger from his hose. "And our father only claimed one son. The king signed your death warrant."

Alan bellowed like a caged lion. "You lie! You'll not be here to see the riches I am granted. All of the Highlands will fear me. I will cut off your head and impale it on a pike above the gate as a testament as to who is the better son." Baring his teeth, he grasped Sean's hair, swinging his blade back.

Time slowed.

The cannon boomed with a long drawn-out blast.

Sean watched the blade rise then focused on the pulsing vein in Alan's exposed neck. He could hear the thump of his brother's heart. A drop of Alan's sweat splattered on his cheek. *He will never touch Gyllis.*

Before their father's sword began its downward momentum, Sean sprang up and sliced his dagger across MacCoul's throat.

In mid-swing, the sword's edge embedded deep into Sean's shoulder, but he didn't feel a thing.

Stunned and grasping at his throat, Alan fell onto Sean. "I am the eldest son," he croaked.

Sean wrapped him in his arms. "I wish it had been different between us, brother."

Alan let out a long hissing breath. His last.

Sean rested his brother's body on the floor and passed a hand over his face to close Alan's vacant eyes. Aye, he'd done what he must, but this was not victorious.

When he started to stand, Sean's head spun. He glanced down at the gash in his shoulder. Thick blood oozed down his hauberk. He reached for the chair to steady himself, but it was just beyond his grasp. Grunting, Sean fell forward and collapsed atop Alan's body.

Chapter Thirty-One

Gyllis and Meg clung to each other in Duncan's tent while the battle raged. Every blast from the cannons made Gyllis quake in the oversized kirtle Meg had borrowed for her. "When will it be over?"

"I know not," Meg's voice trembled every bit as much as Gyllis's did. "But we will be victorious. There is no other option."

A man screamed, followed by a bone-crunching thud. Gyllis didn't want to think—but her mind's eye still pictured a warrior falling from the battlements.

She forced herself not to scream. "What if Sean or Duncan is hurt?"

Meg grasped her shoulders firmly and looked Gyllis in the eye. "We will not think on it."

"I hate hiding in this tent. What more can we do to help?"

"Pray."

Meg had always been pious and Gyllis grew inordinately guilty about having cursed at God the day before. She cringed. "I yelled at the heavens when I couldn't find Sean. God could be very upset with me this day."

Meg clasped her hands, squeezing tighter with her claw. Meg only used that hand when she was dead serious. "Did you find Sean?"

"Aye," Gyllis whispered—of course Meg knew she had.

"Well then, sometimes you might need to yell to be heard." She closed her eyes and recited the twenty-third psalm. Gyllis followed along, mouthing the words. Evidently Meg didn't feel it necessary to yell, because she kept her tone even and somber.

When Meg finished, an eerie hush hung over the encampment. Gyllis stood and turned full circle, hearing not a single scrape of a sword.

"The siege is over, long live the king!" someone bellowed.

A roar of triumphant voices rose around them.

Gyllis grinned at Meg and pulled her hand. "Come." Together they made their way over the barbican bridge and into the inner bailey as fast as Gyllis could manage. Men were celebrating, running past them with their weapons held high, but the women fought through the crowd. When they reached the donjon, Gyllis clapped a hand to her chest and caught her breath. "Have you seen them?"

Meg turned full circle. "Not yet."

A fallen man clutched at his stomach, lying in a pool of blood. "Help. Someone, please help me."

Meg pointed to the doors. "You go—I cannot leave him."

Gyllis needed no more encouragement. For all she knew, Sean could be laying in his own pool of blood. When she pushed into the great hall, all she saw was madness. Duncan's men were rounding up the usurpers and had them lying on the floor with their hands behind their heads. But the King's solar was above stairs. Pushing through the crowd, she made her way to the stairwell.

As she climbed, pounding grew louder. When she reached the landing, Duncan and Mevan were chopping the solar door with a battleax. She didn't need to ask. Sean was in there, and so was Alan MacCoul.

Dread iced through her veins while she watched them beat down the door. When they finally had it clear, she rushed in. "Sean!" Her heart stopped. Sean didn't move. Slumped over the body of MacCoul, all color had drained from his face.

Blood pooled thickly on the floor. Splatters covered everything.

"No!" *He cannot be dead.*

Tears stinging her eyes, she threw herself over him. "Sean. 'Tis me. We've won!" She shook his shoulders. "Sean. Wake up. Please. Wake."

Duncan grasped her shoulder. "Our dear friend is gone, lass."

Ice coursed across her skin. "No," she cried through her tears. "I do not believe it."

Duncan again tugged, but Gyllis clamped her arms around Sean. "I will *not* leave him." She turned and glared at her brother. "Carry him to a chamber."

"But—"

"Do it." She pointed. "Now!"

Duncan nodded his head once and beckoned Mevan. "There's a bedchamber next door. The women will be able to prepare his body there."

Gyllis grasped Sean's hand. His fingers were frigid— and there was a deep gash on his shoulder.

"Stand aside," Duncan said.

Sucking in her tears, she allowed the men to lift Sean's body. His head flopped back and his arms and legs hung limp as they hauled him into the next room and placed him on the bed. "Send for Lady Meg," she snapped.

Duncan hesitated for a moment, but he didn't say a word.

They left her alone, holding Sean's hand.

Chapter Thirty-Two

In the dimly lit room, Gyllis threw herself over Sean's lifeless body, a wail erupting from her throat. "Please God, no." She could scarcely utter the words through her fitful sobbing. She held up her blistered palms, still so painful from rowing to Kerrera. "You did not guide me to Kerrera only to see him killed here!"

She prostrated herself atop him.

"I do not believe it."

"I do not believe it."

"I. Do. Not!"

Reaching down, she threaded her fingers through his and kissed them. "You told me you would be careful."

A pained cry caught in the back of her throat.

"Why did I allow Meg to talk me into letting you fight? I knew you were weakened, yet I trusted everyone and *ignored* my own heart."

Spittle leaked from the corner of her mouth. "Please, God. D-do not take him from me."

She scooted up and cupped his face with her palm. He seemed so peaceful—not dead, but in a deep sleep. How a man could be so beautiful, she could not fathom. And this man had loved her in spite of all her adversity, in spite of her limp, in spite of her every weakness.

"I will always love you." She pressed her lips to his and closed her eyes, praying all the while. His lips were far warmer than his fingers—warmer than the chill within the chamber.

Sean's chest rose and fell.

Gyllis jolted up. "Sean?"

He didn't move.

She held a finger beneath his nose. A faint puff of warm air caressed her finger.

Clapping a hand over her mouth, she gasped. "Oh, thank God." She limped to the door as fast as she could and swung it open. "Fetch Lady Meg. Sir Sean is alive!" Gyllis latched on to an arm of a passing guard. "Did you hear me? Fetch Lady Meg at once."

She must have been assertive or half-crazed, because the guard saluted. "Yes, m'lady. Straight away."

Swiping away her tears, Gyllis hastened back to the bed. "Lady Meg is coming. We must see to this horrible gash on your shoulder." Her heart fluttered. "You will be fine. I know it."

There wasn't much left of his sleeve, so she tore it away and pushed the remaining cloth aside to inspect the wound. It was deep, but she couldn't see bone. That had to be a good sign.

Meg rushed inside. "I've sent Mevan to fetch my basket."

"His chest heaved and I felt warm air from his nose."

"Thank heavens." Meg inspected Sean's arm. "I'll need to stitch this straight away." She grimaced. "But 'tis so deep, he could lose the arm."

"What's an arm compared to a life?"

"Let us pray we can save both." Meg faced her. "Regardless, I'll need your help. The injuries out there are horrendous. You'll have to tend him all night—keep a cool cloth on his forehead, spoon willow tea into his mouth. Can you do that?"

"Of course. I will do anything."

"I've your basket, m'lady," Mevan said from the doorway.

Meg beckoned him. "Bring it here, then go help the others. I'll head to the hospital tent as soon as I stitch up this wound."

Mevan set the basket on the bedside table and hissed. "Bloody hell, MacCoul nearly took his arm off."

"'Tis none too pretty." Meg fished for a whalebone needle and thread. "Gyllis, you'll need both hands to hold Sir Sean's flesh together."

"I'll do anything you need."

"Good." Meg smiled. "I hope you have a strong stomach."

Gyllis would have a strong anything if it meant Sean would live. When she moved to Sean's shoulder, she ignored the pain in her palms and bore down with all her strength, matching the two sides of his skin. She watched Meg's every stitch until the last one was tied off.

Meg swiped off the blood with a cloth and secured her needle in the basket. "Remember what I said. Keep his forehead cool. Keep the wound doused with avens oil. Have the chambermaid bring you willow bark tea and ale. Keep spooning it into his mouth until he wakes."

He wakes. Those words were like angel's bells. "I'll keep a vigil for a month if I must."

"If things grow worse, send someone to fetch me." She put the basket over her arm. "I fear this will be a long night for us all."

***

As she'd promised, Gyllis maintained a vigil at Sean's side. Blood seeped from his wound, but she saw that as a good sign—God's own form of cleansing. The past few days had sped past in such a blur. She sat beside him on the bed, allowing herself to doze only for brief moments in between dousing the cloth in cool water. She hummed and talked as she worked—partly for her sake and partly for Sean's. If he could hear her, she wanted him to know she was there—would always be beside him.

The witching hour must have come because Gyllis's eyelids refused to stay open. Sleep kept trying to claim her mind. Her head continuously bobbed. She got up and paced the floor, but her toe stubbed repeatedly, making her stumble. Walking, exhaustion and the latent effects of paralysis did not go well together.

She pulled a wooden chair beside the bed and sat, realizing the hour glass had run its course. Once she turned it over, she picked up the tankard with the tea and a spoon. "Time for another tincture, my love." She ladled a few drops in Sean's mouth—his lips were still so chapped. "Did I ever tell you about the time Helen and I were spying on you and Sir Eoin MacGregor?"

"Nay," a raspy voice answered.

She held the spoon completely still, her gaze shooting to Sean's face. His eyes were still closed. "Nay?" she asked, wondering if her mind was playing tricks.

His Adam's apple bobbed. "N-nay," he said.

"My goodness, you heard me?"

He nodded slightly.

"Are you in pain?"

"Aye." His eyes opened a wee bit. "Come here."

She set down her things and nestled beside him, careful not to disturb his wound. "They thought you were dead, but I wouldn't believe it."

A chuckle caught in his throat. "I'm glad you did not." He licked his lips. "But I'd expect no less from my woman."

Her heart squeezed. "I'll take care of you, Sean MacDougall. I shall care for you until I draw my last breath."

"I'm the one who should be uttering such words of chivalry." He blinked then widened his eyes. "You have my vow, I will protect you forever. You will always be the keeper of my heart. Never again will I be so foolish as to walk into battle when I ken I am weak. That bastard nearly killed me."

"Hush." Gyllis placed her finger to his lips. "You did what you must. Now let us spoon some willow tea in your belly. It will help keep the fever at bay."

"Nay. All I need is you beside me. A wee bit of sleep and I'll be right."

"You're a rugged man, Sean MacDougall." She snuggled into him and pulled the bedclothes around their shoulders. "Everything will be better on the morrow."

***

Her mind was in a fog when the door burst open.

"Heaven help us, you are ruined." Mother rushed inside, slamming the door behind her.

As soon as Gyllis heard the voice, she bolted upright. "Ma? What are you doing here?" Devil's bones, she needed about another sennight of sleep.

"You expected me to sit idle when news of a battle arrived at Kilchurn? And I was right to come. Look at you. In bed with a *man*! If that's not bad enough, there are armies of people everywhere. You are *scandalous*!" She clapped a hand to her forehead and paced. "The family will be disgraced. I'll never find husbands for Marion or Alice. All three of you will be ruined."

Gyllis glanced downward at her borrowed, ill-fitting kirtle and then across to Sean's naked chest—he hadn't awakened with Mother's tirade. Gyllis shook her head to clear the cobwebs and swung her legs over the edge of the bed. "He's been unconscious most of the night. God's teeth, Ma, Lady Meg assigned me to his care."

"Watch your vulgar tongue." Mother held up a finger. "That didn't mean you should climb into bed with the man. Who has seen you?"

"N-no one. I stayed awake until I could no longer hold up my head."

Ma stopped pacing and glared across the room. "I must have Duncan speak to Sir Sean at once." She walked up to the bed, as if she'd only realized Sean was still sleeping. "The only way to avoid a scandal is for him to propose marriage this day." She patted his cheek. "Sir Sean?"

He didn't move.

Gyllis grasped Mother's arm. "Please, let him rest. He was severely injured—was close to death." She swallowed her urge to smile and led her mother to the chairs in front of the hearth. Had she honestly used the words *propose marriage*? "I've wanted to talk to you in earnest about Sir Sean for a long time. Perhaps we can have a word whilst he slumbers."

Mother pursed her lips as if the thought didn't appeal. With one last glance over her shoulder she relented and sat.

Gyllis leaned her head in and kept her voice low. "Did Helen speak to you?"

"Aye," Ma whispered.

"So you know Sir Sean visited me…um…frequently when I was at Ardchattan?"

Mother nodded.

"And you are aware we wish to marry?"

"Wheesht." Ma grasped her hand and squeezed. "For some ridiculous reason, Duncan has never approved of Sir Sean's affinity for you, so you'd best wipe that smile off your face and play along if I am to have any chance of success." She violently shook her finger. "This is scandalous," she raised her voice. "You remained the entire night in this chamber alone with Sir Sean? How could you? Now *only* Duncan can keep the entire family from ruination!"

Gyllis hid her face in her hands. Evidently Mother had arrived at Dunstaffnage with a well-thought plan of her own.

***

Every inch of his body ached, but Sean forced himself to open his eyes. For some mysterious reason, he could have sworn he'd heard Lady Margaret's shrill voice shouting about a scandal—and he was the rogue at the bottom of it. He'd been the center of a scandal before, but definitely couldn't admit to any foul play last eve.

"But Sir Sean could have died had I not been here to tend him," Gyllis said.

The women were near the hearth. Sean tried to sit up, but unholy stabbing pain stopped him with a bellow. "Bloody hell."

"Sean," Gyllis hastened toward the bed. "You're awake."

He gritted his teeth, biting back the pain. "Aye, and there'll be no scandal. Let the old windbags talk. I'll marry Gyllis this day."

"Sir Sean." Lady Margaret rushed to the head of the bed. "I knew you would see reason." She brushed the hair from his forehead. "If you are to be wed, we must have time to plan." She held up a finger as if she had everything scripted. "A betrothal will be quiet sufficient. But first you must have words with Lord Duncan."

The door swung open. "What the blazes are you doing here, Mother?" The Lord of Glenorchy strode inside, hair mussed, shoving his shirt into his breeks.

Once the door closed, the lady marched up to him. "Are you aware your sister spent the entire night with this man?"

Gyllis pattered in behind Ma. "But he was unconscious. Lady Meg told—"

"Enough," Lady Margaret cut Gyllis off and returned her attention to Duncan. "We have no choice but to insist Sir Sean makes a proposal of marriage to Gyllis this very day, else she and your sisters will be ruined and I shall never find husbands for them all."

Duncan cast a heated look in Sean's direction. "Bloody Christmas, Mother. How the devil did you arrive so early? Do not tell me you rode all night."

"And why ever not? After I received word that my son, my daughter and the mother of my grandchild were embroiled in a battle with a ruthless scourge. Of course I gathered the guard and rode all night." She jabbed her finger into Duncan's sternum. "But that is not the issue at hand. You must have words with Sir Sean. There are people mulling about *everywhere*. News of my daughter's indiscretion will run rampant."

"But—"

Mother stretched a bit taller. "I'd be surprised if the rumors haven't already spread."

"I do not—"

"Thank the good Lord I arrived when I did. The only way to avoid a scandal is if you accept his proposal of marriage to your sister forthwith."

Duncan scratched his head. "Are you finished?"

With a satisfied and aristocratic rise of her chin, Lady Margaret took Gyllis by the hand. "Follow me, dear. We must leave the men to talk." On the way out she shook her finger at Duncan. "I do not want you to leave this chamber until you have come to an agreement."

Despite the excruciating pain in his shoulder, Sean withheld his urge to laugh. Aside from Lady Meg, Lady Margaret was the only person Sean had ever seen make Duncan eat his words. But he had no illusions that his friend would be in a bear of a mood. Sean eased to his good side and forced himself to sit up.

Duncan faced him and glowered. "You're the only man I know who could cause a scandal whilst out senseless."

Sean tried to smile, but his lip split. "Aye, and I didn't even chance to have any fun." He winced, Christ, sometimes he didn't know when to keep his mouth shut.

"Bloody damnation and ballocks to that." At least Duncan didn't hit him. "You look like shite."

"Feel like it, too." He licked the blood from his lip. "You ken I've always been in love with Gyllis."

"Aye, but I've fought your affinity for my sister for years." Duncan sat on the bed beside him. "You'll have to put an end to your womanizing, else I'll be forced to tell Ma the girls are ruined."

"You'd do that?" Sean forced a grin. The lusty laddie moniker had to go. He hated to admit it to Duncan, but it was time to bare his soul. "I haven't looked at a woman other than Gyllis in over a year. Even after you sent me to the miserable borders, I kept to myself." God, his head hurt. Everything hurt as if he'd been bludgeoned within an inch of his life. "I love her, Duncan. I would die for her."

"Even after her paralysis? You ken she may never be graceful—never dance again."

"Do you think I care? I love Gyllis for the angel she is in her heart." Sean swiped a hand across his chapped lips. "I've loved her since your mother forced us to take part in all those silly dancing lessons, and my love for her grew tenfold after Gyllis, stricken with paralysis, rowed from

Dunstaffnage to the southern tip of Kerrera because she remembered a threat Alan MacCoul made months prior—a threat *you* heard him utter."

"And yet I didn't believe her. I, too, can be a dunce at times." Shaking his head, the corners of Duncan's mouth turned up. "Very well, I shall agree to your betrothal, but you will not spend another moment alone with my sister until after your vows are sealed."

Sean held up his palm. "Just allow me a modicum of time."

Duncan eyed him.

"I'm in no condition to take advantage of the lass—and she needs a proper proposal."

"Very well." He held up a finger just like his Ma had done only moments ago. "But keep in mind, I will be right outside."

When Duncan opened the door, Lady Margaret, Lady Meg and Gyllis all stared up at him as if they were trying to pretend they hadn't overheard a word. He ushered Gyllis into the chamber. "Sir Sean wants to speak to you for a moment and that is all I will allow."

When the door closed behind her, Gyllis tiptoed inside with her hands steepled to her lips. "I am sorry all of this had to happen whilst you are in so much pain."

Sean stood, his legs wobbling beneath him. The past few days had nearly sent him to an early grave.

Gyllis rushed forward and grasped his elbow. "You should still be abed."

"Mind you, that's exactly where I'm headed, but there's one thing I must do first." Thank God he didn't fall on his face as he went down on bended knee. He took her hand in his palms.

Her wee gasp made his blood thrum anew.

Taking a big inhale he stared at the eyes that had enraptured him since boyhood—the only lips he wanted to kiss, the woman who had grown to mean so much to him. "Gyllis Marietta Campbell, you have shown me courage beyond that of any man I know. You have shown me perseverance to rival the greatest of men, and you are the dearest and most stunning creature I have ever seen. I love you more passionately than life itself...You have claimed my heart. Will you do me the honor of agreeing to be my wife?"

By the time he'd finished the brief proclamation of his undying love, a tear spilled from Gyllis's eye and splashed on the back of his hand. Keeping her palm in his grasp, he first kissed her salty tear, then turned her hand and pressed his lips against it.

"Aye," she whispered. "I will marry you, Sir Sean MacDougall."

Chapter Thirty-Three

After Sean's proposal, they had decided to hold the wedding at Kilbride Church on Dunollie lands. In front of the polished copper mirror, Gyllis sat in the chamber where she'd tried to sleep that first night when she'd visited Dunollie—the one where she and Sean couldn't return to Ardchattan due to the flooding.

Helen straightened Gyllis's gold veil which was held in place by a circlet encrusted with emeralds. "You make a beautiful bride."

Gyllis offered a sheepish smile. "If only I could have been at *your* wedding."

"It was nice, though not as well attended as yours." Helen toyed with Gyllis's collar. "My, Mother must have invited half of Argyllshire."

"I believe she did." Gyllis chuckled. "And how is life as the Lady of Ardnamurchan?"

Helen glanced toward the window. "I enjoy running the keep—just as I always thought I might."

"And Sir Aleck? Is he treating you well?"

"Aye, I suppose. He's an unusual man when he's home. He's oft away—embroiled in the feud with the MacDonalds." She reached for a bottle of rose oil sitting atop the sideboard. "He's as fierce a warrior as I've ever seen."

"Oh my, that is saying something, with Duncan Campbell as our brother and the Highland Enforcers always mulling about Kilchurn Castle."

Helen dabbed a bit of the oil behind her ear. "True." There was sadness in her voice.

Gyllis placed a palm on her sister's arm. "Is he tender with you?"

"Not really." A wee tear glistened at the corner of Helen's eye. "If anything he's gruff. But I needn't worry overmuch. Thus far, he's not been around long enough for it to be a bother."

Gyllis pulled Helen into her arms. It didn't seem right for her to be so happy when her sister was not.

"Enough of that." Helen backed away and grasped Gyllis's shoulders. "We are here to celebrate your marriage to Sir Sean MacDougall this day. At least one of us caught the man of our dreams."

"And you must know you are welcome at Dunollie at any time with or without your warrior husband."

"Thank you. One never knows. I may end up on your stoop with a satchel over my shoulder."

Gyllis dabbed Helen's eye with a kerchief. "I'm sure things will improve."

"Aye, Mother said the same. She told me the first year is always the worst. As you recall, hers was an arranged marriage, and things did not start well between her and Da."

Gyllis chuckled. "I remember the stories well."

A rap came at the door. "It is time." Duncan stepped inside. "Are you ready?"

Butterflies flitted in Gyllis's stomach as she glanced around the room. "I was ready sennights ago."

***

Sean hadn't been this nervous when he went before the king on the day of his knighthood. Why he was anxious at all baffled him. He loved Gyllis, and had waited throughout an agonizing month while her mother invited half of Scotland to the wedding feast…but still, he paced in front of the altar.

It seemed like an eternity had passed since Duncan had left to fetch Gyllis. What if she suddenly had a change of mind? Sean clenched his fist. *Gyllis wouldn't do that.*

The church pews were filled with people. In fact there were so many in attendance, groups stood at the back of the nave. *Where did they all hail from?*

John Campbell took his place in front of the altar, holding a black prayer book. "You could sit until they arrive. You look like a caged dog."

Sean shot the priest an annoyed glare. But he did sit—for about two blinks of an eye and then he was back on his feet. "Sitting only makes it worse."

John frowned—probably because he thought he should. If the former knight hadn't gone off and joined the priesthood, he'd be laughing and giving the Dunollie Chieftain a good rib about now.

When the double doors finally opened, Sean held his breath. Duncan led Gyllis inside and they stood at the rear of the aisle. She smiled. Sean's insides melted. By God, she was stunning. Wearing a golden headdress, the silken wimple framed her face, enhancing her vivacious coloring. Green eyes, pink cheeks, lips as red as rubies. She wore a high-collared, woven red-and-gold mantle over a silken kirtle that made her look as regal as the queen. When they proceeded down the aisle, Sean hardly noticed her limp. God, she was amazing. It hadn't even been a half-year since she'd contracted paralysis and look how far she'd come.

By the time she arrived beside him, Sean's nervousness had been replaced by complete and utter adoration. Duncan offered her hand and he grasped it, hoping never to let go. "I've missed you."

Her radiant smile melted yet another piece of his heart. Gyllis inclined her lips toward his ear. "I though this past month would never pass."

"I cannot wait until the feast is over so I can whisk you above stairs," he whispered out the corner of his mouth.

She leaned into him and winked. "But we shall need sustenance first."

If he hadn't been in a church, Sean would have burst out laughing.

John cleared his throat. "Shall we begin?"

Sean gave a nod and the Latin mass commenced. There was only one thing he could focus on, and that was the face of the incredible woman who stood before him. How such a lady could love a man such as he, the Chieftain of Dunollie—former Lusty Laddie—he would never know, but he loved her with a fire so passionate the torch he carried for Gyllis could never be snuffed.

Author's Note

Thank you for joining me for Gyllis and Sean's journey. This was an interesting story to write, indeed. Because there are so many people named John in this series, I used "Sean" for the hero's first name. As you may have guessed, the 11th Chieftain of Dunollie was John MacDougall, of MacDougall. I also left the date of this story ambiguous, because I believe John was much older when he actually married Gyllis Campbell.

The facts in the genealogy record do detail that John MacDougall's uncle, the Lord of Lorn (also named John) asked for protection from the MacDougall Clan during his wedding at Dunstaffnage Chapel. Alan MacCoul, MacDougall's illegitimate brother, stabbed Lorn outside the chapel doors. The Lord of Lorn took his vows while he was dying, thus granting his son the lordship. Alan MacCoul then laid siege to Dunstaffnage Castle and did imprison John MacDougall in irons on the Isle of Kerrera where he almost died.

The Campbells (reported as being led by Colin Campbell, the Lord of Argyll) fought and reclaimed Dunstaffnage, and Alan MacCoul is said to have slipped away. The record says nothing about who actually rescued John MacDougall from the cave, thus it was convenient to have Gyllis perform that act of heroism.

Next up in the Highland Dynasty series is Lady Helen and her abominable marriage to Aleck MacIain. With luck, Eoin MacGregor might perform his own acts of heroism in *Highland Knight of Rapture*.

Excerpt from Amy's Next Release:

Highland Knight of Rapture

Highland Dynasty Series ~ Book Four
Coming July, 2015

Chapter One

Mingary Castle, the Highlands. March, 1493

Clenching every muscle in her body, Helen bore down with her remaining shreds of strength. She'd crossed the threshold of her endurance hours ago. Pain no longer mattered. After twenty-four hours of labor, she needed to expunge this bairn from her womb if it killed her, which may very well come about.

Her body shuddered as she shrieked through her grating voice box, pushing until her eyes bulged. "I…" she panted. "Cannot. Take. Anymore!"

"You can," Glenda shouted. "Just a bit longer, m'lady."

Helen sucked in a gasp of air. If she weren't on the brink of death, she'd give her chambermaid a strong rebuttal. But before she could open her mouth, the blinding pain intensified. Panting, she gripped the bed linens and clenched her teeth so taut, they might just shatter. "Eeeeeeee," she screeched.

"I see the head, m'lady. Keep. Pushing!"

Helen loved Glenda, but by the saints, the woman had to be the spawn of the devil to encourage this mounting torture.

Straining so hard her skull throbbed, Helen gulped one more deep breath and pushed. This had to be the end. Swooning, she could take no more. Stars darted through her vision. Her insides ripped and tore. Many women died in childbirth.

Would she, too?

Blessed Mother Mary, help me, I must survive.

Then as if her prayer had been answered, the bairn slid out between her legs. Her pain subsided.

Helen collapsed against the pillows.

A slap resounded through the chamber. A wee cry sang out.

Helen's heart soared.

"'Tis a lass, m'lady."

She could have floated to the canopy above. Pushing the sweat-soaked hair from her brow, Helen smiled. "A wee lassie?" Joyful tears welled in her eyes. Suddenly, all the pain and agony seemed worthwhile as the infant's angelic voice gasped and cried. It was the most delightful sound she'd ever heard. She reached up. "I want to hold her."

"Let me finish cleansing her, and then you can make the bond," Glenda said from across the chamber.

With a sigh, Helen gazed at the scarlet canopy above. She'd never been so elated, yet so exhausted.

Glenda came into view, a wide grin on her careworn face. She settled the bairn in Helen's waiting arms. "What will you call the lass, m'lady?"

Helen regarded the beet-red infant yawning at her. She had a tiny bow-shaped mouth, enormous blue eyes and a smattering of black curls atop her head. "You shall be named Margaret after my mother, but I shall call you Maggie, because you are the most adorable wee bairn I have ever seen." She kissed the top of her daughter's head. "And your second name shall be Alice after my younger sister. I like the sound of *Alice* ever so much."

With a fragrance as fresh as morning's dew, Maggie turned her head toward Helen's breast and nudged.

"She can smell your milk, m'lady." Glenda untied Helen's linen shift and opened the front. "Hold Maggie to your teat. She'll ken what to do."

Helen moved the bairn in place, and just as Glenda had said, Maggie started to suckle. But it burned. Alarmed, Helen gasped and shot a panicked look at her chambermaid.

"Do not worry, m'lady. It stings a bit at first, but eases as soon as your milk starts to flow."

Again, Glenda was right and the stinging lessened as quickly as it had come on.

Watching the miracle in her arms, Helen sighed. "I do not ken what I would do without you, Glenda. You are so wise with these things."

"Aye?" The chambermaid chuckled. "Having three bairns of my own gave me all the learning I needed, I suppose."

Helen stiffened when the door opened. Her husband strode into the chamber, his heavy boots clomping over the floorboards while the sword and dirk belted at his waist clanked against his iron hauberk. She would never grow accustomed to Aleck MacIain's harsh mien. With a bald head and black steely eyes, she'd yet to discover his compassionate side, despite five years of marriage. That the bulky man entered wearing his weapons, along with muddy boots, spoke volumes about his lack of respect for her.

Though Helen's skin crawled, she feigned a smile— the same one she always used to mask her fear. "Come meet your daughter, m'laird."

He stopped mid-stride and glared. "You mean to tell me that after five miserable years of waiting, you only manage to produce a lass?"

Helen tensed and glanced to Glenda. The chambermaid met her gaze with a frown, then snapped her attention to gathering the soiled linens. No one in the clan dared confront the Chieftain of Mingary, lest they be turned out to fend for themselves. A knot clamped in Helen's stomach. Aleck may be a tyrant toward her, but he would respect their daughter. "She is our firstborn—a lovely, healthy bairn. 'Tis not always a misfortune for a daughter to come first. We will have other children, of that I am certain."

He dropped his gaze to her exposed breast and frowned. "I have misgivings about your ability to be successful at bearing lads, given the length of time it took to conceive a lass." He grunted. "At least you've gained some shape to your udders, though I doubt they'll stay that way."

Helen turned her face away, heat prickling the back of her neck. Bless it, she'd just birthed *his* bairn, and he hadn't a kind word to say? She bit back the tears threatening to well in her eyes. A long time ago, she'd vowed Aleck MacIain would not make her weep. She'd spent every day of the past five years trying to please him—looking at every insult as another chance to better herself. But her efforts had never been enough.

If only I could do something to make him like me.

She regarded the helpless bairn in her arms. Hit with an overwhelming urge to protect Maggie, she pulled the comforter over the lass to shield the child and her breast from Aleck's stare.

Glenda clapped her hands. "I'm afraid Lady Helen is very weak, m'laird. She has lost a great deal of blood and needs her rest."

Aleck's gaze darted to the chambermaid as if about to spit out a rebuke. But his lips formed a thin line and he nodded. With one last odious look at Helen, he turned on his heel and left.

Helen allowed herself to breathe.

Glenda dashed to the side of the bed. "I'm ever so sorry, m'lady."

"'Tis not your fault. I kent Sir Aleck wanted a lad." Helen smoothed her hand over Maggie's downy soft curls as the bairn continued to suckle. "He just doesn't ken how precious a lass can be."

"No, he does not. I doubt he ever will."

"Wheesht, Glenda," Helen admonished.

The woman crossed her arms. "I'll not pretend. I disprove of his boorishness, especially toward you, m'lady."

Her serving maid had never been quite so forthright. Helen should scold her further, but presently she hadn't the wherewithal to do so. At long last, she held Maggie in her arms and even Aleck MacIain could not quash the joy in her heart. Helen grinned. "She is beautiful, is she not?"

"A more precious bairn does not exist." Glenda reached in. "'Tis time for her to suckle on the other side."

***

After a fortnight living in solitude with her newborn cradled beside her bed, a bout of melancholy attacked Helen today. Aleck had ordered the bairn to be moved from Helen's chamber to the nursery. He'd cited the unbearable racket at all hours of the night screeching through his adjoining chamber walls. *Such is the affection of my husband.* The fortnight hidden away with Maggie had been a heavenly reprieve. But even Helen knew her bliss wouldn't last. Henceforth, Maggie's care would be entrusted to the nursemaid and Helen would resume her duties as lady of the keep.

Standing in front of her polished copper mirror, she clamped her hands to her waist and pushed in on her stays while Glenda laced her bodice. "I'm afraid I'll have to ask the tailor alter all my gowns."

"You've slimmed down a great deal since Maggie was born."

Helen regarded her bosoms, now swelling above the neckline of her blue gown. At least she was more voluptuous. Aleck seemed to prefer women with more shape. Perhaps he would now look fondly upon her. The thought, however, turned Helen's stomach. She'd been married to Aleck long enough to shudder any time he suggested paying a visit to her bedchamber. In addition, by his frequent derisive comments, she suspected he wasn't overly fond of bedding her either.

Alas, arranged marriages often did not come with a silver lining…or love. But Helen had a duty to her clan, and now to Maggie, and she would see to everyone's care with forthright, if not stoic dedication.

Glenda finished tying the bodice and gave it a pat. "How is that, m'lady?"

Helen released her grip and inhaled. Her head spun. "I must admit I haven't missed wearing stays during my confinement."

The chambermaid frowned deepening the lines in her jowls. "These new contraptions are devices of torture if you ask me."

"True, but fashion dictates ladies must wear them."

"Aye?" Glenda placed a matching mantle of blue, adorned with gold threaded fleur de lis over Helen's shoulders. "Next the powers above will be convincing Scottish women that iron corsets are the style."

Helen laughed. "If that comes about, at least there will be no need for women's armor."

"Armor?" Glenda gaped, pinning Helen's silk veil in place. "Do not tell me the women at court wear armor?"

"Of course not, silly. But ladies might be a bit more secure if they did."

"Do you believe so?" The chambermaid brushed her hands along Helen's skirts. "But isn't that what menfolk are for?"

"Aye." Helen turned sideways and regarded her profile in the mirror. "Though perhaps we would gain a bit more freedom to move about if we were more self-reliant."

Glenda gestured toward the door. "Sometimes I think you live in a fanciful dream."

"I suppose I do." *I would have withered under Aleck's harsh nature by now if not for my vivid imagination.* Helen picked up her skirts with a sigh. "Besides, I like my stories. They help me escape, if only for a brief interlude, and I see no harm in it."

"Nor do I." Glenda opened the door and bowed her head. "Enjoy the evening meal, m'lady."

Helen smiled while her stomach squelched. She dreaded rejoining Aleck at the high table. But like the books she so loved to read, her time of solace had come to an end. She stood tall and headed to the stairwell. The voices below stairs rumbled with a familiar hum, reminding her of all the duties she must resume as lady of the keep—caring for the villagers of nearby Kilchoan, and menu preparation being at the top of her list.

The jumbled conversations grew stronger as did the aroma of rosemary herbed lamb. When she rounded the last few steps, she stood at the bottom of the stairwell and looked across the tapestry-lined hall. The tables, filled with her kin, were lined end-to-end forming two long rows. She nodded to those who noticed her, then focused on the dais.

Aleck presided over the throng from his oversized chair as usual, but Mary the widow sat in Helen's seat. That the buxom woman had been invited to dine at the high table didn't surprise her, but the fact that the pair was being openly affectionate did. Upon Helen's confinement, Aleck had wasted no time finding a leman. Helen had felt slighted, of course, but he'd been reasonably discrete—aside from the lewd noises coming from his chamber at night. Fortunately, Helen was the only one privy to such a disturbance.

Mary wrapped her arms around Aleck and mashed her breast flush against him. In fact, the woman leaned so far forward, she not only gave Aleck a peek at her wares, the clan's highest ranking men seated at the high table could see as well. The scene was scandalous. Mary hadn't even respectably covered her brown tresses—she was, after all, a matron.

Something must have been inordinately funny because they laughed raucously, until Aleck looked up and spotted Helen. Then he puffed out his chest as if he was proud of consorting with his leman in front of the clan.

The rumble in the hall silenced.

Helen lifted her chin and affected a pleasant smile. All eyes fixated on her as she proceeded to the dais. The swishing of her skirts in concert with her footsteps echoed clear up to the rafters. Aleck shifted in his seat and glared with a look Helen knew well. She was to keep her mouth shut. Mary released his arm, but remained in Helen's chair.

Lovely.

"You're late," Aleck groused as she neared.

Ignoring him, Helen climbed onto the dais. Head held high, she strolled to the place reserved for the lady of the keep. "Good evening, Mistress Mary. My *husband* requested my presence in the hall this eve." In the folds of her skirts, she clenched her fists and forced a serene expression. "I believe 'tis time to remove your person from my chair."

Aleck inclined his head to the seat at his right. "Och, Helen. Mary has already portioned her trencher. It will not pain you to sit over here for a meal."

Heat flooded her cheeks, but she did not falter. How she'd expected *him* to support her assertion was beyond Helen. Clearly, he cared not about her humiliation upon arriving in the great hall to see a woman pressing her breast into her husband's arm. Then to be swatted aside with a "sit elsewhere" was almost more than Helen could bear.

She pursed her lips and slid into the chair at Aleck's right, then looked out over the hall. Stunned faces gaped back—faces of people she'd grown to love, and she hoped had also developed a fondness for her. She spread her palms and offered gracious smile. The banter resumed and a servant placed a tankard of mead in front of her.

Helen bowed her head in appreciation. "My thanks, Roderick."

On her other side, Grant, the MacIain henchman, dipped his head politely. "'Tis good to see your bonny face this eve, m'lady."

He'd learned his manners from Glenda, his ma. *Thank heavens all MacIain's are not brutes.* "I'm glad to be well enough to dine in the hall, though it was difficult to leave Miss Maggie."

"Och, the bairn will be right with Sarah. She's a fine nursemaid." Grant held up a trencher of bread and offered it to her.

"Aye, she is," Helen said, reaching in.

Before she could tear off a bit from the loaf, Aleck stretched in front of Helen and snatched the tray from Grant. "When I said it was time to return to your duties, I expected you to be attentive to the ram's horn announcing the evening meal."

Helen drew back her fingers and clutched her fist to her chest. "Forgive me. I had a bit of trouble fitting into my gown. The one I wore for my confinement is now too large, and this one…" She gestured downward.

He arched a brow and glanced at her breasts. "I reckon a bit of fat on your bones is not a bad thing."

She pulled her mantle across her open neckline. "I was thinking of asking the tailor to let out one or two gowns to provide a bit more comfort."

His shoulder shrugged. "Do what you must."

When he started to turn toward Mary, Helen grasped his arm. "It would be ever so nice if you would pay a visit to Maggie, m'laird. She changes every day."

Aleck brushed her hand away and gave her a steely glare. "I'll not be visiting the nursery until there's a wee lad occupying it. I need a son to inherit my name, not a daughter. You'd best heal fast, wife, for I've no option but to visit your bed again soon."

She preferred not to have this conversation in the hall, but now that he'd mentioned the bedchamber, Helen would have her say. She leaned closer so only he could hear. "And once you return to my bed. Will you stop keeping company with the widow?"

"Wheesht and mind your own affairs." He grasped her hand under the table and squeezed. Hard. "I'll not have any lassie yapping in my ear like a bitch. I need your noble arse to bear my son, and that's the last I'll hear of it."

Suddenly not hungry, Helen pulled her hand away and rubbed her fingers. How could her brute of a husband treat her with such disdain? And how in God's name was she to endure his boorishness for the rest of her life? Yes, her mother had always repeated the words: *that which cannot be helped must be endured.* But Da had treated Ma with respect, even in the beginning. Though Helen's parents had an arranged marriage, they'd grown to love each other, and in short order, too. Helen glanced at Aleck's bald head. She no longer harbored hope of love ever growing between them—tolerance was the best she could hope for.

But I must try harder.

The big oak doors at the far end of the great hall opened with a whoosh. A sentry wearing the king's surcoat emblazoned with an orange lion rampant stepped inside. "I've a missive for Sir Aleck MacIain."

The Chieftain stood and beckoned him. "Are you blind? Bring it here to the *high* table."

Helen huffed. Decorum would never be her husband's strong suit. Who on earth would not be aware the clan's chieftain sat at the high table? And flaunting the fact by being rude only served to promote discourse among those who paid fealty to him.

Aleck drummed his fingers while the man strode through the hall and climbed up to the dais with all eyes upon him. The room hummed as people mumbled, clearly impressed that a king's man had come all the way to Ardnamurchan to deliver a missive to their chieftain. Aleck snatched the velum from the man's fingertips and sliced his eating knife under the seal. Leaning toward the light of the enormous candelabra, Aleck knit his bushy eyebrows as he read.

Helen craned her neck in a futile attempt to see the writing. "What news, m'laird?"

With a frown, he shoved the missive into his doublet and looked to Grant, completely ignoring Helen's question. "The king has requested my presence at Stirling Castle. We must leave on the morrow."

Amy Jarecki

"Stirling?" Helen clapped her hands together. "Oh it would be lovely to purchase some new fabric at the castle fete."

"Aye, but *you* will not be accompanying me."

Helen frowned. It was no use asking if he would bring back a bolt of gold damask. He wouldn't do it. And making such a request would only give him another opportunity to berate her.

Grant stood and bowed. "I'll ready the men." He looked to Aleck. "We'll take the galley to Dunstaffnage and ride from there as usual?"

"Aye."

Helen nearly melted when she heard the henchman say *Dunstaffnage*. She had many fond memories of that castle. It was only a short ride from Dunollie where her sister, Gyllis, lived with her husband, Sean MacDougall. If only she could stow away on Aleck's galley with Maggie. Helen could visit Gyllis, and then travel east to Kilchurn Castle and see her mother. How wonderful such a holiday would be. She hadn't seen her kin in years.

Alas, Aleck would be in too much of a hurry to take her and Maggie to Dunollie—only four miles south of Dunstaffnage.

However, in her usual mien, Helen chose to see the positive side of this turn of events. Perhaps this journey would take Aleck away for an entire month. She smiled. Indeed, his absence was something she would welcome.

End of excerpt from Highland Knight of Rapture

Other Books by Amy Jarecki

Highland Force Series:
Captured by the Pirate Laird
The Highland Henchman
Beauty and the Barbarian
Return of the Highland Laird (A Highland Force Novella)

Highland Dynasty Series:
Knight in Highland Armor
A Highland Knight's Desire
Highland Knight of Rapture

Pict/Roman Romances:
Rescued by the Celtic Warrior
Celtic Maid

Visit Amy's web site & sign up to receive newsletter updates of new releases and giveaways exclusive to newsletter followers: www.amyjarecki.com

If you enjoyed *A Highland Knight to Remember*, we would be honored if you would consider leaving a review. *~Thank you!*

About the Author

A descendant of an ancient Lowland clan, Amy adores Scotland. Though she now resides in southwest Utah, she received her MBA from Heriot-Watt University in Edinburgh. Winning multiple writing awards, she found her niche in the genre of Scottish historical romance. Amy loves hearing from her readers and can be contacted through her website at www.amyjarecki.com.

Amy Jarecki

CPSIA information can be obtained at www.ICGtesting.com
Printed in the USA
LVOW11s1845160616

492904LV00001B/47/P